D0062377

Mina

The Dracula Story Continues

Marie Kiraly

BERKLEY BOOKS, NEW YORK

THE BERKLEY PUBLISHING GROUP
Published by the Penguin Group
Penguin Group (USA) Inc.
375 Hudson Street, New York, New York 10014, USA
Penguin Group (Canada), 90 Eglinton Avenue East, Suite 700, Toronto, Ontario M4P 2Y3, Canada
(a division of Pearson Penguin Canada Inc.)
Penguin Books Ltd., 80 Strand, London WC2R 0RL, England
Penguin Group Ireland, 25 St. Stephen's Green, Dublin 2, Ireland (a division of Penguin Books Ltd.)
Penguin Group (Australia), 250 Camberwell Road, Camberwell, Victoria 3124, Australia
(a division of Pearson Australia Group Pty. Ltd.)
Penguin Books India Pvt. Ltd., 11 Community Centre, Panchsheel Park, New Delhi—110 017, India
Penguin Group (NZ), 67 Apollo Drive, Rosedale, North Shore 0632, New Zealand
(a division of Pearson New Zealand Ltd.)
Penguin Books (South Africa) (Pty.) Ltd., 24 Sturdee Avenue, Rosebank, Johannesburg 2196,
South Africa

Penguin Books Ltd., Registered Offices: 80 Strand, London WC2R 0RL, England

This is a work of fiction. Names, characters, places, and incidents either are the product of the author's imagination or are used fictitiously, and any resemblance to actual persons, living or dead, business establishments, events, or locales is entirely coincidental.

MINA

PRINTING HISTORY
Berkley mass-market edition / September 1994
Berkley trade paperback edition / December 2007

Berkley trade paperback ISBN: 978-0-425-21746-7

PRINTED IN THE UNITED STATES OF AMERICA

10 9 8 7 6 5 4 3 2 1

With thanks to Georgette Gouveia,
who provided the first spark of inspiration,
and to Elaine Bergstrom,
who knew what to do with it.

FOREWORD

In writing *Mina,* I have tried to remain as faithful to the story of Dracula as possible. The novel *Dracula* is written as a series of first-person accounts by Van Helsing, Jonathan and Mina Harker and the others. Near the end of the story, Mina's first-person accounts are abandoned and her feelings about her ravishment by the vampire never described save by the men. Perhaps Stoker was uncomfortable dealing with the musings of the damned. Perhaps he was attempting to convey the notion that Mina was being lost to the men as Lucy had been earlier in the story. In any case, Mina's voice, so strong through the early parts of the novel, is abruptly silent.

I begin my novel here.

While faithful to the original novel, I restore Mina to her rightful place in the final struggle with Dracula, then follow her back to London, and to the new struggle to move into the future with a memory that, like Bram Stoker's novel, and Dracula himself, can never really die.

PART ONE

Dracula

CHAPTER ONE

From the journal of Mina Harker, written on the train to Varna.

October 13. I am writing this account in a small notebook separate from the diary I keep in my traveling bags. That diary, which details our desperate search for Dracula, is too public, and though Van Helsing would never read it without good reason, I fear there may be reason enough before this journey is done. This notebook will record my most private thoughts. I intend that it stay with me always. It is written in shorthand so that should it ever be lost or should I die, the others will require the help of my husband in order to transcribe it. My dear Jonathan, if they ask this of you, I beseech you to read no further. If I am dead, truly dead, burn it. If I am missing, gone to him or lost during our quest, keep it safe for me, for these thoughts are mine alone to share only as I see fit.

I shall begin this account on the night at Dr. Seward's that I can never forget. We met after dinner in the doctor's study. There, the five of us who had been involved in the sad affair since the beginning—Quincey Morris; Arthur Holmwood,

Lord Godalming; Jack Seward; Jonathan and I—listened as Professor Van Helsing told of the nature of the creature we faced. As Van Helsing requested, I wrote down everything he said. I made only a few references to my own thoughts, and those were centered on my concern for Jonathan. During his journey into the count's feral land, his dark hair had become streaked with grey. Though he was scarcely twenty-two, lines of worry were permanently etched on his handsome face. He had been through so much at that fiend's castle that I feared even a discussion of the vampire's nature would tax his sanity.

As if Van Helsing didn't tax all of ours. In an accent that grew thicker as he went on, he described bats, wolves, mist, dust with terrible relish, as if we were all children and he some sadistic uncle filling us with fear of the night. The inmate Renfield had sounded saner on my visit that afternoon than Van Helsing seemed that night. If I had not heard Dr. Seward's account of poor Lucy's true death, I would have laughed at how seriously the others listened. Instead, with my free hand pressed tightly to Jonathan's, I listened with horror all the stronger for my belief.

When he had finished, the men did something that I have never attempted to understand. In spite of all my assistance to them, they decided to shield me from any knowledge of what they would do from then on. In the months before this, I had traveled alone to Budapest to be at Jonathan's bedside. I had helped nurse him. I had listened to what had seemed at the time to be his ravings of pale female monsters, and of some obsessive fixation on their incredible seductive beauty. I listened to it all, knowing that somewhere within the fever and delirium my dear Jonathan was trapped. I never mentioned his ravings after he recovered. Until the others asked me to transcribe his shorthand diary, I never read them. Once I knew the truth, I accepted it with as much courage as any of them, yet these men, these dear, brave men, felt the need to protect me. For my own part, I felt no resentment for their chivalry. No, my only resentment was self-directed for I was too well bred to say an honest word of protest, though I recited enough of them inwardly in the hours that followed.

When the men had left to go to the ruins at Carfax and begin their hunt for Dracula's coffins, I went upstairs to bed. Everything Van Helsing had said that evening weighed heavy on my mind, and now that I was alone to reflect on his account, I felt a terrible fear. Jonathan had described the creature they would face. Van Helsing seemed to know even more about Dracula's powers, yet he led them to the abbey to begin their search at night rather than in the light of day, when the vampire is most helpless. I knew the men went with sacred hosts, holy water and crosses, but after so many centuries, would a creature who Jonathan reported had rejoiced at having a church on his property really be repelled by blessed symbols that were not even of our own faith?

Had the vampire been buried in consecrated ground the first time? Had he, like some profane messiah, risen anyway? Crosses. Holy water. Fools!

These were the thoughts racing through my head and keeping me from sleep, until sleep became impossible even if I had been ready. Dogs began barking outside. Their cries apparently roused Renfield, for I heard his mad screams in the asylum wing of the house, screams soon echoed by the other inmates until the asylum resembled less some orderly haven than the bedlam of a pauper's madness. It occurred to me then that I was utterly alone, and terribly vulnerable.

In this state of mind, fear began to multiply until I longed for relief. I went to the table near the hearth and poured myself a glass of sherry. As I did, some motion in the crack between the heavy velvet drapes caught my eye. With my arm extended so I could keep my body as far from the window as possible, I slowly pulled one drapery back. Though I expected to see a bat or worse staring in at me, there was nothing but the usual evening fog rising from the murky waters of the Thames. As I let the curtain fall, a new sound shattered the pressing silence of the night.

I wish that I could say that I thought the cry had come from Jonathan or one of the others exploring the ruins of Carfax, for that would have been a far better excuse for opening the window than the cry of an animal in pain. I thought that perhaps one of Seward's dogs had wounded a rabbit or hedgehog and the poor animal was suffering in the bushes beneath my room. Knowing the dangers that night now held, I ran to the bed stand and found the blessed crucifix Van Helsing had asked me to keep with me always. With this firmly in my hand, I unlocked the window and pulled it open.

A cold, damp breeze poured over me, carrying with it a heady scent like some exotic perfume. Though I wanted to shut the window, I backed away. A mist too thick to be natural rose outside. I saw eyes glowing red in the center of it.

A face slowly formed in the cloud, a face that could only be Dracula's. His expression was lonely, defiant, as if he read my thoughts and mirrored them. In his hand, he held the limp body of a rabbit. The blood glistened as it seeped from the wound in the animal's side, and I knew it was the poor creature that I had heard cry out, the animal Dracula had killed to meet his terrible needs. He looked younger than Jonathan had described, hardly older than Jonathan or I. It seemed that he was telling me that any blood would satisfy him, that he did not need to kill men to survive.

He was dressed entirely in black. His face and hands were pale in the wan firelight and his deep-set green eyes that had been red—perhaps mirroring the use of his dread power—were human now, though dark and strangely lightless, like those of a dead man whose tears no longer moistened them.

Yet he had an arresting face—with high, arched brows and a long, rather thin nose with flared nostrils. I had expected a mustache, for that was how Jonathan had described him, but now he was clean-shaven, his hair the length of any proper Victorian gentleman, his sideburns neatly trimmed. He had mirrored Jonathan's grooming so well that he would fit in perfectly in London. Noble, rich, foreign, he would be the rage at social gatherings where the exotic—in food, drink and guests—was always revered. He had laid his plans so well, save for Van Helsing's arcane knowledge and the determination of our little band.

I suddenly longed to meet the creature the men feared. To hear his voice. To learn, perhaps, what he intended to do about the threat my husband and the others gave him.

I, not Renfield, invited him inside; not with a word but with my heart and my thoughts and my damned curiosity. In the moment when his body separated from the mist and stood before me, I understood. The dark powers at his command could touch some passion deep within the human heart and use it for his end.

He stared at me, and for a moment, I had an astonishing revelation of where his mesmerizing power lay. All his thoughts were fixed on me as no other man's had ever been. Even Jonathan, on the day I agreed to be his wife, had a portion of his mind elsewhere. But with Dracula, I was the center of all his attention, the one who could satisfy his terrible need, give him strength. The others were protecting me. This creature would use me—willing or no—for his own ends. The understanding gave a heady feeling that made me weak with a desire I found horrifying. The room closed in around me. At the end, blind, entranced, I felt only his arm supporting me, his pale hand, as cold as the death that had come to him centuries before, brushing away the hair that covered my outstretched neck. His eyes were fixed on mine. I smelled the cloying sweet scent of his hair as it brushed against my face. The quick prick of pain which followed led to—I can only admit it now!—an ecstasy I had never imagined could exist in this life or the next.

It was nearly dawn when I heard Jonathan tiptoe into the room. Shamed, wanting to wait and sort out the night's terrible events before I confessed to what I had done, I kept my eyes shut. Jonathan's hand touched my forehead, and he left me. As soon as I was alone, I glanced at the window and saw that the drapes were drawn, the sash latched. I stood in front of a mirror and examined myself carefully. There were no marks on my skin. Last night had been a dream, or a delusion born from worry, nothing more.

I vowed to keep my dream a secret. The men were being strong for me; I would be the same for them. I closed my eyes and slept. When I woke, the clock in Dr. Seward's study was chiming eleven.

It was too late for breakfast so I rang for a maid and asked for tea. While I waited for it, I reread the account I had made from all our notes and journals, looking for some clue that would help the men in their terrible task. A strange exhaustion had taken hold of me, and I found my mind wandering so often that I had to work to keep it on the task.

I thought of Lucy as I read the account. I miss her laughter, her jests, the gossip we shared with one another only months ago. I found it impossible to believe that she can really be gone . . .

No use dwelling on what cannot be changed.

Nonetheless, the sorrow of her death brought tears to my eyes, and I might soon have been crying outright had the maid not arrived with my tea, biscuits and preserves. She also brought me a recent copy of *Lippincott's Monthly*, which featured the beginning of a new story by Oscar Wilde. Critics of *The Picture of Dorian Gray* implied that the piece was somehow scandalous. I found it intriguing, the moral that beauty could conceal terrible evil certainly apropos in our circumstance. Jonathan had long ago passed judgment on Mr. Wilde, and I made certain that the magazine was returned to Dr. Seward's study before dinner so my husband would not find it in my possession.

Dinner was strained. Jonathan, especially, seemed pained by the thought that he must keep the men's actions from me. I have no idea what sort of horrors they had faced the night before, though I suspect my imagination is far more lurid than the truth would be. I said good night to them early, hoping that sleep would come more easily. I was not so fortunate.

Instead, as on the night before, I dreamed of Dracula rising in the fog outside my window, of my hand throwing back the sash, of his white face above me and, dear Lord, his body pressing mine against the bed. When I woke, Jonathan slept beside me. He had stripped off only his outer clothes, and his shirt and pants smelled of smoke and dampness. His work is so dangerous, so important, I dared not disturb his sleep. I carefully rested my hand on his shoulder and closed my eyes once more. Dreams. How could I avoid them when Jonathan was in such danger and I could not be a part of it?

That thought was the last thing I recalled until I woke late that morning. As I slipped out of bed, a sudden dizziness made me grip the bedpost for support. I took a deep breath and steadied myself and went to the window and cracked open the drapes. The day was foggy, but in the distance I could just make out the crumbling walls of Carfax Abbey as nothing more than a dark shadow in the gray light. I turned and, as I had for the last two nights, examined my neck in the mirror. There did seem to be a pair of raised places on the skin, but these were hardly the seeping welts poor Lucy had on her neck. Perhaps these were nothing more than the product of my own hysteria, as the stigmata were for the medieval Catholic mystics and saints.

I decided I would not have the men worrying about me when they had so much else to think of. That night I drank a sleep potion that Dr. Van Helsing mixed for me. It was, as he promised, very light—so light that I recalled quite distinctly everything that happened that night and saw in the pattern of what occurred some semblance of the nights before it.

And much of what I told the men later was a lie.

Dracula came as he had before, in a mist that flowed through the cracks in my latched window. He needed no invitation; I had already brought down the barriers that might have kept him at bay. Though I could not move, I was more conscious than I had been on the nights before. I could see Jonathan lying beside me in a deep sleep. I was afraid to call his name because in the moment I saw who was in our room, Dracula told me that my husband's waking would mean his death.

I did not trust my body to remain passive under the vampire's touch, so I slipped carefully away and stood in the center of the room, before the one I already thought of as my master.

"You shall be my vengeance," he whispered, moving closer but not yet close enough to be a threat.

Such a strange choice of words. "Vengeance?" I asked. "Vengeance for what?"

He did not answer, but for an instant only, I saw pain in his eyes.

I lifted the crucifix I wore around my neck, keeping the small bit of silver between us. "Not that," I said softly. His presence gave me a strange, desperate courage. When he had lived, he had been a barbarian prince, taking life as casually as he did in his eternal altered state. He could kill me if he wished, but I would not be his pawn.

"No?" He cocked his head and smiled. His teeth were white and moist, the canines as Jonathan described them—long and pointed. My hand shook. Then he did something I had never expected. His fingers wrapped around the silver cross, pushing it down and away with such ease that all my strength seemed no more than a child's against his. "Do you think such symbols really repel me, especially when wielded by one with so little faith?"

My voice no longer worked, yet my will if anything seemed stronger. I stared at him, determined that I would not cower even if I could not run. He untied the lacing of my nightdress, pulling back a flap to expose one shoulder. I trembled, but I was frozen, unable to do anything but stand helpless as he pressed his open lips against my skin, sucking in a bit of flesh, biting down.

He tasted me then drew back, his expression mocking. I fought down my fear and looked defiantly at his dark eyes. "I will not cower," I whispered, "not even at the moment of my death."

"No?" he asked. I felt his mind release me, but I did not move; I did not flinch even when his pale hand brushed my cheek, wiping away a tear. Only then did I realize that I was weeping silently. Later I repeated to my husband and the others the words he had spoken. "Flesh of my flesh. Blood of my blood. Kin of my kin. My bountiful winepress for a while." I knew that he meant my blood, my life, when he said those last words, but I felt little fear. As I watched silently, he exposed his own chest and, using one sharp nail, opened a wound above his heart. I recoiled at the sight of the blood welling across it, dark beads on the skin that seemed so white in the cold moonlight. Then he drew my head forward with such force that I had no choice but to press my lips against the wound, to drink.

His blood tasted familiar. I wondered if he had done this to me before. He had called me his vengeance, yet as I drank, I knew that I could be more than that. I sucked greedily. I tilted back my head so he could drink. I undid the rest of the lacings of my gown and pressed my bare breasts against his waiting hands. For the time that he held me, all the restraint I practiced in my nights with my husband vanished. For the time he held me, I was as wanton as the vampire women Jonathan had met in Dracula's castle. The women—my blood-kin.

This could not be damnation. But if it were, the fire was far too sweet to resist.

"Jonathan," I whispered, looking back at my husband sleeping so innocently beside the place where I had lain.

"He will not wake," Dracula whispered and kissed me. I tasted my own blood. I tasted his. I reveled in both. I would have died and gladly that night, prepared to awaken into another life, had there not been the pounding of feet on the stairs, the trying of the locked door.

Dracula gripped my wrists to push me away, but I would not be denied one more taste of his dark eternity. As my lips pressed against the wound, he held me close for one final moment. I heard him draw in breath, then let it out in a human sigh of fulfillment. Then the door slammed inward, and Quincey, Dr. Seward and Arthur rushed into the room.

With deliberate scorn, the count pushed me back against my sleeping husband. As the men advanced with crucifixes held out like swords against a mortal enemy, I watched Dracula slowly retreat. Was their faith so much stronger than mine, or did he only toy with them, making them think such trinkets could repel him?

The moon which had given the only light to the room vanished behind a cloud. When Quincey lit a match, Dracula was gone. The faint tendrils of mist curling across the red carpet on the floor gave the only sign that he had been anything more than a terrible dream among so many others.

I covered my face with my hands, trying to hide my shame. I recall nothing else, though Dr. Seward wrote that my expression was dazed and filled with terror, my moans pathetic to hear. Ah, if he had only known the guilt that was the cause of them. When at last Van Helsing and Dr. Seward managed to wake Jonathan, he comforted me without the slightest thought that I might have deserved some blame for my fate. It was in that moment, with his arms circling me with such fierce affection, that I decided to keep the terrible knowledge of my passion a secret forever.

Nonetheless, we were allies against the monster. In the morning, I told them what I could recall of the night and the nights before it. The half-truths added to my guilt. In the hour that followed, as Jonathan held and comforted me, I found myself thinking of the future and the hopelessness of the men's task. I thought of the risks they would take for me, and death seemed suddenly the sweetest, easiest means to end my curse.

It was not like me to be so despondent. Nonetheless, the rightness of my decision seemed more clear the more I considered it. Later that morning, when I hinted to the others that I would kill myself rather than harm any of them, Van Helsing said aloud what I had already suspected. "It is his blood already tainting you. In death, you would become as he is, condemned as he was. No, Madam Mina. You must not die. Especially not by your own hand."

Could they stop me? I suppose Seward could have put me in one of his padded cells, but otherwise the decision was mine. A single stroke of a knife would end my life. Or I could go to the river and throw myself from a high point on the bank. The water is brackish. My body would not be easily found. I would have time to wake, to walk the night as he does, perhaps even to search out my new kin.

Yes, though it was hard to accept, Van Helsing must have been right. The thought of suicide seemed so sweet because the vampire was already calling to me!

Yet the terrible, alluring thoughts that were not entirely my thoughts tumbled round in my mind. I managed to hide them well until the moment when Van Helsing had finished leading us in prayer then lifted the host above my head and called upon God to protect me. As the wafer touched my forehead, I thought of my passion, of the vampire's blood flowing so willingly in my veins, and I felt the searing pain the host gave to my flesh.

I screamed. I cried. I was damned and would not be comforted, not even by Jonathan, who left a message in his journal that should I become vampiric, he would join me in my terrible eternity. He knew I would transcribe it with the others. Perhaps his decision was genuine, motivated by the love we have for one another. Perhaps he thought to give me one more reason to live. I cannot condemn him for that, but I have grown cynical in the days since I drank Dracula's blood. I see things more clearly, and I am not so trusting as I once was, not even with my husband. They all manipulate me.

When they saw the mark the host had made, the men became desperate. Though it pained Jonathan to leave me, they departed for London to search out more of Dracula's earth boxes and, perhaps, find the monster himself and destroy him when his powers were weakest. Van Helsing says they must do this. If Dracula escapes, I will never be free of him, and when I die, I will rise into his world of eternal night.

I remained at the asylum listening to the constant cries, the swearing of the guards, the smell of urine and feces that permeated even these private rooms. By afternoon, unable to bear the confinement any longer, I slipped outside. I was certain to let no one see me leave, for I did not know what orders Seward had given his staff concerning me.

The sky seemed unusually bright, the grass and trees of the sloping asylum grounds iridescent green. The brilliance of it hurt my eyes, and I hurried forward to the shade of a thick stand of trees that grew along the wall separating the asylum from the grounds of Carfax.

It was daylight. Mortal time, not his, and I felt the need to see what the men had done to his home, to see if he could indeed walk the exorcized grounds or sleep in the boxes defiled by hosts and holy water.

I searched the wall until I found a low wooden door hanging partway open, enough that I could squeeze my body through.

On the opposite side, the once beautiful gardens were overgrown with weeds and scrubby bushes. The abbey church that had undoubtedly once been beautiful was covered with dead ivy that surrounded the vaulted stone frames empty of their holy glass.

What had happened to the order that had once lived here? Did their ghosts still walk these quiet grounds, desolate souls among broken dreams?

Did the vampire's soul walk with theirs?

"Dracula," I called.

A sigh on the wind answered me, coming it seemed from the church.

I went into the building, through the dark, empty hole that had once held its doors. He might be waiting for me in its darkness, but he could not harm me any further. I was mated to him now. The worst had already been done.

Inside, I smelled the ancient earth scattered all around me. As my eyes grew accustomed to the darkness of the space, I saw the broken boards, the scattered earth still damp with holy water, the crumbled hosts strewn above it.

"Dracula," I called again.

No response, yet I knew I was not alone.

I walked toward the great stone of the altar and saw that it was slightly skewed from its base.

I did not see him, but I knew he rested in the hollow beneath it like some ancient saint. All I had to do was find a stake and a stone to drive it, and all our trials would be over.

"Revenge," I whispered, not as a warning for what I would do but as a justification.

The reply, too soft to be a whisper, formed in my mind. "For Lucy."

It was not my voice but his that spoke in my mind. I fled.

That night, as the men discussed the work they had done in London, I sat with them, picked at my food and said nothing about what I had seen or felt or heard.

And now it seems that Dracula is always with me. I see him on the edge of my sight, especially at night, when his dark eyes burn red in the center like a smoldering fire ready to flair and devour. His expression is filled with hunger and with lust. Even now, when I am an accomplice of those committed to destroy him, I long for him as I longed for him the moment I first saw him, before his blood made me a part of him forever.

When Dracula left England, I made the men take me with them when they pursued him. I need to see the outcome of this chase with my own eyes. If Dracula escapes them or, worse, destroys them, I may as well face my doom at his side. If Dracula is destroyed, then his death is on my conscience for if I had not weakened and let him close to me, only Van Helsing would have pursued him with such diligence.

Van Helsing is driven by a desire to destroy Dracula. If I dared, I would ask him what makes him such an expert on vampirism and such an enemy to the creatures, but I am afraid to do so. The closer we get to Dracula's native land, the more often Dracula seems to be in my mind, and I would not wish to give the vampire some information that would put Jonathan and the others in danger. I would also not want Van Helsing to assume I am in an alliance with the vampire. He is so obsessed with this chase that I think he might kill me if he believed that. I am like-wise certain that he would kill me if I became undead.

I have begun writing this account after telling the men that the smell of their cigar smoke nauseates me and their talking keeps me from sleep. They comment often on my lethargy but go to the smoking car to sit. I hope that they will do so often on this journey for I wish to be alone with my thoughts. I need this time to sort truth from lies and half-lies, my real feelings from those his blood has aroused in me as well as those the men believe I have. Through it all, I must practice deceit though it galls me to do so.

My world has suddenly become so filled with tragedy. I don't . . . Wait, I hear Van Helsing and Dr. Seward speaking together in the hall outside our compartment. Later . . .

CHAPTER TWO

I

"It is nearly sunset, Madam Mina," Van Helsing said softly as I hid my book in my pocket. He entered the compartment followed by Seward. Without waiting for my assent, he folded his glasses and put them in his pocket then took out the watch he used to hypnotize me. Behind him, Seward stood ready with the pad and pen he used to record my thoughts.

As always, Van Helsing could barely contain his excitement. For a moment at dawn and dusk, he can use me to touch the mind of the vampire. It thrills him to be able to use science against such evil, and it somehow thrills him even more that I have been able to form the idea of attempting this contact on my own. As he reminds me and the others far too often, I have Dracula's blood in my veins, which makes me a most unpredictable ally.

Going to Dracula with my mind is always strange. In the beginning, the mental journey frightened me and made me dizzy, as if I were actually flying across land and water to meet him, with only the tenuous tie to Van Helsing's mind keeping me aloft. Now I am more used to it, but as always, I have nothing new to report. Dracula is still at sea, still in a state of half sleep, using what power he dares expend to order the storm that sweeps the boat, the *Czarina Catherine,* swiftly toward the Black Sea.

The bond broke quickly this time. "Do you suppose his power is growing now that he is so close to home?" Van Helsing asked me. I nodded. "I feel his mind close to mine so often now," I told him.

"And how do you feel? Does he try to control you?"

"No." I hesitated, weighed my words carefully and decided to tell the truth. "I believe that he knows that to make me truly his ally, he must allow me some independence. He is testing my resolve. So far, at least, I am up to it."

Van Helsing knelt in front of me. He studied my color, took my pulse. Afterward, I opened my mouth so he could part my lips and examine my teeth. I wonder what he would think if I bit him at that moment. Would he be concerned about being infected? More likely, he would question my misplaced sense of humor, or my sanity. He would be right to do so. So much that is tragic strikes me as humorous. So much I used to ignore seems tragic. "You should join us for dinner," Van Helsing said with an uneasy smile as he patted my hand.

"In a moment," I replied, closing the compartment behind them.

Soon after, I tiptoed down the dark and narrow hallway to the door where Seward and Van Helsing had paused. I smelled the smoke of Seward's meerschaum pipe, Van Helsing's cigar. Just out of sight of them, I stopped, leaned against the wall and eavesdropped on their conversation.

"How is she?" Seward whispered.

"Worse." Van Helsing's voice became even softer. The noise of the train made hearing nearly impossible, but I believe he said, "You are prepared to do what must be done?"

"If it comes to that." Grief made Seward's reply much louder, and I had no difficulty hearing his words.

"I fear it will be soon."

Soon! I backed up a few feet then strolled down the hall toward them, bumping into Dr. Seward. He started as if he expected me to suddenly turn into a wolf and lunge for his throat. I felt a pang of pity that would have brought tears to my eyes had I not fought them down. Seward was a reclusive man. Like so many others, he had found his love late in life. Though Lucy chose another, he loved her still and had been horrified by the creature she later became. If "true death" would save my poor soul from her fate, he would gladly help deliver it.

I find myself pitying Jack for his loss, all the more because it would be impolite for him to mourn openly as Arthur does. What is stranger yet is that I do not fear Van Helsing. I have always trusted my intuition, and it rarely fails me. It is a good sign for the future!

Exhausted by the constant focus on their enemy, the men discussed their work over dinner. While he is away, Arthur has placed his affairs in the hands of a trusted friend. Seward has able assistants at the asylum. Quincey, of course, is touring Europe and can go where he wishes.

During the discussion, I noticed that Jonathan had become quite withdrawn. Van Helsing did as well and laid a sympathetic hand on my husband's arm. "I too left my work suddenly," Van Helsing said. "We will be back to it much sooner than you think."

"The Hawkins staff has a reputation for dependability," Arthur added and instantly regretted his choice of words.

"Mina is more important than the firm of Hawkins and Harker," Jonathan said softly.

"I meant that they will manage well in your absence," Arthur replied.

"Of course they will, darling," I said and impulsively kissed his cheek. As I did, I noticed Seward lean forward in alarm.

If I had any desire to devour my husband, did he think I would do it in the dining car? The thought of such an act struck me as hilarious. I hid my smile behind my napkin, my laughter behind a feigned cough. Quincey seemed to have shared my thought, but his reaction was concern not amusement.

When dinner was over, Jonathan decided to join the other men in the smoking car for a game of cards. Quincey offered to see me back to my room. When we arrived there, he paused then asked awkwardly if he could come in for a moment and speak to me. Once inside, he came directly to the point.

"On the frontier in America, women have to be armed just like the men. I have something for you." He reached into his coat and pulled out a short-barreled pistol with a tooled leather handle. Without asking whether I wanted it or not, he proceeded to show me how it loaded. "It doesn't have the distance of the rifles, but if it comes to using it, the bullets are as lethal at close range as those from a Winchester." He handed the pistol and a box of bullets to me. "Take these," he said.

He was not suggesting the pistol as a defense against vampires, for, as had already been demonstrated, bullets had no effect on them. I knew whom he feared, and I had a perverse desire to force him to give a name. Instead, polite as the Mina I had been only days before, I merely said, "Thank you."

"It will be our secret," he replied.

I took Quincey's hand in one of mine and saw him looking down at my fingers with a sense of wonder. Had he expected them to feel something other than alive? "I am quite all right and fully intend to remain that way," I told him as brightly as I could and warmed to his smile. Quincey is so honest, so much more open-minded than the others. I imagine that the American frontier must be a wild place filled with all sorts of rare and exotic creatures. If so, it would be quite unlike England, where everything is so static that it is a wonder that only the houses are covered with ivy and moss. "Why did you come with the others?" I asked him.

"To avenge Lucy. To see the last European frontier." He smiled sadly. "And, forgive me, I mean nothing but respect when I say, for you."

I kissed his cheek and whispered, "Lucy loved you so much. I understand why. Your nature is like hers. You give so much."

I felt his unease, his uncertainty about what my words meant. Not wishing to embarrass him, I pulled away too quickly then realized it must look as if I were indeed doing something improper. He glanced over his shoulder at the door, and I saw the pulse quicken in the vein in his neck. Dear Quincey! For all his rough edges, he is as civilized as the rest. I wonder what he would have said had he known that my only desire at that moment was to lock the door and taste of him. I would have been chaste, gentle, but no less insistent than Dracula had been with me.

I wrapped the gun and bullets in a scarf and put them in my traveling bag. As I did, Quincey retreated toward the door and I told him good night.

Afterward, I recorded these thoughts. My odd fantasies! I would never act on them, yet the very fact that I have them at all fills me with shame and dread. My future is in such turmoil, my soul in such peril, yet as I write these words, I feel nothing except a vague affection for my companions and curiosity about my fate.

II

October 14. This morning, Dracula woke as I touched his mind. I saw his eyes open to the blackness of the box in which he rests, smelled the dry earth on which he lies, felt his terrible hunger as if it were my own. The strength of it, and the pain, forced my immediate withdrawal, and I found myself suddenly staring, dizzy and disoriented, into Van Helsing's piercing eyes.

"What has happened?" he asked.

I lied and told him that I did not know. However, I am certain that at the time my mind touches Dracula's, my thoughts are known to him. I find this consoling. I still hope that I can somehow be free of his control without causing his death or the deaths of the men who travel with me. Though I have never confessed this to the others, Van Helsing guesses my feelings and reminds me often that my soul depends on our destroying the vampire. I disagree. My soul is mine to save or destroy. To say that its fate depends on another's death means that there is no justice to be had from God. Such blasphemy!

During the journey, I find myself thinking too often of Lucy's true death. When I first read Dr. Seward's account of her last days, I thought that if she had known the exact nature of the creature that preyed on her, she might have had the strength to fight back. Now I am not so certain. Lucy was always frivolous. She would have been easier to seduce than I was—than I am. And yet there was strength to her as well, a strength born of knowing she could defy convention and survive the consequences with her reputation only slightly blemished and her virtue securely intact.

Think of it! She received three marriage proposals in one day from some of the finest men I have ever met! Not since Queen Bess has anyone been so sought after. And when she made her choice, she let the others down so gently that they loved her still.

When I consider this, I wonder about poor Lucy's freedom once the count claimed her for his own. Though she drank the blood of children, she did not kill any of them. Had she some choice in the matter? On one hand, it comforts me to think she did. But if so, then what a terrible thing the men did to her out of ignorance.

My thoughts were fixed on this throughout our evening meal. I scarcely heard the men's plans, or even noticed the taste of the food I ate. As always, the men urged me to eat more. I did as they asked until I could scarcely breathe, yet I felt terribly unsatisfied and strangely sleepy. Nonetheless, when we stopped at the train station in Hungary to take on coal and water, I got out with the others to stretch my legs. While standing on the platform, I noticed a pair of passengers saying good-bye to their families. They were young men in simple woolen coats and pants. From the looks of them, I would say they are peasants. Perhaps they have been conscripted or are going to sea, for everyone was crying openly as if the separation may be permanent.

A woman kissed one of the passengers in a way I would have blushed to kiss Jonathan in the privacy of our bedroom. I saw the man's hand slide beneath her heavy coat to brush against her breast, watched her press close to him and kiss him again. As they parted, the woman noticed me staring and smiled as she wiped away a tear. The gulf between our worlds is so wide, yet I feel a longing for her freedom, her passion. I am so constrained—my emotions as contained as my body is beneath the bone corset correct civilization demands that I wear even in a land that would not notice its lack.

I don't feel "correct" any longer, and the farther we get from home, the wilder my thoughts become. It is his blood in me that makes it so. How will I control my thoughts when I finally walk on the soil of his native land?

The following morning on the way to the dining car, I saw the two peasants sitting in the nearly empty coach sharing bread and sausage, laughing heartily as they did. I would have asked where they were going, but I did not know their language.

On our travel through the night, the land had become wilder, the mountains more craggy. As I sat with the others, eating slices of fine white bread that had all the dry taste of flour in my mouth, I looked down at drop-offs to swift cataracts in the valleys below. Wild. Barely settled. His country. I would have known it even if I had not been told that we would be transferring in Bucharest within the hour and arriving in Varna by evening.

As I sat listening to the others conversing as if our journey were no more than a pleasant adventure, I listened to the wheels of the train rolling over the tracks, pounding like a pulse . . . blood and blood and blood.

My expression must have given me away. Van Helsing took my hand and looked carefully into my eyes.

I gazed back at him as innocently as I could. As I did, I found myself wondering what would have happened if Dr. Seward had never written him. Would I have woken one night to find Lucy sitting beside me on my bed? Would she have killed me then? Would she have loved me with the dark passion I had always sensed just beneath the veneer of her aristocracy? Would I have been able to resist her charm—the charm of my only close friend?

"Are you all right?" It was Jonathan speaking, his voice full of love and concern.

"It's the height. It makes me uneasy," I replied, pulling my hand away from the professor's and leaning against Jonathan.

"Perhaps Dr. Seward should see you back to your room?" Van Helsing suggested.

My hand squeezed Jonathan's more tightly. "I will," he said.

"I'll come as well," Jack suggested, resting a hand on Van Helsing's shoulder as he stood.

I knew what they were doing. They meant to keep us apart because they do not trust me. This makes me furious, yet they are right to do so.

Blood . . . and blood . . . and blood.

October 25, Varna. This afternoon, Dracula came to me, his presence so real that for a moment I was certain that his body actually stood before me.

We have been staying for the last ten days at a hotel in one of the finest sections of Varna. The rooms are spacious and clean and always warm. The food served here, the men tell me, is exquisite, though I can scarcely taste it anymore and eat only to please them. The leaded glass windows that cover the entire east wall of the dining room overlook the harbor. Jonathan and the others often stand by them watching boats sailing in and out. The *Czarina Catherine* is expected soon, and they all hope the struggle will then be over. After his visit, I knew otherwise.

By noon, the strange lethargy smothered me completely, reminding me most unpleasantly how often I had claimed exhaustion to the men throughout the journey. I retired to my room and did not even try to write in my journal. In truth, little had happened and so I did not feel uneasy when I slipped into bed and, I think, immediately fell into a deep sleep.

I dreamed of the water, the reeking hold of the ship that carries him here. Then he was with me, rising from the mist in the center of my mind. A moment later, I joined him and willingly clasped his outstretched hands. I sensed no uneasiness in my actions, as if this dream foreshadowed that change in me that he expects will soon come. I spoke. Though I could not hear my words, I know I told him every part of the men's plans. I sensed his thanks, and recall the words of his reply as clearly as if I had written them down.

"I will travel on alone for a while longer," he said. "When the men face me, it must be on my own land, where I am most powerful. I promise on the honor I once possessed as a prince and general that I will do my best to end this chase without them coming to harm."

"And me?" I asked. "What price do I pay for your mercy?"

He paused before answering. I heard the hiss of his indrawn breath as he prepared to speak. "Only this—you must pledge to follow your desire and do as you will rather than as your husband and the others direct. If you agree, I will release your soul."

"Did you ever have it?" I asked.

"I will release it," he repeated with more force.

"As you released Lucy!"

I had issued a challenge, nonetheless he took little offense at the intent. "Get up from your bed, Mina Harker. Take out your little journal and write down the words I speak. Later, when you are awake, read them and think carefully on their meaning."

I did as he asked. Later, when I woke and found them written in the back of the journal, I pulled them out of the book. Now I record them as they were written, along with my thoughts of everything else that happened during that dream. If it was indeed a dream. To leave them as they were, divorced from the rest of my account, would seem unnatural, as if dream and reality had twisted and broken apart into two unmatched halves. I cannot allow that. To lose my hold on my thoughts would likely destroy my mind.

I recall rising from my bed as he demanded, locking the door and sitting at the little table. I recall writing furiously, often thinking not of anything but the act of writing itself. He stood beside me, pausing often to let me catch up and to force a deep breath of air into his lungs.

"I had wanted to take the three women with me to England; but their needs were too great," he said. "We never would have survived the journey. We four together would have soon devoured the crew of a ship twice the size of the *Demeter*. I had promised them that I would make a place for them in your new, crowded land and that later they could come and be with me as they had been for years upon years in the past. The arrangements would take some time, but as you know, my blood-kin and I have time to spare."

Another pause before he went on. "I had not counted on my loneliness, especially for the fair one, my last mortal lover. And the loneliness was all the greater for the life surrounding me in England. I sensed it, even as I slept, and it made my need for someone, anyone with whom to share my existence, that much stronger.

"Ah, I see the pity in your eyes, Mina Harker. I suppose it is inevitable when I bare my soul like this.

"Oh yes, I have a soul, and it is much as it was when I lived. When I first saw Lucy on a crowded Whitby street, her brown hair shining with its golden highlights even in the foggy afternoon light, I felt loneliness. Such a wonderful land, your gray-shrouded England, where I can walk even at noonday without fear of the sun. I joyfully followed her. My intent then was not to use her, for I am of noble lineage and know the danger of preying on the wealthy and powerful. No, my intent was simply to observe her, to hear her laughter, to see her smile.

"You and she were together, but in truth, I noticed only Lucy. I watched her climb the hill to a great house and despaired. I had hoped she was staying at some public house where I could go inside and order some food that I could not touch and sit and listen to her voice, perhaps even share a brief conversation with her.

"Such loneliness is dangerous, no? I knew that even as I went on, staying well behind so she would not see me following her. Afternoon turned to twilight while I stood in the protective shadows of the trees and watched the house. I don't know why I stayed. Perhaps because the spot is so beautiful, the view of the harbor so magnificent. I watched the ships swaying on the tranquil evening sea and thought how free mortal men are. They can travel anywhere while I, trapped by needs, had been forced to plan my journey so carefully, going even so far as to be certain that the ship's crew would be large enough to sustain me.

"Am I speaking too fast for you, dear Mina? No? Good!

"I stayed until night, thinking of this. Then I heard men's voices whispering in the trees. I knew they were thieves, for their dress and actions were the same as thieves throughout the world.

"I could feast on one and kill the other. Their bodies could be pitched into the rocky strand. The tide would account for the loss of blood, the marks.

"I had moved closer to them when a figure coming from the quiet house startled us all. The men retreated, but I, for whom darkness conceals nothing, knew it was Lucy coming to me. She had sensed me, and I had not even called except through desire."

"She walked in her sleep," I told him. "She did so before you arrived in England. We always feared what might happen to her."

"Silence!" His voice seemed to thunder in the little room. "She came to me, else why would she have chosen the exact spot at which I waited?"

"We often picnicked there. The place has the most ideal view of the harbor."

This time he let my comment pass and went on. "Her gown was thin. I could see the outline of her breasts, the cleft of her sex, and I sorrowed for I could not love her as a man loves a woman. That was gone with so many other possibilities centuries before.

"Even so, I gave her pleasure, and when I tasted her, she felt no pain. The sigh, that tiny perfect sigh she made as my teeth pierced her, I noted it, recalled it in the nights that followed. When she was strong enough, I came back and used her again and later again."

"You killed her," I replied savagely.

"*They* killed her! Yes, she had my blood in her, as you do. She would have survived and lived her natural years. Later, I would have claimed her, restored to her youth after a long and hopefully fruitful life, as my bride.

"Instead Van Helsing came and knew what she would become. My only hope for her future was to claim her and take her away. Do you think she died in Van Helsing's absence by accident? No, I chose the night of her death carefully, so that I would have time to find a new and safer resting place for her body before Van Helsing persuaded the others to help him destroy her."

"But the men found her in her own coffin," I said.

"I would not have a slave for a bride! Lucy did not lose her will when she died. She was confused, yes, but stubborn, and she would not go with me. Had there been no Van Helsing, she would have learned to understand the need to exist under my protection, and to choose my life over true death."

"To harden her heart to killing," I responded.

"You are so perceptive. Had there been no Van Helsing, she could have risen, could have stumbled from that cold tomb into the beautiful night and slowly learned what was necessary to survive. Instead, instead . . ."

His pale hands were clenched with rage, the nails digging into his palms. I saw him as he would have been when he was alive, the savior of his people, slaughtering the enemy, rejoicing in battle. Seeing him like this made him more human, and somehow more powerful. "Instead they killed her," he said bitterly. "They destroyed one who had done nothing to deserve that end."

I lowered my head to the table and cried.

He looked closely at me as if he had never seen such sorrow before. "You grieve for her?"

"I grieve for her, and for the men who did that to her," I replied.

He shook his head, and again he seemed so wise, so good. His words did not surprise me. "No, Mina, you must not. In time she would have had no choice but to be as I am. No will is stronger than our power and our need."

"And yet you say that you can release my soul."

"If you follow your desire."

I had always prided myself on being independent. What he asked was no more than what I would have done. "I agree," I whispered.

I waited to hear him acknowledge what I had said, but he had already begun to fade into the misty shadows of my mind . . .

Now that I have put the words I wrote of my dream in their proper place, I begin to understand Dracula the man and I pity him. Of course, he may be lying about freeing me. He may mean to kill the men and take me, willing or no, to be his eternal companion. And yet I feel a strange sense of peace and acceptance of an end that can only be inevitable. If Dracula passes us by, what recourse will we have but to pursue him? I can only trust him as I trust Van Helsing. Neither of them will destroy me until this struggle between them is over.

And if the choice becomes Van Helsing's stake or an eternity of blood, I honestly do not know which fate I would desire.

It is his blood tainting me. Can I ever be truly free of it?

October 28. The telegram I had expected came. During last night's fog, the *Czarina Catherine* bypassed Varna and went directly on to Galati.

"Galati!" Quincey Morris spoke the city's name as if it were a curse. "How could he have known we were here?" Of all of the men, he seemed the most surprised by the news, the least willing to give up the chase. The others were merely disheartened that Dracula's ship had been swept on to the Romanian port some hundred miles north of Varna.

My face grew white with the realization of the vampire's power. I said a prayer of hope that what Dracula asked of me was for the best, then looked at Van Helsing as I spoke. "It was a chance we had to take," I said.

"We know much, thanks to Madame Mina," Van Helsing responded. He would have taken my hand and patted it, as is his way, but I had my fingers clasped together. I did not want to touch him, or any of them, now. I am dying and their life calls out to me.

"The train," I whispered to him and told him that one would be leaving for Galati in the morning, for I had recently looked up the time. They asked me to bring the schedule to them. Though I closed the doors behind me, their wood was thin enough that I could overhear Van Helsing. As I suspected, he knew that Dracula had read my mind. He told the others to keep the knowledge from me, as if knowing it would somehow undo me. I'm stronger than that, stronger than any of them suspect. Haven't I proven that so many times in the last few weeks?

Some time later, with the train schedule in my hand, I returned to them. Then, quite directly, I told them that I believed Dracula had read my mind and that they must not put me in contact with him again. My honesty had the effect I hoped it would. I am now in their confidence once more, and we shall continue our pursuit. I am certain that it will end as Dracula wishes it to end, at his terrible mountain aerie.

On his own land, they will be no match for him. I tried to warn Jonathan in private, but he will not be turned from the chase and the others are equally committed. I find myself contemplating the outcome as if life and death no longer hold any meaning for me, save the thrill of using my power. While I listened to the men planning the final strategy of the chase, I fed on their affection for me the way the vampire feeds on blood.

Is that so loathsome? More and more I wonder if Dracula has freed me rather than made me his slave.

And when the chase is over, however it ends, can I go back to being Mina Murray Harker, the same prim Englishwoman I was only months ago?

That future holds more terror for me than eternity at Dracula's side. And yet the words I write in my more public journal are true. I love my husband. I only hope that when this is over and we go home to our civilized world, our social confinement, he can still love me.

CHAPTER THREE

November 4. It has been days since I have been able to write. I do not know where to begin save at the moment that we arrived by rail in Galati only to discover that Dracula had eluded us once more. Through inquiries, we learned that he had departed by riverboat toward the center of his domain before we were able to search the ship that brought him back to his homeland.

As the fox retreats to his den, so the hunters quicken their pace. The men have their reason, and they make certain that I know it.

Jonathan and the others often comment on my strange emotionalism, the dull lack of energy with which I move through the daylight hours, as well as my difficulty sleeping at night. Van Helsing notes that my pulse is weaker and slower. Their observations are likely true, but the changes do not trouble me. I remind them often that the journey has been a hard and tiring one, and the tears and laughter I often display natural in a woman on the edge of exhaustion. Perhaps that is all it is, but they will not allow our quest to go unfinished. I suppose I should be grateful. If we broke off now, I would be under a cloud of suspicion for the rest of my days.

And when I die, they would treat my body as they did Lucy's. I tell myself that I would be past caring and that my fear for the shell that once held my soul is illogical. Still, the thought terrifies me.

Though I have no reason to trust Dracula, I take comfort in his promise to spare those I love. I reminded myself of it often while I wrote down my thoughts on what the men should do in order to continue the chase. After I showed them the map of the area and explained that the count had most likely arranged to be taken by boat as close to the Borgo Pass as possible, I saw them take heart once more. "All is not yet lost!" Quincey exclaimed. Van Helsing embraced me as if I were a daughter. Even Jonathan, who had been the most despondent of any of them at this new setback, seemed infused with new energy for the chase. I was prepared to insist that I be allowed to accompany them, but before I could, Van Helsing made a suggestion that I accompany him by coach while the men follow Dracula upriver on a launch.

"I cannot allow it," Jonathan said. It was the first time he had countered any of Van Helsing's instructions. I felt a rush of love for him, for I understood that, like me, he feared Van Helsing's obsessive concern with my change.

"Cannot?" Van Helsing bristled, contained his temper then went on soothingly. "I am an old man. I am not able to travel as you do. Though there is danger in taking Mina to the heart of his so-dark land, I will do it to save her."

I thought of the pistol in my traveling bag and how a vampire's strength was incredible. I could defend myself against Van Helsing. If it came to a struggle between us, it would be better if Jonathan did not witness the outcome.

"The professor is right," I said sweetly, taking Jonathan's hand. "He knows so much about the monster we face, I will be safer with him than with any of you."

Was it only weeks ago that my aunt sat with me in her parlor and warned me that in our marriage I would always be the stronger, the more intelligent? With my mind blinded by love and concern for Jonathan, I had politely ignored her. Now I understood the truth of her words. I wish Jonathan had disagreed with me for a while longer. If he had, I would respect him more. Instead he nodded and, with his hand holding mine, listened as Arthur and Quincey discussed the arrangements for our pursuit.

Within hours, I was at the riverbank saying good-bye to Jonathan. He and Quincey will travel on the water, hoping to overtake the barge that is carrying Dracula home. Jack and Arthur will travel by horseback along the river. Van Helsing and I will take a carriage to the Borgo Pass. Hopefully one party or the other will do "what must be done," as Jack Seward is so fond of saying.

Throughout the first day of the journey, Van Helsing acted the parts of father and physician, watching me constantly for any sign of fatigue so he could order me to sleep as if I were a stubborn child. I understood that the difference in our ages was partially responsible for his behavior and hid my resentment. As it was, I needed the sleep and lay in the back of the carriage, wrapped tightly in the fur coat and throws Van Helsing had purchased for our journey. Each time I woke, it was with greater difficulty. I would sit silently beside Van Helsing as we traveled through country increasingly more rugged and remote.

We stopped in midafternoon at a farmer's cottage to exchange horses. I smelled stew cooking and suggested to Van Helsing that we purchase a meal. The farmer's wife, a portly woman with flashing black eyes, smiled happily at the amount we offered and invited us inside to warm ourselves at the hearth, where a half dozen children waited for dinner. They stared at me with dark, slightly slanted eyes that made me understand just how far east we have traveled.

I unwrapped the scarf from around my face, exposing the scar the host had made on my forehead. The woman's eyes grew wide. She held out her index and smallest finger toward me and glanced at the door, as if assuring herself that the sun was still high in the sky before dishing out the stew. I smelled the garlic in it, and though it was spicy, I ate it anyway. Everyone looked at me so intently that I knew the food was a test of my nature and I dared not refuse it. Once I had taken a few bites and commented on the flavor of the bread, the family seemed to relax and fear turned to curiosity.

During the meal, I tried to speak to the woman, using a few of the words I had learned when I had come east to find Jonathan, but the dialect in this region was too different. However, as I was finishing the meal, the woman suddenly pressed a plain brass crucifix into my palm. I thought she was giving it to me, but she pulled it back then gestured that I hold out my hand. I did as she asked, angling my palm toward the firelight so she could see that the cross had left no mark. Relieved, she gripped my hand, made the sign of the cross over me and recited what I thought was a quick prayer.

"She recites a charm to protect you from the vampire," Van Helsing told me and translated. "May this sign protect you from the soulless ones who hunt the night."

I held out my hand as she had done. "This sign?" I asked in her language.

The woman nodded solemnly and, for a moment, the barrier between her world and mine crumbled. She placed two fingers on the scar on my forehead. She pressed her lips to my cheeks and mumbled something else, *"Binecuvintat."*

"She blesses you," Van Helsing said.

Tears came to my eyes. This time I could not hold them back. The woman hugged me as I sobbed, understanding without words the pain I was in. "Tell her thank you," I said, then repeated Van Helsing's words to her, *"Multumesc."*

As soon as Van Helsing was outside to help hitch up the fresh horses, I pointed to the cross and pulled a pair of gold pieces from my bag. Though the woman eyed my fortune with a blend of awe and greed, she would not make the exchange. As the professor and I drove on in the deepening gloom, I looked back at their little house with its thatch roof, at the woman standing outside it with her sheepskin boots and long brown woolen shawl. How vulnerable they were. In their isolation they would be such perfect prey. Yet it seemed to me that their very simplicity gave these people added protection from the vampire. They believe in this evil while civilized London would have been at Dracula's mercy. "I think they would have killed us had the cross burned my hand," I commented to Van Helsing.

"Be thankful it was unblessed," he replied.

I thought of the couple's poverty. The money I had offered had been the equivalent of months of work for the pair, yet the woman had refused. The cross had been blessed. I was certain of it. No, it was not damnation that left this scar on my face but rather a reflection of my own guilt and passion for the creature. Even if I had wished to argue with Van Helsing—hardly a good idea under the circumstances—I was far too tired, and a little ill from the food as well. I recalled crawling into the back of our cart, wrapping myself in the soft furs then nothing for hours.

* * *

WHEN I woke, it was after dark. I felt as if I had slept for days— refreshed, incredibly alive. Van Helsing noticed the change in me. It seemed to make him angry, perhaps because I could have guided the wagon as well as him. On the other hand, he was so exhausted from the journey that I took pity on him. He seemed terribly anxious and refused to give me the reins. Often he looked at the drop-offs on either side of the road as if fearful that were I in control, I would tip our tiny carriage over the side. I tried to make him relax, but he only did so after he had found a stand of rocks to shelter us and our horses for the night. "Have you ever seen such incredible mountains?" I asked him, for the jagged peaks around us were dark and beautiful against the evening sky.

"A place of evil," he commented. "We are near the Borgo Pass and the road to his castle. Be wary."

I built up the fire and tried to sleep, but after a day of rest I hardly needed it. I tried, however, until I saw Van Helsing nod off. I placed a second fur rug over him and walked a bit away from our campsite. As my eyes grew accustomed to the dark, the light grey around me, and for the first time in my life, I saw the incredible beauty of a wilderness sky. I inhaled and smelled pine and the musky scent of rotting leaves and earth just beginning its spring thaw.

City-bred, city-raised, I thought of how I had been blinded by the gaslights of Whitby and London, how the scents of burning coal and wood masked all others. I thought of how my emotions had been bound by convention and expectations. I found myself fumbling excitedly with my clothing, intending to rip off everything and run carelessly through the forest. I had begun to undo the first buttons of my jacket when I stopped and forced myself to think.

There is a blood tie between me and this land. The emotions I feel are too new, too alien and far too strong to have come from within me. I am being called to my death, or worse.

"How dare you!" I whispered to the darkness around me. "You swore to give me my freedom. Keep your pledge and I keep mine."

I turned back to Van Helsing, sleeping so soundly by the fire. I moved close to him and sat, thinking of little save that I remain there, until morning. For the first time in days, I was able to pull out my little journal and write this account. Unlike the journey on the train, the writing gives me no comfort, for I have suddenly noticed how easy it is to read my own words in the flickering fire.

My senses are becoming like his. No wonder I think of this land as beautiful.

November 5, dawn. I am alone, utterly alone in this snow-covered wilderness, and I am thankful for my solitude. The last day and night have been the most fascinating, and the most terrible, of my life, and I need time to think—to sort reality from delusion, to plan.

Yesterday began with frustration. Once we left the main road at the pass, Van Helsing and I traveled down roads that seemed no better kept than footpaths, backtracking often when we were certain we had gone the wrong way. We might have asked directions, but no one seems to live in this land of jagged peaks and towering mountain pines. I find myself realizing that it is not only Dracula that we must fear. The land itself, desolate and gripped by the savage winter, holds its own dangers. Without our team of horses and our well-laden wagon, we would be utterly lost.

By midmorning, the terrible lethargy gripped me again so that I was forced to sleep and let poor Van Helsing do all of the work. Concerned about my condition, he spoke to me often, calling to me loudly when I dozed off and did not reply. I was furious at being disturbed, and yet, after the temptation of the night before, I understood what troubled him. Dracula's hold on me is growing stronger. Soon all I will need to do is agree to the change and I will be as he is. The very fact that this nocturnal pattern seems so natural horrifies me most of all.

When I woke, it was late afternoon. Van Helsing was dozing with the reins held loosely in his hands. The horses had somehow found their own way to our destination, for the rotting walls of Dracula's castle, exactly as Jonathan had described it, loomed on the hill above us.

I reached for Van Helsing, intending to wake him, but my hand never touched him. Instead I fell asleep until dark. Then I apparently woke with great difficulty for Van Helsing was shaking me roughly and calling my name with some alarm until I opened my eyes.

As happened last night, I became agitated and excited immediately after sunset. Van Helsing took my pulse and felt my teeth. He did not have to say a word. My tongue had already confirmed what he feared. They were longer, sharper, ready for use. I trembled while Van Helsing wrapped me in the fur rugs we carried then marked a wide circle around me in the snow. As I watched, curious for my body's reaction, he crumbled two of the sacred hosts he had brought into the circle until I was surrounded with a blessed barrier. I sat, horrified by the understanding of what he was doing. Bloodless, cold as death itself, I watched him work.

"Come over to the fire," he called to me when he had finished.

I understood the test he was making. His eyes gleamed in the light; his hands tightened around the stick he was using to tend the fire. I wanted to go to him, to prove once and for all that I was not damned. I stood and took a step toward him.

As I did, the wind shifted, carrying his scent to me—stale sweat, garlic from last night's meal and, over all, the smell of blood. The attraction of the last overpowered the others. A hunger coursed through my body as the blood coursed through his. I could fight the desire to feed on him, indeed my dislike of him somehow made the act of feeding more despicable, but the feeling was too new, too strong. I dared not trust my will.

My expression must have given my thoughts away, for Van Helsing stared at me a moment, his eyes so clear in the half-light, so filled with relentless understanding. "You will destroy me if I become undead," I whispered. He might have seen this as self-pity, or a need to be certain that he will end my life if it is necessary. Perhaps he even understood that I meant this as no more than honesty, an acknowledgment that this truth should be stated. I would never know. Without a word, he returned to tending the fire.

Through the evening, the horses had complained often, protesting the cold, the absence of any real shelter, the distant howling of a pack of wolves. Later they began to whinny with fear. Van Helsing went to them, stroking them and talking softly to calm them. As he did, I detected the sound of seductive laughter carried on the winds of the night from the castle to my mind. The moon that had first given some light was soon covered by clouds, and a heavy wet snow began to fall.

I knew what this meant all too well. My sisters were coming. I sat hugging my knees, rocking my body, waiting happily for them—my new kin!

When the snow was at its heaviest, a glowing white mist rolled down the path from the castle, bringing with it what seemed at first a rush of lighter snowflakes. The flakes whirled in a vortex that could be seen but not felt. Indeed, the air was strangely still. The laughter I had heard only in my mind became audible, and following it, their bodies took form. As they did, I saw Van Helsing make a slow circle, reciting a prayer as he held out his last host. I dared not ask him to come and seek protection with me, and he knew enough to not do so.

Dracula's brides may have been ordinary in life, but in death their power made them beautiful. As Jonathan had described, two were dark and resembled Dracula. The third was very fair, in the manner of Irish women, with honey-colored hair and eyes blue as an autumn sky. Her smile was so coquettish that I could not help but see the resemblance to poor Lucy.

Their voices tinkled like strings of tiny brass bells in a spring breeze. Their lips were red against their teeth like some bold harlot's, their voices sweet as they called to me, "Sister. Sister, come and join us."

I wanted to! But in spite of their allure—perhaps because of the crumbled host circling me, or Dracula's promise, or only my own stubborn will—I knew I had a choice. Yet there was one temptation that could not be resisted. I held my hand beyond the circle.

"Stop!" Van Helsing cried, but even as he rushed forward, he dropped his last remaining host. It fell into the shadows of the snow-covered ground. I heard his cry of frustration as he knelt and groped for it. As he did, the darkest of the three vampire women stepped forward and eyed my outstretched arm. Though I recognized the hunger in her gaze and knew she could easily pull me from the circle and end my human life, my arm was steady. I had to touch her!

She clasped my hand in both of hers. I felt the hardness of her flesh, sensed the incredible strength of her delicate hands as they pulled me to the edge of the sacred circle.

That touch, light as the brush of a wind-tossed feather, changed my life forever.

I whispered her name—Illona—then leaned forward, willingly letting her hands explore my face, her lips brush the scar on my forehead.

I had already decided that God would not damn me without my full consent. Consent requires knowledge. In Dracula's absence, this woman shared hers with me. Good and evil, ecstasy and terror flowed into me with a swiftness that made me weak. Her hands on either side of my head were all that kept me from collapsing as I sank slowly to my knees before her.

I had guessed the age of these creatures by Dracula's history, but the years had meant nothing without some understanding of their passing. She gave me that. She and I watched the last battlements of the crumbling castle erected in the months after she came here as his child bride.

Yes, she had loved him, admired him, shared his cause as a true wife must. She even damned herself for him.

As their enemies grew, she made a pact with the Lord of Darkness. I saw her standing alone in one of the castle rooms, her body bathed by firelight and incense. The room was cold, so cold that in spite of the blue woolen cloak she had tightly wrapped around her, she kept close to the fire. I shared her resolve, her incredible courage as she watched the grotesque form of the master she had chosen lumbering from the shadows of the room toward the place where she stood so still, as if death had already claimed her. "I believe," she whispered and knelt to kiss the ruby ring on his finger, to grasp his dark and taloned hand.

She had hoped to drink from him—only to drink—but he

wanted more. With growing horror, she watched his yellow reptilian eyes study her lithe body, watched his hands move toward her cloak and pull it from her. "My slave," he said, his voice soft and sweet, so at odds with his ugliness. I thought of Eve in the garden. The snake would have spoken in a voice such as this.

Then he kissed her, sinking his long fangs into his own lips as he did so. She shuddered as she kissed him, but with the first taste of his blood, her loathing turned swiftly to desire.

I understood too well the horror she felt, for I had glimpsed some measure of her passion when I drank from Dracula. But he had once been a man, still had the semblance of a man. This creature had never been human, had never known love or tenderness, only the dark beauty of suffering, the fulfillment of pain.

As his blood moved swiftly through her, turning her instantly into the creature she had longed to become, his savagery increased. He could do as he wished to her for she could no longer die.

When he was sated, when her body lay ripped and bleeding on the cold stone floor of the room, when her tortured, hysterical sobs no longer amused him, he left her to pull the tattered remnants of her soul back together and live forever in eternal life-in-death.

He gave her his dark gift. When the change was complete, she could not die and those who tasted her blood would share her immortality.

How she begged her husband to accept her gift! How she swore that nothing within her had changed, that they could love one another forever. Her lips were warm as they kissed him, her touch more wanton than ever before. In the end, out of love and need to protect his people he weakened and took the blood she offered then left to command what could well be his legions' final battle.

The Turks were breaking through Dracula's last defenses,

when Illona threw herself from the castle walls in full view of them. I sensed her terror as she fell, then nothing until the night she wandered the carnage of Dracula's final battlefield, searching for his body among the rotting piles of the dead. There were so many that had fallen on both sides, yet only one was truly of her blood. As she pulled the reeking corpses from the mound where Dracula lay dressed in the coat of a common soldier, she saw that his wounds had already begun to heal. In the bowels of the castle, she laid him in the tomb she had prepared for him. She nursed him with her own blood. That and his native soil slowly restored him. It took months for the wounds to heal completely. When they did, he rose into her life.

I saw his face when he first woke. How radiant it had seemed, how filled with wonder. How quickly that wonder died.

The pair had done this for the sake of their people, but after the change, the needs of mortals meant nothing to them. They lost all concern about the people inhabiting their lands. Blood, after all, is the same. They were mad for a while, reveling in the carnage their powers allowed them.

The memories took hours to sort and place in order, the words themselves so many minutes to write, yet all this was thrust into my mind in only a moment. In the next, Van Helsing, armed with the crumbling host, moved between me and the woman.

She retreated. Van Helsing pursued her until she joined her pale sisters, then he ran to the protection of his sacred circle.

As for me, I lay facedown in the snow. What happened between them seemed unimportant to me in the face of one terrible final revelation.

The bargain the woman had struck could have been made by others. There could be dozens of these creatures scattered throughout the world.

"Come to us," the three called to me, holding out their delicate hands. "Be with us, a sister forever."

I didn't move. Instead I knelt in the center of the circle, horrified most by the temptation their offer held for me. Seductive. Powerful. Eternal. So beyond the judgment of God Himself. What of my love for Jonathan, my responsibilities to the family I had left in England, the life I had led?

"Sisters," I whispered, I begged. "Sisters, please give me time. Leave us in peace."

The fools turned their attention to Van Helsing instead. I saw them bare their bodies before him, showing him the perfection of life-in-death. They kissed one another, touched one another, their hands moving seductively, their lips parted with a passion I often felt deep inside but never dared express. They had one another, used one another in an incest perfected through the centuries. Their laughter grew husky, sensual, inviting as they moved to the edge of Van Helsing's circle and stretched out their bare arms to him.

In spite of his age and his intellect and his determination, Van Helsing was affected by their passion. His mouth hung slack, his hands rose, seemingly of their own accord, to reach toward them, then, fists clenched, Van Helsing the hunter, the slayer, the righteous one began to force them back to his side. As he did, they grabbed his arm, pulling it out of the circle. With their eyes turned seductively toward his, they held his hand against their breasts, they brushed their tapered fingers over his lips. The boldest of them licked Van Helsing's wrist and bit deep. For an instant he was helpless, frozen by the touch of her lips and the enthralling passion that touch gave. I sensed his anger at his own weakness, his abhorrence of their seduction. They did not understand the righteousness of the man they faced, or they would not have tempted him so.

"Go!" I cried to them again. "Leave us now!"

The fear in my voice made them pause and look at me. Understanding that I spoke a warning, they smiled and drifted away from us. Some time later, the horses that had been whinnying in fear ceased their sounds. The women reappeared momentarily, their faces flushed with the blood they had consumed. The fair one blew me a kiss, her smile young and filled with delight as they faded into a mist that dissolved at the touch of the pale dawn light.

CHAPTER FOUR

November 6. I recalled nothing more until I woke to find the sun had risen. The day is dark. There are wolf prints in the new fallen snow around the campsite, yet Van Helsing is gone. Only one thing would make him leave me unarmed and at the mercy of the unseen pack—he has gone to destroy the women. I expect that soon I will know the outcome of his quest, one way or the other. The women were fools to try to tempt him. Their terrible beauty may have aroused him, but it only makes his path more clear. As to the women's power, it is daylight—his time, not theirs.

I found it easy to leave my holy circle, but there was nowhere to go. I have built up the fire as best I can. Now I sit beside it, watching the gray shapes of wolves moving in the shadows of the trees. I am so tired, yet sleep could well be fatal. So I wait, hoping that should the wolves decide to attack me, they will kill me quickly and finally. The pack has grown in size . . . I must pause in my writing and watch them . . . Van Helsing, where have you gone?

An hour or more passed while the wolves grew bolder, circling closer to me. Often I had to pull a flaming branch out of the fire and stab at them to scare them off.

Finally, they tired of the sport and found an easier meal in our dead horses. As I watched the pack at their feast, once more the blood lust was upon me. I waited until the pack had eaten their fill then lifted a flaming branch and walked toward them. My display of courage confused them, and they retreated, allowing me to kneel beside the warm carcass, to press my fingers against the bloody meat then lick them clean.

The scent. The taste. Finer than the richest wine, the most exquisite meal. I yielded to my hunger, dipping my hands into the mangled carcass, feasting as I had not done in days on Van Helsing's charred meat. It had been so long since I had felt so satisfied. When I was done, I looked down at my bloody hands, the bits of flesh sticking to the fur of my wrap. I had become an animal. No, worse!

Van Helsing must never know what I had done! I ran to the fire, melted some snow and washed all traces of the meal from my face, clothes and hands then took out this journal and wrote these words.

Though it can hardly be past noon, the sky has darkened and a heavy wet snow falls once more. I am sitting in the covered back of the wagon writing this account. An exhilaration has taken hold of me. Whatever the outcome, soon everything will be over. My entire future depends on the next few hours, yet all I feel is curiosity, as if I have already died and am about to view the manner of my ending.

The snow falls harder, dancing in the wind. Whorls of it move closer to the carriage. I see the faces of my sisters in it. I am alone. No one can stop me now as I go out to dance with them . . .

The women were only there in spirit. Even when their garments moved in the wind, brushing against my outstretched hands, I could not feel them touching me. Spectral hands reached for mine, spectral arms circled me. "Van Helsing has gone to destroy you. You must not stay with me," I cautioned them, feeling no remorse for my warning. "If you are able, go back to your bodies, leave your sleeping room and hide."

The fair one smiled with lips together to hide the strangeness of her teeth. "What can he do? He will never find us," she said, laughter rippling through her voice.

"Jonathan Harker is my husband. He found your resting place. He told Van Helsing where to look."

The dark-haired one who was Dracula's wife grew even whiter, if that were possible. She opened her mouth, as if to agree with my warning, but no sound came from her. Instead, I saw the vision begin to fade. As it did, a sudden gush of blood burst through the white skin of her chest, staining her diaphanous gown. Her terrible shriek of agony vanished in the winter wind.

Her blood was my blood, her pain my pain. I doubled over, clutching my chest as if to shield them all from Van Helsing's stakes. The screams continued, borne on the wind as the three vanished from my sight, one bloody apparition after another, the fair-haired one the last to go. Though I saw her wince, saw the blood spread across her chest, she remained silent. As she vanished, I saw an expression on her face that seemed inexplicably one of triumph, as if what had happened were meant to happen.

It seemed that I was to be killed as well. A great weight pressed against my chest. I tried to take a breath and found it impossible. My heart pounded, and I folded slowly to my knees as darkness closed in around me.

Sisters, I thought. Sisters, may your souls wait for me.

* * *

WHEN I regained consciousness, snow was falling heavily though the sky seemed lighter, giving some promise that the storm would soon end. Van Helsing had returned and stood near the fire putting on a clean coat. A second, bloody one lay on the ground beside him. I looked at him, horrified by the knowledge of what he had done.

"It is all right. I am not hurt," he said, then went back to his washing, hoping perhaps that I would return to sleep. I stood and walked to the fire.

"When the sky clears, it will be colder. The castle could give us shelter," I suggested. "The men are sure to come there."

He shook his head. "You especially must not rest within the walls," he said.

"Because of the bodies?" I asked him, the sharpness of my voice betraying my anger.

He looked at me curiously, paused for emphasis, then said, "The women are dust, Madame Mina. Their souls are at peace. No, you must not go because it is his lair. The very walls will call to you. No . . . you must not."

I didn't have the strength to argue. Instead, I helped him collect our bundles. Then, burdened by the weight of our baggage and the exhaustion the day always gives me, slipping often on the snow-covered rocks, I followed Van Helsing down the path to the distant road.

We had traveled less than a quarter mile when we saw fresh wolf prints in the snow. A bit later, I saw a pair of the beasts on the path below us. "Professor," I whispered and pointed.

Two more appeared, the pack blocking our descent. Van Helsing scanned the rocky ground around us and motioned me into a little hollow. There, an overhang made it impossible for the wolves to attack from above, and the narrow entrance assured that they would have to pass into the space single file. "We shoot them if they come," he said, lifting a revolver. I pulled Quincey's pistol from my pack and crouched beside him.

The wolves seemed content to stop our journey. Hours passed and they did not attack. Though the snow continued, occasional clear patches of sky to the west showed the height of the sun. We waited anxiously as the afternoon stretched on forever.

"Is the vampire close, Madame Mina?" Van Helsing asked.

I nodded and pushed myself to my feet. As I did, I noticed that the valley below us was visible from the stand of rocks. On the road that wound through it, I could make out a number of riders and a cart of some sort heading toward us. Even more distant were two riders—no doubt some of our party in pursuit. "They're coming," I called to Van Helsing.

Van Helsing looked from the road to the setting sun, measuring the time the men had before Dracula woke. I did not need to look. Dracula was already awake in his box, waiting for the moment when he could rise in his own land—powerful, ready for the kill.

I felt Dracula's rage rise in me as well, and fought it down with horror. Whatever I had become, I was still Mina, wife to Jonathan. I recalled how much I loved my husband. The thought was all that sustained me as I helped Van Helsing collect our furs.

"We go down to them," he told me. "There is a path . . . see it?"

I considered the road we had been traveling—icy and treacherous even before this heavy snowfall. To me, the straight descent appeared impossible. "Wait," I said and scanned the landscape below, pointing to a second pair of riders coming from the west. "This is the only road to the castle. If we remain here, they will have to pass right by us," I said.

Van Helsing smiled. "Ah, dear Mina, you are right. We stay and trap them. We shall make certain that the cart does not pass."

I nodded my agreement, and the two of us waited as the cart and riders began the ascent on our path. There were nearly a dozen of them, all colorfully dressed, with turban-shaped fur hats covering their heads and ears. Some carried rifles, others only knives. It seemed to me that our little band was terribly outnumbered, but I knew Jonathan and the others coming up behind them were desperate.

Through the windblown snow, I could see the sun nearly touching the peaks in the clear western sky. The men would not reach the cart in time. "Remember your promise," I whispered to the creature being carried toward me.

"Madame Mina?" Van Helsing said. "Did you speak?"

"A prayer."

"Good," he replied and crouched lower behind the concealing stones.

As the gypsy leader approached the place where we were hidden, he raised his hand and the group halted. I thought we had been spied, but he gave us no notice. The terrain may have been dangerous or he may have glimpsed the wolves. When they continued forward, it was with greater caution.

Van Helsing muttered something under his breath. I glanced sideways at him and saw the gleam in his eye as he waited for the men to reach us. It was the same expression I had seen when he sat in Dr. Seward's comfortable parlor and described the powers of the vampire, as well as when he faced the three vampire women. Whoever served Dracula was an enemy—human or not, they were easily destroyed. I suddenly felt less guilty for my duplicity. There, on that snow-covered incline, I understood what an implacable enemy Van Helsing would be.

I had no time to contemplate this, for Jonathan and Quincey were riding hard up the path, closely followed by Arthur and Jack.

The gypsy band halted and drew their weapons. Without slackening his pace, Quincey fired, hitting the gypsy in the back of the cart. Another returned fire. I saw Quincey recoil, but though he had been hit, he drew his knife and charged toward the band. Taking advantage of a break in the gypsy ranks, Jonathan jumped onto the cart and began prying at the clasp on Dracula's crate while Quincey single-handedly held off the band until the others rode up to help him.

They were too late. The sun, no more than a pale ball of light beneath the clouds, sank behind the craggy mountains, the shadow of its passing rolling over the land.

From the place where I was hiding, I could look down on the cart. I saw the lid of the crate flung back, Dracula's eyes open and glowing with triumph as they met Jonathan's. The vampire's timing had been nearly perfect. Even so, Jonathan did not hesitate to do what he had been told would save me. He stabbed his knife downward at Dracula's neck while Quincey aimed his for Dracula's heart.

The look of malice on the vampire's face became one of peace. The body vanished into a dusty mist that whirled in an ever-widening circle and was lost to the rising wind. The gypsy leader motioned silently to his men. With those who had been in the wagon riding double with those on horseback, they fled down the mountain. Van Helsing watched them go, his brow furrowed in puzzlement at their sudden retreat.

As he did, the sky above the castle darkened and the wind became a gale, swelling as if demons themselves ordered it out of revenge for their fallen comrade. As the storm grew, snow began to fall so heavily that I could no longer see the men. The sound of their cries and the whinnying of the horses seemed to come from all around me.

And with the storm came a compulsion so strong that I am certain it could only have come from Dracula or others of his kind. Unable to stand in the force of the terrible wind, I crawled slowly uphill toward the castle.

The outer gates were open. Snow drifted in the courtyard and softened the jagged edges of the crumbling walls. I pushed open the carved wood doors and wandered into the hall. Though I had read a description of the place in Jonathan's diary, it seemed even more familiar to me, as if I had seen it firsthand many years ago. I found a torch where I expected to find it, a flint box on a ledge beside it. The smoky light it threw was scarcely enough to illuminate a portion of one wall. Had I the time, I would have looked at everything, would have run my hands over the carved rail of the stone staircase, studied every detail of the ancient paintings on the walls. Instead, I quickly made my way to the lower chambers where the women had slept.

When I reached the stone passage that led to their hall, I lifted the torch I carried and surveyed the walls. They were decorated with tapestries of oriental design. A few were of delightful landscapes. Others, far more profane, showed naked couples in the varied positions of lovemaking. Had there been anyone with me, I might have been embarrassed, but alone I found them fascinating and, in spite of my weariness, arousing. I suppose that was their purpose, for any visitor who would wander so far would be ready for the sensual trap the women would have waiting in their chamber.

The room where the women lay was as vast as the upper hall, yet signs of Van Helsing's carnage were everywhere. Blood coated the stones beneath the caskets and formed dark collars around the heads that rested together on the ground. Their expressions made it clear that the women had not died in peace. Rats, surprised at their feast, scurried away as I walked toward the caskets. As I expected, the bodies had not crumbled into dust. In horror, I stared at the wooden stakes pounded between their exposed breasts, the blood covering their smooth flesh.

Throughout this terrible journey, I had noted Van Helsing's obsession. Often he had hinted at some ancient hatred he had for the vampire. I had no doubt that Van Helsing believed he served a righteous purpose, yet I knew otherwise. The seductive power of these women had unnerved him. A man such as him had no choice but to destroy.

I thought of Van Helsing ripping open their gowns, stopping to marvel at the perfection of their flesh. Had he touched them before he began the killing? Had their beauty made him pause at all? I doubted it.

I ran my fingers over the tips of their delicate hands, then, bolder, over the cold breasts that might have suckled children centuries ago. "I'm sorry," I whispered to each of them. "Sorry that it came to this." I knew from the color of the body which had been the fair one. She wore a silver filigree ring with a ruby stone. I slipped it off her finger and onto mine. Then I kissed her blood-soaked flesh. Though the blood still tasted sweet, it held no warmth, no memories. I said a prayer for all of them and for myself as well, for I had never felt such despair.

I looked around me, hoping to see some sign that what Van

Helsing had done had been justified. All I saw was a pile of animal bones, stripped clean by the vermin. Recalling Jonathan's journal, I looked closely at the pile but detected no remnants of human victims.

There were no settlements in the area, I quickly reminded myself, nor even any farms. The natives had vanished—fled or devoured. I wondered why the women had not followed them, traveling as Dracula had to London, instead of living on animals and occasional unwary travelers.

The only other thing of interest in the room was a wooden box on a table near the door. I lifted the lid and found a book with black leather cover and parchment pages. It appeared to be a journal, written in a delicate script in a language I did not know. The last entry was not dated, yet the writing seemed fresh. Had one of them kept an account as I did? What might she have recorded in all the years of her life? I placed it in the inner pocket of my coat, vowing to find someone to translate the account the woman had set down.

But there was one thing more I had to do. I lifted the torch and set the tapestries that adorned the room to burning. Without a backward glance, I made my way through the passage and started up the too-familiar stairs.

My soul was mine, as Dracula had promised. My choice was mine, and he had promised that as well. I could have died in that room, by my own hand, and awakened to his world. Instead I had chosen Jonathan and the world I knew. I brushed my forehead and felt the smooth skin. The scar left by the host had vanished.

I would be wife to Jonathan, someday mother to his children. And yet I wonder. Is Dracula alive? I think of him beaten in one more battle, utterly alone in his dark castle. He has had centuries to grow used to loss. He will find others to replace the women Van Helsing killed, and in time he will forget about me. But if he is indeed alive, what consequence is his blood in me?

A crash in the chamber behind me must have opened some

passage directly to the outside, for suddenly the stairway I climbed filled with smoke. Holding my breath, I climbed faster. My cloak tangled around my legs and I fell. Instinctively, I took a breath and coughed. My eyes watered, and on hands and knees I climbed the stairs. The air grew hotter. The inferno rose to claim me.

"Jonathan," I whispered, and as I looked at the now-glowing smoke, I thought I saw my sisters waiting for me. I smiled at them, lay my head on my arm and closed my eyes. Death was coming. I could feel it a long way off, but moving closer. I didn't care to struggle any more.

November 9. We are on the train, this time heading west. Our little group is smaller. Only Dr. Seward, Jonathan and I are traveling to England. Van Helsing chose to stay in the area and continue his research on Dracula and vampirism. I understand his need to do this all too well, for he knows that nothing is really settled. As for Arthur . . .

Order, Mina! Even in this private journal events should be recorded in order, particularly now that the others have finished their accounts of this terrible adventure and this will be the only recording of its aftermath.

I woke in the courtyard of Dracula's castle with my head resting on Jonathan's knees. He had been using snow to wipe the soot from my face. I think the coldness of it shocked me into consciousness. My lungs were still filled with smoke, and I coughed and gagged until I caught my breath. When I did, I looked around me. The winds had diminished and a light snow fell, the huge flakes softening the jagged stones of the walls, the pitted ground of the courtyard. Wisps of smoke still rose from the open castle doors. The fire must have died before it reached the upper floors, no doubt because the passage had been made of stone.

"Are the others with you?" I asked when I was able.

I saw sorrow in Jonathan's expression, heard the pain in his reply. "The others are with Quincey. The gypsies shot him and he is dying, I think. He lost a great deal of blood. I could do nothing for him so I came to find you."

"Do the others know I've come up here?"

"We couldn't see anything in that storm. Don't you remember?"

"I do." But I wanted to be certain, absolutely certain. "Van Helsing told me not to come here. He said the walls themselves would tempt me. But . . ." I paused, loathing the idea of telling him how I had been drawn here. ". . . But the storm came so fast, I lost my way. The only thing I could see in the gale was the castle wall above me. I knew there would be shelter here. And then . . . Oh, Jonathan, I had to see the place where they had lain and be certain they were truly gone. You'll understand when Van Helsing and I tell you everything that happened to us."

"Did you find that place?" he asked in a low voice.

I wanted to tell him about the bodies and Van Helsing's lie, but everyone had been so concerned about me that I feared to do so. "I found the coffins. Then I burned their chamber, but the fire grew so fast."

He held me tightly. I had never felt so thankful for his arms before. "When I brought you outside and saw that the scar had vanished from your forehead, I was so afraid. I thought it was a sign that you were dying," he whispered. "Now it's over. We can go home."

"The others, we must go to them," I said.

"Not yet. Rest awhile."

"Take me to Quincey, please. I want to say good-bye." Jonathan helped me to stand, and I leaned heavily against him, fighting the terrible dizziness as we descended to the place where Van Helsing and the others tried with no real hope to save Quincey's life.

Nothing could be done. As Jonathan watched, I walked forward and knelt beside the brash American, making certain that he saw my unblemished forehead. "Ah," he said and smiled and let out one final breath. The vapor hung in the cold air then dissipated in the frigid wind.

They unloaded the box that had held Dracula, wrapped Quincey in some of the fur rugs and started back to Galati. Arthur decided to book passage to America and take Quincey's body home. Van Helsing seemed triumphant at their victory over the vampire. The others only mourned.

As we traveled down the mountain, Van Helsing looked up at the castle, noting the wisps of smoke rising from inside its walls. He glanced at me and I met his gaze steadily. "Let it burn," I said.

He did not question me.

* * *

WE held the final meeting of our quest after we returned to Galati. Arthur, who had lost his love and one of his closest friends, seemed the most affected by the events, the most sedate as we discussed our future. He had already decided to take Quincey's body back to America. Van Helsing declared his intentions to remain in the area and continue his research on vampires.

"Everything is finished. We've won, haven't we?" Jonathan asked with concern.

Van Helsing knew the truth as well as I, but he replied, "Of course. But there may be more of those creatures. We must be careful." Van Helsing looked directly at me as he continued, "And you must keep silent about what we have done, particularly what happened to Madame Mina."

"I hadn't intended to speak about any of it," Arthur said. "But why shouldn't I?"

"I obtained my knowledge from others who are just as determined as I to end the vampires' curse. Some of them are not so trusting in God's grace and goodness. Do not draw their interest."

Van Helsing had been fanatic enough. I gripped Jonathan's arm and nodded. I was thankful that I had not mentioned to Jonathan the journal I had taken from the castle, for he would certainly make me give it to Van Helsing.

When the others retired for the evening, I stayed behind to speak to Van Helsing in private. I think he waited for me to confess that I had seen the women's bodies. Instead, I spoke as candidly as I dared, dreading his reply. "It isn't really over, is it?" I asked.

He took my hands, his own shaking slightly with fatigue or age or emotion. "I know much, Madame Mina. I know not everything. Here I will hope to learn more. Go home. Be wife to your husband, the strength he needs. I will write, hopefully to say that all is as well as I believe it to be."

He kissed my cheek and held me tightly. "Daughter," he whispered as he let me go. I saw that the word had not been said lightly, for there were tears in his eyes.

PART TWO

Mina

CHAPTER FIVE

On the train ride west, Mina finally gave way to the exhaustion of the long ordeal and slept late the following morning. At breakfast time, Jonathan knocked lightly on the door to Dr. Seward's compartment and received no reply. Thankful for the time alone, he dined quickly then retreated to the smoking car. The crystal chandeliers tinkled lightly from the swaying of the train, reminding him uncomfortably of the laughter of the vampire women. He ordered a double brandy neat and stared into the glass, thinking how luminous their skin had been, how glowing their eyes.

Now they were dead and he was alive and everything could be the way it had been. Except . . .

He explored his despondence, finally focusing on the truth of what he had done.

He was a solicitor. The others had been interested in revenge and adventure and, particularly in the case of Van Helsing, a rigid form of righteousness. Jonathan had joined them because he had no choice. With Mina's soul hanging in the balance, he should have reveled in the act.

Instead he had suffered the quest with stoic misery, fighting his terror every step of the way. Even when he and Quincey were in hot pursuit of the cart carrying Dracula's helpless body home, Jonathan had decided there was something to be said for being a poor rider. He would not be the one to reach the cart first. Then he had been caught up in the final heroic moments and, determined to insure that his wife would not turn into one of those terrible and alluring creatures he had faced in the castle, he had gripped the cold hilt of the huge kukri blade he carried and spurred his horse onward. He hardly recalled the final moments of the ride, or how he had jumped from his horse to the cart. He recalled only that he had killed.

Try as he might to rationalize that Dracula had died centuries before, he knew he had killed.

In spite of the crimes of his victim and all Jonathan's certainty that there was no other outcome possible, this did not sit well with his conscience.

And why were the vampire women still on his mind? Why had he, only an hour before, looked down at his sleeping wife with her slightly open lips, her tiny hands and delicate arms resting so beautifully on the brown wool blanket, her tousled chestnut hair, and wished that her brows were darker, her hair thicker, her lips more red.

Mina! If these were his thoughts, what must hers be?

The final question numbed him. He ordered a second brandy then, without any real plan in mind, purchased the rest of the bottle and carried it back to the compartment he was now able to share with his wife. He found her awake, sitting at her dressing table with her traveling cape covering her nightdress.

She had been writing something in a thin journal. When she saw him, she closed the book without letting the ink dry and placed it in her pocket. "You're still taking notes, I see," he said uneasily.

"Just a few thoughts. So much has happened." She hesitated then added, "Poor Quincey."

She faced the mirror and began pinning up her hair. "Let it lie free," he said.

She turned from the little mirror on the door of their tiny closet. Her brow was furrowed, her expression puzzled. "Jonathan?" she asked.

He poured her a drink and held it out to her. "I know it's early in the day," he said. "But we've been through so much, I thought you might like to join me in a toast."

"A toast?"

"To Quincey, who was such a brave man and . . ." He had to say it, as close to a confession of his thoughts as he dared go. ". . . to Dracula, who was once a great general, a protector of his people. May his soul now rest in peace."

Why did Mina seem so suddenly remote?

"Do you think it's wrong to raise a glass to him?" he asked.

"No. I think it's admirable." She lifted the glass and touched it against his, sipping her brandy then setting the rest on the bed-stand.

"Even after what happened to Quincey?"

"Forgiveness is always . . ." She hesitated and looked at him. She had always been perceptive, but now the talent seemed heightened, as if something of Dracula's mental power remained in her. She seemed to forget what she was going to say and looked down at her hands, clearly flustered.

The silence became long and awkward. "How do you feel?" he finally asked.

"Like myself. The sleep did me good. And I suspect dinner will taste marvelous."

"Dinner is not for another hour at least." He sat beside her, aware of the warmth of her body even through his coat and shirt. He took her hands in one of his—so soft they were, so warm!— and with the other turned her head toward him and lifted her chin for a kiss.

What was intended to be a light kiss between husband and wife became something more. He ground his lips against her, forcing her mouth open. He felt her indrawn breath—surprise, then an even more surprising response. Her arms wrapped around him, pulling him close.

Yes, she was perceptive. She knew what he wanted and was willing to give even that. Stunned by what he demanded, humbled by his love for her, he drew back and saw the tears in her eyes.

"Mina, I'm sorry," he whispered.

"I love you, Jonathan." She spoke as if he felt some doubt.

He recalled with sudden clarity a moment ten days before when he and Quincey were alone together in a compartment such as this. The two of them had earlier come upon Van Helsing and Seward whispering together in the smoking car. The subject apparently changed when he and the American joined them; the conversation remained awkward until he and Quincey left to return to the compartment they shared with Arthur. At the door, Jonathan had turned back and seen the two speaking once more, their heads close, the voices low.

"How can you tolerate the way those two are always watching Mina," Quincey had said when they were alone. "They act like she's dying when it's clear she is better than she's been in weeks. You should be with her, not cooped up in here sleeping triple with Arthur and me."

"Van Helsing doesn't think that wise," Jonathan had replied carefully, not certain how to respond to Quincey's American directness.

"You've been married for what, six weeks . . . Well, I'm sorry. I guess I just don't see things with quite the same reserve as the English." Quincey hardly sounded apologetic.

Jonathan had waited until Quincey was asleep before slipping out of the compartment and going to Mina. He had stood at the foot of her bed, staring at his wife, so innocent save for the terrible scar on her forehead that was visible even in the moonlight shining through the window. Though she had been sound asleep when he arrived, she seemed to sense his presence and held out her arms to him. He kissed her once, chastely, but she pulled him closer to her, responding with a passion he had never felt in her before.

"Mina," he whispered, stroking back the locks of hair that had fallen over her forehead.

"Promise me that they will not be harmed," she whispered. "I will do anything if you only promise me."

"Of course," he replied and moved away from her, guessing what presence she thought was in her room, the bargain she would strike with the vampire to save his life. He retreated before he gave in to the petulant temptation of waking her and telling her what she had promised.

Now he found himself wishing that she would display that passion to him. It was unreasonable to be jealous of a vampire, a creature who could force Mina to respond to him, yet Jonathan was. How could he be so cruel, so blind! He reached out and gently wiped the tears from her eyes. "I'm sorry, darling," he said. "It was callous of me to come to you so soon."

She was about to say something, but he could not bear to hear her justify his action. "I'll come for you when dinner is announced," he said and left quickly.

The train had stopped to take on water. Through a window that had been cracked for air, he heard it flowing into the tank car, felt the vibration its rushing caused. He paused to listen, to think of what he could do for Mina, but she would not remain in the center of his mind.

What were the women's names? he wondered. What sort of lives had they led before they became Dracula's terrible brides?

Dr. Seward opened his compartment door. "There you are! Care to join me for drink and a cigar?" he asked.

"Just a moment. I bought a bottle," Jonathan replied and went back into his own compartment to retrieve it. Mina stood looking out at the town. "Craiova, isn't it?" she asked without looking at him.

"I think so."

"When we leave this land and the terrible reminders it gives us both, things will be better," she said as if trying to assure herself of it.

"Of course." He kissed the back of her neck and fingered a lock of her hair. "I love you," he added. She turned and wrapped her arms around his neck, pressing her face against his shoulder. "I came back for the bottle. Jack and I are going to have a drink. Should I have him go on without me?"

She shook her head. "I'll join you in a little while," she said.

As he left, he looked back and saw that she had turned her face toward the window once again. He was certain she was trying to hide her tears.

Why shouldn't she hide them? he thought as he sat in the smoking car with Dr. Seward. Every time she had acted the least bit emotional, feminine as his father had once called it, Van Helsing had responded with concern. The entire trip east had been terrible for Jonathan, evoking all the memories of his weeks in Dracula's castle. How much worse must Mina have felt? Fool! he thought and must have mouthed the word, for Dr. Seward looked up from his paper.

"Are you all right?" Seward asked.

"Just preoccupied." It occurred to him that this might be the most helpful person he could talk with—but only about Mina. His own problem was easy enough to identify. "It's Mina. I'm concerned that what she's been through will have a . . . a sort of delayed effect on her."

"Has she given any sign that there's a problem?"

"Just. Well, she was crying today. And yesterday . . . she seemed so passive. That's not like Mina."

"Don't worry about her. She's been so strong through this ordeal that it's about time she let her emotions out. She's healthy—emotionally as well as physically. She'll recover with no scars, I promise you."

"Of course, she is quite all right now."

Jonathan hadn't asked a question, but Seward sensed his uncertainty. "Van Helsing assured me that when the vampire died, the scar would vanish from her face, and it did. He said that when the vampire died, his blood in her would die as well. I have no way of checking that last, Jonathan, but I trust Van Helsing. The scar is gone. What other proof do we need?"

Mina's assurance, Jonathan thought. That was what had not been given.

Soon after, the two men and Mina sat together in the dining car. White linen covered the table. Broad-based crystal goblets and silver utensils circled the plates. Though they had eaten here three times already, this was the first time Jonathan had noticed the luxury and how right his wife looked sitting in the midst of it. The cameo she wore on her high-necked blouse was the same color of peach as her cheeks, and her hair, falling in ringlets over her velvet jacket, shone brilliantly in the afternoon sun.

The weeks since their marriage had been filled with tragedy. All that would have to change. Hadn't he inherited a fortune from his employer, a house in Exeter, a position as head of a firm well established in London business? When the steward came past, he asked for wine and raised his glass in another toast. "To the future," he said.

Mina smiled. It was so good to see her smile, if only for a moment. Then the remote expression returned to her face, like a dark curtain falling between them, cutting off their view of each other.

That night, he lay beside her, holding her lightly in his arms as they planned to move her belongings to Exeter. They talked for an hour, but when he rolled her sideways and began to stroke the side of her face, he felt her stiffen.

"Mina, it's over," he said.

"I don't feel the same as I did before he came to me," she confessed, shuddering as if the revelation gave her pain.

Neither do I, Jonathan thought. Everything might have been different had he only said the words aloud, but he could not. The admission would have wounded her too terribly. "We'll give it time," he said.

CHAPTER SIX

I

Just after he and Mina left England, Jonathan's aunt Millicent Harker—maiden aunt, as she was fond of calling herself—had moved into the house Jonathan had inherited in Exeter.

"The mysterious honeymoon," as she referred to their journey, had taken place so suddenly that Jonathan's last, indeed only, request before leaving was that Millicent travel from Reading to Exeter and take up residence there. Otherwise, he wrote, he would be leaving the house and belongings in the care of servants who might have been loyal to Mr. Hawkins but had no reason to be the same to him. There had been no time to catalog the possessions, and while he would not refuse a servant some cherished memento of his former employer, he made it clear to Millicent that he had no desire to allow a dishonest few to steal him blind.

Certain that a surprise assault was in order, Millicent did not post Jonathan's letter authorizing her to act in his behalf. Instead, she arrived unannounced at the spacious Tudor-style home near the cathedral. Having dismissed the hired cab with a two-penny tip, she knocked on the front door with all the force of someone bearing a proclamation from the Queen herself.

James Chapel, Mr. Hawkins's personal servant for the last sixteen years, opened the front door. In his early sixties with a siz-
able inheritance from Mr. Hawkins, he could have moved in
with his daughter in Cornwall. However, he was a trim man
whose hair was still a rich brown. He looked and felt a decade
younger than his actual age and was hardly ready to retire.
Jonathan Harker had suggested that he live in the house until
they returned from their trip on the Continent. Chapel had
done so in the hope of reaching some arrangement with the
Harkers. He had met Jonathan and Mina a number of times before his employer's death. In the few days the couple had spent
there, he had helped Madam Mina adjust to managing a household staff. Both of them, particularly the wife, were charming,
unassuming people. He suspected that they would get along
well.

Millicent, with a drab olive-green cloak covering her stout
body and the black hat perched on her dull gray hair, was a different story. She waved her nephew's authorization in Chapel's
face and pointed to her bags. Chapel looked from the parcels to
the woman. She was short, with the look of one prematurely
old, her round face permanently lined and tanned by sun and
wind. "You weren't expected so soon. If you had wired, we would
have had porters meet you at the train," he said.

Millicent snorted as if he had suggested something unseemly.
"Perhaps another servant can help," she said sharply.

"I am the only one here, madam. A maid was hardly needed
in the Harkers' absence, so I thought to save them the expense."

"Well then . . ." She hoisted the largest two parcels and swept
past Chapel into the foyer. "Show me to my room, please."

"The guest room? There are three on the second floor and another plus sitting room on the third. If you will leave your bags
here, I can show the rooms to you." As he spoke the last, he
moved past her and out the door, hesitating just outside to de-
bate whether to get the rest of her things or—such a deliciously
wicked thought!—simply leave her to fend for herself.

Duty and habit won. When her five bags were safely on the inlaid wood floor of the foyer, he took her on a tour.

She hid her amazement at the magnificent dining room—at its red brick fireplace, oak wainscotting and windows overlooking a small rear yard enclosed by a stone wall and iron gate. She seemed more at home in the parlor, where Chapel himself spent most of his idle hours in the empty house, and warmed her hands against the small gas heater. Later, in the kitchen, as she examined the cupboards and stove and, with great curiosity, the water heater, Chapel finally understood her behavior. She was not wealthy, nor even exposed to wealth, and now that her nephew had acquired it, she was convinced it could be as easily taken away as it had been given.

Chapel took her through the second floor. She noted that the main bedroom with its east-facing windows and the smaller attached room that Mr. Hawkins had used for a private study would be perfect for Jonathan and Mina. "The little room will make a fine nursery," she said in a conspiratorial tone, as if children were the furthest thing from Mina Harker's mind.

"Mrs. Harker said the same," Chapel noted dryly. "We've already moved the couple's clothes in here, Madam Millicent."

She was looking away from him, so he sensed rather than saw her approval when he called her that. When she turned to face him, her eyes were softer, her mouth less rigid. "Miss Millicent," she said.

The other bedrooms—two across the hall from the main one and a third at the top of the servants' stairs above the kitchen—were not private enough for her taste, so he took her upstairs.

The third floor had a wall dividing the two large rooms and a water closet in the front from the three small servant's rooms in the rear. Once, the front quarters had been used as the children's room and sleeping space for nurse, nanny or, when the children were older, tutor. The rooms still had their original mauve walls and whitewashed floors. Just before Mr. Hawkins died, he had ordered them to be washed and the old velvet curtains replaced with white Irish lace. The iron bed had a lace coverlet and there was a large oak armoire and dresser along one wall. The room had most recently been occupied by Jonathan and Mina. After Mr. Hawkins died, Chapel had ordered the master bedroom painted and had the Harkers' clothes moved into it. Now these were the best empty rooms in the house.

"I'll move in here," Millicent declared.

"They suit you, Miss Millicent," Chapel said. "Before you settle in, shall we have some tea?"

They sat together in the parlor, where, in the next few hours, Chapel learned a great deal about the new owner of what he privately considered "his house." With an affection for her nephew that bordered on adoration, Millicent told him of Jonathan's history. "His grandparents had been dairy farmers, his father a shopkeeper in Reading. When Jonathan was a baby, they would take him to work with them. His first year was spent surrounded by bolts of linen and lace, spools of thread and notions. When the store grew prosperous enough, my brother opened a second. Jonathan's mother managed it, and until Jonathan was old enough for school, he lived with me."

"He was their only child?"

She nodded. "My brother's wife was not a strong woman. Jonathan was her one blessing."

"And yours as well." Seeing her frown, he quickly added, "Considering how much you love him."

"I raised him," she responded. "Even though I did not learn to read until I was nearly an adult, I knew the value of an education, Mr. Chapel. I taught Jonathan his alphabet, his numbers and his prayers. When he started school, his progress . . . well, if I'm biased, so were his teachers.

"His father taught him to keep the business ledgers, and he did so meticulously. His mother used to comment that he worked too hard and that he should spend more time doing things he liked such as sketching and writing. Jonathan ignored her—not disrespectfully, of course. Jonathan was never disrespectful. He was serious, though, far more than his mother."

"I wouldn't doubt it, Miss Millicent," Chapel responded.

"And it was the frivolous attitude of hers that caused my brother to lose the second shop."

Chapel did not approve of gossip, especially not of the dead. He poured more tea from the delicate blue-and-white porcelain pot then carefully changed the subject. "And how did you get by?" he asked.

Millicent's smile was tight-lipped, filled with satisfaction. "With great care. The terms of our parents' will gave me their house and my brother nearly all the land. He sold his acres while I used mine. Every square meter of that soil produced, Mr. Chapel, and every milk stall in the barn was occupied. In the early years, I did the milking and delivered the calves myself. Six years later, I bought my brother's land back from the new owners. Once I was too old to run the dairy, I sold off the stock and rented the land. Now I live off that."

Hard work was admirable, Chapel knew that lesson well, but something in her tone made him uneasy—as if she judged the world entirely by her ethics. "And you never married?" he asked.

The relaxed intimacy Chapel had created vanished, and he was certain that the question concealed some terrible secret. "No," she said curtly.

"Then Jonathan and Mina are your only family?"

"Jonathan. Mina . . ." Her voice trailed off. "Mina is the woman Jonathan loves, and he has always been so sensible, so of course I care for her because she is his choice. But my loyalty is to my own, Mr. Chapel, as I am sure your loyalty is to your own."

Chapel had been most loyal to Mr. Hawkins, who had treated him less like a servant than a brother. Nonetheless, he nodded.

"Now I should like to move in," she said. "After, I think I would like to cook us dinner."

Before Chapel had a chance to clear the tea service, Millicent had carried the tray downstairs to the kitchen. There, she rinsed the cups and pot and placed them in the cupboard, running a finger over the shelf and tsking in disapproval when it came away dusty.

They carried her bags to her room. This time she took the lighter ones and paused at the first landing to catch her breath until Chapel, concerned for her health, told her to put them down and made an extra trip. While she unpacked, Chapel found fresh blankets and sheets, then took her list and went shopping. As he picked out the ham and the vegetables she had asked him to get, he thought again of how difficult it would be to live with the woman.

A dairy maid, in the third-floor guest rooms. "Miss Millicent," he said aloud as he lifted the grocery bag and started out the door. A challenge, he thought, as he stopped at the end of the street and, with his own money, purchased a bouquet of bright pink chrysanthemums from a florist stall.

Millicent had said she intended to rest, but when Chapel returned to the house, he discovered that she had put on a work dress. In his absence, she had scrubbed the china cupboards and was now on hands and knees using the soapy water to wash the floor.

Chapel stopped in the doorway and stared at the scene a moment. Acting solely on instinct, he crouched beside her and held out the flowers. As she took them with hands reddened by the harsh lye soap and scrubbing, he shook his head sadly. "My dear Miss Millicent. Hard work is admirable, but if you care for your nephew, there are some things you must no longer do."

He saw her anger rise then dissipate, to be replaced by doubt. "What do you mean?" she asked.

"In your nephew's house, you can be one of the family. If you wish to work, perhaps you could run the household, though, in one as small as this, that is usually the wife's duty. If you have a special talent for cooking, you could do that on a daily basis and oversee the planning of special dinners. But under no circumstances can you act as the scullery maid. Never! Now, come." He pulled her upright and pointed to the sink. "Wash your hands. We'll make dinner together and then we will talk."

In the hours that followed, Chapel told her about Mr. Hawkins's early life, the struggle that, only in the last decade, had finally brought him wealth. "He acquired a very important client, a nobleman, who paid him well. The money was valuable but even more so were the people his client knew. Mr. Hawkins was suddenly being received in society, and he was perceptive enough to know that he was unskilled. He found the means to educate himself and he prospered."

"What did he do?"

"He hired me. No, don't frown. I am telling no more than the truth. He hired me because I have worked all my life in the houses of the very wealthy and, more importantly, in the houses of the nouveau riche. I know manners, Miss Millicent. I know what must and must not be done if one is to prosper in society, and I would consider it a great privilege to teach someone as well intentioned as you."

"To teach?" Millicent said. Had Chapel known her better, he would have understood that the vague tone of her voice was disapproval.

"Yes," he replied.

"And I could be cook?"

Chapel looked at the remains of the meal—the ham with its rich honey basting, the turnips and carrots baked with it, the biscuits as perfect as any he had ever tasted. What could the woman do with desserts, he wondered, or with stocks? "Without a doubt," he replied. "I think the Queen herself might hire you."

II

By the time the train reached Rotterdam, Mina was once more ill. She could eat nothing, drink only a little broth. The symptoms frightened her and Jonathan, but Dr. Seward noted the fever that accompanied them. "It's nothing more than in-fluenza," he told them, "and not a very serious case."

"We'll put off crossing the channel until you're better," Jonathan said.

Mina shook her head. "I'll keep warm. I'll sit inside close to the stove through the entire crossing."

"Is that wise?" Jonathan asked Seward.

"I want to go home," Mina insisted, looking to Seward for support.

"The boat can hardly be more drafty than the halls on the train," Seward commented.

They crossed to England during a downpour. Every window in the steamboat's passenger room was tightly latched. The wind, blowing relentlessly from the west, carried the engine smoke through the vents used to provide a draft for the wood-stove that gave the only respite from the frigid North Sea air.

Mina sat close to the stove, on the end of one long, wooden bench. Jonathan dozed beside her, his hand holding hers, as if protecting her even while he slept. Dr. Seward sat nearby drink-ing tea with an acquaintance also making the crossing. Mina's body beneath the fur stole, thick wool coat and socks and high leather shoes was wet from fever and sweat. She uncrossed her legs, and the cold draft against her thighs set her to shivering once more. She controlled it as best she could and looked outside at the angry gray sea, shrouded in mist.

It reminded her of Carfax. Of him.

Would she ever be free of his memory? The thought made her angry. Impatience was no virtue, she reminded herself. She had time, years to forget, all the years she would share with Jonathan. Soon they would be home, in the house in Exeter that Mr. Hawkins had willed to them. There had been so many changes, but none could equal the change she had already en-dured.

A pain, born perhaps of memory, started deep inside her, growing as she focused on it, until she was doubled over, one fist clutching her midsection while the other hand remained in Jonathan's grasp.

When he saw the agony in her expression, Dr. Seward moved toward her, but she motioned him to remain where he was. Her stomach was churning and she needed air—that was all the pain signified. She slowly withdrew her hand from Jonathan's, but as she began to stand, a dizziness as insistent as the pain made her stumble. She gripped Jonathan's shoulder for support.

He woke immediately, his eyes instinctively seeking her, his arm supporting her as she fell heavily onto the bench. She had been flushed with fever earlier. Now her skin was white, her lips almost as pale.

"Mina!" Jonathan cried.

"I can't breathe," she said, looking alternately from Jonathan to Dr. Seward to the curious passengers who had formed a circle around them. She saw something more than a physician's concern in Seward's expression and thought of what she had read about Lucy's last days. Her symptoms were far too similar for her to feel anything but terror.

An older woman stepped forward, tapped Seward on the shoulder and whispered a few words to him. A moment later, she helped Mina to walk to the head and latched the door behind them. The room was even closer than the passenger shelter and reeked of vomit and excrement. The woman pulled open a porthole then began unbuttoning Mina's jacket. A wash of salt spray and a gust of cold air blew against Mina's face. She shivered, but the fresh air made the pain subside enough that she could manage to loosen her corset on her own.

"I suggest you take that thing off and pitch it out the window," the woman said with a good-natured chuckle.

"I couldn't," Mina replied, shocked at the suggestion.

"You haven't told your husband yet, I take it?" the woman commented.

"Told him what?"

The woman smiled. "You didn't know either. It must be your first."

"A baby?" Mina asked.

"I had six, all of them boys. Believe me, I know the signs."

"Dr. Seward told me I had influenza."

The woman snorted. "I never knew anyone who learned she was pregnant from a doctor, especially one who would let a patient cross the Channel with what he believes to be the flu." She noticed Mina's expression, the shock, the dread. "What's the matter, girl, don't you want a child?" she asked.

Mina faced the porthole as she replied, as evenly as she was able, "Oh yes, but not so soon." When she turned and faced the woman, her expression was as serene as it had been on the journey to Varna, her emotions once more perfectly under control.

She readjusted her clothing and moved close to the porthole. The spray on her face felt wonderful, the cold air bracing. Terns circled the boat. She heard their harsh cries and wished she were on deck, watching them, feeling the beating of the wind on her body, hearing the thunder of the waves.

He had controlled even this power, and now he was gone.

Would she be condemned to think of him in times of ecstasy? Would her nights with Jonathan be marred by the memory of his hands, his lips and her own surrender? And the child? How could she ever look at the child and not wonder . . .

No, they had done much but nothing that could have led to conception. The blood in the child was another matter.

If there were a child. How could anyone be certain so early? She tried to remember her cycle. If anything, her monthly was not even due yet. "Please don't say a word about this," she told the woman. "Since we're already traveling, there's no reason to worry the men."

"Of course. You look much better. Shall we stay here awhile?"

"Please."

A pounding on the door made that impossible. Mina and the

woman went out and sat close to the door talking of their lives. In the hours that passed, Mina listened to the woman describe the bookstore she and her husband owned in Cambridge and the constant trials of dealing with the university students who were often so poor they couldn't help but become thieves. The conversation was so pleasant that Mina almost forgot her concerns, remembering them only at the times when she was forced to lie about their trip and what had preceeded it.

The sea had calmed and the passengers were on deck when the steamer pulled into Grimsby hours later. The harbor was filled with sailing ships, both British and Scandinavian, the docks covered with barrels of halibut, plaice and mussels. The water that covered the fish, like the sea itself, glowed silver in the soft evening light. Sounds were muted by the damp, colors faded. Mina sat beside Jonathan, guarding their bags while Dr. Seward hired a carriage to take them to the train station.

They ate on the train, saying little to one another. The past that had linked them so tightly was not one any of them cared to mention, and their futures were so different. Their good-bye was too quick to be awkward; then, on a second train, Jonathan and Mina started for Exeter and home. Mina stared at the dirty tenements, at the ragged urchins picking clinkers of coal from the ditches at the side of the rails and contrasted it with the bundled children eating stew in the peasant cottage in Romania. Progress—how little it gave the poor, how much it took away.

A strange thought but fitting. She could already feel the weight of society, its demands for her future pressing down against her. She closed the curtain, took out a book and tried to read.

III

In the weeks that followed her arrival at Jonathan's house, Millicent had doggedly learned manners and dress, hoarding each small fact with the same sullen avidity a miser did his coins. By the time Jonathan and Mina returned to Exeter, pale and exhausted from their journey, Millicent had rearranged the kitchen to her liking and hired Laura—a petite Irish girl with huge shy eyes who rarely raised her voice above a whisper and obeyed all of Millicent's orders with frightened perfection—to clean house.

Millicent, Jonathan and Mina ate dinner together at a small table in the parlor, the gas heater and candles giving the only light. When the meal was finished and Laura had cleared the dishes, Millicent launched into a lengthy account of all she had learned and her assessment of what the household needed. "Laura, a cook and a butler. Three could run the house quite nicely," Millicent said to Jonathan, then looked at Mina, daring the young bride to contradict her.

Mina had no intention of doing so. The thought of servants seemed an invasion of privacy, so the less of them the better. "Do we need so many?" she asked. "There are only two of us."

"Mr. Hawkins had four and he rarely entertained. However, Mr. Chapel does agree with you. He told me that he is getting too old for full-time duties. He has gone to Wellington to be with his son for the holidays. After the new year, he would like work here in a part-time capacity to manage the hired staff when you and Mina entertain."

So there would only be a cook, a maid and an occasional Mr. Chapel. Mina smiled, grasped her husband's hand and said, "Aunt Millicent is right, darling. I had learned to type so I could help you with your work. But that would hardly be appropriate now that you head the firm. Instead I shall manage the household and be the best possible wife for you. Now, if you do not mind, I still feel ill and would like to retire."

"Would you like some sherry first?" Jonathan asked her.

Mina ignored the older woman's disapproving expression. "Please," she said softly and took a glass from her husband. He had filled the stem goblet nearly to the rim, and she sipped it awhile then carried it upstairs with her.

"Is that her custom?" Millicent asked when Mina had gone.

"It helps her sleep. It was a difficult journey."

"Where did you go? What did you see?" Millicent, who had never traveled farther than London, was nonetheless fascinated with foreign countries.

Jonathan could never explain the horrors they had witnessed, the things they had done. The memory of the creature that still kept Mina awake at night for fear of the dreams that would come when she slept was not one he wished to share. Besides, his aunt was a stolid woman, her feet firmly planted in a reality that had no place for wolves, gypsies or vampires.

He decided to lie and listed places he had already been. "Amsterdam. Paris. Zurich. It was primarily a business trip for Lord Godalming. I thought Mina would enjoy it, but during it she became quite ill. One of our party died of the same strange fever that affected her."

"Wine is hardly a cure for illness."

"A glass. One glass to help her sleep."

"That was how your mother started, remember? Jonathan, you are the master of your family. You have to be firm with Mina."

The way his father had never been. Did Millicent know the pain she caused each time she reminded him of that past? "Please, Aunt . . ."

Millicent's eyes, dark like her grandmother's, flashed with an anger that Jonathan recalled far too painfully. Her voice was as cool as ever. "Promise me that you'll at least speak with her."

His aunt didn't understand, indeed couldn't, Jonathan thought. Nonetheless, his aunt might have some reason to worry. "Very well," he said. "I'll talk to her tomorrow."

IV

In the room upstairs, Mina was preparing for bed. She had little energy to undress, none at all to write in her diary or in the journal still hidden in her traveling cloak. It seemed now that the only journal that mattered was the one she had taken from Dracula's castle. She dug into her traveling bag and slipped it into her pocket, then opened each of the drawers in her bureau. One held her slips and chemises, another corsets and stockings, the others less intimate clothing. All the garments were neatly folded and arranged. It seemed a violation of every ethic she held dear that someone should be paid to do this work for her, yet that would be her life now unless she fought for it to be otherwise.

She didn't have strength to spare for that battle. The fatigue that had plagued her in the last days of their quest had lessened, but still it seemed to surround her like a dense fog muffling her emotions, and her ability to concentrate on anything beyond the hour to come. Nonetheless, she had to plan.

There were answers in that journal, she told herself. Her main goal must be to have it translated.

She pulled the bottom drawer out of the bureau and put the journal in the space beneath it then replaced the drawer. Hardly a secure hiding place but the simplest one for now. With that done, she washed her face and went to bed.

The dreams came. They were expected, for, in the days since she left the vampire's castle, the dreams had always come when she felt most helpless. His form was shrouded by the mist. His face was turned to her, but she could see only his lips, the fangs that were the mark of his terrible curse, and his eyes so filled with need.

Her arms lifted, her lips parted. When he touched her, she moaned with delight.

And, as always, reacted with horror. She cried out in her sleep for him to stop, beat the covers away with her hands. On the train that brought them back to a world of orderly cities and civilized men, Jonathan had always lain beside her, had always awakened and comforted her. Now she fought on her own and, when she woke, he was not with her.

"Jonathan," she whispered, certain that in all her life she had never felt so totally, so terribly, alone.

The room smelled of rose sachet, a scent she had always associated with her youth, with her mother, with an innocence she had lost so suddenly only weeks ago. Loneliness and memories pressed too close, and she wrapped a blanket around her shoulders and went into the hall. At the top of the stairs, she halted.

The house was dark except for the light spilling into the foyer through the open parlor door. She smelled the smoke from Jonathan's cigar, heard Millicent speak her name.

She sighed when she heard the woman's voice. Did Millicent ever smile? Ever laugh even when she was young? Mina doubted it. No, to her, Millicent was one of those women who saw life as a trial, her virtue constantly at risk. The heaven Millicent hoped to achieve with this behavior would hardly be any better.

Before her journey with the men, Mina had not been one to eavesdrop, but now she was less certain of herself, less willing to trust that people who cared for her intended the best for her. She descended halfway down the stairs and, in the shadows of the landing, sat listening to their conversation.

". . . few weeks Chapel has taught me so much," Millicent was saying. "And you know how easily I manage things. If Mina is still ill, I could rent out my cottage the way I do my lands and stay on as cook. In the beginning, I could also handle Mina's duties so she can rest and recover. Jonathan, I'm worried about her. She hardly ate and drank nothing but the sherry. She seems so pale and fragile, like an empty glass."

The woman had no way of knowing how appropriate the metaphor was, Mina thought, as she listened to Jonathan mumble some agreement.

"I'd like to help you . . . both of you in any way I can."

Mina clasped her hands together and closed her eyes. "Say no, darling," she whispered. "Please say no." Even as she spoke the words, she knew the truth. The woman had raised Jonathan. He could never turn her away.

"She is still weak. Yes, I suppose, if Mina agrees."

And what could she do but agree? Mina thought. Millicent

would see through every excuse she would give for managing the household on her own. Mina would never be forgiven if she demanded that the woman be asked to leave. Millicent was, in her own devious way, far more deadly than Dracula had ever been, because Jonathan loved her.

"And there is the matter of the sherry, Jonathan," Millicent said sternly. "You cannot just talk to her. You must be firm with her. Promise me."

Mina did not need to hear her husband's reply to know what it had been. Feeling suddenly chilled, she pulled the blanket more tightly around her shoulders and moved slowly up the stairs, her bare feet making no sound on the thick green carpet.

She had just reached the door to her room when she noticed a growing light on the servants' stairs at the opposite end of the hall. A moment later, Laura, in a white nightdress, reached the second-floor landing. Mina was lit by the gaslight coming from her room, Laura by the oil lamp she held. Each stared silently at the other.

Laura took a step toward Mina. Mina, alarmed, put a finger to her lips, motioned the girl away and retreated to her room.

She had just returned to the warmth of the bed when Jonathan joined her. He undressed quickly and put on a nightshirt, then slipped into bed beside her. She pressed her back close to his chest. The warmth of his body felt delicious, his arms so comforting as he held her. "Were you sleeping?" he asked.

"Off and on." She took one of his hands and kissed it. "I was waiting for you."

She heard him murmur something in a voice too low to be heard. His hand moved to her breast. She rolled over and faced him, willing herself to be passive, to let him take his pleasure while thoughts of the vampire and the passion he had aroused in her coursed through her, potent as blood.

"Jonathan," she whispered and, just for a moment, yielded to the pleasure. Her body tightened. She kissed his chest, pulled his head down to find his lips.

But it was already over as suddenly as it had begun, with no fulfillment for her save in her memories.

She could sleep now that Jonathan was with her, his warmth and presence comforting her. For the first time in days, she did not dream. A new set of problems had replaced the old. The present dispersed the past.

Mina woke with Jonathan the next morning, to see him off on his first day at work as head of the firm. She sat across from him at the small table in the parlor, drinking tea and eating biscuits Millicent had baked for them the night before. She tried to think of something encouraging to say, but every attempt only seemed to make him more insecure.

Following a long silence, he mentioned Millicent's concern about the sherry. "I couldn't tell her why you needed it and I promised her that I would speak to you. Try to sleep without it and, when you can't, put a bottle in the cabinet here so she doesn't see you drinking it."

"Jonathan, you make it sound as if a glass of sherry is a sickness. Besides, what business is it of hers?"

"My mother . . . was very cruel to Aunt Millicent, especially when she drank too much. Millicent tolerated her tirades, most likely because she would not have been allowed to care for me otherwise. Please, don't drink in front of Aunt Millicent any longer."

He paused to look at her face, her lips pressed together, her eyes soft with sorrow. "I don't like to speak of what she and I endured," he said, pulled her to her feet and hugged her tightly. "We'll banish the past together, I promise you."

CHAPTER SEVEN

I

Winston Gordon, Lord Gance, liked to compare himself to Lord Byron, the distant uncle who shared his surname. Both were poets, he was fond of asserting publicly, though only his close friends were allowed to read his creations and they made little comment on his skill. His intimate friends were more likely to agree that both were libertines. The similarity ended there. While the poet had been short and somewhat fat, with a sanguine complexion caused by a blend of heredity and drink, Gance was tall and exceedingly pale, with eyes of such a pale gray that they often looked colorless in bright light. In spite of an appetite for food to rival that for sex, he was also slender to the point of emaciation. Only his profile, with its classic nose and thin, delicately curled white-blond hair above the receding hairline, and his direct, often insolent, stare, showed the blood tie between the men born nearly a century apart.

In spite of his heritage, Gance was a businessman, not a romantic, and revolutions held little interest for him. Indeed, he was quite committed to the empire, for India, along with sundry investments on the Continent, had made him wealthy beyond the dreams of his ancestors.

His father had been the first noble to employ the legal services of Peter Hawkins, noting to young Winston that Hawkins had more honesty and skill than the advisors to the Queen. In the years that followed, Hawkins had proven his worth, and Lord Gance saw no reason to abandon a successor who seemed nothing more than a younger duplicate of the scrupulously honest Hawkins himself.

Gance had arrived at Harker's office to sign some papers for the purchase of a winter estate in southern France when he passed a young woman coming out of the offices. Though he was certain he had never met her, she seemed startled, almost fearful, when she saw him. She stared at his face a moment too long then modestly looked away. She was pretty, but there was little remarkable about her except her magnificent chestnut hair, which she had tied back somewhat hurriedly it seemed, and her complexion, which was pale enough to rival his own. Then she glanced at him again. Her eyes, he decided, were incredibly beautiful, and her expression managed to be both frank and sad. He was certain some terrible business had brought her here. "I just passed a woman going out," he commented to Harker's clerk. "What is her name?"

"Mrs. Harker, sir, Wilhelmina. She and Mr. Harker were married on the Continent only a few months ago," the clerk replied, the evenness of his expression hiding his distaste. Gance's excesses were well known to anyone who listened to gossip.

"And is Mr. Harker free?"

"He will be in a moment, sir."

Gance took the time to sit and consider everything he knew about the Harkers. After his business was complete with Jonathan, he asked how Jonathan liked Mr. Hawkins's house.

"It's beautiful, particularly the view of the cathedral and its grounds."

"We share an appreciation of that. My own estate is just to

the north of your home. Since we're neighbors, I'd like to invite you and your bride to a holiday dinner I'm giving on the fourteenth." Harker knew him well enough that Gance expected him to attempt to decline. Before he could, Gance added, "It will be a formal affair. A number of your other clients will be attending along with some of our neighbors. I think it would be wise for you both to attend."

"Thank you. We . . . will do our best. My wife and I recently returned from a trip to Austria. Since her return, she has not been well."

"All the more reason to buy her a new gown and give her a chance to get out. I'll count on you both." Gance smiled, genuinely it seemed, and left before Harker could refuse.

Harker could, of course, refuse later, but Gance doubted that he would do so. On the walk home, Gance noticed Mrs. Harker going into a dressmaker's shop and stopped to watch her through the window. She moved confidently among the satin and laces, viewed with interest the woman's sketches. Mina Harker knew fashion. She knew what she liked. He decided that she was beautiful. If she had been single, or married longer, he would have managed to meet her now. Instead, he waited until she had left the shop then went inside. He'd done business with the owner a few times, and she had always done perfect work. Now he drew her aside from her other customers and explained that heirs had just moved into the Hawkins' house. "I've invited the Harkers to my house for dinner next Saturday. The chestnut-haired woman in the green skirt who just left here is Mrs. Harker. She will need a gown, I think. I suggest that you contact her."

"And how can I be of service to you, sir?" the seamstress asked.

"By making her look as lovely as possible for her husband's sake. I suggest that you make her a gown of this fabric." He pointed to the bolt of green velvet, with a color so deep it appeared nearly black.

The woman knew him well enough to understand. "I will try

to convince her," she said. "With her coloring, I'm certain she'd look stunning in it."

Gance tipped her well and went on his way, happy in the thought that he would see Mrs. Harker again and soon.

II

We have been at home nearly two weeks, and I think fondly of the snow that fell in the mountains of Transylvania, of the deep blue skies and marvelous sunsets, Mina wrote in her journal the following night. *It is odd to think of that place as beautiful when such tragedy happened there, and yet, after weeks of fog and chilly rain, I would do anything to see the sun. I ordered Laura to clean the parlor and dining room windows and to rehang the velvet draperies to let in more light. Though Millicent complained that the draperies look strange pulled back so far, it is now possible to read a newspaper in the afternoon without use of the gaslight. I mentioned the savings to Millicent, who only looked at me oddly, as if guessing that she was being placated and not certain how.*

As I expected, Jonathan is working a great many extra hours. Having the position as head of the firm fall on his shoulders so suddenly with Mr. Hawkins's death has placed a terrible burden on his conscience. He is terrified of not living up to the firm's reputation, or of making some mistake that will remove all the good fortune that came to us. I tell him that Mr. Hawkins had faith in him for a reason, but it does little good. I wish I could help him, but I know so little about his work that he will not allow it, nor does he have the time to teach me.

She hesitated, then continued on in shorthand.

In spite of her apparent kindness, I find it impossible to be at all comfortable in Millicent's presence. All her affection is centered on Jonathan. With our age and temperament so different, we have nothing in common at all. Nonetheless, she is the only family Jonathan has left, and I will learn to accept her for his sake.

I have begun to meet some of our neighbors as a result of an invi-

tation to a client's dinner party—a relation to Lord Byron, imagine! It is a formal affair, and Jonathan asked that I have a gown made. I knew no one, but a seamstress whose shop I'd visited had a card delivered to me. I stopped by this afternoon and had a fitting. While I was there, a number of local women came in to place orders or pick up dresses. I spoke to a few of them, and one of them, Winnie Beason, invited me for tea tomorrow afternoon. Mrs. Beason is somewhat older than I, and though her hair is darker than Lucy's, her skin that magnificent shade Jonathan calls Cornish ivory, she reminds me of Lucy. They share that same happy interest in life and an independence that has no respect for petty conventions.

At the dress designer's suggestion, I picked a French design for my gown. It has a sea-green satin blouse and sleeves and a deep green velvet layered skirt, cuffs and collar. She wanted to make a matching evening cape, but I thought the price too extravagant, especially since Jonathan asked me to order three additional gowns, one more formal and two for afternoon wear. I chose cream for the formal, pale blue and white for the others. The white is probably too thin for winter wear, but even with the holiday season and the dinner we are giving for Jonathan's staff, I cannot imagine the need for four new gowns in the next few months. I told this to Millicent, certain that she would agree, and she said that socializing was one of my duties—as if a party were some sort of chore to be endured! I think sometimes that she must have had a sad and lonely childhood and wish we could be better friends.

When I went into town yesterday, Jonathan took me to lunch and we laughed with as much joy as we had when he courted me. Last night, I waited eagerly for him to come home, but at dinner, he was as solemn as always. It is what Millicent expects from the little boy she still thinks him to be, and it is what he gives her. I would give anything to hear him laugh so happily in her presence.

As Mina put the diary in the drawer of her dressing table, her eyes focused on the bureau, the place where she had hidden her journal and the book she had taken from Dracula's castle. She opened the door to her room and listened in the hallway.

Jonathan was downstairs in the study, working a few extra hours before bed. Millicent had apparently already gone to sleep, for the stairs leading to her room were dark. Mina shut her door carefully and pulled her journal from its hiding place. She slipped into bed and, in the light of a single lamp, began to write hurriedly in shorthand.

I have tried to find a translator for the book I brought back but so far have had no success. Exeter is not the cosmopolitan city that London is, and I hope that, sometime in the future, I can go to London and find the help I need. Jonathan said that Mr. Harker often had to travel there on business. Perhaps when Jonathan goes, he will take me and I will have a chance to slip away.

I wish I could tell him what I have done and why, but I do not dare. Van Helsing's warnings would make Jonathan uneasy, my doubts even more so. Besides, Jonathan seems to have put the ordeal behind him. I will not be the one to remind him of it.

In a way, I thought I could forget as well. This is the first time I have opened this journal since our return to Exeter, and I do so with some sorrow.

The fainting spell on the boat seems to have been an isolated incident. I've felt no nausea, no recurring fever to signal a pregnancy. As a result, I am nearly certain I am not pregnant, though I am somewhat late. Anxiety can cause that, I have heard, and I've certainly had reason enough to be anxious in the last few months. Still, a child for Jonathan and I would be a respite from what looks to be an endless life of leisurely boredom. If only I could work as I did before Jonathan and I were married. As it is, between the solicitous Laura and Jonathan's aunt, there is nothing here for me to do.

Now Jonathan is working downstairs and I am alone as always. I find myself longing for those days on the Continent, when we were so close, so caught up in the horror and adventure of the chase. I feel restless, anxious. I think of the pledge I made to Dracula in my dreams. I would follow my desires, I said. I thought it easy then. It has not been so.

A light knock on the door startled Mina. She softly closed the book and capped the ink, placing both in a drawer. "Who is it?" she called when both were out of sight.

"Laura." The girl cracked the door. "I saw your light. I was just going to bed and thought you might need something."

"Nothing, thank you." Mina blew out the candle and lay back in the bed thinking of Jonathan working in the study below her. As soon as she was certain the girl had gone, she placed the book back in its hiding place and returned to bed, shivering with cold, to wait for Jonathan so she could sleep in peace. The clock in the foyer chimed the hour then the half, and still Mina was alone.

Enough! she thought. Enough. She put on her dressing gown and went downstairs.

The smoke from his cigar drifted into the hallway. His chair was turned so his back was to her, and he seemed to be looking for some reference on the bookshelves that covered the wall behind the desk. She saw a crystal flask full of brandy on his desk, an empty glass beside it. It looked as if he had had one drink, perhaps two. This was not like Jonathan. She wondered if he had drunk some in an effort to relax.

The pool of light and the door that framed her made her feel small, vulnerable. She took a breath, intending to call his name.

"Damn it!" he muttered as he pulled a volume from the shelf. He checked the contents and returned it, then reached for another.

Not so certain of her welcome, Mina nonetheless called, "Jonathan?"

He turned, the momentary irritation at her interruption turning to duty, then welcome. "Mina. I thought you were sleeping."

"I . . ." What? she wondered. I thought you were my lover, my husband. I need you beside me. "I was lonely. I came to see how long you would be."

"Lonely?" He smiled and reached for her hand, but even as she walked toward him, his focus shifted from her face to the pile of papers on his desk.

Mina bent over, and as she kissed his cheek, she whispered, "Don't be too late. Exhaustion causes its own mistakes."

"He died," Jonathan said, resting his hand palm down on the papers covering his desk. "He died," he repeated, and Mina realized that he was a little bit drunk. "He left me all that was his, and then he died before he could even begin to explain what I had . . ."

Mina recalled clearly the hospital in Budapest where Jonathan had lain raving about wolves and bats and women with fangs. In his fever, he had sounded much like this.

"Jonathan!" she said sharply, and as he looked at her with dull surprise, she kissed him. "Jonathan," she repeated more softly. "It will be all right. I know it. How can it be otherwise now that we have gone through so much and survived?"

He did nothing but hold her hand as he sipped the dark amber liquid. She understood that he wanted nothing more than for her to leave.

She would not. Instead she would be bold for his sake. She poured more brandy into the glass, drank some then passed it to him, beginning a silent ritual that continued until the glass was empty. Standing, she pulled him to his feet, not letting go as she led him through the study with its soft gaslight and up the dark stairs to their room, where a single candle burned. In the doorway, she paused and turned toward him. Illuminated from behind, her body was a warm shadow beneath her thin white nightdress. Thinking only of his need, he followed her as she backed inside.

Her hands reached up and cradled his chin as, on tiptoe, she kissed him. If his mind had been elsewhere, it was on her now and remained there as they tumbled onto the bed. Their fall set the velvet canopy of the bed swaying, its breeze extinguishing the candle, leaving them alone in the wanton dark.

She kissed him shamelessly, as she had always longed to kiss him, then—more wickedly!—placed his hands where they would pleasure her most. It took little brandy to make Jonathan clumsy. Mina put herself astride him, moving long after he had finished, demanding her own pleasure.

Mina woke in the center of the bed, the quilts wrapped tightly around her. She recalled falling asleep in Jonathan's arms, but that had been hours ago, it seemed. She felt warm and sated and far too tired to wonder where he had gone. She drifted back to sleep as the clock in the foyer struck one, slept on through two and three. When Jonathan finally joined her again, she did not wake, nor did she stir when he left her in the morning. If she dreamed at all that night, she did not remember.

CHAPTER EIGHT

I

A half hour before Mina Harker was to arrive, Winnie Beason pulled the fresh scones from the oven, put out her cigarette and went upstairs to dress. When she had invited Mina, she'd known that this was the week her cook went to Hampton to visit her mother. However, Winnie was not only capable of baking her own sweets, but actually enjoyed it. Besides, she and Mina would be uninterrupted for most of the afternoon, a much better means of discovering if her new neighbor was as independent a woman as she believed.

Strange rumors had preceded Mrs. Harker to Exeter. Jonathan Harker had been a simple clerk in the Hawkins firm until Hawkins had sent him abroad. When he returned, it was with a wife and, not only an incredible promotion, but a future inheritance as well. Then, only days later, Hawkins died. No one suspected the Harkers, for Hawkins had been ill for some time. However, the Harkers' disappearance so soon after the funeral aroused some curiosity. Winnie was not one to pry, however; Mrs. Harker's fortune had risen as suddenly as her own. Through that bond she hoped to have found a friend.

She served Mina coffee kept warm in a samovar, heated with a candle at the base, and offered her a cigarette, which Mina refused. The initial reserve both women felt soon vanished, for they did have much in common, including a daring that women raised more protectively might have found far too masculine to be fashionable.

"You went all alone to Budapest to marry?" Winnie asked, less amazed than envious of Mina's adventure.

"I had to," Mina replied simply. "I had no one to go with me."

Winnie looked at her, expressing no sympathy for the lack of parents or siblings. As far as Winnie was concerned, family ties were a curse that strangled any real opportunity.

"And what did you do before you married?" she asked.

"I was a teacher."

"A tutor?"

"At first, but I wanted to do something more, well, more worthwhile, so I left to teach school in London."

"London! Dear, what an experience. Tell me about it?"

Mina did, pleased to find someone so interested in her ragged youngsters. She supplied details with only occasional prompting while Winnie refilled their cups.

"There are over forty women in the Exeter Ladies Society. We have organized a school for poor children and raised money to hire teachers," she said when Mina had finished. "We also run a charity hospital. We've hired a doctor, and the rest of us are volunteers. We learn as we go and do our best. I work at the hospital tomorrow. I'll show you around if you wish."

Mina smiled. "Did you invite me here to convert me?" she asked.

"Convert? An appropriate word. Actually, Mina, when I met you, I sensed that you are a woman who looks at her surroundings. So many choose not to do so. Blindness is so convenient, you know."

"I know," Mina replied. She mentioned the children she'd seen collecting coal beside the tracks.

"Last week one had his foot caught beneath a tie. He lost one leg and most of his second to a train that could not stop in time. I think it was better that he died."

"In Romania I saw peasant children working the land with their parents. They must have been terribly poor, but they seemed so healthy."

"So you believe in Rousseau's theory of the noble savage?"

"No." Mina fought the urge to smile. The expression would have revealed too much. Later, when Winnie knew her well enough to be certain of her sanity, Mina might tell her of Dracula. Not yet. "But I believe in the responsibility that we must all share with those less fortunate."

"Please come to the hospital tomorrow. I must show you what we've done."

"I'm not certain I can get away," Mina lied. She wanted to speak to Jonathan about the Exeter Ladies Society and make certain it was more than a suffragette front before she got involved in it. Throughout the afternoon, Mina had been keeping track of the time through the glass-domed anniversary clock on the mantel. Though she would have gladly stayed the evening, it seemed polite to go. "Is it really five already? I ought to leave," she said.

"It's getting dark," Winnie said. "Margaret should be back by now." She rang a bell, and a girl no more than thirteen came running up the stairs from the kitchen. She wore a plain gray dress with an embroidered white collar. "Mrs. Harker, this is Margaret. She will see you home."

Margaret curtsied pleasantly and went for her coat.

On the walk, Mina could not coax more than a dozen words out of the child. Through those she learned that Margaret was an orphan, and had lived with the Beasons for two years while attending the Exeter school. With the first hint of emotion, Margaret proudly said that she had made her dress herself. "Even the collar. Madam Winnie taught me needlework."

"Does anyone else live with the Beasons?"

"My brother did. But he was already sick when he came there and he died." She said it simply, as if she had seen so much death that its tragedy no longer touched her.

They walked in silence until they reached Mina's home. There Mina paused then had Margaret come inside. She hastily wrote a note, telling Winnie that she would definitely visit the hospital tomorrow. "Something to do," she said happily as she removed her hat and arranged her hair in the hallway mirror. Jonathan would be home soon. She wanted to look her best.

Dinner was not pleasant, Mina wrote in her diary that night. I described my afternoon with Winnie and decision to visit the hospital. Millicent made her disapproval known. "This is hardly the time to spend energy on charity work," she grumbled, speaking to Jonathan rather than to me as if he were my master not my husband.

"Some of the wealthiest women in Exeter volunteer there," I responded, looking at Jonathan as she had when she'd spoken.

Jonathan hesitated. I could almost feel him considering the most tactful way to placate us both. Staring directly at his aunt, he replied, "You have been such a help to us that Mina has nothing to do. And she is right. The contacts she makes could be valuable to all of us."

"There's other work, Jonathan. There's the preservation society, the literary clubs. I know about all of them. She doesn't have to work with all those poor." Millicent spoke the last words as if poverty were a curse.

Perhaps it was to her. Nonetheless I did not hide my anger. "How can infants and small children have any blame for their misfortune?" I retorted. "You may not have been a wealthy woman but you were never penniless, you never lacked for food to eat or a bed for the night. Decency demands that we share—"

"Mina!" Jonathan exclaimed, cutting me off. I saw not anger but anguish in his expression. Peace. Above all, he wanted peace.

"Winnie Beason works two days a week there. If I approve of what I see, I will be doing the same," I said evenly, left the table and came upstairs to write this. I notice that my hands are shaking, but I said what I felt, as calmly as I was able. I consider that a triumph.

II

The Exeter Charity Hospital was located in one of the older, poorer sections of town. Its front doors opened onto a wide street where carriages could come and go, dropping off not patients but the wealthier women who volunteered their time. High brick walls flanked both sides of the old hospital, and the building itself, while sturdy, looked windowless and ugly from the front. Judging from the area, Mina thought that at one time the building might have been a warehouse or factory.

The waiting room was cheerier than Mina had expected. A large open hall had locked cupboards along one wall, mismatched chairs and davenports in the center. Since there was no one to receive her, she followed the instructions posted on the wall and rang the bell. The faint smell of lye hung in the air, a smell that became stronger when the inner doors opened and a stern-faced young woman motioned her inside.

Winnie stood next to one of the beds, spoon-feeding a youngster who had both arms in splints. She gave the duty to the woman who had brought Mina in so they could tour the building.

They walked past rows of cots placed so close together that the nurses could only approach the beds sideways. Girls were on one side of the huge room, boys on the other, and a screen that could be moved from bed to bed provided the only privacy. Mina noted sadly that there were no empty places.

"Winter is one of our most difficult times," Winnie said. "Malnutrition and this terrible damp cause so much disease. If any more patients come in, we'll have to double up the babies to make room."

"Are there always so few nurses?"

"It's nearly Christmas, Mina, hardly a time to risk becoming ill by working here. This is also the ward for the oldest children. Most of the women prefer working with the babies, so this section is always understaffed. I would be here every day, but Mr. Beason will not allow it. Ever since he learned that microbes are responsible for disease, he has a terrible fear of this place. As a result, I am only allowed to work here on days when he is certain he will be at the office until late, and I must bathe and have Margaret scrub my clothes before he comes home. Fortunately, Mr. Beason also has the hugest heart of anyone I have ever known. I should like you and your husband to meet him."

It was an opening, Mina knew, but she was not sure how to respond. "I would love to have you both for dinner," she said. "Sunday, perhaps."

"Sunday," Winnie said. "Definitely." She linked her arm through Mina's and led her to the infants' ward.

The ward faced south. Tall windows let in the sun, making the room both bright and hot. The smell of lye, sour milk and dirty diapers made Mina's eyes water. There were no cots in this room. Instead long tables were arranged in front of every window, and on them unpainted cribs held infants and toddlers. Many were dull-eyed from fever, their faces and bodies marked with sores. Others appeared nearly well, playing happily with stuffed dolls and strings of painted beads. Mina had expected to see more mothers there, but only a handful sat beside their babes. Two mothers were nursing, and as soon as the children had finished, they rearranged their clothing and left. "Most of the mothers work," Winnie explained. "And most of them have other children to care for."

"The babies have no clothes," Mina commented, looking at all the tiny pale bodies around her.

"If they did, we'd have more to wash—scrub actually, since so many of the children have infectious diseases. The room is warm and blankets and diapers are work enough for the staff. Besides, Mr. Beason has very definite ideas about cleanliness."

"Your husband?"

"Mr. Beason founded this hospital. He may never set foot in it, but I assure you, he is as much a part of it as any volunteer."

One of the toddlers had escaped his crib and crawled beside Mina, gripping her skirt for support as he stood. His shoulder and the side of his face were burned, the depth of the wounds making it certain he would be scarred for life. Mina wanted to lift him, but his hands and knees were dirty. She wished she had dressed more simply.

Winnie picked up the child. Before putting him back in his crib, she carried him to the huge porcelain sinks and washed the dirt from his knees and palms. "Do you know that this building used to be a slaughterhouse?" Winnie asked as she carried the child to his bed. "Now water and lye goes down the drains instead of blood. I like to think of that. The history of the place makes our work all the more fitting somehow. Mina, what is it?" she asked, and followed Mina's fixed stare to the crib behind her.

The infant in it had a long, deep gash across his cheek. A thick bandage wrapped tightly around one of his arms was soaked and dripping fresh blood, and blood stained the bedding as well. Winnie glanced from Mina to the child. "Esther!" she screamed. "Esther, come and help me, William's stitches have opened!" She pushed Mina aside, unaware of how pale her friend's face had become, and lifted the unconscious child.

The babies around them, startled by Winnie's call, began to cry, their noise drowning out Mina's soft plea for help as she gripped the side of the empty crib for support. It tipped toward her, and she fell with the bloody linens falling above her. A scream, seemingly from a great distance, followed her descent, and she wondered vaguely if it had come from Winnie or herself.

The scent of blood was all around her—the child's mingling with the scent of her own—and for a moment its terrible pervasiveness blocked out sound, and speech.

She felt herself pulled along the floor then lifted by more than one person and carried to a cooler, quieter room, where she was placed on a cot. She felt someone grip her hand, heard Winnie calling her name. "If you don't open your eyes, I am going to have to wave smelling salts under your nose, Mina dear. They're quite disgusting. I'd rather not."

"I'm still here," Mina whispered.

"I'm so sorry, dear. It was an emergency. The child . . ."

"The child is dead," Mina finished for her and squeezed her hand.

"How could you know? Well, perhaps it was obvious, the poor little thing. It's a wonder he survived his accident at all."

Mina opened her eyes and focused on her friend's face, on the tears on Winnie's cheeks. They weren't for her, she knew, but soon they would be. She felt the pain that had made her so faint on the channel crossing, like a hand gripping her womb with relentless strength. Her thighs were wet and sticky. "Please send for a carriage," she said, wanting nothing more than to go home and somehow get to her room and wash and change. Afterward, she could go to bed and plead illness until the pain subsided.

Her body would not allow it. As she sat on the edge of the cot and reached for her cloak, a wave of pain coursed through her. She pressed her hands against her stomach and moaned.

"Mina, you're hurt!" Winnie exclaimed.

Mina shook her head. "No, I'm not certain but I think I may be losing a child. I've never felt a pain like this before."

"How late were you?"

"About ten days."

"Then it's far too early to tell. Even so, after what happened you need a doctor. While he examines you, I'll send for your husband."

"No! Winnie, please. Just take me home."

"Not yet, dear," Winnie said. Her eyes focused evenly on Mina's, and her voice was firm, that of a nurse to a patient. "Just lie back and rest. I'll take care of everything."

Winnie did. Throughout the next few hours, she left Mina's side only to bring her gauze and tea and, when the bleeding increased, bringing with it an increase in pain, laudanum.

That evening, after helping Mina change into one of the gray hospital work gowns, Winnie took her home in a hired carriage. At Mina's house, she asked the driver to leave and helped Mina to the door.

Laura answered the bell. Noting her mistress's pale face and how heavily she leaned on the woman with her, she immediately went for Millicent. By the time the two returned, Winnie had helped Mina upstairs to her room. "Who is this woman?" Millicent asked.

Mina, giddy from the pain and the drug, giggled. "Madam Winifred Beason, wife of the founder of the Exeter Charity Hospital for Children," Mina replied. "And my nurse. Winnie, this is Miss Millicent Harker, my . . ."

"A nurse?" Millicent asked before Mina could finish. "Why on earth do you need a nurse?"

"She suffered a fainting spell while visiting the hospital," Winnie replied for her. "Now, please, Miss Harker. Mina is still very weak. I must help her undress."

"Where are her own clothes?"

"Being washed, madam. They were soiled when Mrs. Harker fell. Now, please, would you go downstairs and ask the maid to bring a sponge and hot water so Mina can bathe?" As tactfully as she could, Winnie began forcing Millicent back toward the bedroom door.

"I am quite able to take care of my nephew's wife myself, Mrs. Beason," Millicent replied.

"I'm sure you are, but since I brought her home and it is my training, I might as well see her safely into bed. Some tea would make her feel better, I think. If you would please summon a servant." With one final step forward, she forced Millicent into the hall and shut the door.

". . . my husband's aunt." Mina, finally able to finish the introduction, smiled weakly.

"Should I have let her stay?"

"No. I want to be the one to tell my husband." She sat on the edge of her bed and removed her bonnet and coat. Winnie helped with the rest then sat with her until, finally, Mina slept.

Though Winnie had aired the room before she left, the smell of blood was still strong, its reminder drawing Mina into the

nightmare of a terrible, bloody birth and a black-haired child
with dark knowing eyes that glowed red in the center as she
nursed him. Horrified, her dream self screamed. Laughter answered, and the three vampire women floated toward her, each
carrying a child of her own who suckled their naked breasts
though blood, not milk, dripped from their nipples. "Sister, what
a gift you bring!" they cried in their cold and beautiful voices.
They surrounded her, lifting the child from her arms. Milk
dripped from his tiny mouth. His tiny hands gripped their hair
as they raised him to their lips and began to feast on him one after the other.

She would have thrashed, fought until she woke, but the laudanum Winnie had given her allowed no release.

"How can you do this! How can you let them destroy your
son!" she screamed to the darkness beyond the women's hovering forms. There was no reply, no salvation to be found in calling
him. Dracula's powers did not extend this far. The women
moved toward her slowly, their hands rubbing her swollen
breasts, her stomach still painful and swollen from the recent
birth. She opened her mouth to cry out, and the fair one covered
it with her own. She felt the life leaving her body, blood through
her womb, breath through her parted lips.

* * *

WHEN Jonathan woke Mina that evening, she was sticky with
sweat. She shook as he held her, then lay back and took his hand.

"Did the fever return?" he asked.

She shook her head. "I fainted, but I'm certain it's for the last
time."

"How can you know?" he asked.

"I can't be certain, but I might have been pregnant, Jonathan.
I'm bleeding now. I may have lost a child."

"Child?" Comprehension came slowly, followed by a grief that
brought its own sharp pain. She saw him wince, his eyes blinking
to hold back the tears. She rested a hand on his sleeve. It seemed
so pale against the dark gray wool, so small and delicate as he

wrapped it in his own. She felt more helpless than she ever had, more in need of his comfort, as if she were a little girl and he her father not her husband. "Oh, Mina. Are you certain?" he asked.

"No, but my monthly was late by three weeks and the pain . . . I've never felt such pain." She lied about the days, but the rest was true enough. Birth must feel like this, she thought.

"You would have conceived before . . ."

"Definitely, Jonathan. Before."

Neither of them mentioned the name. Dracula. He drained their life force even now. They feared him even now.

"I love you," he whispered, and kissed her hand.

The tragedy brought them close, closer than even their desperate journey had, because now there was only her and him and no one else to share the sorrow. He would understand what she had done, she decided. She took his hand intending to tell him everything that had happened in her days with Van Helsing, and of the book she had found.

Millicent's footsteps in the hall outside stopped her. "Don't tell her about the child," Mina whispered. "She'll treat me like an invalid."

Jonathan looked at her, astonished by what she'd said. "Darling, since you'll need her care, you can hardly hide what has happened. Besides, pampering is exactly what you need."

"Jonathan!" she whispered.

"Please, Mina. We've kept enough secrets from her."

Mina lay back, too weak to protest. Millicent entered with a pot of tea and some soup for the three of them. "Mina thinks she might have been pregnant," Jonathan said.

"Oh, child! Now you've lost it?" There was genuine sorrow in Millicent's eyes.

"I fainted at the hospital, but the room was so warm. Perhaps it was only heat or exhaustion," Mina suggested.

As they ate together, Millicent described Winnie's rude behavior. Though she did not blame Mina at all, she made certain that Mina's part in it was mentioned, and suggested, as tactfully as her temperament allowed, that Mina's visit to the hospital might have been to blame for her condition. "You weren't completely well and that's the truth," she said to Mina. "You went out too soon, and to a place such as that."

Jonathan would certainly take her side now, Mina thought. She had not counted on his habitual sense of duty. "Yes," he said quietly. "Until you're completely well, you must stay at home, darling." With that simple assent, those almost loving words, Mina's desire to confide in him vanished.

She was silent throughout the rest of the meal, stayed silent when Millicent left and they were alone. That night, for the first time in so many, he stayed with her and held her—possibly because he was certain that tonight there could be nothing but affection between them.

Millicent has been clucking over me like a stern mother hen, she wrote in shorthand in her private journal a few nights later. *I admit that I like the attention, but not the smug way she gives it. I suppose I should be thankful that the woman treats me as a daughter-in-law rather than a rival and in her own dour way seems to have my best interests at heart.*

I have not felt so despondent since we left Transylvania. It seems as if a huge weight were pressing down on me, making it difficult to move, even to breathe. All that is left is sleep. Fortunately, the loss has brought Jonathan and me closer together. He is with me each night, and as long as he is beside me, I sleep without dreams.

This amazes me, for the scent of my own blood seems to hang heavy in this room, reminding me of all the tragedies that have occurred to mar our happiness. I tell myself that things will get better, and yet, though my intellect is certain of this, my soul cannot believe it. Even when I thought I had lost heaven forever, I did not feel such despair.

And now I have lied to Jonathan. Well, in a month I will know for certain if I have lost a child or am on the road to losing my mind.

CHAPTER NINE

When days had passed without any word from Mina, Winnie sent Margaret to the Harker house with a note. The girl returned with no reply. Winnie visited Mina personally the following day, but Millicent said curtly that Mina was resting and could not be disturbed. Winnie left a second note, but when that was also ignored, she became convinced that the messages were being thrown away before Mina could see them.

She recalled that Mina had spoken as fondly of her husband as Winnie herself spoke of Mr. Beason. With that in mind, her visit the following afternoon was to the firm of Hawkins and Harker.

When Winnie Beason swept into Jonathan's office, filled with polite indignation at being turned away from his home, he saw in her a spark of the old Mina, the one of decisiveness and courage. He desperately wanted that woman to return, but force of habit made him follow Millicent's sensible suggestions.

"She told you what happened?" Winnie asked.

"About the child, yes."

"It is a loss, Mr. Harker, one that a man for all his love and sympathy cannot fully understand. She will dwell on it. Her body gives her little choice. It is something that she must force herself to throw off. I'd like to see her, to counsel her."

When Jonathan had come home last night, Mina had greeted him with a wan smile. When he left the bed this morning, she had not stirred. He had stared down at her, amazed at the ashen color of her skin, the lack of luster in her hair, as if her body responded to the hopelessness gripping her mind. She needed sympathy, of course, but even more than that, she needed rest, a concept he doubted that Winnie understood. "I don't think it's possible to see her yet. Perhaps next week."

Winnie considered arguing and decided against it. Instead she made a point of calling on a friend who lived on the same street as the Harkers and served on the hospital board. As the women sat in the parlor, Winnie positioned herself so that she could watch the street. When Millicent passed by outside, carrying a market basket, Winnie excused herself and walked to the Harker house.

What she planned was most improper, but she consoled herself with the thought that the worst that could happen was she would be turned away at the door. After adjusting her hat and straightening her coat, she rang the bell. When no one answered, she rang again.

After a third try, she checked the door, found it unlocked, and went inside. "Mina," she called softly and heard light footsteps on the servants' stairs.

A young maid rushed into the hall, her hair falling loose from its net, her face smudged with dirt. "I would like to see Mrs. Harker, please," Winnie demanded.

"That isn't possible. Miss Millicent and Mr. Harker gave orders that—"

"I've just seen Mr. Harker. Is Mina upstairs?"

"She's sleeping."

"Then I'll peek in and see how she is. You needn't show me the way; I know it." Winnie walked up the stairs slowly, certain that any speed would send the flustered girl running after her.

The heavy drapes were drawn over Mina's window. Though the fire had nearly burned out, the room was warm from the earlier blaze. Mina lay in bed, sleeping so soundly that Winnie's hand on her forehead did not wake her.

"No fever. Well, that's good, Mina dear." She spoke louder; "Now you must wake up!"

As Mina began to stir, Winnie went and pulled open the drapes. A rush of sunlight, its rays diffused by the dust falling from the curtains, forced Mina awake. Her eyes, red and swollen from crying, squinted in the harsh light as she tried to focus on her tormentor. "Laura, is that you?"

Winnie sat beside her. "I suppose after that awakening, you'll want me to go," she commented.

"Winnie! I was expecting you, but I assumed I would get some warning."

"Warning!" Winnie laughed. "Mina, I nearly had to break down the door."

They spent the next hour alone together. During it, Winnie kept up a constant stream of chatter, coaxing Mina out of bed, sitting behind her at the dressing table, working to comb the many tangles out of her hair. "Does Millicent know what happened to you?" she finally asked.

"Yes. But it's so strange. My bleeding stopped two days ago, just as always. I had heard that when you're traveling, it's natural to be late. But if it had been nothing more than that, shouldn't the pain have subsided by now?"

"Physical pain?" Winnie asked, concerned that some infection might have set in.

Mina shook her head. "I think of the life I may have lost. The lack of certainty makes it worse somehow."

"Even if you weren't certain, it will be hard to forget. I know. I had four miscarriages before Mr. Beason and I decided to remain childless. The last time, I was in my sixth month."

"How did you go on?"

"By doing what I always did. Every day the anguish would be

a bit less." She took one of Mina's hands in both her own, the way Van Helsing had done so recently, while Mina stared into the mirror at both of them. How pale her face seemed, how colorless her eyes.

"What was it you wanted to do before this happened, Mina?" Winnie asked.

"Wanted?" Her little journal and the book she had taken were still safely hidden. Secrets, Winnie, she thought. I wanted to keep secrets from my husband and his aunt, even from you. Now the last didn't seem right. Someone besides herself ought to know what she was planning. Perhaps Winnie could even help. "Winnie, do you consider yourself to have an open mind?"

Winnie laughed. "As open as possible. About what?"

"About . . . the devil, and creatures that serve him."

Winnie stared directly into Mina's face, an amused smile on her lips. "Mina Harker, are you inviting me to a séance? If you are, I assure you that I shall be certain to attend."

"Not a séance. I need to tell you about the last few months of my life. I don't expect you to believe any of it, but I assure you that it is true. Jonathan has the journals and notes that we all wrote locked in his safe. I would rather not ask him for them just now, but you can check some of the facts for yourself through the newspapers. I remember the dates quite clearly. It began when Jonathan left Exeter the end of April . . ."

An hour passed. Millicent brought up tea, set it on the bedside table and left without a word. After that short pause in their conversation, Mina talked until four. She had just finished describing Lucy's death when Winnie said she had to go. "I'll come back tomorrow if you like," she said.

Mina nodded. "Come at one. I will be in the parlor waiting for you."

"Dressed for a walk, I hope."

"If you wish." Mina looked down at her hands. "Winnie, I said I would understand if you did not believe me, but I want you to." She took a piece of paper from her writing box and scribbled some dates. "The first is the date the storm blew the ship called *Demeter* into Whitby harbor. The story ran in the Whitby papers for some days. I'm sure you can find mention of it here. The second is the day Lucy Westerna died. The third was the day we read about the molesting of children in Hampstead. I haven't come to that part of the story, but it is important to my tale. The Exeter newspaper keeps back issues, does it not? Please go and check them."

"Mina, I have no reason not to believe you."

"You will," Mina replied. "Be assured that you will. Now, please. I need you to be completely convinced. Do as I ask."

"All right, but no matter what I discover, even the plague could not keep me from coming tomorrow to hear chapter two."

In spite of what she said, Winnie did want to check Mina's dates. Curiosity would not let her wait for morning, and she arrived at the *Exeter Telegram* just as it was closing. A healthy tip kept the office open an extra half hour while she paged through the back issues.

The strange story of the Russian ship *Demeter* had the most prominence for, as its writer asserted, "Never before had a ship reached harbor with a dead man at the wheel." Follow-up stories on the boxes of earth inside and the diary of the captain gave credence to Mina's story. Actually, Winnie realized, Mina's story of a vampire feeding off the crew made more sense than the madman theory that finally closed the case.

Lucy Westerna's death in mid-September was briefly mentioned, primarily because she had been engaged to Lord Godalming, who owned a house in Exeter. As for the mysterious "Bloofer Lady" preying on children in Hampstead, Winnie remembered reading that odd story when it ran two months before.

That night, as she and her husband ate their dinner, he commented that she seemed strangely silent. "Preoccupied," she replied.

A one-word answer to a question that would normally keep Winnie conversing for hours alarmed him. "You're not ill, are you?"

"No, merely thinking of something I was discussing this afternoon." She put down her fork and stared at her husband. "Do you believe in ghosts?" she asked.

"Of course. Many sane people do these days, particularly since they seem to be turning up everywhere."

"And do you think that the soul of a person could somehow . . . well, animate the body it once occupied?"

Emory Beason chuckled. "Not for very long, my dear, though I could well imagine some moldering body appearing like Grendel in the midst of a roomful of aristocratic dabblers in the occult. The sight would ruin a perfectly respectable séance, not to mention the effect of the smell. Now, whoever gave you that idea?"

"Just a conversation I had at tea. Nothing serious."

But it was. Whatever Mina told her, she was prepared to believe. She reminded herself of this as she rang Mina Harker's bell the next afternoon.

Mina answered the door herself. Her bonnet was already pinned on, and she carried a coat and bag. "If I don't leave immediately, Millicent will find some excuse to keep me inside," she whispered as if she were a disobedient child. Her pace began slowly then quickened. While they walked, Mina looked at the sunlit winter sky, the frost her breath made in the air. She drank it all in eagerly. "This is the medicine I need," she said and looked at Winnie with thanks.

They went to a confectioner's close to the market, where they ordered cocoa and shortbread and took a table close to the windows. Beyond the lace curtains and polished rolled glass, people walked back and forth on mundane errands, while inside, Winnie sat watching the smoke rise from her cigarettes as Mina went on with her story.

Mina had just begun describing their chase across Europe when she noticed that tables were filling up around them as people came in for afternoon tea. "The rest I haven't even told Jonathan," she whispered. "I can't go on talking here."

"We'll go to my house," Winnie suggested. "Mr. Beason will be working late. Send a note home and stay for dinner."

Mina finished her story that evening. In the last moments of it, when she described finding the bodies and taking the journal, Winnie sat with her hands gripping the chair, her eyes fixed on Mina's. If Winnie was not fully convinced, Mina knew she was nearly so.

"And now you think the vampire is still alive?" Winnie asked.

"Not for certain, and yet it seems that he must be. I still feel his blood in me. I still feel that passion his touch aroused."

"That's hardly surprising. You're a married woman. You now have permission to be passionate," Winnie replied.

"You're right, but it's more than that. I have dreams, terrible dreams. And the smell or sight of blood is . . . attractive, far too attractive, and the attraction itself unnerving. I wonder if I really did lose a child or if what I felt when I began to bleed was something less natural. If so . . ." Her voice trailed off, and she looked away to hide her fright. "Now, I keep waiting for all of these things to diminish, but if anything they all grow stronger." She tried to shrug. "I fight it. I put on a magnificent act even though I feel my will crumbling slowly inside me."

"Have you spoken to your husband about this?"

"A little." Mina knew her deceit must sound strange, particularly since she was newly wed. "He went through so much at Dracula's castle, that any reminder of it is painful to him. If I tell him about the journal, then he will want to know how it came into my possession. I'm hoping to keep it a secret until it is translated, and even after that if there's nothing in it of any importance. I suppose I'll have to go to London to find an expert to work on it. If I do, we'll have to write back and forth. Jonathan is sure to discover it."

"Well, if that's necessary, you can have the letters sent here. But perhaps you won't need to leave Exeter. I know of someone here who has ties all over eastern Europe, even into Russia itself—Lord Gance."

"Truly? He's one of my husband's clients," Mina said. "We're invited to a dinner party at his house on Saturday. Now Jonathan is trying to beg off because I've been ill."

"Ill! Despondent is more like it. That party is exactly what you need, Mina Harker. Tell Jonathan so! Mr. Beason and I will be there, so you'll know someone. After you meet Lord Gance, it will be easier to approach him about the book."

"But he knows Jonathan," Mina protested and reminded Winnie of the need for secrecy.

"Lord Gance manages to be both a hedonist and an astute businessman. As a result, you can rely on his discretion. He makes a point of it, particularly since he has had to rely so often on that virtue in others." Winnie concluded that summation with a sly smile.

"And for all that, you still sound as if you like him."

"In one respect, I do. He's donated a great deal of money to our hospital, for no reason whatsoever that I can determine unless . . ."

"Unless?"

"Unless we've been treating his bastards. More likely, he actually possessed some noble sentiment. Other than the regular drafts, however, I've never seen signs of it."

"No wonder Jonathan was trying to wiggle out of the invitation."

"Well, don't let him. One of Lord Gance's parties is not only socially acceptable, it is probably the only interesting event you'll attend for months in Exeter. Now, promise me that you'll go."

"I don't know. That's up to Jonathan."

"Damn it, Mina! Tell him you'll go without him if he refuses." She noticed Mina's shock and added, "You stood up to a creature who controlled the winds and wolves, who once led armies, who lived for centuries. I think you're more than able to face down one proper English husband."

"In that case, I think it's time for me to leave," Mina responded.

Winnie seemed ready to apologize, and Mina laughed. "You are so wise, Winnie dear, but gentle persuasion is better than a battle of wills. I think some time alone with my husband is all I'll really need. I think I'll stop by the firm and drag him away from work early enough to stop by the dressmaker's with me. Once he sees the gown and how anxious I am to go, the matter will be settled."

Jonathan commented on how delightful it was to hear my laugh, Mina wrote the following morning in her diary. *He said the dress was almost as magnificent as the woman who would be wearing it. By the time we reached home, there was nothing Millicent could say that would keep him from agreeing to my every request.*

Millicent did not mention my absence. Indeed she seemed quite cordial at dinner. I was pleased by this. If being strong-willed wins her respect, I am quite up to the task. I think she knows this now. I think that perhaps, as time goes by, we may even become friends.

PART THREE

Gance

CHAPTER TEN

On the afternoon of Lord Gance's dinner party, an early winter storm covered the city with a wet, heavy snow. Mina, who decided to lie down and rest for the afternoon, had sent Laura to get her dress. Though the girl had been given instructions to return in a cab to protect the package, Millicent brought the dress up with its brown wrapper soggy, its hem coated with snow.

"The clumsy thing dropped it just as she was coming in the door," Millicent complained. "That's what happens when you let the seamstress work until the last minute. You've nothing else . . ."

Mina sat up in bed, her back rigid, her expression determined. "Then I shall have to wear it as it is." Millicent's disapproval made her smile and add sweetly, "Aunt Millicent, we live near our host. So do a number of his expected guests. There will be many damp hems around his table tonight."

"You should look perfect."

"And we should be rude because I won't? Millicent, dear, listen to me. We both love Jonathan. We both want what is best for him. But you must trust him more, and trust the choice he made when he chose me."

Millicent looked at her, her stern expression dulled with shock. Mina had never spoken to her so frankly before, and Millicent responded with honesty of her own. "Everything changed so suddenly," she said.

"Of course it did, but Jonathan can handle the responsibility. And, Millicent, so can I. Now, please help me dress. I want to make the best possible first impression on our neighbors."

While the dress lay over a chair near the fire so the hem could dry, Mina piled her hair high on her head and curled it in loose ringlets, lightly powdered her face and shoulders, and colored her lips in the careful manner that made it seem she had done nothing to them at all.

Jonathan arrived just after she'd finished. He had little time and quickly changed into his frock coat with its wide silk-faced lapels, matching vest and small-checked trousers. "You're always so calm," he commented as he tried to knot the new wider tie he'd purchased, wincing at the white polka dots on it. "This tie may be the fashion but I feel like a fool."

"You look splendid," Mina said.

He managed to finish without her help, then held her at arm's length to look at her. "So do you," he said. "So serene and so beautiful. And that green velvet, whatever made you pick that color?"

"The seamstress suggested it. When she held it up to me, I understood why." She took his arm. "It is a lovely night for a walk, Mr. Harker."

* * *

CASED candles lined the cobblestone drive from Lord Gance's estate to the street. As Mina approached the wide stone steps leading to the doors, she saw a statue beside them, a tiny brass satyr peeking out at her from behind a pair of rust-and-gold chrysanthemum bushes, their last blooms bright against the snow-covered ground. The statue seemed so out of place amid the classical gardens and the tall stone portico in a Greek design. Mina reminded herself that the satyr was a Greek myth, one that might have stemmed from the passion buried in the most civilized man. Had she been alone, she might have crouched for a closer look at the little statue. Now she only gripped Jonathan's arm and lifted her skirts as they started up the stairs.

Winnie waited in the foyer for them, and judging from how warm her hands were, Mina assumed she had been there for some time. Her dress was pale blue satin and lace, a beautiful compliment to her rose complexion and dark curly hair. Tonight, with her hair carefully pinned up, a bit of rouge on her cheeks and lips, she was no longer the determined nurse with the plain, generous face, but a woman of almost dramatic beauty.

Mr. Beason was exactly what Mina had expected. Shorter than his wife and somewhat stout, he had a receding hairline and wore thick glasses both of which made him seem far older than her as well. After the men were introduced, Mina followed Winnie into the music room, where women were using the huge mirror above the spinet as a place to rearrange their hair and make final adjustments to their gowns.

"You look lovely tonight," Winnie said. "And much happier, too."

"I am. I believe Millicent and I are on our way to some agreement on how to live together. I found our common ground."

"Your husband?"

"Exactly. We both agree that we love him so," Mina said seriously. Then, seeing Winnie's amused expression, she laughed. As she adjusted her hair in the mirror, pinning up a stray lock that had fallen on the windy walk, she asked, "How long have you been married, Winnie?"

"Eleven years. I was just eighteen when we married."

"And you feel as attached to him now as before?"

"More. Before I loved him. Now I also admire him. And now, my infatuated bride, I will take you upstairs."

* * *

As Mina climbed the broad steps to the second-floor ballroom, she felt as if she had been in this house before. The scent of it—a blend of polishing oil, aged wood and cigar—could have belonged to any old house, but there was another smell as well, of musk or incense or some exotic Indian tea. The pattern in the oriental carpeting of the stairs also seemed familiar, and the violin music— yes, she had heard the same piece played just as beautifully sometime in a distant past.

Her mind often played these tricks on her, but never so strongly before. And with the strange memories came another, darker, feeling, one so full of despair that she gripped the rail, certain she was about to fall.

Jonathan, who had been waiting for her at the top, noticed her falter and rushed toward her, but she motioned him back. "I tripped," she said, "but I caught myself in time."

Winnie glanced at her. "Are you all right?" she whispered.

"Almost. Do you know the history of this house?"

"The house is over a hundred years old. Byron himself once held a masked ball here. Why do you ask?"

"Just curious," Mina replied lightly. "It's such a beautiful place, but I have a feeling that some great tragedy happened here."

"Lord Gance's mother died in a fall down these stairs. Perhaps you sense that. I have a friend who often feels events long after they happened. She believes that places have memories, just like people."

"Well, this one's are terrible." Mina walked more quickly up the stairs, then moved to Jonathan's side, taking his hand as they walked through the doors and into the brilliantly lit ballroom.

Just inside, she paused and turned to say something to Winnie. As she did, she noticed a man coming in behind them, his skin and hair so pale in the dark outer hallway. Mina recognized him as the man she had seen entering Jonathan's firm, the one who had reminded her so much of Dracula. She stared at his face, and as he returned her gaze, his eyes caught the light, glowing silver for an instant. It wasn't possible! They had left this all behind!

As she stood, frozen by the sight of him, something wet touched her hand. She stifled a cry and looked down at a massive wolfhound with a gold link collar around its neck. Its eyes, nearly the same shade of pale gray as its owner's, looked up at her expectantly.

The spell which had seemed almost deliberately cast, was broken. Gance took her hand. "I see the coincidence has made quite an impression," he said after they'd been introduced.

"Coincidence, Lord Gance?" For a moment she wondered if he had read her mind.

"You needn't be so polite, Mina dear," Winnie said as she moved beside her.

"The velvet," Mina said, realizing that they wore the same shade and texture in coat and gown.

"I think the color looks far better on you than it does on me, Mrs. Harker," Gance said. "Under the circumstances, my guests will understand if I absent myself for a little while."

"It's hardly necessary, Lord Gance," Mina protested. "As you noted, it's only a coincidence."

He shook his head. "In my house there are no coincidences, Mrs. Harker. Later, you must dance with me." He left her, followed by the dog, then the butler as he went out the doors.

"How strange," Mina commented to Jonathan. As she did, she noted that those nearest them had stopped speaking and were looking at her curiously. Winnie moved close to the pair, dragging them into the nearest group, introducing them both then adding that they were recently married on the Continent. As the group began asking the couple the usual questions, Winnie excused herself and moved to a second group then a third. Sometime later, Mina noticed her standing alone at the window. She asked Jonathan to get her a glass of eggnog and joined Winnie there.

"Would you care to explain what's happened here?" Mina asked.

"This is Lord Gance's holiday party. In the past, he has often invited his mistress and they have always worn matching colors. Under the circumstances, he had to change. Otherwise, I suppose he would have had to make some announcement. It would have been highly amusing, but also a terrible embarrassment for both you and your husband."

"And for Lord Gance."

Winnie laughed. "Dear Lord, no! He'd revel in it." She waved toward the elaborate buffet and out the window at the extensive gardens glowing with their hanging Chinese lanterns, at the ice sculptures on the terrace below. "He has something suitable to wear, Mina. Don't doubt it. Here comes your husband with the eggnog. Be careful of your later glasses. I think the brandy content increases as the night wears on."

After Jonathan handed Mina her glass, Winnie pointed across the room. "Now that I have you both together, come and meet the Andersens. They live nearly across from you at number forty-nine and have been anxious to meet you. Afterwards, perhaps we should simply move to the next address and the next until we've covered everyone."

Mina laughed. Jonathan merely smiled and held his wife's arm somewhat more tightly than necessary. Mina knew he was not afraid of losing her to some group, but simply holding on to her for her support. She felt far more at ease in this gathering than he did, interested rather than intimidated, as he was, by each new arrival. Poor Jonathan! she thought and gave him frequent, encouraging smiles.

* * *

GANCE had intended to hold the party in the first-floor solarium. If the weather had been as fine as earlier in the week, he would have ordered the doors opened and let the party spill into the terrace and garden. The sudden freeze had changed all that, and preparations had shifted to the second-floor ballroom.

A string quartet had been hired to provide the entertainment for his sixty guests. The house staff had done the rest. They had labored with remarkable efficiency, without a word of complaint because, though Gance's reputation was tarnished in polite society, his staff adored him. The feeling was mutual. Abandoned by his self-absorbed parents, Gance had been raised by the family retainers. As a result, he did not believe in caste. He wished he could invite his servants to these socials, for he frequently took his meals in the kitchen with them and found their banter to be far more interesting than the strained amenities at these formal affairs.

In keeping with Gance's mode of entertaining, the dinner would be served buffet style. In the meantime a selection of cheeses, hot rum and cider, and cold eggnog were being served at a table close to the fire. For those less traditional, a butler carried glasses of champagne.

While Gance was changing, the music had begun. Now he stood in the doorway, watching his guests talk and dance. This was the way the house was meant to be—filled with people and laughter. The more socials he held in the mansion, the more he seemed to exorcize the tragedies of its past.

"David, what is the piece being played?" he asked his butler.

"Part of *Scheherazade* by Rimsky-Korsakov, sir."

"Ah!" Gance paused, listened a moment then said, "Order the candles lit and the gaslights turned down."

He moved through the room, stopping often to talk with his guests, circling ever closer to Mina. He waited until Jonathan was with her before approaching them both. "I came to collect my dance," he said to Mina, then turned to Jonathan. "With your permission, of course."

Jonathan watched them walk to the center of the floor. His lips were affably upturned. Only his eyes revealed his concern.

"Emory?" Winnie asked, glancing from Jonathan to Mina. He nodded. Without a word, Winnie drew Jonathan onto the dance floor, placing her hand on Jonathan's shoulder just as Mina and Gance swept by.

Damn that woman! She behaves like a venomous ex-lover, Gance thought as the pair stayed just within hearing distance. He had hoped to be charming, to make an impression, and instead found himself nodding politely to Mina's husband. "I hear you were married in Hungary," he said to Mina.

"Yes. Jonathan was on a business trip. He fell ill. He had no family to go to him, so I did. We were married in Budapest."

"You visited that country again, didn't you?"

"Business. Jonathan thought I might like to go along since I did not get to tour the country properly the first time."

"Did you, the second time?"

"No."

"One of your group died, didn't he? Quincey Morris, the American?"

"Where did you hear about that?" Mina asked, astonished by his knowledge.

"I handled some of Lord Godalming's affairs in his absence. He later wired that he had to go to America. Poor Arthur. First a fiancée, then a friend. Mr. Morris became ill, I take it?"

Mina nodded.

"It is a lovely country, though. I've been there a number of times."

"Do you speak Hungarian?" Mina asked, thinking of the book she intended to show him.

"Enough to get by. I have no great skill with languages. Fortunately, others do." The music stopped. He held her at arm's length for a moment. "I do believe the color looks better on you than me. I promise never to wear that green in your presence again. Unless you request it, of course."

She knew what he implied, but he had done it so skillfully that the blush that colored her cheeks seemed only to reveal the nature of the gossip she had heard. When the music started again, she danced with her husband, resting her head on his shoulder so she would not have to speak at all.

Dinner was served a quarter hour later. Huge silver trays of sliced roast beef were surrounded by pieces of pudding. Whole salmon baked in a pastry crust followed, and the main dishes gave way to glazed carrots, potatoes, creamed leeks, pickled vegetables, breads, cold meats and a selection of sweets.

When the guests had all been served and were seated at the tables scattered around the edge of the hall, Gance clapped his hands.

Servants brought in three slender urns, each half the height of a man, then filled them with pitchers of oil. One burned red, the other two bright orange. The gaslights were turned down even further, until all the light in the hall seemed centered in the urns.

Gance clapped again and five men came into the hall. Each was dressed in a white cotton turban and loose trousers. Their swarthy skin looked even darker against the flowing white fabrics. Three carried drums and stood beside the oil burners. The others carried stringed instruments. Someone standing close to Mina whispered to a companion that they were a tanbur and a lute.

Without waiting for an introduction, the group began to play an intricate melody so unsuited to Mina's ears that she could only distinguish the deepest drum and the tanbur, which whined at such a high tone that it seemed to be buzzing in her head. Attention was centered on the door, and a moment later two men and a woman entered.

The men wore white cotton shirts and trousers, but instead of turbans, their heads were shaved. The woman, her face and hair and body covered with thin silk veils in clashing shades of red and gold and purple, moved at their center like a butterfly among camellias. Though her entire body was covered, except for her eyes and her hair, the way the thin fabric clung to her made it obvious that she wore little underneath the outer gown.

She took a place among the musicians while the men who had come in with her began to move in time to the music— swaying, whirling, apart then together, until Mina was certain they were not Arabs or Turks but dervishes from India. When it seemed that they were incapable of moving any faster, the men began a tumbling act, bouncing off each other's shoulders and arms. Each trick was more complex than the last, and the audience applauded enthusiastically.

The music shifted, becoming slower, more sensual. The woman stepped forward and began to dance. The sinewy movements of her arms, the soft motion of her bare feet on the wood floor had an exotic beauty. Though her body moved in the most provocative way, the mask on her face gave her a remoteness that kept attention fixed on her art.

Mina tried to focus only on the dance, though the way the dancer moved beneath her flowing silks reminded her—No, not here, she admonished herself so sternly that she nearly said the words aloud.

Mina glanced at Jonathan. His eyes were focused on the woman, his hands beating time against his thighs. His mouth was slack. Had they been alone, she would have kissed it. Instead she merely looked away, letting the music lead her thoughts.

The woman danced through three more songs then fell to her knees, signaling that her performance was over.

One of the musicians whispered something to the dancer then unhooked the veil that covered her face.

The woman's arms remained at her side, but Mina saw them tense, fighting the urge to cover her face. The men applauded; a few women did as well, but only out of politeness. Mina did not applaud at all. She saw the woman's expression. She knew exactly what the musician had done.

How dare the man! she thought. And how dare Lord Gance allow it. Didn't he understand what that act meant to the woman? "Jonathan, it's getting late. Would you take me home?" she asked when the performers had left the room.

As they said good-bye to their host, Gance noted Mina's disapproval. He drew her aside and whispered, "The man was her husband, Mrs. Harker. He had the right."

"And you the power to stop it," she countered.

Gance watched them go and thought, happily, that he had broken through her defenses. Yes, he would definitely see her again.

CHAPTER ELEVEN

I

"You were so lovely tonight," Jonathan said as he helped Mina unhook her gown. He lit the candles beside their bed and on her dressing table, then turned out the gaslight. As he did, she unpinned her hair. It fell over her shoulders in a warm cascade. He loved her hair—its color, the subtle perfume of the shampoo she used. She reached for the brush, but he took it instead and stood behind her, running it through the tight curls. "Gance wasn't the only one watching you, though he was the most obvious."

Mina laughed. "Should I wear something less revealing next time?"

He kissed her shoulder. "Let them look," he said.

But Jonathan knew he didn't mean it, at least not where Gance was concerned.

Jonathan's jealousy astonished him, for he had never felt anything like it before. On the journey with the men, he had noticed Seward watching Mina with more than clinical concern. He had understood that they all loved her, all respected her strength and common sense, and he had even taken some comfort in knowing that if he had died, one of them would have eventually married her. But those were all good men, who would have seen to her needs and welfare. Perhaps his jealousy stemmed more from Lord Gance's reputation with women. It was said that Gance seduced them, used them, abandoned them. There were even rumors of suicide connected with his affairs and, so barbaric in these times, a duel.

And that creature had held Mina, had stared at her breasts— so beautiful against the dark velvet of her dress—had touched her hair, inhaled the scent of her perfume.

Jonathan had almost lost her once, he would never allow it to happen again. He wished there were some prayer he could say to guard her against every evil, human or otherwise, some way to ensure that a creature like Gance could never touch her. A way . . .

"Jonathan?" Mina turned sideways. "Jonathan, if you're not going to use the brush, give it to me."

He stroked her hair a few more times, watching the sparks he raised flicker in the dimly lit room, then set it down. Taking her hand, he pulled her to her feet, turned her to face the mirror and began to undress her, the articles of clothing falling one after another like Salome's veils. She tried to touch him, to kiss him, but he would not allow it. With this act, he claimed his ownership of her. He would not excuse it, or apologize for it. It had to be done. I alone see you like this, he thought. I alone. No one else.

When he'd finished, he stepped back and undressed quickly, watching her all the while. So beautiful. His Mina. His wife.

He pulled the covers back, drew her to him and onto the bed.

He had been so careful with her until now. In the beginning, when he had been recovering, he had so little strength. Then . . . well, he would not think of that, or the child. There would be children enough in the life that stretched ahead of them.

As for now, though they had slept together for weeks, this seemed like his wedding night. The passion that flowed through him was more than sexual, more than love. He had been touched by evil and survived, and she was another of his kind.

His lovemaking—if this could be called by so civilized a term—was intense, over soon after it began, leaving him with no strength to continue. Jonathan rolled up on his elbow and kissed Mina's forehead. As he did, he noticed how bright her eyes were in the soft candlelight, and how quickly she turned her head away when he noticed the tears.

He didn't ask what was wrong, for he was certain he already knew. He had approached her too soon, too roughly. Indeed, he had acted as if she were his mistress, not his wife, a creature to be used solely for his own pleasure, as Gance undoubtedly used the dancer Jonathan had seen tonight. He gathered Mina into his arms, murmured that he loved her and closed his eyes.

Sleep eluded Mina. She lay thinking about what she had almost done, frustrated by what she had almost felt.

Had almost done what? Lost that terrible control that had been pounded into her soul from the time she was a child? Submit, do not enjoy. Love, do not desire.

Passionless. Shame-filled. It wasn't right. The vampire's blood still strong in her screamed that it wasn't right. If she had been alone, she would have satisfied herself. Instead she lay and let silent tears flow as she mourned the freedom she wished she had.

. . . Then the room in the castle where the women lay took shape around her. Mina had just torched the tapestries, but when she tried to move toward the staircase, she saw that the floor was covered with newborn kittens, pawing at one another, their helpless mewing terrible to hear. She looked at the flames and tried to brush their tiny, almost hairless bodies out of her way so she could run. The attempt was useless. So many, so many. She ran anyway, and as she stepped on them, they mewed and crumbled into dust . . .

* * *

SATURDAY morning, as always, Jonathan rose early, dressed quietly and went to work. Mina woke later. The room was cold, and she hastily lit the wood Laura had arranged on the hearth and ran back to bed. Her daily diary was in the drawer of her bedside table. She took it out and began recording last night's events in shorthand. Near the end, she added a personal comment.

As I whirled with Lord Gance though his ballroom, I found myself strangely attracted to the man. Perhaps this is because of all I have heard about him. It is a heady feeling to be with a man in public who would be dangerous in private. A plea for mercy would fall on deaf ears, a plea for restraint—well, if half of what Winnie tells me is true, he would only laugh. It is a potent fantasy, and nothing more. Still . . .

She paused in her writing. This was the diary she kept where Jonathan could read it at any time. With perverse pleasure, she realized that she wished he would. She was no angel, no carefully clothed porcelain doll, but a woman. If he read this, he would not mention it any more than she could voice aloud the following words.

But if he read them, he might understand. With excitement, she went on.

. . . it was a pleasure to see the jealousy so clear in Jonathan's expression, to stand in the center of our bedroom later and watch him claim me as his, to be wanton and demanding in his arms. I need this passion. I need it desperately. Too often I fear that I will only feel it a few times in our marriage and that, tragically, I will never know the moment when it ends.

There was much to be done before Christmas. She put the book away, put on a simple gown and went downstairs, where Laura had been cleaning the dining cupboard. The silver service was large enough to serve the firm's clerks and their wives, but the linens were yellowed, many in need of mending.

"Not one to entertain, was he?" Laura commented.

"My husband used to say that Mr. Hawkins was like all good solicitors. All he needed was a box of hand-rolled cigars, twenty-year port and a client, or better yet, two." Thinking Laura might misinterpret her remark, Mina added, "Still, though he may have been something of a recluse, he made Mr. Harker and I feel at home. Would that he were here to share the house with us as he planned."

Laura had begun dusting the china when the front bell rang. The girl ran for the door and returned a short time later with a wrapped parcel for Mina. Inside she found a mound of shredded green velvet and a note which read,

Dear Mrs. Harker. I am sending you my coat as it now is. I do this so that you will never hesitate to wear the gown which so enhances you own beauty. Yours truly, G.

She put the note in her pocket, and handed the box to Laura. "Go downstairs and burn this in the stove," she said. That night, when she wrote in her diary, Mina devoted only a single sentence to the parcel, adding no thoughts of her own save one—*What he did seems so terribly strange that I do not know what to make of it.*

II

Gance's offices were located on the east side of Exeter, in the second floor of a private house. The businesses he had inherited from his father were far-flung, his interest in them purely financial. He could have easily managed the accounts through Harker's firm, but he wanted a place he could keep the records and conduct business that was separate from his home, and the office his father had established here years ago was perfect. He was fond of the owner too. An old woman with no children of her own, she doted over him with more maternal warmth than his mother had ever displayed. Always ready with tea and sweets and critical comments about his guests, she reminded him most of the housekeeper in those droll detective stories by Doyle.

The woman paid little attention to gossip and therefore did not know anything about his third house in Exeter—the small and private retreat by the river that had once housed his father's mistress and now held his. His mistress was a quiet creature, exotic in the manner that Hindu women usually were. In the beginning, there had been fire in her blood. They had often fought, and he had found it difficult to win the battles, though win he had. Now she appeared utterly devoted to him, but sometimes, when she was not aware he was looking at her, he saw a terrible hatred in her eyes. Getting her to converse had become impossible, though in every other respect she did her best to please him.

Any other man would have found her irresistible, but she bored Gance in every way except in bed.

Weeks ago he had vowed to break it off with her, go out and find someone that would challenge him, and amuse him, and fear him just enough to make their relationship interesting. Someone married and of his own class would be ideal, he decided. He loved the game of seeing his lover on her husband's arm, dressed for the opera or a play or just a day in the park, watching him slyly and with just a hint of fear at how easily a wrong word or gesture could reveal their sins.

He had once thought that Winnie Beason would be perfect, but one evening at a social when he had whispered that suggestion to her, she had smiled and told him, "I am passionately in love with my husband," turned and walked away.

He would never have guessed it, for she threw herself passionately into causes—the hospital, the school, the women's crusade. Philanthropy was usually a sign of trouble at home. Then she said she passionately loved Emory Beason, that portly round-eyed bookworm! Perhaps, he thought, she was passionate about everything. She certainly showed signs of it in how passionately cruel she had been to him since he had made his discreet pass.

A pity that she had become so close to Mina Harker. More the pity that Mina Harker's note had made it clear they were coming here together this afternoon. Still, after waiting nearly a week for her to contact him, he was encouraged by her note.

"Mina, dear Mina," he whispered aloud. "You with the sad eyes, so filled with secrets." While he waited for the women to arrive, he pulled Lord Godalming's last letters to him—the first written the day before he left for Hungary in the company of the Harkers, the second just a quick scrawled note saying he was going to America and would be back before the new year.

Arthur had mentioned that there'd been a doctor in their party, he recalled. Or had he said two? Hardly an auspicious beginning for a marriage.

The women arrived with Winnie's usual punctuality. Mrs. Harker wore a hat with a veil, Gance noted, as if she were not comfortable with coming here. And though she looked him in the face as they talked, at first she had trouble doing so. Both these signs pleased him. He wanted her off balance. Women off balance often did the most inexplicably wicked things.

He offered them seats on the divan and sat opposite them in the black leather Chesterfield chair that always made him look paler than he actually was. He noticed that Mina Harker watched him intently. "Your note said you wanted to discuss a business matter," he commented.

He expected her to approach the problem obliquely, as nervous women usually did. But she pulled an old leather-bound book from her handbag. "I need someone to translate this," she said and handed it to him.

He opened it, glanced at the writing and frowned. "Why did you bring this to me?" he asked.

"You told me that you spoke Hungarian."

"Some. But this is not Hungarian."

She seemed genuinely surprised. "Then what is it?"

He studied the script more closely. "A dialect, I think. I recognize some words." He pointed as he went on. "Child . . . home . . . journey . . . It seems to be a diary."

"Exactly. Do you know someone who could do the work?"

"I have an acquaintance in London. If he doesn't know the language, he will know someone who does."

"Could you give me his name, please?"

"He will see to the request more quickly if the journal comes directly from me."

Mina hesitated, then, with her back even stiffer than before, she went on. "This is a private matter. Even my husband does not know that I have this book. I would not have brought the request to you if Mrs. Beason had not assured me that I could trust your discretion."

"You ask me to give you a reference. Why should I?"

Though the question was natural, its bluntness astonished her. Yes, she was attracted to him, intrigued as well, he believed. "I suppose because I requested it," she replied. "Would you like me to pay for the information? I can if you wish."

"Not at all." He laughed, took out paper and a pen, and wrote a name and address. "He will ask for payment, you can be sure of that. Now, would you care for some tea?"

Mina hesitated. Winnie Beason did not. "I must get to the hospital this afternoon," she said.

"Would you stay?" he asked Mina.

"No. That is, I'm going with Winnie."

"I see. You'd rather risk the microbes than me, eh?" He laughed. "You're right to be so wary, after everything that Mrs. Beason has told you about me."

Mina Harker didn't deny any of this, did not even blush as so many silly women would have. When they said good-bye, he noted that her handshake was as firm as any man's. As he looked down from his front window at them walking toward the hospital in the black skirts, tightly fitting coats and silly plumed hats that all liberal women of means seemed to find so socially acceptable, he felt quite certain that he would see Mrs. Harker again and under far less correct circumstances.

In the meantime, he might as well learn more of the mystery of her marriage and her strange visit to the Continent. He knew exactly where to begin.

CHAPTER TWELVE

Arthur Holmwood, Lord Godalming, was despondent over his recent losses—first of his fiancée, then of his friend—and even more by the manner of their deaths. He felt as if his entire world—beautiful and lighthearted—had a volcano at its core, ready to erupt and destroy everything he valued.

On his voyage to America, he had made no shipboard friendships, shared no journeys from his past. He often took his meals in his cabin. People knew he accompanied a body back to Texas, assumed he was in mourning and left him to himself. The journey from Boston to Texas troubled him as well, for the sights along the way reminded him of how when Lucy had been so ill, he had promised to bring her here and show her the sights of this savage, new land.

When he had done his sad duty, he could not bear to return to Boston. Instead, he traveled to New Orleans and stayed through Christmas. Though he did not admit it to himself, he hoped that this city—so civilized, so cosmopolitan, so beautiful—would lessen his despair. Instead, the city only increased his sorrow for he sensed too strongly in those chilly rain-washed streets that dark undercurrent to life, the evil that ended in sudden violent death.

He booked passage on the next ship to England and arrived in Exeter five days before Christmas. The holiday season was in full swing, but he had no gifts for anyone, no explanation of where he had been save the story that the survivors had made up, of Quincey's dying of some illness in Austria. The story seemed so preposterous to anyone who knew Quincey well that Arthur was more honest with Quincey's family. Quincey had been shot by gypsies in Romania, he said. It seemed to comfort them to know that Quincey's life had ended through the same romantic wanderlust by which he had always lived, and that he had died in some exotic place. Quincey's youngest brother had even pulled out an atlas and asked him to point to the area where Quincey had died.

Arthur thought of that often. He dwelled on the map and the boy with the same wanderlust in his eyes, and the lies he had told, as he sat alone in his house in Exeter. He barely touched his meals, dared not drink alone, for the dreams that followed intoxication were vivid and terrible. He sent a quick note to the Harkers, letting them know that he'd returned and begging them to tell no one that he was at home.

Gradually, though, word of his return leaked out. Friends came to call and were turned away at the door. He dined Christmas Eve at the Harker home but left early, pleading exhaustion from the trip though he had already been back for over a week. It pleased him to see Jonathan and Mina so happy, so ready to put the recent tragedies behind them. Yet, mean though the thought might be, their very happiness gave him pain. His love was gone, and others laughed.

And he had to deal with the saddest thought of all. He wanted someone to take Lucy's place, needed that someone desperately and condemned himself for his weakness.

Arthur was sitting in his study, staring at the flames in the fireplace, watching the wood slowly consumed, when Lord

Gance rang his bell. He heard his butler give the usual excuse, and then heard Gance's rude response: "The hell he's ill! He's brooding. And he needs company. Now, tell me where he is!"

His butler did not reply, but Arthur was certain the man must have silently agreed and pointed toward the study. A moment later the door banged open and Gance entered, bringing with him a rush of crisp winter air. His pale hair glistened with snowflakes, his dark cape was white at the shoulders. "I did not come all this way in this disgusting weather to hear that you were ill, Arthur, when it is perfectly obvious to anyone who knows you that you are not. Now, have I offended you in some way?"

"Not until this moment," Arthur replied with a wan smile.

"Has anyone?"

"No."

Gance went to the sideboard and poured a brandy, then a second for his host. "So what in heaven's name are you doing here?" he asked.

Arthur spread his hands. "Why, nothing. What concern is it of yours anyway?"

Gance thrust the drink into Arthur's hand and laughed. "Everyone who counts in this city has made it *my* concern. They knew there was no one else obnoxious enough to push past the barricade of your devoted retainers."

"What do you want, Winston?"

"A revolution. The overthrow of Lord Godalming and the return of the *Honorable* Arthur Holmwood—a young man of wealth who knew how to enjoy himself most thoroughly. Seriously, Arthur, I met your beautiful Lucy a number of times, often enough to know that she would not appreciate seeing you holed up this way."

"Damn you, I am in mourning!"

"If you had died in her place, she would not have missed the holiday season, Arthur. Now, don't look so furious. I'm only speaking the truth. Put on something somber. Wear a black arm band or even a widow's veil over your head if it pleases you, but come to tonight's dinner party at the Ellisons'. Otherwise, I will be forced to bring everyone back here afterward."

All the emotions Arthur had managed to hide surfaced now, with anger and despair the most potent. He pushed himself to his feet with such difficulty that Gance wondered how long he had been brooding in that chair. Swaying slightly, Arthur tossed his glass into the fireplace and watched the brandy sizzle and briefly flame in the heat of the embers. "Whatever I have seen or done is my affair, Winston. Now, I am asking for the last time that you leave my house!"

"I'll bring you a plate of sweets. I hear Ellison's cook is even making a rum torte strong enough to put Lady Grayson in her cups."

Lady Grayson's activities in the temperance movement were notorious, but Arthur did not smile. Instead he walked toward Gance, his expression filled with fury. He was larger than Gance, stronger as well. Gance wisely retreated, stopping only when he had the front door open behind him. "Good God, Arthur, what did you see?"

"The devil," Arthur whispered. Gance stood outside; all Arthur had to do was close and lock the door behind him and he could return to his solitude. Gance, with his cadaverous body and pale beauty, brought the memories back too vividly. But, oddly enough, Gance was the one most likely to banish them as well.

Arthur hesitated. "Am I to leave or stay?" Gance asked.

"If you promise not to ask where I've been, stay. Tell me everything that's gone on this season. Be precise. Be sarcastic. Take my mind off all the deaths."

"Gladly. First I'll pour us both another drink. Even second-hand, the Exeter holiday season is best approached while slightly tipsy."

One drink, Arthur thought, or two at most. Enough to make me sociable, no more. "All right," he said, and returned to the comfort of his chair, the consuming warmth of his fire.

Gance talked. Arthur drank. Each glass numbed him a little

more, each burst of laughter made him feel better, though it was a frantic kind of pleasure. It would end, Arthur knew, end as soon as he was alone. Already he could feel the blackness growing around him, like a pit from which the only escape was to imagine happiness, though he knew it was an illusion.

Sometime during the course of the evening, Gance mentioned Lucy once more, and Arthur unexpectedly began to cry. Arthur recalled Gance sitting on the arm of his chair, a comforting hand on his shoulder.

Arthur remembered another drink, then nothing, though when he woke, he was in Gance's nightclothes in a guest room in Gance's house. It would be like Gance to drag him out, but to take him home was a different matter.

A servant brought him breakfast. Gance came in later with a deck of cards. They played for an hour, then Arthur napped until dinner. As he went downstairs in clothes rumpled from days of wear, he discovered Mina and Jonathan with his host.

Arthur picked at his food. Gance devoured his quickly then sat sipping a glass of wine and listening for some news of the others' journey. Though they had been together for weeks, they did not mention the trip.

The group took tea and dessert in the warmth of Gance's parlor. As they went in to it, Mina stayed behind with Gance for a moment. He expected her to mention the parcel, but instead she whispered, "Thank you for calling us. He does seem worse than when we saw him last week. I'm glad you forced him out."

"He was raving last night about the devil in human form. Could he be possessed, do you think?"

Gance said it so seriously that Mina could not tell if he was joking. "I think not," she said.

"There are legends in Romania, of wolves and bats that can turn into men. Vampires, I believe they are called, though they're hardly as silly as that Varney character in the penny dreadfuls. They infect their victims, I hear, enslave their souls or something like that."

"Please, Lord Gance. I doubt that your friend has been infected by anything," she replied. "I'm amazed you consider such things possible." It surprised Gance that she did not smile. He had intended the notion to be utterly outrageous.

"Madam, if God can work miracles, why not His greatest enemy? However, I only wondered about the stories since Arthur kept repeating something that seemed so odd."

"What was it?"

"*Denn die tolten reiten schnell.* You know German, don't you?"

"No," Mina answered, though she knew that phrase well enough.

"'For the dead travel fast.' I find that most interesting, especially since I can't help but think of poor Arthur as haunted."

They sat in near darkness, with the burning logs in the marble fireplace and the candles on the table shedding a dim golden light on them all. Gance had set a specific mood, Mina thought, one ideal for ghost stories and primitive legends, but none of them had any desire to speak of those. The thought of discussing any of what they had seen or heard disturbed Mina. Yet, there was poor Arthur, as helpless as she was, both of them unable to shake the memories of that journey. Perhaps together they could exorcise their ghosts.

As they were leaving, she took Arthur's hand, then looked at Jonathan. "Darling, I'd like to come tomorrow and see Arthur. Do we have any plans?"

"None. Perhaps Winnie would accompany you."

"I'll ask her," Mina replied, though she knew Winnie would be spending the day at the hospital.

* * *

MINA went over the household accounts with Millicent during breakfast the next morning. She would have preferred to eat and do the work afterward, but Millicent did not like to waste time. When they'd finished, they discussed the menu for a holiday party she and Jonathan were giving the following week for Jonathan's clerks. Millicent argued against all of Mina's suggestions, noting quite correctly that she did the shopping and knew what was available. "There are no lambs to be had, dear, only yearlings and mutton, which are too strong for curries. The sturgeon are at their freshest in winter. Beef is marbled and tender." She went on planning a menu nothing like the one Mina had in mind. In the end, Mina let her have her way. Millicent had an affection for food that Mina would never understand, though she respected and enjoyed the result.

But the kitchen was the only part of the house Mina would cede to Millicent. Her own life, and the running of the house, had gradually fallen into Mina's control. She had become used to dealing with Laura and the other hired help, but Millicent's position in the household was too nebulous. And now that Millicent was established here, Mina saw no polite way to ask her to leave.

Mina avoided the woman as best she could. She did so now, waiting until Millicent had gone to market before leaving the house herself and walking the short distance to the Gance estate.

A servant answered Lord Gance's door and showed her upstairs, where she discovered Arthur sleeping soundly. The draperies were closed, but in the dim light she saw a scratch on his cheek, and on the side of his neck a pair of marks that might have been a shaving cut, an insect bite or . . .

She wanted to run or to shake him awake. Neither seemed correct, but the latter, at least, would set her mind at ease. "Arthur," she called, lightly so as not to alarm him. "Arthur, please wake up."

"Lucy," he whispered and opened his eyes. A smile touched his lips just for a moment; then, when he saw Mina beside him, it vanished, to return as something polite rather than blissful. "I was dreaming of Lucy," he said. "Did I call out her name?"

"You did. Are you better?"

He laughed without any real humor. "Better than what? Than self-pity, Winston would answer, but then he has never really loved anyone. I used to feel sorry for him. I envy him now."

"He seems to care a great deal about you."

"Of course he does," Arthur replied. "We amuse one another. And how are you? Do you still have nightmares?"

"Sometimes." She promised herself she would tell him the truth when he was better, thought of Lucy and added, "Nearly every night and they seem to be getting stronger."

Arthur nodded sadly. "So have mine. Does Jonathan dream?"

"I don't know. I've asked him, but he won't talk about them."

"That would be like him. He'd bear them alone if he did. I think he'd die before he worried you."

"That's a terrible thought."

"Yes, it is, but it's something all good men do for the women they cherish." Though the honesty clearly pained him, he added, "I think sometimes that's what killed my dear Lucy. Seward loved her too much."

"It's over," Mina said, though privately she agreed with him. "Whatever we might have done differently is all sad and useless speculation."

A maid carrying a tray interrupted them. Conversation stopped while she poured for them, and after she left, whatever secrets their conversation might have revealed had ended. They finished in silence, then Mina left, promising to come again the following day.

As soon as she had gone, Arthur lay back. His head pounded from the brandy he'd drunk last night. Now that he was alone, he realized that there were also strange gaps in his memory. He was getting too old for intoxication, he decided. Too old to waste time on self-pity as well, but in spite of this, he'd rather sit home and brood than endure any more of Gance's forced dissipation.

He dressed slowly then took stock of himself in the mirror. He looked about as well as could be expected after a two-day drunk, with the pale stubble on his face, his red and swollen eyes, the cut on his cheek and . . .

The marks! He had to look at them closely before he dared to touch them, to feel that they were not bites but scratches, most likely made by his own nails while he slept and dreamed of fighting off the beloved he longed to hold in his arms.

To hell with the etiquette of saying good-bye to his host, he decided. He could send a note to Winston later. He took his coat and hat from the cupboard and started toward the stairs.

He moved too fast, or perhaps his tea had been drugged, because the walls of the hallway seemed to be falling down on him, the floor moving beneath his feet. At the top of the stairs, he gripped the banister and sank slowly to his knees.

Her fragrance. Her beautiful hair. Her lips. "Lucy," he whispered as someone gripped his arm and helped him to stand. "Lucy," he said again as he was led back to his room. There, someone laid him on his bed and began to undress him.

"Lucy, I'm so sorry. I did not mean to kill you," he moaned.

"Killed her? Tell me why, Arthur. I must know," Gance said.

Arthur turned his head sideways and saw Gance sitting in a chair beside the bed.

How dare he! How dare Gance interrupt a moment like this! Arthur wanted to throw Gance bodily from the room, but he had no strength. She was pressing down on him, all her sweet honey-colored hair cascading over his face.

He closed his eyes and surrendered to the reality of the dream, the drug, his love, his nightmare.

CHAPTER THIRTEEN

Mina paused just inside the front door of her house. Around her was the dark polished wood of the foyer, and beyond the open French doors the sunlit parlor with its great stone hearth carefully piled with wood. She could go in and sit by the fire or go upstairs and change, pour herself a glass of sherry and stretch out on the divan beside the window with a book or magazine. She could write one of the many letters she owed to old friends still trying to keep in touch. So many things could be done in these magnificent old rooms if only the walls didn't close in around her, all her options, like her perception of the rooms themselves, narrowing until there was only one—sleep. Sleep, dream and remember.

She wished she were still with Arthur, even wished that Gance had joined them. He made her laugh and she had need of laughter. It would be impolite to return there, and it occurred to her that she had no place else to go.

She heard the clock chime three. She had not intended to stay with Arthur so long. She went downstairs to the kitchen, where Millicent was preparing to bake meat pies for the evening meal.

"You went out?" Millicent asked, disapproval clear in her tone.

"Just for a walk."

"It's so cold today. Do you think you're well enough?"

"The air did me good, though I am tired."

"Go lie down, Mina. You'll feel better after a nap."

How could Millicent know! How could the woman ever comprehend her dreams. "You're right, but I want to come down for tea," Mina said and went up to her room, where her bed, soft beneath its crisp lace-trimmed sheets, waited, sinister as a rack.

She would not sleep, not now. But she could rest for just a little while. She undressed and piled the pillows high so she was reclining rather than lying down. Among Jonathan's Christmas gifts to her was a leather-bound collection of works by Emily Bronte. She had read *Wuthering Heights* before, but the poems were new to her. Carefully, trying to capture the cadence of the lines, she began to read.

> Cold in the earth—and the deep snow piled above thee,
> Far, far removed, cold in the dreary grave!
> Have I forgot, my only Love, to love thee,
> Severed at last by Time's all-severing wave?

She read on, wondering if Jonathan had read these lines before he bought the book, or if he had and bought it anyway. She lay the book on the bedside table and closed her eyes.

. . . Somewhere in the tower above her, she heard Jonathan calling her name, drawing it out in a moan of anguish and pain that rose and fell in the darkness and stench of these rotting walls. "Minaaahhhh."

She went to him through the darkness, moving on faith up the winding stairs, her tread so light she did not seem to touch the ground at all.

Had she already grown so much like them?

The thought that had once terrified her held no terror now.

"Minaaahhhh."

The women were all around him, floating insubstantial as the mists that surrounded these ancient walls. Wraiths long dead, yet stronger than ghosts. The transparent white hands held his arms above him, his legs apart. She watched, unable to move to help him or to flee as they stripped him, his clothes flung away from his body in tattered strips.

"Come Mina, come sister," they called in voices cold and beautiful as ice. "You loved him once, give him our gift."

Gift! It was no gift. She moved away, toward the open door, as they laughed and lowered their red lips to his wrists, his thighs.

Blood flowed too fast for them to drink it, but even as his body grew whiter, his struggles weaker, she saw how hard his penis had become, how aroused their touch made him, how ready he was for whatever they offered.

"No!" she cried and rushed toward him. As she did, she felt her eyeteeth lengthen, sharpen. Felt the blood lust rising in her.

"No!" she screamed, then whirled and ran.

The door was shut, the smell of Jonathan's blood all around her. She beat against the ancient wood, beat until her hands were scraped and bloody, beat and screamed to God to save her . . .

"Mina!" A voice, so familiar, called her from another time.

"Mina! Wake up!"

Her eyes opened. Her legs gave way, and she collapsed in front of the door.

Millicent knelt beside her. "You were screaming, Mina. And you walked in your sleep."

Mina looked down at her hands, the scraped knuckles.

"You were pounding on the door."

"I had a nightmare." How to explain? "All I recall now is that it was terrible."

"Terrible enough. The entire street may have heard you. What must they think?" The question was only what Mina expected from the woman, the sympathy in her tone was the real surprise.

That we torture our servants, Mina thought, and suppressed the urge to giggle. After being pulled from that dream, laughter of relief, of hysteria, was so appropriate. She had never felt so thankful to anyone as she did toward Millicent at this moment. The woman helped her to stand, to walk to her bed.

"I was taking some tea upstairs. It's on the table outside. I'll leave it for you."

"No! That is, please, just stay with me for a little while."

"Perhaps you'd like to get dressed and come upstairs with me," Millicent suggested. Without being asked, she sat and waited until Mina had tied back her hair and put on a gown so that they could climb the stairs together.

Mina had never been asked to Millicent's room before. She had expected it to be spotless but not nearly so bright or so cluttered with mementos from Millicent's past. Mina sat on the chaise in the sunlight and, to dispel the seductive horror of the dream, studied the curios, drawings and photographs arranged on the chest and shelves above it.

"The pictures are all of Jonathan, aren't they?" she asked with surprise.

"I never had any children of my own," Millicent said, her voice defensive, as if Mina would reproach her for this show of pride. "His mother was always having him pose for drawings or photographs. Such a waste of money, but after she died, it would have been more of a waste to throw them away."

"Did Jonathan make the drawings? They look like his work."

"He did. I thought he gave all that up long ago."

"Oh, no. When I met him here in Exeter, he was sketching in the gardens around the cathedral." She sensed the woman's disapproval and thought it odd considering how many of his drawings Millicent possessed. "It was on a Sunday. He said the pastime helped him relax."

Millicent handed her drawings of Jonathan's father and his mother, and one of herself when she was younger. She had far too round a face to be beautiful, but Jonathan had accentuated the candor and intelligence in it.

"I'd like to set some of these on the sideboard in the parlor, if you would not mind."

"Your things belong there, Mina."

"And they are. But I have so few treasures and nothing of Jonathan when he was young. Spare me one. This one." She reached into the back of the display and pulled out one photograph of Jonathan when he was about sixteen, standing in front of Millicent. Millicent's dress was light, and there was a rose pinned to the collar. From the look of it, this must have been the picture from which he had done the drawing.

"It was taken on my birthday," Millicent said softly. "Jonathan gave me the flower. I treasure it so much."

An idea came to Mina, a way of mending their bad start with each other. "Aunt Millicent. This picture of Jonathan is so precious. Would you part with it for a little while? Jonathan's birthday is next month. I can have the picture of him turned into a painting to hang above the parlor mantel. It can be a surprise from both of us."

She saw the natural thriftiness in Millicent's eyes and went quickly on. "In the Westerna house there was a delightful picture of Lucy's father when he was a young man. They had it hanging in the dining room. All good families pose their children. We're lucky to be able to do it after the fact."

"All right." Now that it was decided, Millicent was eager to begin. "Where can it be done?"

"There are portrait artists here, but I don't know much about them." An idea came to her, one absolutely daring. "Jonathan told me of one in London. Very good, and quite reasonable. I'll have to take it there personally. I wouldn't trust this to the post. What if Jonathan misses me?"

"If you make it a day trip, Jonathan will never have to know you've gone. If the train should be late getting back, I can say you are at Mrs. Beason's."

"Jonathan always works late on Tuesday. I'll send a wire today and make certain the man will be there."

* * *

ON the way to the train station, Mina stopped at a local artist's studio and dropped off the picture. With the order complete, she went down to London to meet with Lord Gance's acquaintance at the Audley Bank in Mayfair.

William Graves was a huge man, naturally muscular in spite of his sedentary job, and slovenly in appearance. If his eyes had not been so clear, Mina might have suspected him of drunkenness. He certainly looked as if he had slept in the suit he wore.

The intent way he examined the book reminded her of Van Helsing. "I'm sorry, I can't help you," he said after looking at a number of sections of it.

"Can't?"

"You see, this is not Hungarian. I think it may be a Rumanian dialect, or possibly a dated version of the language, perhaps written by a scholar who wanted to ensure his privacy. What do you think this book might be?"

"A novel in diary form I was told. I purchased it on a trip through Hungary."

"Ah! Well, in that case, I am doubly sad I cannot help you. Most of my work is so dry. Lord Gance wrote that you were from Exeter. Is that correct?"

"It is."

"A pity. I know of no one there. On the other hand, there was a small bookstore in Bloomsbury run by a Romanian family. The son, James, was born here and does not speak Rumanian, but his father was quite a scholar in his own country. If he is still alive, Ion Sibescue might be willing to help you."

"Do you have any idea how I might find him now?"

"Start in Bloomsbury. For all I know the family might still live there. The shop was called Guggums Imported Books and was on the east side of Huntley Street near Bedford Square." He handed back her book slowly, as if reluctant to part with it. "I wish I could do more, if only because I would like to read this. I'm fond of old things."

For the first time since she came to see him, Mina smiled. He returned it. "What do I owe you?" she asked.

"Nothing. It's been a pleasure, Mrs. Harker. Good luck to you."

Luck, indeed! she thought as she left the bank. There wasn't time to visit Bloomsbury today, which meant another clandestine trip to London. She considered other means. In spite of Van Helsing's warning about keeping their journey east private, she could think of only one way to find a translator.

She stopped for lunch and, while eating, wrote a pair of letters, one to the bookstore and the second to Ion Sibescue, care of his son, James, and addressed both as simply Huntley Street, Bloomsbury. As exactly as she was able, she made two copies of the first two sentences of the journal and enclosed them as well.

Twenty words in dated Rumanian would hardly attract a fanatic, if they were even a real concern in London. Yet the return address had its own problems. Jonathan would not read her mail, but Millicent would be sure to question any reply. In the end, she decided to use Winnie Beason's name and the hospital address. Winnie would certainly understand. She posted them both then hurried to the station to catch the train that would take her home. The rocking of the train lulled her seductively to sleep.

. . . The day was cloudy, with a chilly wind blowing from the southwest. There were only a few hardy souls touring the cathedral or walking around the gardens, where even the evergreens seemed miserable and impatient for spring. He had been sitting on one of the wooden benches, one arm holding the sketch book steady while he drew. Curious, she walked behind him. The picture was of an old woman, her face concealed by shadow, her thin, lined hand stretched out, dropping seeds for the birds.

She looked from the sketch to the grounds in front of them. There was no woman there. As she glanced at the artist once more, she saw that he was watching her. "She was here yesterday. I'm drawing the memory."

"Wouldn't that be simpler somewhere warmer?"

"But this is where she was." He grinned, and all the seriousness seemed to vanish from his face. "Well, it's how I work anyway."

"Are you a professional artist?"

"No. A law clerk. Head clerk, actually, for Peter Hawkins. This is just a hobby."

"You're very good. May I?" She took the pad and studied his other drawings—the café on Exe Street, the great oak on Lord Summer's estate, a dull still life, a boat on the river. He had a sense of movement and a sensuality to his work that made him intriguing. If she had not seen the book, she would have thought the dark-haired young man far too straitlaced to be interesting.

He bought her coffee. Afterward, they walked to the river and watched fishermen setting their nets. He looked so distinguished in his black coat and trousers, and he looked at her with such love in his gray eyes that she silently blessed the impulse that had had her walk this way rather than toward the center of town.

"Mina," he whispered, pulling her close. "Dear Mina."

The pressure of his arms was like a vise. She could not breathe in them, could think of nothing but escape. As he tried to kiss her, she turned her face away. He called her name, his voice insistent now, demanding. "Mina."

What choice did she have? She would not submit, not even to the one she loved. How many times had she done this in the past? She could not remember even one, and yet her arms tightened as his had. Her lips pressed against the side of his neck, warmth against warmth. "Jonathan," she moaned and bit deeply into his flesh.

All the bright red blood flowing over the white lace of her dress, the white linen of his carefully pressed shirt.

Someone was screaming. Jonathan! Her! . . .

"Miss! Miss, wake up!"

Someone was shaking her roughly. Mina opened her eyes.

The pounding of the train, the uniform of the steward, the faces of those who shared her car told her where she was. "I'm so sorry. I had a dream," she said.

"Enough to wake the dead!" a woman exclaimed.

How perfectly she put it. Mina smiled. Then, realizing how out of place it must seem, she placed a hand over her mouth to hide it. "I'll be all right," she said to no one in particular. "How far are we from Exeter?"

"Two more stops, miss." The man who had shook her spoke kindly, afraid, no doubt, to upset her further. "If you like, I can arrange a carriage to take you home."

Mina shook her head. "Thank you for your concern," she added, and picked up the magazine she had been reading. The crowd around her slowly dispersed. When she was alone once more, she leaned her head back and stared desolately at the countryside flowing by outside her window, wishing there were some way to exorcise her memories.

"Jonathan," she whispered aloud, unaware of how hard her hands gripped the arms of her seat.

As she had expected, Jonathan had worked late that night. Millicent met her at the door and handed her a note that had come from Van Helsing that afternoon. She slipped it in her pocket and carried it upstairs to read in private.

Nothing Van Helsing could have written her would have shocked her more than the single statement on the card enclosed: *Dear Madam Mina. All is well. Van Helsing.*

"Well!" she whispered and thought that perhaps it was better that she had read this statement in her room. Millicent would never have understood why she felt so compelled to laugh.

CHAPTER FOURTEEN

I

Dr. John Seward had tidy compartments for his memories. Some were always open. Some were usually locked. A terrible few could be contained only with effort. He thought of his weeks on the Continent with Van Helsing and the others as little as possible, but try as he might, he could not bury the memories.

They came to him when he was alone, so he plunged into his work. Even then, they haunted him, and with them came the disquieting knowledge of how much a man's sanity depended on others' belief. If he told anyone what he had helped do to Lucy and Dracula, he would be locked up with his lunatics. A new man would be placed in charge of his asylum.

His entire future depended on his silence. Like Jonathan, he hid his turmoil well, so well that not a single soul in his employ had the slightest idea where he had gone so suddenly, or what he had done.

The envelope sent by Van Helsing from Romania irritated him. He dismissed the emotion, locked the door to his study and opened the envelope. A letter and news clipping from a Budapest paper were inside. He began with the letter, dated in early December.

My good friend. I have sent Madam Mina a note telling her all is well. Indeed, it seemed so at the time. I even heard that some brave thieves had gone to Dracula's castle and looted it. Later I discovered that the thieves went by light of day to be certain they would escape alive. Even so, there were no reprisals on the villagers nearby. I felt heartened then, but I am not so certain since I read the news account I have enclosed. I translate for you—

Though winters in the Carpathians are known for their sudden storms, none in memory have equaled the one that swept down from the mountains three days past. The snow fell so quickly that the railroad tracks from Galati to Buhusi were impassible. A train with nearly a hundred passengers was stranded in the mountains for three days while the storm raged around it.

One of the German passengers, who asked to remain anonymous, has given us the following account.

"I have seen the devil at work firsthand. Its name is snow.

"I was one of over a hundred passengers on a train to Galati. When we stopped to take on coal and water in Buhusi, the sky was gray but there was no sign of snow. All that changed when we reached the high mountain pass. The wind howled like some animal in pain, the snow fell so thickly that our train moved at a crawl then finally stopped, our engineer coming through the cars to tell us that he feared going any farther until the storm abated. We all moved into the car closest to the engine, and from there the porters were able to bring in pails of coal for the little stove. We took turns huddling around it as the storm raged.

"Night passed, and the better part of another day, and still the snow continued. We did not despair though the hours grew tedious. We had no dining car and hence no food but what we had brought, and that was soon gone. Afterward, we contented ourselves with tea and coffee which we made by heating water on the stove and passing around three cups which the porters used for water.

"When the snow stopped, the engineer dug his way through the drifts then came back and announced that in a quarter mile the snow was much diminished, no doubt due to the heavy wind. He sent the coalmen and porters out with shovels. I and some of the other passengers agreed to relieve them if necessary. We never had the chance.

"At dusk, we heard the howling of wolves, louder even than the constant and terrible howling of the wind. The men clearing the tracks were unable to return to the train before we were surrounded.

"The animals acted bolder than any wolves I have ever seen. They threw themselves at the train's windows. They waited outside the doors so that we were unable to go out for more snow to melt or, sadly, to go forward for more coal for our stove.

"As it grew darker, it seemed that some of the animal's eyes glowed with a fire of their own. Though this was undoubtedly caused by some reflection from the train itself, I have no way of knowing why only some of the animals had this appearance as all of them were watching us intently.

"As it grew darker, many of the dozen or so Romanian passengers became restless and huddled together for protection though it was clear the wolves could not enter the train.

"And then, above the howling of the wind and the howling of the wolves, we heard a high-pitched and terrible cry, like a child or a woman shrieking in pain. I thought of the work crew and feared that the wolves had attacked them. The Romanians apparently did as well, for they crossed themselves in the Orthodox manner, right shoulder to left, and split into three groups, heading for the exits to the car.

" 'They cannot go out there,' I cried. 'Someone tell them that they must not go!'

"In that instant, I heard a beating on the side door, not of a wolf throwing its body against the car, but the insistent, steady pounding of human fists.

" 'Open the door!' I called. 'Let the man inside.'

"One of the Romanians seemed to understand German, for he looked directly at me and shook his head. 'The door,' he said in German and pointed at the lock. The door had not been bolted. If that were indeed a man pounding on our door, all he had to do was open it.

"The pounding went on, booming through the car. It amazed me that the wolves, so bold toward us, had not attacked the man outside. Presently I heard another shriek and saw a dark human form moving on hands and feet through the drifted snow toward the front of the train. The wolves followed.

"Thankful for the respite from their attack, we brought in more coal and huddled around the stove until morning.

"At dawn, I and some of the others struggled through the newly formed drifts to where the work crew had apparently been shoveling last. We found their tools and two ravaged bodies in the snow. There had been five men. The others had perhaps fled the wolves and perished in the storm. More likely their bodies had been dragged off by the animals. We will never know.

"Railroad workers rescued us by evening, and we traveled on to Galati, where the railroad officials had prepared a feast for us which, sadly, few of us were up to consuming. The warm baths we all had afterward were far more welcome.

"The following day, I went to the local police official to see what would be done about the missing men. They all seemed unconcerned. The passes are high, one of them told me. The cliffs fall into raging cataracts. There is nothing to do but shoot the wolves, which villagers do anyway, and hope that the men's bodies may someday be found."

When we embarked on our mission, my friend, we thought there was only one vampire. We found three more besides our Lucy already turned. There may be more, many more. Here, undoubtedly, for this was his home, but perhaps even in England. Was the captain of Dracula's ship treated as Lucy was treated? And Renfield?

Seward put down the letter and began to laugh—loudly, nervously, like one of his inmates. If Renfield were one of the walking dead, Seward would certainly know of it. All of London would know.

I intend to go and find this passenger. I know the questions to ask of him to see if he saw one of the beings we so fear. If what I believe is true, I will go to the vampire's lair myself to be certain that they are indeed dead. Do not alarm poor Madam Mina until I have more certain news. But if she should die soon, do to her as we did to Lucy or, if Jonathan will not allow it, put her body in a crypt and reverently watch over it to be certain that corruption begins. We have no other choice, my friend. I wish it could be otherwise.

Try not to alarm her? Seward thought. What of the rest of us? He read the account once more. Had Van Helsing ever been among frightened men? Men half-frozen, fighting to stay awake lest they freeze while they sleep? The superstition of the Romanians had most likely played tricks with the writer's mind. It was possible for a frightened imagination to conjure up anything in swirling snow.

He took the letter and locked it in his desk then went on with his work. Within a day, the memory of its contents, like the journey itself, was carefully closed off. He would not think of it, dared not consider that Van Helsing might have written the truth. His sanity required that he forget that the letter even existed.

II

Abraham Van Helsing—doctor, writer, psychologist, and expert in obscure diseases of the soul—had spent the last two months in Romania and in that time had learned nothing new about vampirism, and little about Dracula that he had not guessed already.

Yet he sensed that their ordeal was not yet over, for, as with Mina and the others, night brought him little rest. Instead he had terrible dreams of the three vampire women and how they had moved so lewdly before him, tempting him with their bodies. Often he woke with his hands pressed against his neck, his lips bloody where he had bitten them as he thrashed in his sleep.

Less than a month after the others left him, Van Helsing had moved from a hotel to a little house near the center of town. He had it blessed, sprinkled holy water on the doorstep and around the windows, slept with blessed hosts beside his bed. Nothing helped. The dreams continued, growing ever more vivid until he became convinced that his memories would drive him mad.

Days were no better. In spite of the winter storms that had closed the mountain roads, he fought a terrible compulsion to go back to the castle where he had beheaded the concubines and watched their master crumble to dust. Often the compulsion seemed justified. The more he learned about Dracula the man, the more convinced he had become that Dracula would not have been destroyed so easily.

Many natives from the region around the Borgo had settled in Galati, and Van Helsing sought them out. He gained their trust slowly, for they were suspicious of strangers. Once he knew them, however, they were quite open with him. They did not like foreigners, they said, because foreigners were stupid and laughed at their warnings.

"About what?" Van Helsing had asked.

"About everything."

"About the Borgo Pass?"

"They are fools. What do you know of the Borgo?"

"I have been to the castle," Van Helsing replied.

"Ah, then you are different. You went and they let you go." The speaker had clasped Van Helsing's hand as he said this, holding it as if Van Helsing had somehow been blessed by the monsters.

"Why did you tolerate them in your midst?"

"Our ancestors lived in peace because of them. We owe a debt and we are protected," he said and refused to comment any more except to offer Van Helsing another glass of slivovitz, the plum brandy of the region, which brought its own kind of forgetfulness.

Then he read the account of the attack on the train.

He had little difficulty locating the German who'd written the account of the storm, but even when the right questions were put to the man, he could add nothing to his tale.

"The wolf howls sounded strange," he said. "I thought I saw a figure in the swirling snow . . . It was dark by then. How can anyone be certain?"

Possibilities. Nothing more. How could Van Helsing tell Jack Seward to leave his work for possibilities? How could he pull poor Lord Godalming from his mourning? Jonathan Harker from his firm? And dear Madam Mina! What could he tell her to put her mind at rest?

Nothing until he went there and saw with his own two eyes that the castle was empty.

Luck was with him. A few days after he wrote Jack Seward and Mina, a sudden springlike break in the weather opened the pass, allowing Van Helsing to reach the castle. He walked its musty halls and visited the lower chamber where the women had taken their daytime rest. Their headless bodies had been burned but not destroyed by the fire. The flesh that remained had frozen and was only now beginning to decay. The rings still circled their fingers; scraps of lace and satin still clung to their bodies.

So beautiful they had been once, Van Helsing thought, like his wife in all the beauty of her youth. Now the monsters were dead, and if anything remained, it could only be their memory.

He slept in one of the upstairs rooms with a blessed host beside him. His dreams were unchanged save that they had become less vivid, perhaps because of his exhaustion after the journey.

Before he started back to Galati, he blessed the halls in the name of God and those who had been destroyed by the creatures who had lived here. He recited each name slowly in a sort of litany to the dead. ". . . Miriam Sebescue . . . Marie Sebescue . . . Zoltan Somogyi . . . Henry Watts . . . Jacques Munroe . . ."

On and on. Names, all names to him until the last, when finally, after so many years of seeking respite from his sorrow through revenge, he was able to cry, "Maria Van Helsing."

She had loved to travel, marveled at the mountains, the wonder of all these exotic, primitive places. Her mind had been as quick as his, as curious. In his ignorance, he had brought her to the Carpathians, into the shadow of these cursed walls. The villagers had searched for her. When he was finally led to her body, the natives had already done what was necessary to see that she did not rise.

III

The portrait artist had finished his work in two weeks. Jonathan's birthday party was a few days later, and Mina could not wait for a reply to her letters before making her move. Actually, she doubted her letters had ever been received, and so she made a second trip to London. There, she spent most of her day in Bloomsbury searching for the Romanian family.

Owners of the Huntley Street shops could tell her little. Some recalled the bookstore but no one could remember exactly where it had been. As to the old Romanian, one elderly woman remembered him fondly but could only say that he had not lived in Bloomsbury.

She returned on the evening train, stopping at the studio to pick up Millicent's photograph and Jonathan's gift.

"Where is the portrait?" Millicent asked as soon as Mina returned from London.

"I left it at Winnie's. I was afraid to bring it home in case Jonathan was here. I've asked the Beasons to come early so that it can be hanging when the other guests arrive. Do you think we should put it above the dining room fireplace?"

"How is it framed?"

"I've brought a sample. Open the package."

Millicent did. The worn gilt frame the drawing had originally been in had been replaced with a square of polished cherry, richly carved. Beneath it was the old frame.

"I wasn't certain if you'd like it," Mina said.

"It's lovely."

Mina detected her thanks, her confusion and the slight hint of reproach. She could lie and say that it had been included in the price, but she did not wish to. Millicent had to get used to their good fortune as she had done, or they would never get on together. "The frame for Jonathan's picture is that shade, but the wood is much wider, the carving more intricate. I think the tone will go well with the rose wood of the mantel."

"I'll have Laura wash the wall and rehang the old pictures."

"He'll never suspect." She hugged the woman. It occurred to her that it was the first time they had touched out of affection. "And Aunt Millicent, I want you to come to the party."

"But the meal . . ."

"You have planned it. You can start the roasts and mix the puddings, and Winnie Beason's cook can finish. This is Jonathan's birthday. These are our closest friends in Exeter, not some formal gathering. And Jonathan will want you there."

"I have nothing to wear."

"You will," Mina said firmly. "We'll see to that tomorrow." She sensed Millicent about to protest and went on. "We are giving him a present. You must be on hand for that. How will it look to have his aunt, the one relative closest to him in the world, preparing the meal instead of eating it? If Mr. Chapel were here, he'd tell you the same."

"I've never worn anything that I didn't make myself." Mina was about to remind the woman that they had no time for sewing when Millicent added, "You'll come and help me pick it out, won't you?"

* * *

MINA had never seen Millicent flustered as she was in the shop. As she watched the woman studying each garment to determine the strength of the fabric and the workmanship on each seam, she began to comprehend the way her husband had been raised, and his compulsive need for perfection in his work.

They finally chose a simple black skirt and a steel-gray blouse with a trim of pale blue around the high neck and cuffs. It was not a color Mina would have chosen, but it softened the lines of Millicent's face, made her gray hair seem striking rather than drab. Mina was going to suggest that they eat lunch in town but decided not to push her luck with the woman. They ate in the kitchen instead, Mina fixing the potatoes while Millicent sautéed their meat.

On the afternoon of the party, it took the combined efforts of Mina and Winnie Beason's cook and butler to force Millicent out of the kitchen. The effort, and Millicent's incredible anxiety, gave Mina little time to think of her own nervousness. Though they had entertained the firm's employees and their wives with a buffet less than a month before, this was Mina's first dinner party as Jonathan's wife. It was deliberately small, but still she wanted it to be perfect. Laura was busy in the kitchen, but she had brought her sister, who, for a few pennies, scrubbed the hearths in the parlor, the dining room, Jonathan's den and the water closet, and laid wood and tinder in each.

The two girls then swept, washed china and crystal, pressed the cloths and napkins and laid out the table. "So much bother. It's only a meal," Millicent commented.

"Your meal," Mina said, reminding her that the pork ragout and roast beef cooking downstairs had been started by her. "Now, let's get dressed."

Mina was just finishing her hair when Jonathan arrived home.

He joined her upstairs and handed her a tiny box, elegantly wrapped in lace and silk ribbon. "It's your birthday not mine, Jonathan," she protested.

"And so I bought something for my wife. Open it."

Inside was a cameo surrounded by pale pink amethysts. The matching cameo earrings had tiny amethyst teardrops falling from their bases. "I'm glad you wore the cream gown," he said as he fastened the chain around her neck. "They look as lovely together as I thought they would."

So he had noticed the dresses. When Mina showed them to him, his mind had seemed to be occupied elsewhere. She kissed him lightly on the lips. "You had better get dressed yourself," Mina said. "The guests will be coming soon."

"No little box for me?"

"Little! Indeed!" She laughed and left, deciding to check on Millicent before going downstairs.

As she expected, Millicent was more nervous than ever and with far less cause. Her clothes looked beautiful. Her hair, carefully arranged by Laura in a loose bun at the nape of her neck, was flattering and not at all severe. She had a box open on her dressing table and was rummaging through it trying to find some appropriate jewelry when, to Mina, the most obvious choice was lying on top.

"The blue brooch," Mina said, reaching for it.

"No!" Responding to the panic in Millicent's tone, Mina jerked her hand back. "It was . . . Well, I couldn't."

Mina believed she understood. Some treasures held too many memories to be displayed. "The rose quartz brooch?" she suggested.

Millicent nodded. Mina pinned the quartz piece on and, with Millicent following close behind her, checked to see that the guest room was ready for Dr. Seward before going downstairs.

If anyone but Millicent had been with her, Mina would have suggested they both have a sherry. Instead, they inspected the kitchen, the dining table laid out for nine, and sat in the parlor waiting for the first guests.

Jonathan had just joined them when Winnie and Emory Beason arrived. The butler went out and returned with a large gift-wrapped package.

"A surprise from me and from Aunt Millicent," Mina said, drawing the woman close to her. "Open it, Jonathan."

The artist had wrapped his work carefully in layers of tissue. Jonathan lifted out the oval portrait and stared at it a moment. "It's been so long," he whispered, staring at his likeness; then he set it aside to reach for a second package in the box.

"Is there some mistake?" Millicent whispered.

Mina shook her head. Jonathan unwrapped a second portrait, not of Mina but of Millicent. The artist had softened her sharp features, showing the girl she had once been. Like Jonathan's, the portrait was lightly colored, with soft brown hair, a touch of color in the cheeks.

"Do you like them? I do," Jonathan said, handing hers to his aunt.

"Did I really look like that?" Millicent asked.

"You still do," Jonathan replied, kissing her forehead.

"We'll hang them together," Mina said.

Laura was already clearing away the pictures and bric-a-brac on the mantel, revealing two new hangers, not the one Millicent had expected to see. As they walked into the parlor, Millicent looked down at her younger self and began to weep softly. The others noticed but said nothing. Jonathan's portrait was handed up. Then Millicent turned hers around and raised it for Laura. As she did, her expression abruptly hardened. Mina was about to ask what was wrong when the front bell distracted her.

Basil and Amelia Lloyd entered. Basil Lloyd had been Jonathan's first employer in Exeter and had referred him to Mr. Hawkins. The two men had rekindled their friendship in recent weeks, and it had seemed right to invite them. Their presence also made it less likely that the others would begin to talk of their strange journey. Mina certainly did not want to dwell on it, nor did she think it was right for Jonathan to do so.

Lord Godalming had persuaded Jack Seward to leave work for a few days and attend the gathering. Now Seward came alone. "Is Arthur coming?" Jonathan asked.

"Arthur is not well. He sends his regrets but has some hope of joining us later."

"Perhaps for cake," Mina said and noticed how Seward winced at the thought of the man's presence.

When introduced to each arrival, Millicent greeted them mechanically. Mina would have understood nervousness, but not this frigid detachment. Throughout the meal, Mina tried to draw her into the conversation, but Millicent said little, smiling only once when a compliment on the meal was directed to her.

They were midway through their cake and cordials when Arthur arrived in the company of Lord Gance and a young woman, Rose Lewis, who said little but sat close to Arthur with her hand constantly on his arm, his shoulder or, most inappropriately since he still had a black mourning arm band on his jacket, his lap.

Her coloring and features were so much like Lucy's that Mina understood the attraction Arthur must feel for her. As to his behavior, he seemed somewhat drunk. Seward, a teetotaler, must have found his excess infuriating. Even now, in the presence of a woman whose laughter was infectious, he sat in a wing chair and scowled, his expression perfectly mirrored by Millicent, who was, if possible, even more scandalized.

Mina had intended to take the women into the parlor. Winnie was anxious to tell Amelia Lloyd about the work of the hospital. It also would be courteous to rescue Millicent from what she seemed to view as a trying affair. However, Mina doubted she could separate Miss Lewis from Arthur and place her in the company of strangers.

Jonathan suggested that Mina play the piano. Since her talents were somewhat limited, she pulled out sheet music and looked for her easiest pieces. "Let me," Rose suggested, then sat down and began playing a piece by Stephen Foster. "I Dream of Jeannie with the Light Brown Hair."

Before the others could start to sing, she began in a voice so perfectly beautiful that no one dared to mar its quality by adding his or her own. She followed it with the sad song "Come Where My Love Lies Dreaming" and a slower piece from *HMS Pinafore*, "Sorry Her Lot to Love Too Well."

Though the last song was no more than romantic drivel, tears came to Arthur's eyes, and rolled slowly down his cheeks. He did not brush them away.

"Give them something difficult, lovey," Gance called to her when she had finished. She nodded, stood and began a cappella a beautiful aria in a stunning soprano.

"*Aida*," Gance said when she had finished. "Miss Lewis is on the stage. She recently finished an appearance in a revival of *Patience* at the Savoy Theatre in London."

"Where for the few days of her performance the elevators were less interesting than the show," Emory Beason added dryly, commenting on the latest exotic addition to the Savoy's lobby. "I should have recognized the face if not the name, Miss Lewis."

The woman smiled and bent over his chair to kiss his cheek, making certain to hold it long enough to give him a glimpse of her cleavage. "We must go," she said possessively to Arthur. "I have to return to London tomorrow. Mr. Sullivan is staging a heavy round of rehearsals. We open in two weeks with *The Mikado*. Do come."

At the door, she hugged Mina and Jonathan as if they were old friends and kissed Emory Beason one more time. With Arthur on one arm and a scowling Jack Seward on the other, she led the men to Arthur's motorcar. Then they were off, with Rose Lewis driving and beeping the horn.

"The little tart!" Winnie whispered to Mina with mock disapproval.

Millicent, who had heard the comment, added coldly, "I wouldn't be so polite."

* * *

WHEN Mina and Jonathan were alone in their bedroom, Jonathan expected Mina to show some elation. Everything had gone so well, even better than expected thanks to Arthur's amusing friend! Instead, Mina sat at her dressing table, cleaning her face, saying little until she blurted, "I can't see how Arthur can bear to be near that woman when she looks so much like Lucy. How could he not think of Lucy constantly?"

"Perhaps because he isn't thinking at all, darling. Under the circumstances, that may be just as well," Jonathan commented dryly.

Mina laughed. "Jonathan, you sound as wicked as Lord Gance!"

"And so you smile. I should be wicked more often." He brushed the back of her neck. "It was a wonderful dinner and a perfect gift."

She faced him, kissing his lips, then moving to sit on his lap. She was so light, so delicate.

"I have to go to London next week," he said. "I can arrange the meetings for Friday and we could stay the weekend. Seward would put us up."

"Please, Jonathan, not there!"

He kissed her hands. "I'm sorry. Let's stay at a hotel, perhaps in Covent Garden so we can walk to the theaters at night. Would you like that?"

For a moment her expression became remote. Then she beamed with delight and nodded. It occurred to Jonathan that he had been too preoccupied with work lately. The firm was important to them but so was her happiness. He vowed to be more attentive then realized ruefully that he had made the same vow two weeks before then made no real effort to keep it.

* * *

THE house was quiet when Millicent stole downstairs and lit a lamp in the dining room. As quietly as she was able, she moved

a chair to the hearth so she could lower her portrait and be certain that what she had glimpsed earlier was indeed there.

Pasted to the back of the frame was the artist's name and his
address. No, her eyes had not been wrong. The artist lived here
in Exeter.

And Mina had gone to London twice.

Millicent had too little imagination. She could only think of
the obvious reason.

Should she speak to Jonathan? Years ago, someone had told
her the truth about the man she loved. The deceit had ended all
chance for a husband and family for her. She should have been
grateful, but over the years she had grown to hate the bearer of
that news, long after she forgave the man who deceived her. She
might tell Jonathan what she had learned, but only if the need
arose, certainly not yet.

CHAPTER FIFTEEN

Mina sat in their corner room of the Adelphi Hotel in Covent Garden, drinking a cup of coffee and impatiently drumming her nails on her writing desk. This was her second full day in London. After yesterday's useless search, she had given up on ever finding Ion Sebescue and decided to concentrate instead on discovering someone else who could help her.

"What would Detective Holmes do?" she said aloud, looking down at the most recent issue of *Lippincott's Monthly*. Thinking of her search as a challenge rather than an obsession made the work more interesting. By the time she had finished breakfast, Mina had jotted down six possibilities. She began with the most obvious one, the Hungarian Embassy.

"I'm sorry that we cannot help you," one of the employees said. "We come here because of our knowledge of English not Rumanian. But when I want to read something from home, I go to a bookstore in Chelsea. Perhaps they can recommend someone."

"The store's name, please."

"Becks," the man replied. "On Cromwell Road. I'm sorry that I don't know the exact number, but it's near Thurloe Square. If you would like to leave the copy of the writing with me, I could pass it on to the owner next time I go there and he could contact you."

It was nearly eleven. A trip to Chelsea would take most of her precious afternoon. "Please," she replied and wrote Winnie's name and address on the back of the sample.

"You might also try the British Museum," the man suggested. "They have excellent translators on staff."

"I was just going there," Mina replied happily. Things seemed to be falling in place so much better today.

Since it was a weekday, the museum was nearly empty. Surrounded by all the magnificently restored antiquities, Mina could not help but think of the crumbling ruins of the ancient castle, the ancient creature that had inhabited it. Had he visited this place when he came to London? She was certain of it, could almost see his pale face still hovering on the other side of the glass cases with their Grecian urns and Roman swords and ancient Egyptian jewelry.

At another time, she might have spent hours studying all the exotic wonders, reading the description of each magnificent piece. Not today. Instead, she purchased a catalog and noted a few things Jonathan might find of interest then walked quickly to the curators' offices. As she did, her leather-soled shoes beat against the polished marble, setting up echoes in the empty halls like footsteps following after her.

She went to the receptionist and asked if the museum had a specialist in Eastern European documents. Mina was led to a more secluded section of the museum where documents and paintings were cleaned and restored. There, surrounded by shadows and dusty framed pictures, she met a young man with intense, almost black eyes and prematurely gray hair that, in the shadows, seemed nothing more than an extension of his likewise pale skin. When they were introduced, Anton Ujvari's handshake was limp, leading her to wonder if the young man was ill.

Mina waited until they were alone, then explained. "I have a document that I need translated. I brought a sample of the writing." She handed the sheet to him.

He angled his work light for reading. As he scanned it, Mina saw his back stiffen, his hands grip it more tightly.

Why had she been so foolish? Mina asked herself. Van Helsing had not been wrong about the vampires' nature. Why had she expected him to be wrong about those who hunted them? "Are you able to read it?" she asked as evenly as she was able, praying he would say no.

He studied it a moment longer. "I have been in . . . this terrible place for nearly a . . . a century? How unusual!" he exclaimed. His accent, no more than a slight inflection when they were introduced, thickened as he went on, more quickly, his voice reflecting all his excitement. "I do not know if I am a . . . slave or captive, perhaps, or . . . a word for 'mistress,' I believe, of this place." He looked at her intently, his eyes glittering in the shadows of their deep sockets. "What does this mean?"

It occurred to her that to lie about the nature of the journal would not work with its translator. "I don't know," she said. "I purchased a journal in Bucharest. I was told that it was valuable and quite old. One of the pages was loose. I brought it with me." She took a magazine from her handbag and flipped through it until she found the single page from the end of the book.

Ujvari studied the quality of the paper, the shade of the ink. "Not so old," he said. "At least not as old as its author claims to be." For the first time, he smiled, and some of her uneasiness about confiding in this stranger vanished. Fanatics, she thought, did not smile.

"I would like the entire journal translated. Could I hire you to do that?"

"Gladly. Did you bring it with you? It will be very hard to agree on a price otherwise."

"I have it in London but not with me. It has about fifty handwritten pages. I can bring it to you tomorrow morning, and we can discuss the terms then."

"I'm sorry, I won't be working tomorrow. We could meet somewhere else, if you wish."

She suggested the café next door to the Adelphi Hotel. They agreed on ten the next morning. On the way out, she stopped in the main offices once more. "Could you tell me how long Mr. Ujvari has worked here?" she asked the secretary.

"Five years," the man replied.

Long enough to be reliable, Mina decided. And long enough that she would always know where to find him.

* * *

MINA arrived at the café early, ate breakfast and finished her detective story while waiting for her translator. When he arrived, Ujvari seemed even more intense than yesterday, and she decided, with a pang of pity, that as one so enamored with novelty, his job must bore him terribly.

"I finished reading the page you gave me," Ujvari told her as soon as he sat down. "The narrator identifies herself as Countess Karina Aliczni. If you have purchased copy of a journal kept by her, it may solve a very old mystery."

"Why wouldn't it be an original?" Mina asked.

"Because the writing is no more than a few decades old, at most, and the countess disappeared over a hundred years ago."

Mina feigned confusion, not certain that she had done it very well. "Was she that famous?" she asked.

"Her father was wealthy. He assured that her legend would live on. I show you." He pulled a kerchief from his jacket and unwrapped a gold coin. "Many people wrote of the beauty of the young countess. This is a likeness of her. The coins were stamped in the year 1772, just after she disappeared from the Romanian town of Sibiu. Her father ordered the coins circulated in the hopes that someone would recognize her and lead him to her. He promised a thousand more coins like this to the one who would do it."

Mina looked down at the stamped likeness. Even in this, she could see the girl's delicate beauty and the similarity to the fair creature in Dracula's castle, the one who reminded her of Lucy. "Did her father ever get news of her?" Mina asked.

Ujvari shook his head. "But she lives through this coin and the legend that surrounds it." He took the coin from her hand and abruptly kissed Mina's palm. "I am romantic," he said. "I like to think that she found a happier life, perhaps with a lover in some distant land. You have given me a chance to solve the mystery. For that I am so very thankful."

Mina already knew that the truth was far less beautiful. She pulled the book from her bag. "I will need proof that I have given you this," she said.

"I've brought it." He handed her a letter describing the work he would undertake to use as a receipt. They agreed on a price then exchanged home addresses. Mina gave him Winnie Beason's, then, in case it was necessary, the address of the Exeter Hospital as well. Just before Ujvari left, he took a pencil and made a rubbing of the coin. He left it with the letter as they parted.

He'll think it's fiction, she decided, as she watched him go with the wrapped book under one arm. *The more fantastic the woman's account becomes, the more he will be certain that it's fiction. And if he should believe it, well, he doesn't know my real name.*

Now that she had parted with the book, she felt a lightening of her spirits. She had found a translator, had given him the book. There was no use worrying about an outcome she could no longer change, nor any use waiting impatiently for something that would take weeks to finish, and there was even less use in anxiety about what the journal might contain.

She wandered the streets around the hotel, buying trinkets for Winnie and Millicent, some charming carved and painted wooden birds with outstretched wings to hang in the children's hospital. She had tea in the Savoy Hotel, tried on bracelets and rings at a jewelers nearby, fingered lace scarves and bonnets, bought a feather fan to take to the theater that night. So many beautiful things. Exotic things. Expensive things. Things to adorn the body and the home. Things to show taste when manners would do. Things to show affection when a word would do.

All the sunshine of the day faded within her as she saw the world as Dracula must have seen it, the glorious press of humanity—unaware, defenseless—all around him.

It seemed that she had never seen England as clearly as she did on the walk from the Savoy back to her quiet hotel on Floral Street. Near the entrance to it, a flower vendor thrust a small bouquet into her hand, the miniature yellow roses and daisies wilting in the damp winter cold. She paid for them gladly and went inside. When Jonathan was dressed for the theater and dinner, there would be a flower for his lapel, roses for her bonnet, something honest and fresh amid all the gilt of London. She held the bouquet up to her face, inhaling the scent as she went inside.

"Mrs. Harker."

Startled, she looked around and saw Lord Gance coming toward her, one pale hand outstretched. As always, the sight of him brought back memories and emotions she had to struggle to hide. What must he think of her, she wondered as he took her hand and kissed it, his lips just brushing the back of her glove. He did not let go of her hand as he spoke. "I was just about to leave you and Jonathan this note inviting you to dinner tonight after the show." He handed the card to her.

"Dinner? I can ask Jonathan."

"Miss Lewis, Arthur and I are meeting a group at Rules. Tell him that I don't invite him, only you. Him, I order to attend. The new wealth of London will be there tonight. He is so young and honest, he must meet them."

"We are all young, Lord Gance."

"It's the age of youth. May we never grow old." He noted her shock. "Oh dear, if I've said something wrong, I apologize. I was only trying to be complimentary."

He looked so mockingly sad that she had to laugh. "And if I decline?" she asked.

"You won't. These people are more than amusing, Mrs. Harker. They are an adventure, and an education. You must come, especially tonight, since you seem to be looking more beautiful than usual."

Did it show in her face, that passion that flowed from somewhere deep inside her? "And you so witty," she replied with a tiny laugh.

"London does that to me. All the wits bring out a competitiveness in my nature that is utterly useless in Exeter. Promise me that I will see you there."

"I'll do my best." The thought suddenly became more intriguing. She needed the company, the diversion, the chance to laugh. "Yes, I promise."

He closed his eyes and nodded solemnly; then, without warning, he moved close to her. She thought he was going to whisper something to her. Instead his lips brushed the edge of her mouth and her cheek. Her face was still cold from the winter air, and his breath was warm against her skin. "Until tonight," he murmured as if they had arranged a tryst, then turned and left her.

Jonathan arrived at the hotel nearly an hour late. Mina had already dressed in the magnificent green gown she had worn to Lord Gance's dinner. She had piled her hair high on the sides, let it hang in loose ringlets down the back and arranged the rosebuds in a single clasp near the crown.

"Now you look so perfect that I shall have to take you to the Savoy after the show," he said as she slowly turned to show him the dress.

"We're invited to Rules." She handed him the card.

"Gance again," he said with no real enthusiasm. "Do you want to go?"

"Please!" She sounded too eager, she decided, but went on anyway. "Arthur will be there, along with Miss Lewis and others from the cast."

"I thought you didn't like Miss Lewis," Jonathan countered.

"Not her! No, I thought Arthur was using her. Perhaps I'm

wrong. They've been seeing one another quite often, and Arthur seems so much happier. Please, Jonathan, we came for a holiday. Tonight I would like to do something we would never be able to do in Exeter!"

"I don't like crowds," Jonathan grumbled.

Mina recalled that Lord Gance's holiday party had resulted in two new clients for Jonathan's firm. Though it galled her to have to say it, she went on. "Lord Gance said there are a number of people coming whom you should meet."

For the first time, Jonathan seemed to consider her request. "I suppose we could put in an appearance," he said. "Will you promise that we won't stay too long?"

"Only as long as you like," she replied, her happiness somewhat contrived.

They met Gance and his party outside the theater. Rose Lewis, looking flushed from her performance and the three curtain calls after it, joined them some time later. Arthur was already at Rules along with a dozen others. Mina never learned all their names, nor could she recall half of what was said that made her laugh so happily.

She dined on partridge and smoked salmon, drank far more than usual. As the evening went on, she noticed Arthur's jealousy of Gance's friendship with the actress. Rose ignored his barbs, treating both men with equal affection. Unlike Lucy, who had to choose one suitor and marry, Rose Lewis could have two men or more if she chose. Rose also did her best to make Mina and Jonathan feel welcome, but it seemed to Mina that the more she relaxed, and the more she laughed, the less pleasant Jonathan became. Finally Jonathan and Arthur retreated to a quieter table. At first she thought they were merely sulking, later Mina decided that they might actually be discussing business.

She took pity on them both and joined them, suggesting that they walk back to the hotel. The men lit their cigars, and with Mina in their center, her arms laced with theirs, they began a leisurely stroll toward Covent Garden.

The street was more crowded at midnight than it had been at noon, and far more lively. Carriages and riders moved down it, ragged flower girls sold exotic bouquets and street bands played for passersby.

The lights, the scents, even the wine she had drunk lent magic to the night. Mina lifted her face to the sky and inhaled deeply, feeling as if she could also drink in the night. Out of the corner of her eye, she saw something huge and black on the opposite side of the street.

"Jonathan, look!" Mina exclaimed, pulling away and pointing across the street to an organ player with a dancing bear on a leash. "Let's get closer," she suggested and the trio began crossing.

At that moment, the bear stepped off the curb and moved too close to a passing carriage. The driver pulled the team toward the center of the road, and one of the horses reared, its hoof cutting the side of Jonathan's head. Mina screamed. The driver yelled a curse and went on.

Arthur pulled Jonathan to the sidewalk and pressed a scarf against the wound. "Are you all right?" he asked.

Jonathan's only reply was to grip Arthur's arm until he was able to lean against a lampost in front of the restaurant. The blood had soaked the scarf and soiled Jonathan's coat. Mina longed to help him, but the sight of it held her back. She feared that the fainting spell at the hospital would be repeated. In spite of his pain, Jonathan saw her tortured expression and understood. "Go back to Rules, darling. Arthur will see me safely to the hotel and send for a doctor. If I'm able, I'll be back in an hour or so."

"You're not coming?" Arthur asked Mina.

She did not seem to hear him, but only looked down the street, as if something far distant held her interest more than her wounded husband. "The blood," Jonathan whispered for her.

"I understand." Arthur flagged down a cab, helped Jonathan inside then took Mina back to their table, whispering a few words to Rose and reassuring Mina that he would return and tell her how Jonathan was.

Rose had Mina sit beside her, but as the evening stretched on, they moved apart in the crowd. It seemed that Mina's wineglass was always full and, though she made an effort to drink slowly, so much talking in the noisy, smoky room made her thirsty. Two hours passed before Arthur returned. "Jonathan is sleeping. He has a concussion, but the doctor believes that he'll be fine in a few days," he told Mina. "I'll walk you back to the hotel whenever you wish."

She was about to ask to leave immediately when Rose motioned Arthur to join her. Mina watched him go, waited a while for him to return, then found her coat and slipped outside to hail a cab.

Gance joined her. "I told Arthur I would walk you home. I promised him that I would be a gentleman and reminded him that honest solicitors are far harder to find than beautiful women." He took her hand and placed it on his arm, then led her across the street.

"And what do you think makes a gentleman, Lord Gance?"

"A simple thing, Mrs. Harker. As every woman knows and rarely admits, a gentleman is one who always gives a lady no less than what she wants."

"A gentleman can hardly know what is in a woman's heart."

"It is his responsibility to inquire. For example, I wish I knew what you desired, because I would like to offer it to you, now and as often as you like."

Mina blushed, and felt thankful for the darkness that hid it. "I would think you more sincere if you had waited to know me better before saying such things."

"I know you. I know you through your eyes and the tilt of your head and the firmness of your step. I know you by the way you dance, the friends you have chosen, the causes you support, even by your devotion to your husband."

Mina laughed. "You are hardly a romantic, Lord Gance."

"Call me Winston, please. Let me think I am making some progress here. And I am a romantic, romantic enough that I do not understand why the devoted bride is here in the shadow of

St. Paul's Churchyard with another man rather than at her wounded husband's bedside."

"How dare you!" she exclaimed as she pulled her arm away and turned to leave.

He gripped her shoulder. "Because I dare anything," he replied and kissed her, holding her so tightly that she had no chance to resist.

His face glowed in the distant gaslight, his hands gripped her arms painfully, his eyes seemed so dark and inviting. For a moment she was no longer in London but in the little room in Purfleet, and Dracula, not Gance, was holding her.

"No!" she screamed. She pulled herself out of his grasp and ran. The cobblestones were uneven, her balance a bit skewed from what she had drunk. Her ankle twisted and she fell, fighting back the tears. She had not felt so helpless for so long. And the horror was that it reminded her of the past and, more, that somewhere deep within her she reveled in it.

Gance crouched beside her. "Mina!" he exclaimed, and when she did not answer, he repeated again, "Mina, can you stand?"

"I think so." She let him help her up, then tried to walk and winced.

"Here." He held out his arm so she could lean on it. After a few steps, she felt steadier, the pain less acute. "I'm sorry," he said as they went on. "But I cannot believe that was your first stolen kiss. Even if it were, I would never have expected that a woman as strong-willed as you would . . ."

"It was not my first, Lord Gance. It was how you took it."

That part of the street was quieter, darker. She knew she had given him an invitation, but nonetheless she felt brave rather than foolish.

"Gently then, dear Mina." He lifted her chin and looked at her, prolonging the moment until their lips touched. For an instant, she thought that he would not kiss her, and she frowned. It was what he had been waiting for, and he pulled her to him, kissing her with a passion that demanded a response.

It was dark. She had had too much to drink. She had no choice. And there was the matter of the vampire's life, his memory, still too much a part of her. She responded.

He pulled away and smiled down at her. "I think it's time I take you back to your hotel," he said.

They returned in silence, Mina conscious of the motion of his body beside her, the grip of his hand in hers as he supported her weight. At the door, he stopped. "I do not love you," he said. "I do not wish to love you or to replace your husband in your life. But if what I sense is true, you are my mate in ways I doubt your husband understands. It's your decision now, Mrs. Harker. I will wait to hear it."

He turned and left her standing there.

He did not look back.

Jonathan had left a single lamp burning for her, its light so weak it scarcely threw shadows in the dark room. The smell of blood seemed to hang in the air, the scent half real, half memory. As Mina turned up the light, Jonathan stirred. It was her chance to go to him, to see how he was, but she wanted to be alone with her thoughts of passion, and wickedness, and selfishness.

She should have hated herself, and yet as she sat in front of the mirror combing out her hair, her reflection showed a vague smile of satisfaction, a flush of excitement in her cheeks.

If Gance had hailed a carriage, had taken her away to some secluded room, she would not have said a word of protest, or of assent, and could have ended the evening with some sense of virtue intact. Instead, he had left the decision entirely up to her. She realized now how corrupt he was, how careful, and how brutally fair.

* * *

THE doctor had left a codeine elixir for the pain, but Jonathan would only take a little on the journey to Exeter. Once they reached home, however, he gave in to the pain, took a large dose of the drug and went to bed. Mina sat beside him, holding his hand while he slept, squeezing it each time he moaned and whispering to him that she was near. Though she was reading a book, the words meant nothing to her. Her mind was entirely on Gance, as if vice rather than virtue would free her soul from the past.

Later, when Jonathan's sleep became more natural, Mina unpacked the gifts she had brought and took Millicent's downstairs. The woman was reading in the parlor. On the carved oak sideboard, the framed picture of Jonathan and her had acquired a central place. Mina picked it up, commenting as she did, "It looks so right here among our other treasures. I brought you something." She handed Millicent the package, wrapped in lace and satin ribbon.

Millicent opened it and pulled out a lifelike bluebird on a carved wood perch. It wound like a music box and, when the lever in its base was pushed, began to chirp and move its wings.

"Jonathan said there were bluebirds in the fields around your farm. I thought it would remind you of home."

The woman did not smile, did not thank her. "You have been so kind to me, even to the point of letting me into your house," she said, the coldness of her tone so at odds with the words and the intent of the gift she held in her hands. "While you and Jonathan were away, I thought of how sad it was here with only Laura for company. Then I considered how marvelous it was that Jonathan had acquired so much through hard work and ambition. I would not want him to lose it, and since I am convinced that you truly love him, I know you feel the same way."

"Of course I do. Millicent, what is it?"

The woman ignored the question, instead fingering the feathered head of the mechanical bluebird in her palm. "If you do, you will not bring any scandal on him. Solicitors, and their families, must be above reproach."

How could she know about one stolen kiss? It had to be something else, perhaps some silly breach of Millicent's rigid etiquette. "Neither Jonathan nor I have done anything detrimental to his reputation."

"I'm pleased to hear of it. Perhaps you would tell me, then, why you lied to me. The pictures of Jonathan and me were drawn here in Exeter."

Mina hesitated then responded with the truth. "I lied because it was kinder than saying that my reasons for going to London were private. However, my journey had nothing to do with some lovers' meeting or any other scandal. You said it yourself, I love my husband."

"You are flushed, my child. I hope it is out of righteousness." Millicent paused, then added, with apparent sincerity, "Indeed, I'm certain of it."

Tell me a secret, Mina thought, any tiny secret at all. Tell me why you don't like to wear the blue brooch or the real reason you detested Jonathan's mother, and even though Jonathan will object, I will tell you where we went on the Continent and why. You will have to believe it when Jonathan agrees with my story.

She said none of that, however. She had been so fearless when she was among the men, part of their team. Now, in the face of one old woman, she was a coward. "I'm going to bed early," she said. "Good night, Aunt Millicent."

Millicent paused. "Good night, child," she said wearily.

In Mina's absence, Jonathan had rolled over and lost some of his covers. His face was damp with sweat, and when Mina touched his forehead to see if he had a fever, he woke with a start. "Are you in pain? I could get some ice for your head," Mina said.

"Pain? . . . Yes. Just stay with me as you did in the hospital in Budapest. I feel so much better with you here."

She undressed quickly, put on her cotton nightgown and joined him, lying with her back against his chest. In spite of his illness, he was hard. She could feel his penis pressing against the base of her spine. Usually she would roll over now and touch him, and he would kiss her and whisper some loving endearment. Not tonight, she decided, not when he was so ill and she so very confused. She kissed the back of his hand, snuggled closer to him and closed her eyes.

"Mina," he whispered, his hand on her thigh. She did not reply, and in a moment, he rolled over and went to sleep.

A cry that did not seem to be human woke her hours later. In the dim light from the candle she had left burning on the table, she saw her husband's terrified expression. As she reached for him, his hands moved out, pushing some unseen creature away. The cry came from him again, a low, drawn-out howl of misery from deep within him, followed by her name.

"Jonathan, I'm here. Wake up."

He opened his eyes and pulled her to him, holding her as he trembled in her arms. "The drug. It made the pain go away, but what came in its place was far, far worse."

"It helps to tell a nightmare, Jonathan," she said.

"The vampire women. They came for me. They wanted me even though they were nothing more than ghouls, their bodies rank and decayed. I was pushing them away, but they were as strong as they had been when they were alive. If you hadn't been here, I would have died in my dream, I'm certain of it."

"I'll always be here, Jonathan," she whispered, pushing back the damp dark hair from his forehead, checking the bandage though she already knew he had not opened the wound.

Mina lay awake the rest of the night, listening to Jonathan's even breaths, ready to battle the demons that still plagued him. By dawn, she had reached a decision about Gance. She would write him and tell him that she could never consider his proposal. She would do it now. Once it was done, she would never change her mind.

She dared not use the writing desk in her room. Instead, she went downstairs to Jonathan's study and desk drawer for some paper. There, along with his pipe and pens and ink bottle, beside the gold-plated watch that had been his father's, she discovered his pastel chalks. Beneath them lay his sketchbook.

He'd begun drawing again! How pleased she was to see that. If he would not come to her for solace as he once did, he had at least found another outlet.

The first picture was of her as she had looked on their wedding day, with the little white hat and veil the only semblance of bridal dress. She turned to the second page and almost dropped the book. There in plain charcoal gray was Dracula's castle—the ruined walls, the ancient doors, the stark beauty of clouds above it. She went on to the third drawing and stared with astonishment at what he had done.

It was the woman, the dark one who had been Dracula's wife. She stood beside a bed draped in heavy hangings, her pale, naked body so lean, her expression so erotic. If he had drawn her hurriedly, Mina might have considered the work a kind of exorcism. But the woman had been drawn with exquisite care. The cascade of dark hair was exactly as Mina remembered it, the full lips that same shade of red, the nipples of her breasts large and dark against her white skin. And he kept it where he could stare at it often.

"Jonathan," she whispered. If she had been able to feel true righteousness, she would have taken the book upstairs and confronted him in private. With misery, she realized that her sin was so much worse. He was attracted to a memory, playing with it like some dirty fantasy while she considered taking a flesh-and-blood lover to dispel the nightmares of her past.

She returned the sketchbook to the drawer, arranging the chalks and other items as closely as she could recall to how they had been before, then quietly returned to their room. Nothing was settled, she realized sadly. At least, not yet.

CHAPTER SIXTEEN

I

The following Wednesday, Mina received a note from Winnie asking her to stop by. When she got there, she discovered that there had been an answer to her inquiries in London. James Sebescue, owner of Z. Becks Books in Chelsea, had written that his father had retired but was most interested in taking the work.

She read the letter aloud, giving special emphasis to the final sentence, *There are many charlatans who can give you an approximate translation, Mrs. Beason. But my father is from that part of the world. This is his native language, and he will be as faithful to the original document as he is able. Please reply through me.*

"He makes a persuasive case," Winnie commented.

"Far too persuasive. I was in 'that part of the world' as he calls it, and I saw how suspicious the natives were, even of perfectly normal strangers. I'm thankful I found Mr. Ujvari, for he seems a dedicated and sensible man."

"Will you answer Mr. Sebescue's letter?"

"I suppose I should, since he replied so quickly." Mina wrote a short note, thanking him for responding and stating only that she had hired another translator, a young man who she was certain would be faithful to the text. She hoped the curtness of her reply would discourage him from contacting her again.

Business concluded, she sat in Winnie's parlor drinking coffee and discussing her London vacation, the evening at Rules and Jonathan's accident. She did not mention Gance, but he was foremost in her mind, his proposition making her feel more lighthearted than she had in weeks. It seemed a genuine happiness. Someone loved her. Another desired her. She knew how wrong the satisfaction was, for she was not vain, or shallow. It was boredom, she decided. Though the thought of entering the hospital wings terrified her, she nonetheless asked, "Would there be some work I could do at the children's hospital? I don't think I can work as a nurse but perhaps in some other capacity?"

"There is something you can do from home, and it's important. We need someone to raise money for us, and to contact physicians to donate their services. Personal contact is so important. In the past I have done it, but I simply don't have the time to devote to calls. Could you go in my place?"

"I could."

"Then wait a moment." Winnie left Mina alone for a few minutes, then returned with the rough draft of a letter and a list of donors. "These people always give something, but a visit seems to raise the donations considerably."

Mina looked at the donor list and the amounts given. Most of Exeter's wealthier individuals were on it. Near the top, she saw Lord Gance's name. She had expected to see it, but the amount he donated, over five hundred pounds a year, astonished her. "Have any of these people ever visited the hospital?" she asked.

"Lords Somersby, Gance and Fenton. Lady Fenton did volunteer work when we first opened our doors, but soon lost interest. It is not particularly fashionable work. I can understand why she did not like it."

"Have you considered offering tours of the hospital?"

"We held one open house a year after we opened. Five people came, and they would have come later anyway. People don't mind paying to alleviate misery, particularly if they don't have to look at it."

"They look at it every day," Mina commented, and shook her head sadly. Tomorrow she would start her work, sending notes to the top five donors, asking permission to call. Gance was one of them. She wanted an excuse to see him again, to judge him, to decide.

II

Gance fingered the far too formal request to call that Mina Harker had written him. In it, she had made it clear that the visit to his business address was on behalf of the Exeter Ladies Society and their hospital. It was possible that she was intending to reject his proposal. On the other hand, this could also indicate her great discretion. He approved of that. He was not one to boast of his affairs; the few that had become public knowledge had been trouble enough. A tarnished reputation made him interesting; a blackened one would make him an outcast.

He had already made his arrangements for Mina. His mistress had wanted to travel to India and visit her brother. Gance had provided the steamer ticket and two hundred pounds for expenses. She had not asked him to take her to Plymouth to board the ship, nor had he volunteered. They had not said good-bye, but he doubted he would see her again. He briefly considered that she had loved him, then dismissed the thought. If she had loved him, it was of no consequence, save that the emotion had made her less amusing.

He had dressed carefully for this meeting, choosing a businesslike jacket and vest in black wool, white silk shirt and, for effect, a deep blue ascot. The colors made him seem paler, thinner. He had always detested the look, for it made him appear ill, but he sensed that Mina Harker found this appealing. After nights listening to Arthur rave about demonic seductions by the walking dead, he understood why.

How much of Arthur's story was real? How much a shared delusion? Mostly the latter, no doubt, particularly since that idiot Jack Seward was involved. Nonetheless, had he not been attracted to Mina Harker before, he certainly would have been after hearing Arthur's story.

Mina arrived punctually at eleven. Though Gance knew his clerk had asked for her coat, she left it on, no doubt intending to leave as soon as possible. The black fur of the high collar was dotted with snow. There was snow in her chestnut hair as well, and her cheeks were red from the cold. She seemed younger than she had looked the other times they'd met, perhaps no more than twenty. No wonder she had been so coy.

He offered her a seat then sat behind his desk, waiting for her to speak. After all, she had come to see him.

She immediately began her presentation on the hospital—the number of children who had been cared for over the last year, the need it had to expand. Throughout it, she handed him photographs of the wards, drawings of the proposed changes. He suspected that she had given the same presentation a few times before. He doubted she had been so nervous on the other occasions. "So, of course, I came to see you," she concluded. "You have been so generous in the past."

"Of course. I wish to be known for my generosity."

"How oddly you put it," she commented.

He smiled. He'd expected it would take longer to put her at her ease. "Oddly? How so?"

"As if your generosity were no more than an affectation. It makes you seem conceited somehow."

"Conceited? Oh, I am that. But I'm also a realist. I live up to my own expectations. As they are quite high, it can be a demanding chore."

"Are you always so hard on yourself?"

"What do you mean?"

190 *Marie Kiraly*

"That you would deny your own nobility and your higher sentiments?"

"Ah, those!" He laughed. "I have them, but no more than any common man, which is to say that they are most untrustworthy. Self-conceit is a higher emotion."

"Self-worth," she corrected.

"Tell me the difference, if you can. We'll discuss it over lunch."

"I'm sorry, I can't."

"Then tell me on a walk to the hospital. I need a tour to be certain my money is well spent, and I cannot think of a finer person to give it to me."

"I've only been there once."

"Yet you call it a worthy venture and ask me for a thousand pounds."

"I believe in what they're doing, but I don't have the constitution for nursing."

"Nonsense. Jonathan told me all about his fever. He said you nursed him through it. A regular Florence Nightingale, I believe he called you."

"He is not a child, Lord Gance. And he did not have an open wound or an amputation. Those poor children—victims of accidents and neglect. Wounded, delirious . . ." Her voice trailed off.

"Bloody," Gance concluded, and saw from the sudden tightening of her expression that he had hit the mark exactly.

Walking dead. Good old Varney. He wanted to laugh.

She stood and retrieved her leather satchel from beneath her chair. "I've taken up enough of your time," she said. "I'll leave the decision to you."

"I've already made it." He took an envelope from the desk drawer, walked to the door and handed it to her. "You didn't need to come for it. You even knew that, didn't you?" She didn't answer, which he expected, but she was not angry either. He'd hit the mark, all right. "Toying with me is a dangerous thing, Mrs. Harker. I suspect you already know that as well. I think the danger itself is what brought you here."

"I've had enough of danger," she replied, her eyes focused on the door. "May I please go?"

"My time has a price. Look at me. I mean it, look at me."

She did.

"You cannot bring yourself to say yes to my proposal, yet you cannot say no either. What should I make of it, Mrs. Harker? Should I assume the obvious and kiss you again?"

She still didn't answer, nor did she look away, though there was no invitation in her expression.

"Not here. Perhaps not ever. But I want you to trust me enough to come with me now for just a little while. Consider it an adventure, much like your one at Rules. I promise to be a gentleman."

"I recall your definition of gentleman far too well," Mina replied.

"I assumed you would." He reached for his hat and cane and led her through the door. "Mrs. Harker and I are going to lunch, then to the children's hospital," he said to the clerk. "Go home when you're finished."

They rode in silence. The leather bag full of photographs and information rested on her lap. They might have been on the way to a business lunch, with nothing to say to each other. Gance knew otherwise, and there would be time enough for words later.

He found that her presence excited him more than he'd expected. The determined set of her head, the delicate gloved hands folded and resting on the dark leather bag, the pale face above the soft fringe of black fur.

When he was eleven, at an age before shame could destroy his sensuous nature, he had lost his innocence to a cousin eight years older. A quick afternoon away from adult supervision turned into long, exhausting nights. She found him an enthusiastic pupil for the months they lived under the same roof, then left him stranded with his wealth and his needs. He soon learned what wealth could buy. Discovering that each new conquest held all the passion of his first time had been the greatest revelation of his life. The wonder that held had a sadder aspect as well. He would never marry. No woman who loved him would ever tolerate his infidelities, and he would never take a wife for convenience, not after seeing the effect of such a marriage on his mother.

The carriage pulled up in front of a high stone wall with an iron gate in the center. He unlocked it and led Mina through a small courtyard with a fountain. A second key took them into a stone cottage that could not have more than a few rooms.

Mina noticed the smell first, a blend of sweet pipe tobacco, sandalwood incense and old perfume. She stood in the shadows just inside the front door while Gance moved through the lower level of the house, opening draperies, letting in the light. When he'd finished, he sat on a black velvet divan close to the rear windows in the drawing room, his body no more than a shadow against the brilliant noon sunlight. He did not move or speak as Mina walked into the room. Instead, he acted as if she were some wild animal exploring the house, ready to bolt should he make a move toward her.

With the draperies pulled back, nothing marred the winter light or the view of a gentle slope ending at the Exe River. Frozen stalks of rosebushes poked through the snow just outside the windows, giving promises of spring. Mina could see the high wall stretching all around the property, assuring privacy for every act that went on inside of it.

And she could see the opulence of her surroundings. In the days when she had stayed with the Westerna family she had lived among such splendor. Her feet had walked on Indian carpets this thick before, her hands had rested on pieces of Murano crystal to rival the colorful collection arranged on the shelves of the carved oak sideboard. But she had never seen a room so bare of silly clutter, or so tastefully arranged. A person in this room was not lost among the draperies and knickknacks or folding oriental screens. A person made this room complete.

She walked through it into a slate-floored solarium, overgrown with palms and flowering plants. In its center was an iron table on which a Limoges tea service waited for use.

A separate door led to a small kitchen, suitable for nothing more than heating water or an occasional light meal. She went upstairs.

The second floor had two large rooms—a bathroom with brilliantly colored mosaic tile on the floor and walls, and a raised tub close to the lace-covered window. The single bedroom had divans, a round dining table made for two and a bed to rival any in Westminster, though Mina doubted Victoria would allow anything so exotic in her palace.

Its four square posts were intricately carved with flowers and vines. They supported a flat canopy draped in wine-colored satin, its underside a mosaic design in mirrored tiles.

Gance was seducing her with what he owned, and with the temple to pleasure that he had created. Then she glimpsed something at odds with the rest of the room—a portrait above the marble stones of the fireplace.

It was a portrait of a woman of late middle age, yet the beauty in her face gave evidence of having increased over time. Her green eyes were round with a curious blend of amusement and wisdom, her lips were large and sensual, slightly upturned and parted as if she were about to make some witty remark to the artist for whom she posed. The drape over her shoulders hung low in the front so that only the tips of her breasts were covered. She was a buxom woman. Mina thought that she would have been pleasant, jolly, the sort of hostess who charmed everyone. All this was portrayed so perfectly in her face. The portrait's background was of this room—the fireplace itself, the single carved post of the bed beside her.

Mina was conscious of the sound of Gance's feet on the stairs, of his soft entrance into the room. "Your mistress?" she asked him without turning.

"My father's," he replied. "No, I never lay with her, except in the sense that a child may sleep with his mother and dream of something more exciting."

"You knew her?" Mina asked incredulously.

"Quite well. She died a year after my father. I was fourteen years old."

"How did she die?"

"Though my father willed her use of this house and funds to provide for it, his death left her alone. By then she was older and far larger than in the portrait. With her beauty and his love both gone, she died of loneliness."

He paused to let her comment. When she did not, he went on, "The house was willed to me, maintained by a separate fund managed by my uncle until I turned sixteen. It has been in use ever since."

She understood what he meant. It was foolish to remain here, when nothing would come of it. "Thank you for a most interesting afternoon. May we go now?" she asked and walked past him toward the door.

"Did you notice that when we left my office, I took pains that the hired driver never saw your face? No one will ever know, Mrs. Harker. Whatever we do here, no one will ever know. And when it is over, there will be no regrets."

"I doubt that. Now I would like to leave."

"Very well, Mrs. Harker."

She turned and faced him. "Why do you keep calling me that?" she demanded.

"To remind you of who you love and who you are. To remind you of how your husband kisses you . . . how he loves you. To remind you that you are here for one simple reason, you are a woman who knows that regret is a far sadder emotion than guilt."

"I am strong enough to survive it," she retorted and started down the stairs.

"Mina!" The first use of her Christian name made her hesitate, then continue on more slowly.

"Mina, when I kissed you that night, I knew that everything I surmised about you was true. You are my equal in passion as well as intelligence. Don't turn away from what you were meant to be."

She had quick visions of the Countess Karina in her eternal state dealing with him, of the women Jonathan had drawn so sensuously devouring Gance together. She pictured him stretched across the damp stone floor of their chamber, his blood red against his ivory skin. This vision was hardly different from the dream she'd had of Jonathan, but now the thought held no horror. Instead it aroused her more than this house, Gance's presence, his challenge.

Yes, she wanted him. But if he would not take her, nothing would happen, nothing at all. She walked slowly down the stairs, her gloved hand brushing the polished handrail as her bare one might brush . . .

"Mina! Have the courage to be joyful. To live."

He started after her. Once he touched her, she would yield. If she did not display that weakness to him, he would never know. She turned and met him halfway.

As she kissed him, she was amazed at how warm he was, he with the winter complexion and the frost-colored hair.

They went downstairs. She left her coat and fur muff with the satchel and followed him into the solarium, where he left her alone in the sunlight and went to brew them tea. When he had brought it to her and poured their cups, he began slowly to undress, stopping from time to time to sip his tea. By the time she'd finished, he was naked in a light that revealed every part of him, every tiny flaw. Though he must certainly have been conscious of this, his body revealed no excitement. She suspected that, on a dare, he might shed his clothes anywhere and remain as casually at ease.

She had never seen Jonathan naked, not even by candlelight. There was always a nightshirt covering his chest, always blankets over his body. No, she was not brave, only carefully adventurous. Had she been brave, the demands she made would have been to her husband and she would have had no need for the passion of a stranger. If the weeks after their marriage had been normal ones, she might have done so gladly. Not now.

She was thinking of Jonathan when Gance left her and went upstairs.

Mina followed, halting in the entranceway. The door had a simple bolt. Even now, he left her no latitude for self-deceit. Yes, these hours were what she wanted. Almost wearily, as if the decision itself had sapped all her strength, she followed Gance upstairs.

He had closed the curtains, red satin like the bedcovers and canopy, and the room was bathed in deep red. She thought she would have to undress herself, but apparently she had done enough to prove her resolve.

* * *

MILLICENT was napping when Mina returned home, so Mina did not have to deal with the suspicious woman's scrutiny. She stole upstairs, removing her clothing far more quickly than Gance had done and prepared a bath. When all traces of the afternoon had been washed away, she slipped on a wool dressing gown, pulled her little journal from its hiding place and began to write.

I tried not to think at all as he undressed me. Yet I could not help but feel that, though he had made it clear that I was in control, I had lost my senses somehow. Still the desire seemed so perfectly right.

As he unfastened the tiny buttons down the back of my blouse, I felt his fingers brushing my flesh, their touch spreading a warmth through me that I understood all too well.

But last time I had felt such passion I had been entranced, and the excitement had all the focus of an unwilling dream. Now my partner was no vampire, no threat to my life or, though it sounds strange to say it, my salvation.

I moaned when he touched me, kissed him eagerly when he walked around me to slip the lace and linen fabric from my shoulders. He moved to the skirt, the slips, the corset, the tips of my breasts hardening when he slipped back the top of my chemise and kissed them.

I now stood in chemise and shoes and stockings, and though I had forgotten it, I saw in the mirror beside the bed that my bonnet was still on my head, my hair still piled beneath it. The incongruity of the scene was not lost on me. I looked like a trollop purchased for a night of pleasure. The thought seemed so fitting that I smiled as I raised my hands to untie my hat.

He caught them, lowered them and undid the straps and pins himself, working so quickly that I started when my hair fell around my shoulders. His hands followed it, moving the white cotton straps of the chemise off my shoulders, my breasts, my hips. Then he was on his knees in front of me, ordering me to raise one leg then another.

He ran a finger down the outside of my calf and pushed me backward so I was sitting on the edge of the bed. He unbuttoned my boots and removed them, the silk stockings slowly, one at a time, his fingers moving down the outside of my legs, then up the bare center, pushing them apart so his thumbs could press against my sex, reminding me for a moment of what was to come.

Again I tried to touch him; again he held my hands back and swung me sideways so I lay along the length of the bed. "Am I to be only used?" I asked.

"Used?" He did not smile as he raised my arms above my head and wrapped my fingers around the carved wood posts of the headboard. "Tell me if you are used when I am done."

At home with Jonathan, I would have considered myself ready for intercourse, but my pleasure had only begun. I don't remember how many times I let go of the wooden post, or how many times he returned my hands to that place above me. There were moments when I wasn't even sure what his hands and lips were doing to me, only that my response was like nothing I had ever felt before, not even in the vampire's arms.

And I still had not touched him. It was as if his satisfaction hinged not on his release but my response, as if he proved his worth with my cries of passion, my begging for him to please, please stop just for a moment so my body could rest.

He never did, and when I began arching my back, when my hands no longer obeyed him and buried themselves in his hair, trying to pull him up on me, he stopped only for a moment. "Used," he whispered and rolled me onto my stomach, pulled me up on my knees and entered from behind. One of his hands remained in the folds of my sex, its skill, and his organ pounding inside me, keeping my passion at its peak until my body no longer had the strength to respond.

And even then his hands continued their knowing assault, his lips still sucked the tips of my breasts, demanding the last shreds of my passion as Dracula had my blood.

What did I learn in the hours we spent in that room? That men purchase women for a reason. That I was not at all the civilized creature I had thought myself to be. Yet something was missing from that hour of lust and rutting. Perhaps it was the color of the room, blood red in the afternoon sun, that made the longing for the taste of blood so strong in me.

We left together, the veil of my hat carefully in place. We traveled to his office as we had to the house, sitting across from one another in the carriage, never speaking, strangers once more. I knew then that, even had I not loved Jonathan with all my heart, I could never come to love the person who had given me such pleasure. The thought of how he had acquired his skill would always be a barrier between us. Yet if I believed that I would never be alone with him in that house again, I would have been saddened by the loss. I need what he gives me. The creature I have become demands it.

As if guessing my thoughts, he whispered as he left me, "The same day next week? I will meet you here at eleven." I nodded and he motioned the cab on. I had it drop me off at Winnie's so I could leave her the check I had collected for the hospital.

"Fifteen hundred pounds!" she exclaimed when she saw it. "We may have to name the new ward after him."

"Or the birthing rooms," I replied. I smiled while Winnie laughed, delighted at my wit. I felt a pang of betrayal as well. Though I knew he would not mind my jest, he had taken great care to see that a child would not come from our union.

Why have I written of this afternoon at all, let alone in such terrible detail, risking the possibility that someday Jonathan or someone else might read this? I suppose I did it so that, in some future time when our affair is over, I can read my little journal as men read their erotic stories and bring back the passion to share—perhaps with Jonathan, perhaps with another, or perhaps only for my self-satisfaction.

Yet there is so much I did not mention because I cannot put such words to paper. Hints of a few—

The way his body looked in the glaring sunlight. The pallor of his skin. The silver highlights of his hair and the softness as it brushed against my thighs.

The sound of my voice, coming it seemed from some other body, one that Mina Harker, wife to Jonathan, could never comprehend.

CHAPTER SEVENTEEN

In a manner totally at odds with her usual behavior, Winnie Beason had not gone to the hospital after receiving the mail on Tuesday. Though she had opened the envelope from London, the moment she saw the contents she had slipped the pages back into it and sent a note to Mina. Then she paced her parlor waiting for Mina to arrive so they could read the translation together.

Winnie had scarcely shut the parlor door for privacy when Mina fell into a chair and pulled the pages out. "So soon!" she exclaimed. "I thought they'd take weeks to translate." She glanced at the letter accompanying them. "Mr. Ujvari has sent part of the work. Shall I read his letter first?"

"The pages. Read them aloud," Winnie suggested. "We'll share them together."

Mina nodded and began to read.

I have been in this place of horror for nearly a century. I long ago stopped wondering if I am a captive, as I know I have become a willing accomplice to the deeds that go on here. Even so, I write this account in the hope that someone may find it and know my fate, and as a warning to those who may come here. Leave this place, if you can. Leave before nightfall. Even I, who do not wish to kill, have so little control.

The others laugh at me for wanting to write this. He, in particular, reminds me that no one ever leaves this place alive. Yet I have hope. The world around us is more crowded than ever before. Someday, someone may come by day and leave by day. If they do and they are from this region, they may leave me with the true death I long for.

"True death?" Winnie asked.

"It was a term Van Helsing also used. It means that her body will be destroyed and her soul will pass on."

"What a sad thing to wish for oneself."

"Not so sad when you consider how they must live," Mina reminded her and continued.

My name is Karina Aliczni. I was born in the year 1753 in Bratislava, though my family home was in Targoviste. My title then was countess. The title seems so unimportant now that I live with a prince, a princess and a creature who had no title when she was alive though, had she ambition equal to her power, she could rule the world.

When I think back through all the years to my mortal childhood, it seems that I was prepared for only one station in life—to marry and become a wife and mother. My training then was in how to wear clothes properly, how to apply rouge and powder, how to curtsy, how to dance, how to play the spinet and sing.

I was also well educated. I had read of foreign places. My father visited some of them, bringing me back porcelain music boxes from France, gold earrings with tiny opaque gems in shar-shaped mountings from the Pyrenees, a map of the world from Italy. The last only made my longing worse. I would not marry some foolish noble tied to his lands and his traditions. I wanted to travel, to see everything I could of the world. I vowed to find someone who felt as I did, even if it meant joining the gypsies to do it.

My father, of course, had other ideas, and one of them was to expand the family holdings through the proper alliances. My brother wed without any protest a well-dowered girl. Though he swore to me that she was too ugly to bed and that there would never be children from the marriage, she gave birth only ten months later. To my dismay and my father's great satisfaction, they seemed happy. My sister married a year later in a similar arrangement, and I knew I would be next.

I begged my mother for time, pleading that I was too young to be a wife, too frail to be a mother. I was the youngest. She had always sheltered me. She did so now.

Something in the way she saw through my lies but responded to my needs made me more comfortable around her than I had been since I was old enough to realize that parents are not infallible. I spoke to her from my heart, telling her of the need I had to live somewhere as far from our little plot of land and our comfortable home as I could. I hastened to explain that this was not because I disliked our life but because I wanted, with a passion I could not understand, to experience something different.

I do not know if she spoke to my father, but in the days that followed he observed me in a way he had never done before. He would ask me to read to him, to sing. He would order my daily wardrobe and would walk with me in the garden behind our home.

What my mother must have suggested to him seems so obvious now. I was beautiful, titled. I should not be wasted on a local marriage to expand our holdings but sent to the capital to attract a better suitor, and hopefully forge an alliance with a family of great wealth and greater power.

The dressmakers came with their satins and velvets and bolts of delicate lace. At night, my father would teach me the newest dance steps. In the absence of any music, he would count the rhythm as we moved through the steps. When he could teach me no more, he sent my mother and me to Bratislava. In the capital, I was given my final lessons by dance instructors and tutors and the well-paid lady's maid my father hired to educate me in deportment.

I was such an eager pupil and such a quick one. Everyone said so, and yet all his plans, all my work came to nothing. My mother took me to court. I danced. I charmed those around me. I even fell in love, in that innocent way of innocent girls, far more than once in the months we spent there, but no one was serious about a match.

"It's your beauty," one of my servants whispered to me on a night when I seemed particularly despondent. "It puts men off."

I looked in the mirror. I had never thought of myself as beautiful. Instead, I had believed that women smiled at me and men gave me longer, more admiring looks because of the ribbons in my hair, the way my servants had dressed me or painted my nails. Such innocence, such perfect innocence.

While I hid my misery as best I could and hoped for someone to save me, my mother was renewing old friendships, among them one with a woman who had an estate in the mountains near Sibiu. My mother suggested that we visit there. I agreed happily for I needed relief from the constant disappointment.

The estate was huge, with a great stone wall running all around it, and outside its fields and gardens was beautiful country, wild and empty. The lower hills were colored dark green by the dense pine forests, with sharp black peaks rising above them. I loved the land, but the people were a different story. They seemed isolated, suspicious of strangers, even those coming to the land in the company of its ruling family. My mother did not seem to notice, but then all her attention was concentrated on her friend. She had little desire to see the country-side around the estate.

Meanwhile, I had little desire to see another set of tapestry-hung walls, particularly when my entire life would likely be filled with such walls. I cultivated the friendship of the woman's son, Janos, a stupid and rather ugly boy a year younger than I. My charm, which had so little effect on the worldly men at court, was more than enough for this conquest. Within days, he was helping me slip out of the estate so he could escort me for rides through the wild countryside or into the town.

I sensed the vampire's presence the afternoon of our visit to Sibiu. The day had been thick with clouds, so that noon resembled twilight. I had been fearful of a storm, but my companion assured me that such clouds meant nothing in these damp mountains.

How could Janos have known the truth? He was wealthy, as isolated from the superstitions of the peasants as I. With only a knowledge of German and Hungarian, he did not even speak their language. If he had, he might have known that dense clouds did mean something in this or any land. Clouds meant that the dead could walk.

I think it was a little after noon when we reached Sibiu, though it would have been impossible to know this by looking at the sky. We had stopped to visit the priest who lived on the edge of town. I was dismounting when, outside the stone wall surrounding the churchyard, I saw a man watching me. Though his back was straight, his face was deeply lined, and what hair I could see under the black hood of his cloak was thin and gray. Yet his face interested me. His eyes in particular seemed to catch the light of the sky and glow as they watched me intently.

What harm could an old man do me? I had walked toward him, intending to speak a few words to him, when the priest came outside.

"Come away!" he called to me. "Come inside."

My hand was extended toward the man. He had just raised his own to touch me when I pulled back, turned and joined my companions. "Was that someone you know?" I asked the priest.

He nodded and said nothing. Janos, who had been seeing to the horses, turned and looked toward the road. "Who?" he asked.

I looked back and the man was gone. We did not speak of him again, but when we left for the ride back to the estate an hour later, the priest blessed us very solemnly before letting us go. He used a language I had never heard before. When I inquired about it, he told me it was the old tongue, rarely used in our time. As we left, I thought I saw the old man standing in the forest close to the road, watching silently as we passed.

I heard later what happened that night. The priest had said the evening service and left to walk through the churchyard to his little house. He never reached it. Like so many others, his body was never found. I know his resting place well now, the deep chasm where his bones and the bones of a thousand others lie crumbling beneath the weight of the new kills falling above them.

Yes, I am not so innocent now.

The next time I saw the man from the churchyard was while walking in the garden of the estate the following evening. He was sitting on a bench close to the heavily scented wisteria blooms. His body had been restored by the life it had consumed. His hair was black, his face unlined, his hands powerful and young. Only the eyes were the same—dark and intent.

A relation to the old man, I thought, yet the similarity was so strong. And, of course, he knew me enough to call me by name.

Was I troubled by this? Not at all. I was in hailing distance of the house, in the gardens of a powerful family. Their guards patrolled the borders of the property. It seemed that the man must have been trusted with admission. Besides, what possible reason would a thief or murderer have for sitting so openly on the grounds?

Had I known what danger I was attracting, would I have gone to him and sat with him and held his cold, pale hands? I doubt an army could have altered my future once he saw me, and now that my future has been set like a pattern in marble, there is no other known to me, no way to find regret.

He spoke of the land, its history and its customs. I spoke of court at Bratislava, of the clothes the women wore, the wealth of the prince. Then, suddenly, with no real warning, I was speaking not of others but of myself and the walls I would face throughout my life.

Suddenly he was kissing me, his mouth hard against mine, his teeth so sharp that my lips bled. I pushed him away, turned and ran toward the house. When I looked back to see if he would follow, he had vanished as if the deepening night shadows had swallowed him whole.

He had given me no name to call him by, no way to find him again. If I had not thought that I would be punished for approaching a stranger, I might have asked my mother about him. Janos, whom I trusted more, knew nothing about the stranger. The mystery of him only added to my passion, and the following evening, I walked in the garden again. But though I stayed among the rhododendrons, the lilies and the blooming vines for hours, he did not come.

The next night, I woke late and looked outside on the moon-drenched lawn. He stood among the flowers, looking up at my window. Child that I was, I had become infatuated with the strangeness of him. I put on a cloak and stole outside, the dew cool on my feet as I ran to him.

I recalled the night perfectly, the shiver I felt as he brushed his lips against my bare shoulder, the side of my neck. He unlaced my night-shirt. I felt his lips on my breast, a pressure there, and an instant later, whatever innocence I possessed died.

On the last few words, Mina's voice had grown soft. Now she stopped reading altogether, looking from the pages to the flames in the parlour stove. Winnie rested a hand over hers. "You wanted to learn from this account," she said as if expecting Mina to destroy the pages.

Mina handed the remaining two pages to Winnie. "You finish the reading. No matter what I do, you finish it." Her voice shook as the past—the passion and the horror of it—overcame her.

Winnie did, going on in a voice far more dramatic than Mina's flat tone had been. *In the nights that followed, I was mad for him, doing what he asked as he drank from me, as he shared his own blood.*

His marks were not on my neck but lower, on the tips of my breasts, where clothing would hide them. I understand the reasons for that now. In this land, there are too many who know the bite of the vampire and the precautions to take. And any woman would hide such marks even from her servants lest she be accused of having suck-led a devil's child. Yes, I hid them well. No one knew of my assigna-tions. I blamed the weakness the others noticed in me on some vague illness. The excuse allowed me to sleep by day and go to him at night. Then, when I was even too weak to rise from bed, he left me. In all the years that have passed, I have tried to understand why he did not carry me off. I have begged him to explain, but he is always silent.

At first I did not notice that he had gone, but when I had recovered my strength enough to continue my visits to the moonlit garden, I walked alone. I felt the cutting pain of loss, and a terrible rebelliousness.

The days all seemed to fly by. My life seemed so short, so useless. I decided that I would no longer be the obedient child my parents wanted. I would dare anything for a chance to live.

Winnie halted. "Mina, are you all right?" she asked. "You look so pale."

"It's nothing save how well I understand her emotions," Mina replied. "Go on."

I rode the estate lands alone. I broke my promise to stay within its stone walls and went out into the countryside. I was looking for him, of course. This was not love, but passion. I don't think anyone could ever really love him, because he cannot love in return. Now that I am one of his kind and the emotion is likewise lost to me, I can see this more clearly.

As I have written this, I have shared the account with the others and they have laughed at me. They are so old, they have forgotten their past. I remember it. I long for its freedom now, as I longed for him then.

I did not find him. Instead, a creature far more ruthless waited for me and, out of jealousy rather than desire, brought me to this place, this life.

"That's all," Winnie said, "Shall I read Mr. Ujvari's letter as well?"

Mina nodded and Winnie began.

"Since I was born in the part of the world in which the Countess Karina lived, I feel compelled to comment on this story. It is a myth in my land that the dead, if buried in unconsecrated ground or guilty in life of unconscionable deeds, may rise and walk the earth, stealing life from those still living. Liderc, vampir, or strigoiul they are called in my country, and there are those who believe in them even to this day. According to other documents I have read, at the time the countess disappeared many people assumed that it had been one of these creatures which had carried her away. This is, therefore, a fictional account of her life, not a real one, for no educated person would accept their existence.

I had hoped to have the entire translation done in the next two weeks. However, the dialect shifts after this to one with which I am less familiar, and the work may take some time. For that I am sorry. I decided to send you what was done so you would have some idea of the sort of journal you have purchased. Anton Ujvari."

"Karina changed the dialect to hide her account," Mina said.

"From Dracula?"

"No, I don't think she was hiding it from him. She mentions others. His wife made Dracula a vampire, and Van Helsing killed another woman as well. But someone made Dracula's wife undead. There may be others, indeed there likely are."

"I suppose." Winnie replied too quickly. Mina decided that she was being placated until Winnie went on, "Did you learn anything from that account?"

"I don't know. I found the thought that Dracula, or someone, could enter the churchyard and kill the priest somewhat odd. Van Helsing said that a vampire must be invited."

"Once Dracula was the ruler of all that land," Winnie said and laughed as if the notion were somehow preposterous. Her face reddened. "I'm sorry," she said, gripping Mina's hand. "It's just that it seems so strange to be dissecting such a fantastic account."

"Do you believe me, Winnie? No, don't nod, tell me the truth."

Winnie hesitated. "I didn't believe you entirely at first. But then, as you went on with your story, it all seemed so real. And I am not blind, Mina dear. You are quite sane and sensible, so, yes, I do believe it. I do admit, however, that I would feel infinitely better about accepting it if I could see one of these creatures with my own eyes."

"Pray that you never do." Mina felt suddenly weary. She stood and asked for her cloak. "Keep the pages," she said when Winnie tried to give them to her. "When we have the whole account, I'll decide if I want Jonathan to read them."

The day had become unseasonably warm. Rather than hire a cab, Mina decided to walk home. She had just turned onto her street when Gance rode by on a beautiful white stallion. "Good afternoon, Mrs. Harker," he called to her, and continued on. By the time Mina reached the house, she felt chilled by the spring damp, and weakened by her sudden rush of desire.

She stared for a moment at her reflection in her bedroom mirror before taking off her bonnet and cloak. The moment when Gance had spoken to her had made it clear that it made no difference if Dracula were alive or dead. His blood had changed her as it had the innocent countess. Its taint would be there throughout her life, altering her existence, perhaps someday altering her death.

* * *

ONE day flowed swiftly into the next, like a current gathering momentum before the falls. Each morning Mina waited anxiously for another message from Winnie before starting her day, but there were none. She wrote letters on behalf of the hospital and followed each of them with personal calls. Her relaxed charm succeeded where Winnie's intensity often had not. Donations came in more quickly than ever before. Winnie and the other volunteers were ecstatic.

Though Mina longed to tell Jonathan about each successful call, he would come home late, ready for nothing but dinner and bed. So she would sit beside him in front of the parlor stove and listen to him speak of his own day. Duty destroyed all real interest. Passion went with it, but he did not notice that either, or how Mina lay awake long after he slept with her gathered in his arms.

It had been nearly eight weeks since she had fainted in the hospital. Her breasts had continued to feel swollen, her stomach to ache long after the bleeding was done. Now, with so much time elapsed between cycles, she was certain that she had indeed lost a child. She found some comfort in that belief, for if she'd had a miscarriage, the terrible thoughts and dreams would not repeat each month.

And then the relentless pressure around her womb started again, followed by the bleeding. She sent a note to Gance to tell him that she could not keep their meeting, then lay in bed, not daring to sleep lest she dream.

Though she did not ask it of him, Jonathan stayed home from work the following day and tended her himself. "You must rest," he told her. "Exhaustion only makes the pain worse."

"Then I dream," she reminded him.

"You always dream. You've said so often enough," he replied patiently.

"Not like this, Jonathan. I cannot tell you how terribly vivid the dreams become. It's as if he walks the earth again. I'm so afraid." She gripped his hand.

"Sleep," he said. "I'll remain here with you. If you become restless, I will force you to wake."

She tried, but though the dreams were as terrible as before, she did not cry out or stir. When she woke, she found Jonathan had dozed off in his chair. She looked at him, with his chin pressed against his chest, his salt-and-pepper hair tumbling over his forehead, and tried to understand how many hours he worked, and how exhausted he must be. No matter how she tried, she could not help but feel betrayed.

After that, though she tasted the tea he brought her and sipped the cordials like a dutiful wife, she did not finish them lest they contain some drug to make her sleep. Her expression grew dull from fatigue then animated as she moved beyond exhaustion, talking to him in quick, short sentences.

When he dozed off, she would shake him awake, until finally, apologetically, he told her that he had to rest and moved into one of the guest rooms.

Once he was gone, Mina could remain awake only through motion. Jonathan lay in the adjoining room listening to the sound of her bare feet on the rug as she paced like a great cat in its cage.

Then the bleeding ended. The anxiousness vanished, and though the dreams remained, they were not so vivid. Mina slept for nearly a day, then woke and felt very much herself. Her optimism had also returned. These three days had been easier than the last. The next monthly would be easier yet. And the next.

If she just kept her mind occupied, everything would be all right.

* * *

THE following Tuesday, she went to Gance.

She reached his little house by a circuitous route that began with a walk to the center of town to catch a cab. Once inside it, she lowered her veil and waited until they had traveled some distance before calling out the address.

The iron gate was open, the outside door ajar. She barred it as she entered, then found Gance in the solarium, a glass of wine in his hand, a second poured and waiting for her. She said nothing, not even a single word of greeting. Instead, she took off her bonnet, her cloak, and began unbuttoning the high neck of the blouse she wore.

I understood why I had to treat him that way, she wrote in her journal that night. *I needed to make it clear to myself even more than to him that he was not my friend, not even my lover, but a creature to whom I came to satisfy my basest needs, as I satisfied his. I could live with my conscience then, the way Lucy might have lived with what remained of hers had she continued to feed but not kill.*

My remote behaviour confused him. I saw him watching me undress, waiting for me to smile or even be so silly as to giggle nervously. I did none of that, not even when I walked toward him, watching his eyes move over my sunlit body. Finally, when I was close enough to touch him, I reached instead for my glass.

We coupled on the French divan, among the drooping palms and heavy-scented gardenias. The sun had warmed the room, and soon there was a sheen of sweat on his body, a musky undertone to the colognes we wore. At the end, when I was almost beyond sated and he close to his final release, I straddled him. He lay with his arms limp at his side, his head tilted back against the pillows. And in the sunlight I could see the vein in his neck pounding. Was it my imagination that it seemed so blue, his pulse so strong and quick? No matter. Passion released my control. In the instant I felt his body tense, his hips thrust upward to meet me, I lowered my head and placed my lips over the pulsing vein, sucked in a fold of skin and bit.

Salty, yet sweet. I have tasted my own blood, sucked from small wounds to cleanse them, yet that blood was nothing like this. It was as if I tasted his passion and made it one with mine.

I had expected him to recoil. Instead his own passion increased, and he held his hands against the back of my head as Dracula had, holding my lips to the wound so I could not help but drink. We exploded together and I pulled back. With his blood dripping from my lips, I began riding him, feeling his blood move through me as his semen moved through my womb—both the essence of life itself.

What must death feel like? Do vampires kill because they cannot die?

She looked down at the words she had just written and saw that her usually neat shorthand ended in a hideous, almost illegible, scrawl. She slammed the journal shut, not caring that the ink had not dried, and placed it back in its hiding place.

Why had she put those last words on paper? Why had she thought of them at all?

She put her hands to her face and inhaled deeply, but an act intended to calm her only made her more distressed. She smelled Gance's cologne, his body. She licked her skin and tasted his sweat. She stripped quickly and took a hot bath, scrubbing her skin until it was scraped and red and smelled only of violet soap.

*   *   *

GANCE had remained at the house. That afternoon he also bathed, in the footed tub before the lace-covered windows, examining the bite Mina had left on his neck in his shaving mirror. The timing of her bite had been perfect. At that moment of passion he had never felt the pain. Indeed, he might not have noticed it at all had he not seen her face as she pulled away, the hunger with which she looked at the blood leaking slowly from the cut and the terror when she saw that he was watching her.

It's high collars for a while, he thought. He might have dismissed the act as nothing more than an extreme of passion had it not been for Arthur's drunken tale. He could picture Arthur believing anything while under the influence of alcohol or the suggestions of a superior mind, but Mina was more intelligent, and far more levelheaded.

And such a surprise. He had not thought of her as someone of such intense sexual needs, indeed had not thought she would accept his offer at all. But she had intrigued him and that was enough.

Now, she intrigued him even more. As soon as he was dressed, he made his way to the train station, sent a wire to William Graves and caught the next express to London.

He dined with the diplomat at a quiet table in the rear of Tyburn Pub. Graves seemed pleased with his company, even more when Gance picked up the bill and ordered them a second round of absinthe drips and dessert.

"Did the woman I referred to you ever make an appointment?" Gance asked.

"Oh, yes. She seemed very determined and a little nervous. Odd, since she said that the book was nothing more than fiction."

"Did you do the translation?"

Graves shook his head. "I couldn't. I referred her to a Romanian I once knew, though I did not have his address. She apparently hired someone else but not before she contacted Ion Sebescue. Recently, his son came to see me and asked about the book." Graves sipped his drink, commented on its excellence, then went on in a low, conspiratorial tone. "Did you ever meet anyone who you thought was truly lethal?"

Gance laughed. "Daily, William. You lead a sheltered life."

"And you should choose your friends with more care," Graves retorted. "James Sebescue is a dangerous man. When we talked, I felt that he was weighing the consequences of killing me after we'd finished. I became so certain of it that I walked him into the outer office while we concluded our meeting. Later, I decided that I might be reacting to the intensity with which he had spoken. And yet I'm sorry I gave him any assistance at all. Now . . . well, I try to remind myself that I don't really know what's in the journal, so there is no reason to harm me."

"I suppose," Gance agreed, then added wickedly, "unless he means to harm the translator or the journal's owner, in which case he may want to dispose of anyone who could link him to the crime. Did you give him my friend's name?"

"He never asked, and I certainly didn't volunteer the information. But the young woman can rest easy. You see, he referred to her a number of times as Mrs. Beason."

"Ah!" Gance responded, with only a fleeting pause. "Where else do you think my friend might have found someone to do the work?"

"The consulates, though I think I would have heard mention of it if she had. The museum is an even more likely place. I'm surprised I didn't think of it when she came to me."

After Graves left, Gance sat alone at the table and considered his next step. Though he intended to warn the women, he likewise wanted to learn more about what the journal contained. Arthur's ravings had been helpful. Quincey Morris, whom he'd met when Arthur brought him round to the Marlborough Club for drinks, was dead. Jonathan . . . No, it was best to keep well away from the husband.

And then there was Seward. Gance hated the man—his petty superiority, as if he had some monopoly on the human mind, his supercilious manners, his arrogant temperance. No, it would be better to find the translator, he decided. He paid the bill and left.

The night was beautiful, warmer than February ought to be. The breezes gave hints of the spring soon to come. He breathed in the damp air and started back toward his house on Carlton.

It had rained that afternoon, and the streets were still dotted with puddles. As he traveled through them, he had a strange floating sensation, as if, like Jesus, he walked on water.

A woman sitting on a bench near the roadway looked up at him. He thought at first that she had lost her way, until she let the shawl drop from one shoulder to reveal the plunging neck-line of her dress. He looked closer, wondering what tart would have the gall to solicit in the shadow of Buckingham Palace. As he moved toward her, he smelled the liquor on her breath, saw the insanity in her glazed eyes. And her age—her lined face, the thin skin on her fingers, the spots on her hands.

A crone could be tolerated but not a woman who was almost beautiful. He recoiled, ignoring her harsh laughter, the mad taunts that followed him as he walked quickly away.

CHAPTER EIGHTEEN

I

Anton Ujvari was used to shadows. In the corners of the museum rooms where he worked. On the streets he traveled on his way home at night. In the doorway of his house. He had always welcomed them, and the mystery they held. Not any longer. The journal was the source of his fear—that and the myths he had learned as a child.

Before he began the translation for Mina Harker, Ujvari had carefully copied the picture on the old Hungarian coin. He'd softened the lines of the young countess's face, given texture to the hair. She had been so beautiful, and her disappearance such a mystery.

His own mother was only a vague memory from his youth, but the memory he had of her was of someone who resembled the countess. They had the same nose and jaw. And they had both disappeared without a trace.

Someone loved them, he thought, for he was a romantic, and the aged, taciturn father who had raised him had instilled only fear in him. For years after he had run away to England, he waited for the man to reappear and drag him back to Romania, as if he were still a little boy needing to hide.

Three days after he had begun the translation, Ujvari pleaded illness and took a leave from the museum. This document, certainly not from the countess herself, was so strange, so darkly sensual, that he did not want to stop the work until he was done.

He translated in longhand, stopping after the first dozen pages to copy the account on a typewriter. Though they had not discussed the matter, it occurred to Ujvari that his employer might wish to see the first pages of the document as soon as possible, so he made a carbon copy of the work. When he'd finished the first third of the journal, he began to have difficulties with the language. He wrote Mrs. Harker a quick note, sent it and the first pages of the translation off to her and returned to work.

With no dictionary to help him, he went through the translated books and documents, trying to find a similar dialect that he could use as a reference for some of the words. There was nothing, so he went into the storage rooms where uncataloged material from the region was kept. There, among the mummified cats, worn Roman coins, dusty scraps of medieval tapestries, and other paltry treasures, he found a box of letters from the Hungarian empire, they and their translations alike musty and crumbling from years of neglect.

Most were worthless save to the detail-oriented scholar. Many were documents of the Habsburg bureaucracy; a few were personal letters written in Hungarian. None were as interesting as the document on which Ujvari worked, though one was in a similar hand.

Thinking he might have discovered something else by the person who had translated the countess's journal—or created a fictitious one, he reminded himself—he pressed the page between two panes of glass and took it to his well-lit desk.

Though the document was not dated, the quality of the paper and the ink used indicated something far older than the few decades of the journal he worked on. In spite of this, the handwriting was nearly identical. The language, however, was Hungarian—dated, but perfect. With the document close to the light, he had no trouble reading what remained of it.

. . . I do not like it here in Vienna. It is pretty, but too many people seem to mar the beauty of the days, too many lights hide the splendor of the night stars. And there have been too many heartbreaks. I am sorry I am such a disappointment to you, but no one is more disappointed than I. Mama tries to look cheerful, but both of us are ready to come home.

The scrap grew more ragged, the edges of lines missing.

I will do whatever you wish, though in truth I would hope . . . to wait for . . . understand that? Did you not love Mother that way once?

Forgive me. I will do as you ask . . . Breaks in the final sentences, then the closure . . . *to understand. Your obedient daughter, Kar . . .*

Ujvari looked from the faded letter to the journal Mrs. Harker had left with him. Could someone have duplicated the countess's handwriting in an attempt to prove that the original journal had really been written by her? Would it not have been easier to duplicate only the first few pages of the journal in her hand? To continue the charade for the entire journal where the quality of the paper was so modern seemed odd. And yet, he had heard of cases in which forgers could easily continue in any script.

More importantly, he could think of no reason for anyone to bother. The young countess's story was known to only a few scholars. A forgery would have no value.

Unless the journal was not a forgery but the countess's own writing. What if one of these creatures had captured the young countess and had twisted her childish rebelliousness into something dark and sinister?

This notion, the twisted logic of it and his willingness to believe it, upset all Ujvari's assumptions about life and death and his own past. Yes, he knew the legends, had shaken with fear as the stories were told. But he had been a child then, hanging on his stern father's every word. He was older now, and laughed at the superstitions of his native land.

Not anymore.

He had not thought his enthusiasm for this project could increase until now. He returned to his translation, determined to remain at his desk until the museum closed, and to finish the entire work by the end of the week if possible.

The bright lamps on his desk barely touched the darkness of the huge room in which he worked. He went on, heedless of the scurrying of mice in the walls, the distant footsteps of the night watchman making his rounds in the public halls, and the soft, steady breathing from the depths of the shadows, the eyes watching him as intently as he did the faded script.

A guard came around at closing time to tell Ujvari to go. With a sigh of impatience, Ujvari packed up the manuscript and his translation. As he reached for his coat, the old man stepped from the shadows near the door and walked toward the pool of light thrown by Ujvari's desk lamp.

"This is not an exhibit area," Ujvari commented more harshly than was polite.

"A word with you please," the man responded.

Ujvari shuddered. The man was Romanian, the voice too much like his father's. Could they have met before? "Speak quickly. The museum is closing and I have an appointment."

"Appointment. Perhaps with Mrs. Beason?"

"Beason?" Ujvari looked at the man more closely. He had met him before, perhaps at the Orthodox Church soon after he'd come to London.

"The woman for whom you work."

"I work here, nowhere else." Ujvari circled the man and walked toward the doors to the exhibit area.

"You work on the journal of the Countess Karina, the *vampir.*"

Ujvari did not look back.

"I want that book!" the man called. "Give it to me! Your soul depends on it!"

Ujvari continued on. Outside the door, he spoke a few words to a museum guard and, certain the old man would be led away, continued out. All along he had been cautious, some sixth sense warning him that danger approached. Now he understood why.

His countrymen believed. Even here they believed.

And they knew all too well how to deal with the *vampir*.

* * *

THE following afternoon, as Ujvari left for lunch, a guard called him over to introduce him to a gentleman who had just asked for him. "You're getting to be a popular one," the guard whispered to him good-naturedly. "First the young woman, then that old man prying into your affairs yesterday, and now a real gent. Talk to this one, why don't you?"

The sight of Lord Gance made Ujvari somewhat nervous. The cadaverous frame, the pale skin, the light gray eyes whose pupils seemed so sharp as to be piercing made him think too uncomfortably of the creatures whose lives the countess had exposed so unpleasantly.

But the name was familiar, and Ujvari had met Gance at a museum function two years before. Satisfied, Ujvari introduced himself.

Gance offered to buy Ujvari a meal, but the man refused it and took him into his workroom instead. The deserted room was an even better place for the business Gance wanted to discuss. Since Ujvari had said nothing, and appeared most anxious to leave, Gance went right to the point. "Some weeks ago, a woman hired you to do a translation. I came to ask how you are proceeding."

Ujvari stared at Gance a moment then replied carefully, "If someone did hire me, the matter would be between us."

"The woman is a relation of mine. The family is quite concerned about her. You see, it seems that she has been under some delusion about . . . Damn, it is so very hard to admit this . . . about some sort of demons. Her husband fears that she may need psychological help."

Ujvari eyed him coldly, saying nothing.

"Her name is Winifred Beason," Gance went on. "Her husband is Emory Beason of Exeter. The pages you are translating are handwritten, somewhat old. What else do I have to tell you to convince you that I know quite well what you are working so diligently on?"

Ujvari did not look at him. Gance's guesses were correct.

Gance sat in a chair on the other side of Ujvari's desk. With another man, Gance might have lounged, or not sat at all. Now with his back rigid, his hands folded in front of him, he looked at Ujvari with the proper blend of pride and supplication, waiting for the moment when his adversary would weaken.

Ujvari's implacable expression softened for a moment. When it did, Gance spoke the discreet temptation. "The family is willing to pay twenty pounds if I am allowed to read a copy of the book that is obsessing her."

The book is fiction, Ujvari thought, denying everything he had come to believe. It can be nothing more than fiction. Nonetheless, the old man who'd spoken to him yesterday had seemed obsessed with obtaining it. Now Gance offered him as much as he made in a year for what would require nothing more than a few hours' work. If he looked too closely at the motive behind the offer, he would never be able to accept it. "I'll allow you only to read it," he said. "I don't have the work here, but if you meet me later tonight, I'll bring it."

Or change his mind. Nonetheless, Gance had no choice. They agreed to meet at a coffee house near the museum. Afterward, Gance passed the hours touring the Egyptian exhibits, looking at the ornate jewelry on their velvet pillows in the glass display cases. He was wealthy enough to buy a copy of anything he saw. What he could not purchase was the sense of history these inanimate objects held. And the mummies, so carefully preserved so many centuries ago, had the same feel of tragic antiquity.

A small girl and boy were touring the exhibits with their nanny, staring at the linen-wrapped forms, making jokes about the bodies inside. They were scarcely six years old, how could they understand death? Gance did. At forty-one, he had begun to see his future clearly, and all the young women with their innocence begging to be lost could not postpone his fate.

It was dark when Gance left the museum, and an annoying drizzle dampened his hair and wool outercoat. By the time he reached his house in Mayfair, his coat weighed heavily on his back, and the early spring damp seemed to have chilled even his bones. He stood by the hearth in his wood-paneled den, thinking of Mina, the mark she had made on his neck—and of eternity, and of blood.

* * *

GANCE arrived at the coffee house a little before the appointed time, ordered the darkest roast and waited. He had expected Ujvari to be late—wrestling with a conscience was always time-consuming work—but as the first hour passed, he began to wonder if the translator had changed his mind. Finally, he paid his bill and left.

"Mr. Ujvari did not come to work today," a museum guard told Gance when he arrived there the following morning. "He was recently ill. I suppose he's having another bad spell."

Gance wasn't so certain. He left and returned later in the morning, working his way to the back of the exhibits. When he was briefly alone, he disappeared into the storage area, and through it to the room where Ujvari worked. Cold and silent, the room offered no sign that anyone had been there that day. Gance stopped at the museum office, but no amount of persuasion, including monetary, allowed him to obtain Ujvari's home address.

The next morning, he considered Graves's troubling information and, respecting Mina's apparent wishes in the matter, mailed a note to her via Winnie Beason at the children's hospital, detailing everything he had heard during what he termed his "chance encounter" with William Graves. Duty done, he settled into his London house, intending to visit the museum each day until Ujvari returned.

II

The days had lengthened enough that it was still light when Winnie Beason and her ward, Margaret, left the hospital. They took a cab to the center of town, where Margaret left to run an errand. On the way home, Winnie stopped briefly at Mina's to discuss the fund drive and to deliver a letter that had come to her at the hospital. As the cab dropped her off at home, Winnie noticed her front door partly open. Mr. Beason was not expected for another hour, but as his plans sometimes changed, she was hardly concerned. It would be like him to forget to close the door when he entered.

In the center of the hallway floor, she saw lying open the satchel she used for her hospital documents, the papers that had been in it ripped and scattered.

A robbery! There had been enough of them in the area in the last year. She had started to back away from the house when the door to her husband's study swung open. A man stood there, with a revolver pointed at her chest. "I've been waiting some time for you, Mrs. Beason. Please come in and talk with me."

Winnie had never heard a voice so softly cold, so naturally lethal. If she had not been certain he would shoot her in the back, she would have bolted from the room. Instead, she used what courage she had to stare at him boldly, memorizing his features as she walked past him into her husband's study.

The intruder had done more damage here. Drawers had been pulled out, their contents scattered. The beautiful overmantel mirror she had inherited from her grandmother had been pulled from its mountings, its beveled glass cracked so that, as she looked at it, she saw her fearful expression multiplied in a dozen small reflections.

How dare she feel so helpless! How dare this man ravage her home! "What in the hell do you want?" she demanded, amazed at the force in her voice.

"Come into your parlor, Mrs. Beason. I need to speak to you."

She did as he asked, sitting on the chair close to the fireplace, within comforting reach of the andirons. They were a defense, perhaps a futile one, but she felt better knowing they were close.

"Now, Mrs. Beason, tell me about the Romanian journal. First of all, where did you get it?"

"There is a used bookstore on Bow Street. I bought a box of cookbooks and discovered it among them. I was curious and so I arranged . . ."

"Where did you get it? The truth this time."

"Very well." Her stomach was churning, and she thought she would be sick. These feelings seemed so terribly feminine, but she reminded herself that almost any man would feel equally terrified when a stranger pointed a gun at his chest. She tried to relax, crossing her legs and resting her hands on the low arms of the chair. As she hoped, her gesture released some of the man's tension as well, and he lowered the pistol. Winnie found it suddenly easier to breathe.

"I found it on a trip east," Winnie said. "I did not purchase it; I discovered it in an old castle Mr. Beason and I were exploring."

"Better. And what town were you near?"

Winnie considered everything Mina had told her. She had never been very accurate with names, but she did recall one. "Bacau," she replied.

"Excellent!" Somehow the intruder's smile seemed even more predatory than his scowl had been. "Now, Mrs. Beason. Why did you take the book?"

"The castle had a strange history which made me curious. If you want to see it, I can't help you. I gave the book to someone to translate. It hasn't been returned."

"The translator does not have it."

Winnie frowned, "If it's being sent, I haven't received it yet. If I had, I would give it to you gladly just to get you to leave. It's of no real value save curiosity."

"Yet you paid handsomely to have it translated." He waved at the room around them. "You're not wealthy enough simply to indulge curiosity."

Now that she was calmer, Winnie hunted for clues to the man's identity. He was not more than forty, with dark brown eyes and coal-black hair worn somewhat too long to be fashionable. His clothes were tailored but of a slightly dated style. His hands were clean and uncalloused. As she listened to his voice, she detected an accent in the way he pronounced his vowels. Enough, she thought. Any more and her expression would reveal her knowledge.

"You'd be amazed to what lengths I would go to satisfy my curiosity," she commented dryly, and continued staring at him. "I suspect you would as well," she added.

He shook his head. "I know all I need to know. Now, tell me, did the creatures in that castle touch you?"

"Creatures! The place was quite deserted." She hoped she sounded sincere, for she had begun to understand this man's obsession.

He ignored her comment, demanding in a voice loud enough to be heard through the entire house, "Did you sleep there?"

"No!" she replied, but he went on.

"Did you dream of death and blood? Were there marks on your neck in the morning?"

"Were there what?" Good Lord! Winnie thought. The man was obsessed.

Without warning, he pulled her to her feet and dug the gun's barrel into her side. "Tell me what you saw. Confess!" he screamed.

Motion behind her attacker caught her attention, but she fixed her eyes directly on his, keeping them steady. Her mouth felt too dry for speech, and the room spun. For a moment, she thought she would do something perfectly silly, then she decided that fainting was the best move. Her eyelids fluttered and she slid slowly downward, supported only by his weight.

Caught off guard, the man let her go. As he straightened, Margaret brought a coal shovel down on the back of his head. He fell hard above Winnie. Fearful of hitting her mistress, the girl waited too long to strike again. He twisted and shot her as the shovel was coming down for the second time.

Winnie attacked. One hand, unusually strong after so much hard work in the hospital, grabbed the gun's handle. Had the man not been dazed, he might have beaten her easily. Instead, she managed to wrench the gun from his hand, point it toward him and fire. She'd wanted only to wound him, nothing more. Instead, the bullet went high, hitting him in the chest. He exhaled blood that seeped from his mouth and across the dark parquet floor. Winnie had seen death enough to know he was beyond any help.

She ran into the street and, raising the gun in the air, fired two shots. The recoil made her lose her footing, but the shots alerted her neighbors. Men rushed from their houses, one carrying a gun of his own. "Send for the police!" Winnie cried. "And for a doctor. There's been a robbery and shooting." With that, she ran back inside to do what she could to stop Margaret's bleeding.

Mina arrived at the same time as the doctor. When she saw Winnie's hands covered with blood, the body and Margaret on the floor, she fought down the rush of emotions and took a step toward Winnie, intending to pull her away. The doctor was here. Winnie's skills were no longer needed. As Mina stepped forward, Margaret turned her face toward her. The wound on the girl's shoulder opened, and the blood began to flow once more. Mina backed away and leaned against the hall table for support. "Margaret will be fine," Winnie said, then put an arm around her so they could help each other up the stairs.

"I'm so sorry," Mina told her when they were alone. "If Margaret dies, I'll be to blame."

"The man I shot is to blame for everything, Mina dear. Now, are you all right?"

"Yes. Here, let me help you." Mina unbuttoned the back of Winnie's soiled blouse so that Winnie could slip out of it. She watched silently while Winnie washed and changed, then she followed her to the top of the stairs and remained there while Winnie went down to explain what she could to the police.

She had surprised a robber, she said. In the struggle that followed, Margaret had been wounded and she had wrestled the gun from the robber and killed him. She spoke calmly, almost coldly. She had always sensed that she possessed such firm control, but she had never expected to have to reveal it to so many strangers. The men who listened to her seemed to be waiting for some terrible breakdown as she described the killing, and to be disappointed when she did not oblige them.

"What do you make of this?" the officer asked, holding up a pair of short wooden stakes and a mallet.

She understood exactly why the man had come for her, the death and mutilation she had so narrowly avoided. "I haven't the slightest idea," she replied evenly, aware as she spoke of Mina standing at the top of the stairs, her face white with shock.

As soon as the police had gone, taking the body of the intruder with them, Winnie told Mina exactly what had happened. "They say that the man had no identification on him. Though I can't be certain, I think the intruder was James Sebescue."

"I assumed it might be after I read the letter I'd received." She handed Winnie the note Gance had sent.

Dear Mrs. Harker, Winnie read. *I had a chance meeting with William Graves yesterday. He asked how your translation was progressing, then told me that one James Sebescue had come inquiring about the journal. His manner and questions disturbed Mr. Graves enough that he has taken to carrying a revolver. Pass this message on to Mrs. Beason, then come to London. Contact me and I will assist you. Gance.*

"Perhaps you should write a note to Mr. Ujvari and warn him. There might be others . . . Oh, dear!" Winnie's hand covered her mouth. For the first time since Mina's arrival, she appeared shocked. "Sebescue said that the translator did not have the book."

"He could have been lying."

Winnie shook her head. "He was certain. But I don't think the book was his real reason for coming here. I think he just wanted to find and destroy me."

"What did he say to you, Winnie?"

"He said I would change into a vampire. No, he did not say it so directly, but he implied it. I think he believed that no one could enter Dracula's castle and leave without sharing his curse. He would have killed me, Mina, but only after making certain I understood why it must be done."

"And I thought Van Helsing obsessed," Mina commented with incredible calm. "I should have listened to his warning. Now there may be more like Sebescue looking for us."

"I understood why you did not want to worry your husband, but, Mina, I think you must speak to him."

"And tell him what? That everything we did in the east might have been in vain. That I may rise after death? That it may happen to him as well simply because those women touched him? Then I can add that I am not certain. I know exactly what he'd do."

Winnie waited, saying nothing.

"He'd tell me I was wrong. That the shock of all those weeks of fear has made me delusional and that it makes no difference if others are delusional as well. Jonathan is a logical man, and I have no proof, Winnie, save the book from the castle and the few pages of its translation. I must go to London immediately."

"Telegrams travel faster, Mina dear."

"I'll send one before I get on the train."

"Where will you stay?"

Mina took a deep breath and answered honestly, "With Gance. Give me the translation, Winnie. I want to share it with him."

Winnie was about to give her friend a warning, but then she considered the flush on Mina's face and the casual way she'd used Gance's name, as if she spoke it often. Winnie wasn't angry, but she didn't try to hide her disappointment either. Instead she shrugged and said nothing. The day had been terrible enough already.

As soon as they were calm enough to travel, the two went to Mina's. Winnie stayed with her friend while Mina packed a bag and wrote a brief note for Jonathan, which she left in a sealed envelope on his desk.

They were just slipping out the front door when Millicent came up from the kitchen. "You are going somewhere?" she asked, eyeing Mina's bag.

"I am going to London. I've left a note for Jonathan telling him that I'll be home tomorrow," Mina said. "I wouldn't leave so suddenly if it weren't an emergency."

"What sort of emergency? You must wait for Jonathan and talk to him," she demanded.

Mina would not link this affair to the hospital again. Winnie, however, cut in, "A legal emergency concerning the hospital, Miss Harker. With Mina's training, it's imperative that she handle it. I'll see her to the station."

Millicent saw through the lie. Her face reddened with rage and her shoulders stiffened. Mina suspected that only Winnie's presence stopped the woman from slapping her.

She and Winnie said nothing on the drive. But as Mina prepared to leave the cab, Winnie gripped her hand and squeezed it. "Take care, dear," she said. "Wire me tomorrow, please! And if . . . well, if things don't go as you hope, there will be a place for you in our house for as long as you need it."

As Mina stood on the platform waiting for the last train, the chilly evening air pressed down on her. Though she was warm enough in her fur-trimmed coat, she shivered.

She had packed her little journal along with more clothes than were necessary for one night in London. It seemed at that time as if she would never return to her house, or to Jonathan. Perhaps that was a twisted sort of wishful thinking for, when she did return, she would bring back the book and whatever else was finished. She would lay it all in front of her husband and tell him everything.

CHAPTER NINETEEN

Gance was waiting for Mina at the London Station when the train pulled in a little after midnight. Though he was prepared to confess his interest in the translation, and hope that the confession would make him a confidant, she did not question him. Instead, as they walked to his carriage, she told him what he already knew about Ujvari's work on the old journal, then handed him Ujvari's address. "We must go and warn him," she said.

"We'll go in the morning. Tonight we have to talk," he said.

"We go there first, or we do not talk at all," she retorted.

"Very well." He sighed, handed the address to his driver and opened the door.

The wolfhound lay sprawled across the front seat. He raised his head and eyed his master. "Hello, Byron," Mina said and let him lick her hand. Then, unconcerned about the worries of the humans around it, it rested its head on the open window and watched the world move slowly by.

In the hours that Gance had waited for Mina to come, he had decided that he could explain his interest in her journal easily enough. The bite on his neck was only one part of it, her drinking of his blood far more crucial. And since she was obviously as infatuated with him as he was with her, his charm would make his curiosity all the more natural. He rested a hand on her knee and squeezed lightly, feeling the taffeta of her underskirt rub sensuously against her silk stockings. She covered his hand with her own. He raised it to his lips and kissed it, then moved away from her, watching her, the play of gaslight and shadows over her face as they drove on. The deep sorrow he often glimpsed in her was more obvious tonight, adding to her loveliness, her incredible attraction.

Though most of his thoughts were on the night's more serious work, he could not help but think of the bordello chair that he had recently purchased, after hearing it was a duplicate of one designed by the Prince of Wales himself. Once it had exhausted its conversation value in his London bedroom, he would have it moved to the little house in Exeter. Tonight, if all went well, it would see its first use.

Mina had expected Ujvari to live in a flat or apartment. Instead the address he'd given her was for one of a handful of river cottages on a dirt road paralleling a low embankment along the Thames. The night chill was greater here, the river fog thick in the bushes along the road, so that many of the houses were known to passing riders only by the crude numbered posts beside their walks. When they reached Ujvari's cottage, the driver pulled the horse and buggy to the side. Gance lit the carriage lamp and lifted it high, but it only seemed to illuminate the fog. He whistled for the dog to join them. Then, holding the light close to the ground and with a firm grip on her arm, he led Mina toward the house.

The path was lined with overgrown bushes and weeds, its stones loose and often missing, leaving muddy holes. The cottage itself was so small that it could not have had more than two rooms. Though the night was chilly, there was no scent of smoke in the air, nor any indication that someone inside had seen their light.

Mina moved in front of Gance and knocked on Ujvari's door.

No one replied. She knocked harder, and the door, shook from its latch, swung slowly inward. The dog growled and hung back while Mina stepped inside the dark room, alternately calling Ujvari's name and identifying herself. Gance stopped to examine the lock. The door had been broken in, the latch hurriedly remounted to hold the door shut.

He pulled a pistol from his belt and followed Mina across the threshold. In the dim lamplight, he saw her hands, white and trembling beneath the deep blue wool of her coat. "Can you smell it?" she whispered. "Blood. Death."

He inhaled, but the damp air was all around him, flowing into the room. He stepped farther inside, but whatever troubled her still eluded him. "Hand me the lamp," Mina whispered.

Instead, he held it high and followed as she moved from the main room, with its bare wood table and two chairs, to a smaller bedroom. He smelled something then, a scent that brought back memories of his year in India, the sickness and the carnage. Mina's face was blank, her lips pressed together as she swallowed convulsively, trying to keep from being ill. Gance followed her gaze from the bed, smeared with blood and vomit, to the floor, where the hound was sniffing at a dark stain. Someone had been killed here, that much seemed certain, but the body was gone.

"My God, who did this!" Mina finally exclaimed and covered her face with her hands.

Gance moved in front of her and pulled open the door of the large armoire. There were clothes inside, nothing more. He took Mina into the outer room. There, he noticed something he had missed on the first pass through the room. The window at the back of the house was open, and there were bits of fabric stuck in the loose splinters of the rotted sill. "I'm taking you back to the carriage," he said. "Byron and I will look for the body."

"No! I'm going with you," she replied. Her courage astonished him. From the way she trembled, he wondered where she found the strength to stand.

The air steadied them, and after a short walk, they scrambled up the muddy embankment. Here, the fog was even thicker, the riverbank invisible below them. Gance rested the lamp on a rock and helped Mina down to where the water swirled, dark and muddy, close to their feet.

The dog padded down the bank, sniffing and rooting in the mud, stopping at a pile of driftwood tangled in the willow roots just downriver.

"Stay here," Gance whispered to Mina, and was not surprised when she didn't listen.

As Gance expected, the body was wedged there, the pale and bloated flesh almost indistinguishable from the white tangle of rotting branches. Mina forced herself to look at the face, to be certain that it was indeed Ujvari.

She had steeled herself for the sight of a body but not the rest— the bruises and cuts on his face, the rough wooden stake through his chest. She backed away slowly, unaware that she moved toward the river until Gance reached for her. As he touched her, she flinched then fell against him, silent, trembling. "There's nothing we can do. Let's go," he whispered.

"We can't. We have to tell someone."

"We will, but anonymously. Do you want to have to explain how you knew the man?" He didn't wait for an answer. Instead, he ordered the dog to the top of the bank, then, using the leash for support, he helped Mina to climb over it. "Now, I want you to listen to me this time, all right? I'm going to take you to the carriage. I want you to wait there with the driver while I go inside the house and make certain that there is nothing to connect you with this crime."

"I've done nothing. I wasn't even in London until tonight."

"And Ujvari has been dead for some time. But he is dead because of you." Mina stiffened, but Gance went on. "My reputation can survive a link to this murder. Yours is, forgive me, my dear, expendable. But your husband's . . ." He left the thought unfinished, but Mina understood. Solicitors had to be above reproach.

She waited in the carriage, her eyes fixed on the path until he returned from his search of the cottage, the agreement and some letters clutched in his hand, along with the cover of the leather-bound journal that he had found in the stove. It was over. She would never know what had been written in the book now.

"Did anyone come by?" Gance asked his driver.

"Someone did while you and the lady were at the house. A homeless old beggar from the looks of him. I gave him a few coins and he went on." He pointed in the direction the man had gone.

"Go the other way," Gance ordered. "And put Byron up front with you. He's far too muddy for the back."

As soon as Gance sat beside her, Mina buried her face against the thick sable collar of his coat. He held her tightly as they rode away, and scanned the fog through the open window, noting with relief the glow rising through the mists behind them. By the time they reached his house in St. James, Mina's tears had stopped, but her face still showed grief, and the terrible depth of her guilt.

*   *   *

WHATEVER impression Gance's house might have made on Mina was lost by the evening's shock. She scarcely noticed the magnificent brick mansion with its tall white marble pillars. She did not comment on the drawing room with its Parisian uphol-stered settees in rococo shades of plum and gray and teal, or the tasseled pillows scattered across the floor. She paid no attention to the black walls with their patterned stripes in red and green, the oriental lacquer desk with its carved dragon and peacock de-signs or the huge water pipe from India already filled with opium that Gance had purchased to help prompt her confession. Instead, she sat on the edge of one of the padded divans, her back stiff, her hands clasped firmly together in her lap.

Gance rang for his butler, who joined them quickly. Though the man wore a dressing gown instead of a uniform, he listened attentively to Gance's whispered instructions and disappeared to get a carafe of brandy, a warming stand and two glasses.

Gance prepared the drinks himself. After handing one to Mina, he stood behind her, kneading his fingers into her tense shoulders while she drank it. He poured her another. "You should get out of those damp clothes and into a hot bath," he suggested.

"I'm leaving in the morning. I am going home and telling Jonathan everything that's happened. I've been keeping so many secrets. Gance, I think it's time to confess."

"Start with me," he said softly. "Tell me why Arthur drinks so excessively and raves in his sleep. Tell me why that man's body was mutilated so gruesomely. Tell me about this." He touched his collar above the place where she had bitten him. "After to-night I deserve an answer, don't you think?"

"You won't believe it," she said.

"After what I saw tonight, I'm prepared to believe anything." He'd tried to be witty, she knew, but his words only brought back the memory of Ujvari's bloated body. "Come on," he added after a moment. "Bathe while we talk."

"Very well," she said wearily. She pulled the first pages of the translation from her bag then followed him upstairs.

He helped her with the hooks down the back of her blouse then let her undress. She did not ask him to leave the room, nor did he volunteer to do so. They had mated, and the sight of each other's bodies was natural now. While she undressed, he read the pages she gave him. Then he followed her into the bathroom.

As she soaked in the ornate porcelain tub with its gently slop-ing back, she told him about Lucy and Van Helsing and their desperate chase across the Continent. She told him too about how she found the book Ujvari had been translating. Sometime during her account, he left her, and returned stripped of his tie and vest and carrying the water pipe. He set the pipe on the edge of the bath, and took an occasional pull as he listened to her. He offered it to her three times before she took it.

As he promised, the drug moved through her, relaxing her through the terrible revelations of her dark passion for Dracula—of how he had fed on her and forced her to share his blood as well. "Now his life is within me like some caged animal, demanding release. You are a part of that, Gance. I'm sorry. If what I did to you repulsed you . . ."

"Repulsed!" He unbuttoned his collar to show her the purple bruise and the bite still red at its center. "Mina, this mark I hide so diligently is hardly the worst wound a woman has inflicted on me in a moment of passion. If you like I can show you the place where a usually sensible woman . . ."

"Gance, don't make light of this. It's far more serious than I've let on." The room seemed to move around her, in a languid spiral with her and Gance at the center. She took his hand and rested it on her cheek. "I think this will be our last night together and not a good one. And yet, if I dared . . ." Her voice trailed off; she had said too much.

If she dared what? To stay with Gance openly? To flaunt all tradition, all accepted social norms? She felt perverse, unclean even at the thought of it. And yet? Her hand brushed her forehead where the host had marked her. Realizing what she was doing, she pulled her hand away and splashed it into the warm water.

"Mina, don't fear that passion. Let it go. See how far it carries you," Gance said. He helped her out of the tub, took a large towel and dried her thoroughly. When he'd finished, he lit the pipe and passed the stem to her.

"I can't lose control, Gance. I could kill you the way Dracula killed poor Lucy and so many others over his centuries of existence."

"I don't believe that." He rummaged in the washstand drawer and pulled out a razor. He opened it and deliberately made a cut over the mark already on his neck before handing it to her. "I even trust you with this."

She looked at the blade. The few drops of blood on its tip shone in the dim lamplight, more precious to her than any gems he might have offered her. "You must not do this," she whispered. The room was spinning faster. Her voice seemed too soft, too uncertain, while inside her someone unseen laughed at her fear. She saw Ujvari's face as it had been in the café, alive and intense, and as it had been in the river, white with milky open eyes.

Life! The creature inside her, aroused by the sight and scent of blood, was loose and howling for it.

"Come with me," Gance whispered. "Come to bed. Bring the razor, put it on the bed table. If you have the urge to kill, all you have to do is reach for it. I know you, Mina, better perhaps than you know yourself. You wouldn't harm me, or anyone. It isn't your nature." As he spoke, he moved closer to her, a hand reaching out to brush the tip of her bare breast.

"No!" She backed away until she reached the wall. "Get away from me!" she screamed, the blade held high. "Get away!"

He disobeyed. His fingers moved lightly over her cheek, her neck, her shoulder. He reached for her hand, saying softly as he did, "Come, Mina. Come with me."

"No! Not tonight. Not like this!" She slashed down, cutting his palm. Instead of retreating, he turned it toward her, the blood dripping from the cut onto the floor. She stared at it, then forced her gaze upward toward his face. She stopped to focus on the small trickle of blood from the cut on his neck. She fell on her knees before him and pressed his wounded palm to her open mouth, moving her tongue furiously over it.

Gance had only expected her to want a taste. This terrible craving to devour was something unimaginable. "Mina!" he exclaimed, a hint of panic in his voice.

She raised her head. Her lips were covered with his blood, her cheeks and chin smeared with it. One hand had a white-knuckled grip on the razor. Her body shook with an emotion far more potent than fear. He knew it well, for he was an expert at arousing desire.

"This is what I've become," she moaned and flung the razor across the room. "Do you still trust me, Gance?"

He stared at her face a moment then decided to follow the instinct that had always served him so well. He held his wounded hand in front of her, and with the other pulled Mina to her feet. "I do," he said. "Now, come with me."

He led her into the bedroom. As her eyes grew accustomed to the darkness, they focused on the bed, with its mother-of-pearl inlaid tiles and carved dragon posts. He took her past it, to the fireplace, where the first of the logs had already burned to embers. He threw another onto them. Its bark blazed, sending a soft yellow light through the room.

Without letting go of her arm, he pulled a chair from the shadows to the front of the hearth. At first she thought it was nothing more than an oddly designed settee. Then she noted that it had handles rather than arms rising from its side, and a pair of stirrups mounted in its elaborately carved paint-and-gilt frame. A flush spread over her face as he led her toward it. "Gance, is this . . ."

"Silence!" he ordered, holding up the hand that she had wounded. She glimpsed the blood on his palm. Without a word, he pointed to the base, padded like the seat and back, then to a second pair of brass fittings that would keep the partner's feet from slipping backward. He placed her on the seat, arranged her feet in the stirrups and wrapped her fingers around the handles. The one he had grabbed to pull the chair forward had blood on it from his cut. Mina's eyes focused on it. She thought of ritual defloweration, of blood-coated ritual phalluses.

"Gance," she whispered again, and his hand pressed against her lips—feeding her, silencing her. The cut seeped blood into her mouth as he fell on his knees in front of her, his free hand and his lips seeking her. With a moan, she relaxed. He had given himself to her completely. He could do whatever he wished.

Later, as he pounded against her from below, with a rhythm so strong and deep that it brought both pleasure and pain, she began to suck on the wound, blood mingling with passion as it had so many times before, with her doomed immortal lover. When they had finished, they moved to the bed. She looked at his body against the brown satin sheets, pale as the vampire's had been against the darkness of his clothing and the night, pale as Ujvari's had been against the muddy water of the Thames.

As she rolled on her side for still another embrace, she saw that somehow during the night he'd retrieved the razor she'd thrown away and set it on the bedside table. "Gance, you mustn't," she said, but made no move to stop him as he lifted the blade, made a cut on her chest and pressed his lips against it to drink.

"I take what I give," he said and raised his head to kiss her, not surprised to feel a renewed passion in her response.

*   *   *

As Gance slept beside her, Mina licked her lips and tasted his blood. She inhaled and smelled his blood. Sleep would bring no rest tonight, at least not yet.

She put on her chemise, lit a candle and went downstairs to the drawing room. She recalled a small electric lamp, but with the darkness dispelled only by the flickering candlelight, she could not find it. She pulled the chain for the chandelier instead, and the room was bathed in more light than would leak in through such heavy curtains by day. She blinked from the sudden glare. As she did, something moved in the corner. She gave a small, stifled cry then saw that it was her own reflection in a gilt-edged cheval screen. Moving closer, she saw the smear of blood across her cheek, another on her chest. Her eyes were bright, her body flushed with lingering excitement.

She searched the corners until she found her bag. From it, she removed the little journal and a pen. The chandelier, with its blaze of electric lit crystal, was too revealing for her work, so she switched on a small desk light, turned out the others and, embraced by the shadows around her, wrote a detailed account of every act she had committed with Gance that night. She used his name in this account. She would hide no longer.

I wondered often how it was that Gance and I came to be naked in one another's arms while someone had died because of me.

All the horror of the day seemed to vanish when he came toward me, she wrote. *Yet through every act of passion, I thought of the young man who had spoken so touchingly of the Countess Aliczni, and I hoped that at some time before he died, he felt such wondrous ecstasy. I thought that if he had died in grace and God was just, He would let him feel through my body the magnificence of a skilled touch, an unrestrained response. I offered the night as a prayer for his soul, as a memorial to him.*

And through it all, there was the blood. The amount I drank was hardly life threatening, and the desire for it, though as strong as ever, no longer repulses me. This sudden change of heart would trouble Van Helsing, and, I suppose, it should trouble me. Instead, though I know that I have been used, and will certainly be discarded when I no longer please Gance, I am thankful to him. He has freed the woman that Dracula woke inside me, the passionate woman that I always feared.

And created a new fear in its place. How can I return to Jonathan and tell him what I did without promising that I will never be unfaithful again? I see only one way. I will go to him as Gance went to me. I will offer myself with the same frank need that Gance displayed. I will make Jonathan understand that death waits for us all, and the only real regret when life is over is never having possessed the courage to live.

She put down the pen and closed the book. All that was left to write about was Ujvari's death, and she would not delve too deeply into her thoughts on that, at least not now with the darkness all around her. To do so would be to encourage a return of the old hysteria, just when she needed to be as sane and cool as possible.

Besides, she couldn't remain awake any longer. Now that she'd recorded her thoughts, wakefulness seemed less important. Fantasies could be feared as the ancient mystics had feared them, punishing their errant bodies with whips and hair shirts, or they could be cultivated as a private, harmless pleasure. With that idea firmly in her mind, Mina returned her journal to her bag and went upstairs to sleep.

CHAPTER TWENTY

The following morning, Gance and Mina dressed in silence, both uneasy about how the day would end. More than once, Mina noticed Gance looking at her intently, as if there were something important that needed to be said, but that was all.

They had a late breakfast in the second-floor drawing room, where huge windows with tiny panes of beveled glass overlooked the gardens. Mina stared at the morning mist, sipping her coffee and saying nothing. Her silence frightened Gance. He had seen the emotion that lay beneath the cool surface of the woman. How much was she hiding now?

"Why would the killer throw the body in the river?" Gance asked. "Could he have wanted to expose it to sunlight?"

"Running water is a more likely reason," Mina said. "Or perhaps, when the body did not crumble to dust, the killer realized he had made a terrible mistake and wanted to hide the evidence."

"How big a man was Ujvari?"

"You saw."

"The water distorts. And he had been dead some time."

"Ujvari was a little taller than me and rather thin."

"The lock on the door was broken. He had warning of the intruders. Could one man have subdued him alone, do you think?"

"He was young, outwardly healthy." She recalled his handshake. "He didn't seem particularly strong. I . . . I really don't know."

"How big was James Sebescue?" He pronounced the name as Graves had. Ze-beck.

"I didn't see his body, but Winnie described him as a large man. Under the circumstances, you'd expect her to say that."

"I'd expect Winnie to observe his actual weight, place his accent and note any unusual moles and scars before she killed him," Gance responded.

"She guessed his name." Mina gave him a fleeting smile and looked away, her eyes scanning the garden once more. "The lock on Mr. Ujvari's door was broken, but there was no sign of a struggle in the kitchen," she commented when the silence became too awkward. "You brought papers from the house. What did you find?" she asked.

"Very little." He retrieved the papers from his coat. There were a few bills, a copy of the letter Ujvari had given her, and Winnie's address at the beginning of a letter that had never been mailed. "It's to you, I believe," Gance said and started to hand it to her.

Mina frowned. "Read it aloud," she said.

Mrs. Beason, he began. *I feel that I must warn you. An old Romanian man came to see me yesterday. He asked about you and the book. I was also contacted this afternoon by someone who offered what to me is a fortune just for the sake of reading the translation. I almost weakened, then took pains to be certain that the story he told me had some semblance of the truth. As I suspected, he had been lying.*

I think someone was watching me, following me as I left work. I have managed to lose the man, and so I think it is a man and not one of the fantastic creatures Countess Karina describes with such terrible detail.

Under the circumstances, I have taken to securing the book when I am not working on the translation. As you see, the journal is so persuasive that I almost believe.

Gance handed her the letter. "Whatever precautions he took weren't enough," he said. He poured himself a glass of wine, then filled a glass for her as well.

"Gance, you needn't sit with me," Mina said. "I would feel so much better if you would get word to the police."

"Very well." He rested a hand on her shoulder. She didn't respond. "Try to get some rest. I'll be back in plenty of time to get you to the station." He spoke defensively, as if she were already a stranger to him, but if he could think of a way to keep her here, any way at all, he would do it.

He left the house as she had requested and walked only as far as the nearest pub. At this hour, it was filled with old men, the middle-class clerks of two decades ago, now discarded for their younger competitors. He watched them drink, seeking forgetfulness, watched them talking, the bitterness so evident in their eyes. He ordered a black and tan. As soon as the mug had been brought to him, he pulled out the papers and began to read Mina's correspondence to Ujvari, and to read more carefully the translation Ujvari had mailed her earlier.

It seemed to Gance that the men who tortured Ujvari must have assumed that they knew where to find Mina. What could they have wanted from Ujvari? A confession of her nature? A confession of his own? If they believed so strongly in the creatures Mina said she had faced, perhaps finding the papers and making them public might have served their purpose. He read on.

An old man. A dead priest. Hardly proof, and yet Karina Aliczni's words were as compelling and believable as Mina's story had been, as emotionally charged as poor Arthur's ravings. Delusion? Most likely, yet Gance placed great weight on other's beliefs. How could he really know?

He picked up a copy of *The Times* that another patron had

left behind and scanned the headlines. As he'd expected, he did not have to risk contacting the police after all.

* * *

AFTER Gance left, Mina sat for some time in front of the window staring out at the garden. It was probably guilt that made her so certain that someone watched her every move. At least she had come as soon as she knew of the danger and would not have to blame Ujvari's death on her indecision.

Her single bag was packed. All she had to do was sit and wait. The moments between now and tonight, when she would face Jonathan, stretched eternally before her. To pass the time, she went upstairs and picked a novel from Gance's library. There, in the stillness so profound she could hear the downstairs clock ticking, she sat by the window and began to read.

The day brightened. The mists were burned slowly off by the insistent sun, revealing the intricate hedge maze, the stone patio. The lilacs were just budding in the March thaw, the few early bulbs already blooming in the front of the formal beds. If she and Gance had been lovers in the summer, would they have played night games here, naked satyr pursuing naked nymph through webs of greenery? Would Gance have taken her savagely on the scented clover lawn? She tried to imagine Jonathan in Gance's place and found the thought impossible. She forced her eyes back to the pages of her book. As she did, she heard the hound barking in the stable and looked outside. Motion on the lawn below her drew her attention back to the garden. She stood and walked close to the window.

Beneath her was an old man, his coat ragged, leaning wearily on a cane. He was bathed in sunlight, while she was hidden by the shadows of the library. He could not see her, yet he did look up. His face seemed terribly drawn and pale, as if he were ill. It seemed doubtful that he worked here; more likely he had come to beg. Mina had thought of ringing for a servant to see to him, had even looked behind her for the bell, when she heard the front door open, Gance's step on the stairs.

He carried a copy of the London *Times* and pointed to an article on the front page. "A fire destroyed Ujvari's house last night. The neighbors found the body soon after," he said as soon as he joined her. "No one will trace the information to us."

"Did you set the fire?"

"There was nothing of value there, and I might have overlooked something tying you to the crime."

"I see." Mina walked closer to the window. "A man was in the garden a while ago. He didn't appear to be a servant."

"Are you sure?"

"Not unless you dress your servants in rags."

"There's a wall. It would take some effort to climb over it unless, of course, some fool left the gate open."

"I heard your driver mention seeing a beggar. Perhaps the man followed us here. It could even be Sebescue's father, the old man who ran the bookstore."

Gance walked to the window and looked down at the gardens below. "He's not there now. I'll go and look for him."

"I'll come with you," Mina said and followed him quickly down the stairs.

Gance halted at the French doors that led from the dining room into the garden. "Wait!" he said and opened a drawer in the sideboard. The gun he sought was not in its place so he took a knife instead. He was about to ring for a servant when Mina gave a cry and pointed to the French doors leading to the patio.

The old man stood just outside, staring through the glass at them with eyes glazed by the beginnings of cataracts. Though a cape covered his body, Mina could see that his stance was stooped and he leaned heavily on the cane. "Hardly a threat," Gance said. "Let's make certain he's just a vagrant before I have him thrown out." He handed Mina the knife and opened the doors.

The man's expression did not change as they approached him. He stood, one hand on the walking stick, the other hidden beneath his cloak. "You are Lord Gance?" he asked in thickly accented English.

Gance nodded.

"You are Ion Sebescue?" Mina asked.

"Yes," the man replied, his attention still on Gance. "Your carriage was far from its usual route last night."

"A business matter," Gance said.

"A translation," the man responded. "And you found the body my son so pathetically concealed."

"He didn't have to kill Mr. Ujvari," Mina said. "He'd done nothing wrong."

"He attacked my son. James had the right to defend himself. What James did after was a precaution, nothing more."

"Your son did more than defend himself," Mina retorted. "I saw the body. I know what he did."

"Ujvari was your accomplice."

"In what crime?" Gance demanded.

"To the crimes the woman would commit if I do not stop her." Ion Sebescue's voice was bitter, desperate. Gance moved toward him. As he did, the old man raised the gun he had been hiding beneath the cloak. "Sit on the ground," he said, keeping the weapon pointed at Gance.

They did as he asked. "What do you want with us?" Gance asked.

"My son and I have been on a hunt, Lord Gance. We have hunted the woman as we hunt all her kind." He slid his hand down the cane, lifted it and pointed the sharpened tip at Mina's chest.

"My kind?" Mina wanted to laugh, but she was not so certain any longer. "Look at me." She pulled back her lips. "There are no fangs in my mouth." She raised her skirt and pointed to a scrape on her shin. "I received this yesterday. If I were a vampire it would have healed, would it not?"

"The journal you gave to Mr. Ujvari to translate could only have come from the devil's lair. No one can go there and leave of their own free will unless—"

"Dracula is dead," Mina told him. "Abraham Van Helsing told

us what to do. We pounded a stake through his heart. We cut off his head. His body is dust. I saw it crumble." Mina noted the glimmer of hope in the old man's eyes, saw him look almost joyfully from her to Gance. In that instant, he noticed the tip of the mark Mina had made on Gance's neck. He fixed his attention on Mina, noting the cut on her chest, the bruise around it. His expression hardened to rage, his grip on his weapon tightened.

"You lie! They only let you go because though you still live and walk by day, in death you will become one of them. *Nosferatu*. You will rise here, spreading their curse through mankind. Their way is your way, even if you do not know it yet. May God have mercy on both your souls."

Mina had done everything right, Gance thought. She had kept the old man talking, had kept his attention on her as Gance waited for the safest moment to attack. It would never come. "No!" Gance bellowed and lunged. He was a moment too slow. The gun fired, hitting him in the chest.

Sebescue dropped the revolver and charged Mina, the stake held high in both hands. She rolled sideways, lashing out with the hand that held the knife. She had intended to do nothing more than deflect his blow, but the blade slipped off the stake and into the old man's stomach just below his ribs. He fell against her, the weight of his body pushing the knife deeper. His hands clutched her, weakening, trying to destroy with the last bit of life left in his body.

Servants, responding to the shot, were running from the house and grounds as Sebescue died. The cook carried a cleaver; the groom had unleashed the hound. With no foe to hunt any longer, the dog ran to his master and licked his hand. While the butler saw to Gance, the cook rolled the body off Mina and tried to calm her, but she could scarcely hear the soothing words. There was blood on the ground, blood on her hands and arms and white lace blouse, blood flowing far too swiftly from Gance's chest.

So many had died defending her! Too many! "Gance!" she screamed and pulled out of the cook's grasp, crawling toward her lover. As the servants parted so she could go to his side, Mina bolted through the house and out the front doors.

Jonathan! If she could only reach him. Confess. Explain. He would know what to do. He would know.

The servants caught her waving her bloody hands, trying to hail a cab, sobbing because no one would stop. They took her inside and tried to calm her so they could clean the blood off her. She ranted, sobbed and would not allow it. Finally, with no other choice, they held her while the doctor who was treating Gance poured a dose of laudanum down her throat. Afterward, they locked her in the guest room until the drug took effect.

When she was sedated, pliant, lost in her own terrible thoughts, they bathed her and dressed her in a clean gown. She did not ask about Gance, lying unconscious in his bedroom. Indeed, she made no requests at all.

She ate when they fed her, did not protest when they left her with the suggestion that she try to sleep. She did exactly as they asked until the sedative wore off.

When she understood that she was a prisoner here, she began to pound on the door and demand to be released. In her state, the staff dared not let her go, and the doctor refused to drug her further. With his master near death, the head butler did the only thing that seemed right under the circumstances. He sent for Jonathan Harker.

CHAPTER TWENTY-ONE

I

As soon as Mina had left for the station, Millicent walked across town to Jonathan's office. As she described the nervous state Mina had been in when she left the house, it occurred to Jonathan that if Millicent had taken a cab here, he might have reached Mina before the train left. Most likely the thought of him and his wife having a scene at the station had been more of a scandal than Millicent could bear.

When Millicent had finished her story, she handed Jonathan the note Mina had written him. Her expression indicated that she'd expected this betrayal from Mina all along.

Duty done, Millicent sat silently while Jonathan opened the envelope and read the note. *I have urgent business in London concerning our trip to the Continent. When I come home, I will have the means to explain everything. I love you.* It all seemed so damning but for those last three words. She did love him, he had no doubt of it, just as he had no doubt that he loved her. Yet their ideas of love could well be worlds apart. It occurred to him that he had never really inquired what it was she expected from him. He had only assumed.

"I'll go now, Jonathan," Millicent said.

"I'll be home early." For the first time in a week, he thought as he said it, and winced.

Jonathan and his aunt did not speak about Mina that night. They hardly spoke at all. The few times he looked at her across the wide dining table, Jonathan saw a frigid determination in Millicent's expression and tried to mirror it in his own. Mina had no right to leave him with such a cryptic explanation, nor any right to keep secrets from him. He tried to be angry, and failed. He did not sleep at all that night, and in the morning he had no desire for food. Even if he'd wished to go to work, work would have been impossible.

No, he could not idly go about his business and wait for her to return. He said as much to his aunt as he packed a traveling bag. She stood in his bedroom doorway, her arms crossed, her eyes filled with fury. "After what she did, you would abandon you clients to go after her?"

"Aunt Millicent, Mina hinted at things you cannot understand."

"I know enough, Jonathan. This isn't the first time Mina has gone to London on the sly."

"What do you mean?"

"The portraits above the fireplace were not painted in London but here in Exeter. If you like, I can show you the man's card."

"It won't be necessary," Jonathan replied. "I will not judge her until I speak to her. Wire me at Seward's if you hear anything from her."

"Jonathan, you can't go after her."

He looked at her, thinking of all the kindness she had shown him over the years, and all the bitterness in her heart. "Wire me or you will no longer be welcome in this house," he said, buckled his suitcase straps and left.

He stopped at work only long enough to assign others to his own projects, then caught the mid-morning train to London.

He got off at Purfleet station and walked to Jack Seward's. He hadn't wired Seward. Someone was always at the asylum, and Jonathan was known to the staff. The walk led him past the ancient ruins of Carfax, and he shuddered, as if the horrors now vanquished still possessed the power to kill.

Seward was present when Jonathan arrived, along with a full staff and a few additional aids. "Early spring always brings out the lunacy in people," Seward said by way of apology, as he showed Jonathan into his cluttered and dusty quarters. "What brings you to London so suddenly?"

"I seem to have misplaced my wife," Jonathan replied, tried to smile and failed. He piled the magazines cluttering a parlor chair onto a second stack of them on the floor and sat, breathing deeply, trying to maintain his composure.

It took little prodding for Seward to discover what Jonathan knew, only a bit more to learn everything his friend believed, including his guilt for pushing Mina away. When Jonathan had finished, Seward poured them each a brandy before returning to his work, leaving Jonathan alone with the books and magazines and his own despair. As Seward went through his work, he found himself thinking far too often about Mrs. Harker, about what she had been through and about—dare he admit it!—what a fool her husband had become.

* * *

THE message Gance's butler sent traveled by wire from London to Exeter to Purfleet by early evening. It said little, only that there had been an accident, that Mrs. Harker was in need of attention and that Jonathan should come to London immediately.

"To Lord Gance's," Jonathan added bitterly when he'd finished reading it.

"They also write that Mina is ill," Seward noted.

It would be like Jack not to intrude unless invited. Jonathan longed to go alone, yet fear of what might have happened unnerved him. "Yes, I'm certain that's it," Jonathan said. "Please come with me. She may need your help."

Seward said little on the journey. Jonathan thought it just as well. He did not want to be pulled from his memory of the past, when he and Mina were just young, just poor, just foolishly in love. By the time he reached Gance's estate, he was ready to forgive her everything, and try to reclaim that innocent past.

Then he saw Gance's house—the high iron walls, the huge pillared portico, the entrance with its inlaid tiles of rosewood and mother-of-pearl and the electric sconces blazing in the hallway. He only glimpsed the fantasy parlor, the dining room easily capable of seating twenty or more. The wealth did not make him feel insignificant, for Gance had not earned it. Instead it diminished Mina in his eyes, as if she had succumbed to the trappings of the man rather than his worth. That made the most sense. In the years Jonathan had known Gance, he had never seen any hint of real substance.

Midway up the stairs, he heard the pounding coming from somewhere above them, Mina's demands to be released. Jonathan turned toward Seward, but his friend had already been alerted. "How long has she been like this?" Seward asked the butler.

"Since this afternoon. A man attacked Mrs. Harker and Lord Gance in the garden. She isn't wounded, but she's been overwrought ever since. She demands to go home, but we cannot just let her leave in her state."

At the top of the stairs, the butler led them away from the sounds. "I want to see my wife," Jonathan demanded.

"Lord Gance has asked to speak to you first."

Jonathan halted. "Do I see my wife or I do I go for the police?"

"Lord Gance is very anxious to tell you what happened. He has refused sedation while waiting for you."

"Sedation?" Seward asked.

"Lord Gance was nearly killed by the intruder. He's in a great deal of pain."

"I'll see him," Jonathan said. "After I have a moment with my wife."

"As you wish." As the butler walked down the hallway, he pulled out a ring of keys.

Mina's pounding had stopped for the moment, but it started up again as soon as the key clicked against the lock. As the door swung inward, she rushed for it, apparently intending escape. Jonathan caught her, gripping her wrists as she fought him. "It's all right, darling," he said calmly.

She looked at him, her eyes savage for a moment. Recognition came slowly. It brought an end to her struggles but no real peace, no relief.

"Jonathan? Jonathan, why are you here? Did Gance really send for you?"

She sounded anxious. Guilty. All his worst suspicions were true. How many times had she come here to be with him? More than Millicent knew, he guessed. Far more.

"They died because of me!" she cried, shaking in his arms. "All the blood, Jonathan. I didn't know there would be so much blood. All I wanted was to know the truth, and they died."

"Hush, Mina dear. It will be all right. We'll go home."

"They'll find us there. There's more of them, the hunters. Van Helsing is not the worst of them. I thought he was, but not anymore."

"She's hysterical," Seward whispered. "I'll give her a sedative."

"No! No more!" Mina cried. "I cannot bear the dreams!"

"Jack is here to help you, darling," Jonathan said, nodding to Seward as he spoke. "Let him."

"No!" She tried to push them both away, her nails ripping at Jonathan's hands, drawing blood. When she saw it, she stopped her struggles and stared at it, trembling with a new, more terrible fear. She did not protest when Seward gave her the injection, or when Jonathan laid her back on the bed. He held her hand as the trembling diminished; letting her go only when she went to sleep.

Some time later, the butler returned. "Lord Gance must see you now, Mr. Harker," he said to Jonathan.

Resigned to the confrontation, Jonathan followed him down the hall, leaving Seward alone with Mina.

II

While Gance had been lying motionless in the garden following the shooting, he'd heard quite distinctly the physician telling his butler that he was not expected to live. It seemed odd to Gance that a doctor could make such a pronouncement when he was still alive, and equally certain that he would remain that way. Gance clenched his fist and tried to mumble a denial. Words would not come.

Nonetheless, his motion must have alerted someone that he was close to consciousness. He felt the cold pressure of the stethoscope against his chest once, then twice more. "The bullet passed right through. That's encouraging," the doctor said in a tone clearly meant to placate his patient should he hear the words. "And the wounded lung does not seem to be hemorrhaging. If the chest cavity doesn't become septic, well, your master may have a chance."

A chance for what? That one day, hopefully far in the future, when he was too old for anything but memories, the sentence of death would be spoken and meant? Death comes to us all. How many times in how many churches had he heard those words? Now he understood. And as he lay there, more helpless than he had been even as a small child, he despised that end.

And he despised the pain as well, a terrible stab of it each time he tried to take a deep breath, to speak, or to moan.

Now, when life was so tenuous, he found the thought of Mina's vampires both beautiful and comforting. He clung to it as he was lifted and carried inside, as the doctor cut off his shirt and began to cleanse the wound. Then the pain grew, enfolding him, pressing out what remained of consciousness.

Later, Gance forced his eyes open. The doctor sat alone at his bedside, a book in his lap, the dog stretched on the carpet at his feet.

"How is Mina?" Gance asked.

"The woman was hysterical. She's sleeping now. Her family has been contacted."

Gance nodded. He would have done the same, he supposed.

"I'll give you another shot for the pain," the doctor said.

"No." Not yet. He had to stay awake, to think. "I want to be alert when the family arrives. They'll have questions," he said.

Mina, my dear Mina, was the secret in your blood? he thought. Was it carried to me by your bite like rabies even before I tasted your blood? Was I already diseased by it, doomed to eternity?

Doomed! If his side had not felt as if it were on fire, he would have laughed. He lay silent, contemplating the future until he fell into a fitful sleep in which he dreamed, as he often did in times of pain, of his father.

The previous Lord Gance had lain in bed for months before he finally succumbed to what his family privately termed debauchery. Though the man had been no more than fifty, his mind had failed him. Too young to understand what was happening, Gance watched in terror as his father's temper grew less predictable each day. The man demanded drink, foods he should not eat. The servants were forbidden to cater to him.

Gance, who loved him, had.

And when his father finally died—raving in his last hours for his dead wife, and for the mistress who was not permitted to enter his house—Gance had known who killed him.

When Gance was younger, he'd dreamed that his father's ghost had come to punish him. Now, he dreamed that he was in that bed, screaming for Mina, and for all the others he had used, to come and comfort him. He struggled as the darkness closed around him, fighting to wake before he died.

He was roused, some hours later, by the announcement that Jonathan Harker had arrived.

Page 256 — Marie Kiraly

With the horror of the attack and his dreams to strengthen his resolve, Gance replied, "Show him in." Gance did not ask to be made presentable, or to be propped up higher in the bed. His very helplessness would disarm this enemy, and he needed Harker impotent during the words he was about to say.

Gance had observed a number of Harker's moods in the past, but he had never sensed him dangerous until now. With his arms rigid at his side, his face red with fury, Harker refused a chair, standing instead at the foot of the huge Galle bed like some crazed specter from Gance's feverish dreams. "What have you done with my wife!" he demanded.

"I wooed her shamelessly. On the dance floor the night I first met her. At your dinner party. I kissed her in the yard of St. James Church. I think that even then she thought I was someone else."

Gance waited to see some flash of understanding. He was not disappointed. Jonathan sank into a chair. "Someone else," he echoed. The words were not spoken as a question.

"Even that hardly surprised me except that Mrs. Harker seemed to be such a practical, intelligent woman. Later, I discovered that her practicality was all a facade. Nothing else can explain what she did to me." He paused, giving Harker a chance to comment. When he didn't, Gance went on. "Come here, Mr. Harker. Let me show you."

Jonathan moved toward him, all anger dissipated, a terrible expression of fatality on his face.

Gance slowly raised his arm, moaning from the pain the motion caused, and pulled down the collar of his nightshirt. The mark Mina had made on his neck was darker now, a bruise in the shape of a pair of lips, the cut a red streak at its center. Gance heard the quick intake of breath, and Jonathan bent over to look at it. Pressing his case, Gance held out his cut palm. "I told the doctor that the man who attacked us did this, but she cut me here as well just last night.

"She is quite mad, you know, though I admit there is something wildly arousing in her insanity. I have never seen such a passionate woman. I could not believe that she would drink from me with such . . ."

Jonathan's face grew white, but, Gance noted clearly, the confession still did not confuse him. "Why are you telling all this to me?" Jonathan asked.

"Because Mina said that she will. There's some honor in being first and sparing her the words, especially when the lady is so apparently ill. I would not want you to think that her talk of what we did was . . . well, another delusion."

"If you weren't in your sickbed, I'd . . ."

"You'd what? Throttle me? Call me out? Jonathan Harker, I assure you that I would kill you. Then where would your darling Mina be? It's my nature to win even if the outcome is a sentence to the gaol."

"What happened to her?"

How calm Harker seemed, yet how concerned. So he loved his wife still, would most likely forgive her what he would see as a foolish display of passion. Poor Mina, Gance thought. She deserved better.

"Today?" Gance asked. "You've heard part of the story already. An old man, most likely a thief, was in the garden. Mina saw him and became quite agitated. As she had with me, I believe she thought him someone else. I told her I would send the man away personally. I ordered her to stay in the house, but she picked up a knife we had been using to cut fruit and followed me outside.

"I don't think the man would have harmed either of us, but when he saw her so distraught, it must have aroused the insanity in him as well. He raised his gun and shot me. As I fell, Mina attacked him. I never saw such fury.

"I'm thankful to her for saving my life, but I don't think that's why she did it. She called out a name as she lunged for him. Dracula, I think it was. Then another foreign word, *nosferatu.*

"Afterwards, she dropped to her knees beside me. She eyed my wound so intently I thought she meant to place her lips against it as she had against the cut on my hand. When the servants rushed around us, I said that it was me who had stabbed the old man. I shielded her because I did not think she was capable of answering any questions and because . . ."

"I quite understand." Though the words seemed to gag him, Harker added, "And I appreciate your candor. It will be of great help in treating her."

"You may stay here tonight if you wish."

Jonathan shook his head.

"Then use my carriage and driver to get to the station. I think that would be more secure than a public cab."

Jonathan stood and started for the door.

"Wait one moment," Gance said. "I want you to understand something. I pursued your wife because she is beautiful and intelligent and independent. I want you to know that had I any indication that Mrs. Harker was at all disturbed, I would not have gone near her. I have never been indiscreet when it mattered, and I find this situation most unfortunate for all of us.

"I intend to leave for Paris as soon as I am well enough to travel. I think it best under the circumstances that I go away for a while. There'll be talk of the killing, and we need to let the rumors die. Mina was not present when the police were summoned, and you can trust my staff not to mention that she was here." Gance didn't touch on their business dealings. Neither did Harker, he noted.

"And, if you would, ask the doctor to come in when you leave," Gance went on. "He has an injection he has been trying to give me since the first wore off this afternoon."

It had gone well, Gance decided after Harker and his wife had left. His driver would know if Harker had taken his wife to Seward's asylum or, hopefully for the woman, home.

If Mina had told her strange tale to him when he first met her, Gance might have wondered at her sanity. Once he knew her, he was certain something had happened. Now he was utterly convinced that Mina had told him the truth, for the steady, sensible Jonathan Harker had stared at the wound on his neck as if he had seen many like it before. No, they weren't all sharing the same delusion. They had all seen something they believed to be immortal and utterly deadly.

Well, one thing Gance had told Jonathan was true. It would be wise for him to leave England when he was well enough to travel. There were so many parts of the world he had not seen. He tried to recall where Mina had said the Borgo Pass was located. Near Odessa? Galati? No matter, he'd made certain that when he left, Mina would be coming with him. She'd show him the way.

III

Early in the morning, Jonathan conferred with Seward on what should be done for Mina. He began by telling of her affair, concluding bitterly, "I thought her obsession with Dracula was over when we returned from Transylvania. I was wrong."

"Memories survive, Jonathan, and they can be more damaging than the events that created them."

"What can be done?"

"Mina must be taught to control the past, to bury it if need be. It's difficult work, even for a man, and men are less emotional."

Jonathan thought of Arthur, his desperate search to end his loneliness by whatever means he could.

"Leave her with me for a while," Seward said.

"Here? In this house? After all that happened here?" The suggestion seemed impossible.

"I would go to Exeter if I could, believe me. Understand that she'll be safe here, far safer than if she had to explain the cause of her hysteria to another doctor."

"Could there be some grounds for Mina's belief? Have you heard from Van Helsing?"

"A brief note. He said that he had learned nothing new."

"May I see it?"

"I believe I threw it away."

"Van Helsing wrote Mina that all was well. Poor Mina. I wish I could remain here."

"It wouldn't be wise, Jonathan. She must have no audience for her delusions. Go home and let me treat her. In a week or two she'll be calmer and ready to see you again."

Jonathan went to Mina's room. He found her asleep, still in her clothes, with her face turned toward the open window. In the early dawn light, the ruins of Carfax darkened the sky, as much a blemish on the landscape as it was on their souls.

Seward had told him not to let Mina speak of her delusions. What could they say to each other besides good-bye? He placed on the desk the blank journal and pen he had purchased for her, and wrote a note on the opening page. With one last loving glance at his wife, he left the room as quietly as he was able.

PART FOUR

Karina

CHAPTER TWENTY-TWO

I

On the long ride to Purfleet, I lay quietly in Jonathan's arms, thankful that he was content to hold me and ask no questions. By the time we reached the asylum, much of Jack's injection had worn off. Even so, I went passively to the room they offered me, not caring that it was the same room where I had first faced Dracula. I found myself looking at the bed, with its new, overly bright, green coverlet, and at the window through which he had come.

The memory of what he did held no terror for me now, but rather instilled in me a strange peaceful fatality. I am utterly different from the innocent Mina who slept here before, a shy bride with an ill bridegroom. Yet I suppose I have not changed so much from my ordeal. After all, I was innocent enough to believe that I could actually return from the Continent and have everything go back to the way it had been before the vampire altered our lives.

As if memories could die so easily. As if I would have wanted that innocence restored. I looked out at the distant ruins of Carfax, then to Jonathan, who stood so uneasily in the doorway. "It's all right," I said. "The place holds no terror for me now."

"I'm glad of that." His eyes were scanning the room. Wondering

what he was looking for, I turned my face back to the window. On the edge of my vision, I saw him grab a letter opener and scissors from the desk and put them in his pocket.

"I'm not suicidal, if that's what worries you," I said.

"Lord Gance told me about both of you. Is it true?" he asked.

I nodded but said nothing. There was, after all, nothing to say.

"He showed me his neck, and his hand. Mina, my love, why?"

He asked, and I had vowed not to lie any longer. "The blood, Dracula's blood, is still in me. It lives."

"Dracula is dead, Mina. Van Helsing says that once he dies . . ."

Van Helsing! They were always speaking of Van Helsing as if he were the final judge of everything unknown. I hid my anger but not the thought behind it. "Van Helsing didn't know everything," I said. "He even admitted as much when he decided to remain behind. Yes, Jonathan, there is no scar on my face any longer, but it means nothing. Dracula is still alive, I tell you. I have felt him in me since that first night he came to me in this very room. Gance . . ."

"Don't say it," Jonathan whispered, and the anguish in his voice seemed to pierce my heart.

If my future and my sanity had not depended on my honesty now, I would have run to him, hugged him and begged forgiveness. Instead I stood with my hands clasped tightly and forced myself to go on. "I must, and you must listen. Gance aroused the creature I almost became. But it was my choice to let it loose. Now the vampire is alive, Jonathan, he is inside of me with all his needs and power."

"Mina, how can you believe such a terrible thing?"

I laughed. Though I knew he wouldn't understand, I could not help myself. I had been foolish enough to think that words alone could make him understand. I should have waited and shown him. "It doesn't have to be terrible, Jonathan." I saw his reaction, the horror in his eyes. Nonetheless, I continued, looking evenly at him, refusing to be ashamed. "It isn't," I added, certain that this was the bravest act I had ever committed.

Jonathan moved away from me and walked toward the door. I had a premonition that if I let him leave, I would never see him again. It *was a foolish feeling, but so real that I did beg him, "Stay with me, darling. Stay with me tonight."*

"After him, after this?" The softness of Jonathan's voice revealed not a hint of his fury.

"Jonathan, have you ever felt real passion? Dracula showed that to me. And passion free of fear? Gance taught me that."

I saw no change in his expression. He would have faced Gance this way, and Gance would have thought his incredible self-control nothing more than weakness and pliancy. I wish I could have said that Gance and I were nothing to one another, but for my part at least, it was not true. I could not apologize for my deeds, either, nor lie and recant them. I had made a decision. I would not lie any longer. "The dreams are still with me, but I no longer fear them. I can control his blood, Jonathan. I'm strong enough now."

"This isn't you, Mina," he said.

"I saw your drawings of the vampire women," I replied. "You've changed as well as I. Don't fight what you feel, Jonathan. Please!"

For the first time, I glimpsed the grief he hid so well. "Someone else is speaking through you, Mina. Someone I could never love." He turned to leave. I gripped his arm, forcing him to wait.

"I have to talk to you," I said. "So much has happened, you must know of it."

"I am aware," he said, his frigid tone hiding the hurt he must feel. "Perhaps tomorrow."

"Jonathan, your life may depend on it."

"Tomorrow," he repeated firmly and left.

It amazed me that he could go without listening to what I had to tell him. We were allies once, he and Jack and I and all the others. Now, when there was so much he should know, I heard the click of the lock. I opened the window and saw the bars that covered it. This was not a guest room any longer, but a private cell for a privileged inmate. I pressed my face against the bars and listened to the silence. From somewhere deep in the house a woman began to sob, her cries rising and falling in the night. When I slept, I did not dream. I think my life has become the nightmare, and there is no need for any other.

This morning, I found a journal and pen on the desk along with a note from Jonathan. He tells me that he loves me. He asks me to record my thoughts to help Seward treat me. So Seward is to read them. I have written in longhand to save him the trouble of arranging a transcription. I want him to know how I feel. Perhaps through him the others can be warned.

II

Mina's closing words were a lie. When she was not recording the details of last night's conversation, she had been privately considering her situation. It did not occur to her that a lesser woman might remain hysterical, or that the display of weakness she had shown the night before was natural. Instead, she simply resolved to be strong with the same determination she'd had when she resolved to confess everything to Jonathan. He hadn't given her a chance. Now she would have to hide whatever she believed in order to make her visit here as short as possible.

She refused to contemplate where she would go once she left Seward's.

Seward came to see her in mid-morning. He found her dressed, her bonnet on her head, her cloak laid across the foot of the bed. He was prepared for a battle. Instead, she was standing at the open window, looking down at the grounds below. "I feel ever so much better, Jack," she said. "Do you suppose we could go outside for a walk? The view from this window is so oppressive."

"I'm sorry you had to be given this room. The only other one is mine, and it's so cluttered with books and patient files that I could hardly give it to a guest."

"But I'm not a guest, am I, Jack? Perhaps you could put me in the asylum with the other lunatics."

He flushed. "No," he said. "You've had a terrible shock, but you hardly belong there."

She laughed. "Well, that's encouraging, anyway." She walked past him, through the door and down the stairs. She paused on the steps of his house to wait for him, and link her arm through his. "You'd best hold on to me, Jack, or I might fly away like a bird, or should I humor your belief that I am delusional and say 'bat'?"

Seward smiled and patted her hand. They walked on until they came to a little bridge over a creek flowing into the Thames. Willows grew along the banks, and there was a covered gazebo close to the water. He took Mina there and sat beside her. "Tell me what happened yesterday?" he said.

"I cannot start my story there, Jack, because it began long before that, even before we left Transylvania."

She lied, but only a little. She told him that she had found the book in the gypsy cart, below Dracula's box of earth. She told him, too, of the feeling that she had, the feeling that whatever poison had been put in her was still there, infecting her. She spoke of her trip to London to find a translator, of the attack on Winnie Beason. She mentioned the note Gance had sent to her and how they had discovered Ujvari floating in the river.

"I felt so guilty then, Jack. His death was my fault, you see. If I had told Jonathan about the book and about my feelings, we might have contacted Van Helsing for help. Instead, I acted alone and the outcome was terrible."

"Guilt is not hysteria, Mina," Seward explained patiently. "You were hysterical when Jonathan and I saw you."

"The old man in Gance's garden was James Sebescue's father. He was going to kill me, Jack. He called me *nosferatu*." She described the attack as it had happened. "There was blood everywhere. Yes, with the past horror so recent and vivid, I suppose I did lose my mind. So they drugged me, Jack, and I dreamed of Dracula and the terrible night he made me drink from him. I woke. I pounded on the door until my hands were sore." She showed him the bruises. "But no one came until you and Jonathan arrived."

She sensed that he wanted to believe her, to hold and comfort her, but he remained aloof, a doctor rather than a friend, and a friend only because he could not be something more. "We should go back," he said. "I'll have the staff clear my room. You can sleep there tonight."

In a calculated, seemingly impetuous gesture that Lucy would have envied, Mina kissed Seward's cheek. "You always were so kind to me, but the move isn't necessary," she said and pulled him to his feet, starting back toward the asylum, willingly it seemed.

He stopped just inside the door. "I must work," he said.

"I understand, Jack. May I choose a book to take upstairs to occupy my time?"

"Yes. Yes, of course." He led her into his study and pointed to the shelves along one wall. "Take more than one, if you like."

"I would like to know as much as possible about my illness."

"Then take this." He handed her a book by Henry Maudsley. "It discusses the origins of dreams."

"And a novel, Jack. Something light to pass the time." She reached for *The Count of Monte Cristo* because its binding was worn. She assumed it had been read many times.

She was correct. "Have you read it?" Seward asked with a new warmth in his voice.

"Yes," she responded. "It is such a beautiful tragedy. Do you suppose that lovers so perfect for one another can ever find happiness with others?"

"If they can accept that as their fate," he replied.

"Is that what life is, Jack? Acceptance?"

He knew exactly what she meant. "I'll help you," he said.

A servant brought them lunch. After they ate, he showed her back to her room, apologizing profusely before he locked her inside.

In truth, she welcomed the solitude. The words were already forming in her mind. Wincing with the hypocrisy of them, she opened the journal and began to write.

I began to tell Jack all the secrets I had kept from Jonathan with a sense of fatality. Someone must know them, and Jack, like Van Helsing, is trained to listen and understand. I found my confession so easy as we sat by the river, and I felt a great closeness to him. He treats me as an equal, the way Van Helsing did, and the way Jonathan does so rarely now. I think that is why I am able to speak to Jack so easily.

Mina paused. The sudden memory of Seward's daily examinations on their journey East returned. She recalled his fingers lifting her lips, moving through her mouth, feeling her teeth to see if they had grown. She shivered, as if shaking the images from her mind. Thinking only of what had to be done, she went on.

I have become so useless to Jonathan. All our dreams of being helpmates vanished with his sudden success. I have servants to keep house. He has clerks to help him with his work. My position all too often resembles that of an obedient pet—I am pampered so long as I adore. Even the woman's domain, the care of the house, has been ceded to another.

Yet I feel a need to help where I can. Tonight I shall ask Jack if there is some work I could do during my treatment here. I may not have formal training, but I have an instinct for dealing with people. If that isn't possible, I could work in his office. I think he could use some assistance with the files. Like all busy men, he has so little time to organize the clutter in his life.

Was the flattery too obvious? Much of what she wrote was actually true; only the tone was off. Somehow, she doubted he would detect the deceit. When she'd finished, she placed one of her hairs across the corner of the last page and closed the book.

At dinner that evening, Mina noticed that Seward had dressed more formally, arranged to have the table set and included a wineglass at her place. "Do you think it's wrong for me to drink?" she asked as he poured it.

"It is a weakness, Mina. I don't drink because I don't believe in giving in to weakness, but I could certainly understand that others . . ."

"Then I won't have it," Mina declared and set it aside. "I want to get well, Jack. I want you to do whatever is necessary to help me get well."

"And what do you think is necessary, Mina?"

"That I not dwell on the past. That I be useful to someone. You said you were so busy. There must be something I can do."

Seward thought a moment. "There is. We have inmates who cannot read but find stories and poetry a great comfort. If you could just read to them for an hour or two every day it would be welcomed."

For the first time, Seward spoke of his patients as individuals, each with his or her own needs. This revealed a different side of him, one Mina had never suspected. "I would be happy to help, Jack," she said sincerely.

Later, as she sat in one of the quieter rooms of the asylum, reading a poem by Robert Browning to a girl whose face was an impassible mask hiding all emotions, she noticed Seward standing in the doorway. He listened. He watched. For a moment, Mina wondered at the intensity of his expression, then she noticed the girl, tears rolling down her cheeks though her blank expression did not change.

Mina's voice remained steady, but when the poem was done, she set aside the book and gathered the trembling girl in her arms, stroking her matted hair, paying no mind to her dirty clothing or the smell of old sweat that hung about her. Instead, Mina hummed softly, rocking the girl back and forth, comforting her with the pressure of her arms.

I felt humbled by my own instincts, Mina wrote that night. *The girl never spoke. She never indicated any particular poem, yet I chose one that touched her. What a sad past she must have had to have isolated herself so perfectly from those around her. What wonderful work Jack does. And how kind he is to those in his care.*

If Winnie were here, Jack would learn exactly how kind, Mina knew. Winnie would not tolerate the filth of the asylum, the way the staff treated the inmates with boredom and occasional cruelty, or how Seward turned a blind eye to all of it. If her entire focus were not on leaving this place, Mina would have voiced her outrage as well. Instead she hid it as best she could and, when it surfaced, lied about its source.

<h1 style="text-align:center">III</h1>

When three days had passed without Mina contacting her, Winnie Beason grew concerned. She sent a note to the Harker house. It was not answered. Discreet inquiries revealed that Mina was apparently visiting friends in London. Winnie did not believe it. She sent a wire to Gance and requested an immediate reply. None came.

Winnie had met Jonathan only a few times, but she thought she knew him. Honest. Upright. A bit dull. Not at all the equal of his wife in either wit or intelligence and well aware of the fact. In short, he resembled so many other husbands, save that, like Mr. Beason, he was fiercely in love with his wife.

She wasn't solely aware of that because Mina had told her so. Anyone who saw them together could not help but notice it.

Yet Jonathan was in town, going about his business as usual. This puzzled Winnie. She knew that if she were missing, Mr. Beason would be frantic with worry. She expected the same of Jonathan Harker. Therefore, he must know exactly where Mina was. Winnie decided to force the information from him.

She went to his office. Denied an appointment, she sat in the lobby until it became clear that she would wait the day, if necessary, just to speak to him.

What did she expect? she wondered. Since he knew where his wife had gone, he must also know where she'd been. Winnie could hardly expect him to welcome her prying. He seemed only tolerant as he offered her tea. She declined, then scandalized him by asking for sherry instead. He poured her a small glass, slowly, as if measuring just the right amount for a woman.

Winnie laughed. "More, please. I think the amount Mina takes to help her sleep would be about right for this conversation." She saw the shock in his expression and laughed. "Mr. Harker, in the few weeks your wife has lived in Exeter, we have gotten to know one another quite well. She told me about the sherry. Among other things."

As she had last time she was here, after Mina's fainting spell at the hospital, she went directly to the point. She explained how she had accompanied Mina to the station and seen her off on the train for London. Mina was supposed to contact her and had not done so. "I assume that you've heard from her," she said.

"Yes." Jonathan stared down at his desk top. "She is remaining in London for a time."

"Is she all right?"

"You've seen how fragile she's become." He looked her squarely in the face as he finished. "She is quite ill. She is remaining in London for treatment. She'll contact you when she can."

"Is she so ill that she cannot put a pen to paper?" Winnie asked with real concern.

"Not physically, no."

Winnie had intended to push him, but she heard the anguish in his voice and admired his candor. He still loved Mina, that much was clear. Yet his voice held traces of weariness, as if the love had become a chore he'd grown tired of performing. "I'm sorry, Mr. Harker," Winnie said. "Please, give Mina my love. Be sure to tell her that a woman who can face the undead can survive any lesser shock."

Winnie's revelation had the effect she'd desired. "She told you about that?" Harker asked incredulously.

"Oh, yes. She told me about Dracula, and Lucy Westerna, about all of you and what you did in the East."

"You must have thought she was raving."

"On the contrary, I believed every word Mina said because she spoke them." She leaned across Jonathan's desk, as if about to impart some great secret. "You see, I have faith in Mina. But of course you understand that well enough."

"I did." His voice held traces of bitterness, the emotion well hid.

Winnie, finding the clue to how much she could reveal, plunged on. "Until Lord Gance?" she asked.

His expression grew more bitter. "You knew!"

She nodded. "I hardly approved, but I understood. We are taught such rubbish, Mr. Harker. Sometimes it takes a desperate act to unlearn it."

"But that she could love him. It's unthinkable, insane."

"Love!" Winnie wanted to laugh at him. Men could be so incredibly dense when it suited their egos. "Did she tell you that?"

He shook his head.

"She didn't love him. She didn't even care for him. Go and ask Mina what he was to her. The answer won't come as a surprise. I think you already know it."

"I'd like you to go now," Jonathan said.

"Not until you tell me where she is."

"This does not concern you," Jonathan replied. "Now, please go."

"It does concern me. She confided a great deal to me because she saw no way to confide in you."

"Go!" he bellowed.

"Where is she?" Winnie repeated, calmly, as if their conversation were still a cordial one. "I will leave when you tell me where she is."

He stalked from the room, taking his coat from the rack, then slamming the outer door behind him. Winnie sighed and picked up her things. Stopping in the outer office, she noted the sudden silence. As she stood, wondering what to do next, the typewriter began to clatter again, a conversation between a clerk and a client continued.

Though it wasn't a workday for her, Winnie stopped at the hospital and pulled the last three issues of the London *Times* from the stack the volunteers kept for patients to read. She spread them out on one of the tables in the nursery and began to scan the news she usually skipped—the tales of killings, beatings and robberies that seemed to plague all big cities these days.

On the bottom of the front page, she found a follow-up story on Anton Ujvari's murder. The report noted the further mystery that Ujvari's death had taken place days before the fire occurred. Police speculated that the fire and murder were not linked, the fire possibly started accidently by looters who had entered the abandoned house.

Mina had been too late.

And the fire?

The knowledge of James Sebescue's attack and death, her affair with Gance, even the loss of the child would not have been enough to push Mina into the insanity her husband hinted now possessed her. This had to be at the root of her problem.

Winnie tore out the story and finished her work quickly. It was time to go home, she decided, and well past time to have a frank talk with Mr. Beason.

* * *

THE housekeeper had fixed a lunch. Winnie took a tray to Margaret's room and ate with her. She had just finished when someone pounded on her front door. Winnie cracked open the door enough to examine the Scotland Yard identification the man offered her.

"Are you here about the robbery?" Winnie asked after she'd shown the man into her parlor and offered him a seat in her most ornate and least comfortable chair.

He seemed far too young to be an investigator and most aware of it. He sat stiffly on the edge of his chair, twisting the brim of his hat as he spoke. "We've identified the man you killed. His name was James Sebescue."

"I'm sorry, but the name means nothing to me."

"I doubted that it would, but you see, there is another mystery here."

Winnie leaned forward, "Such a terrible affair. My maid was wounded, you know. But mysteries. Sir, I do cherish them so."

"Then you should appreciate this one. It seems that two days after James Sebescue was shot while attempting to rob your house, his father, Ion Sebescue, an aged and somewhat crippled man, was killed by Lord Gance while attempting to rob the Gance estate in London. What do you make of that?"

"Why, nothing. Except, of course, that I know Lord Gance. Everyone in Exeter does; he sees to it." She hesitated, then asked, "Can you tell me what happened?"

"The report will be in *The Times* this afternoon. According to the statement we were finally able to take from Lord Gance—"

"Finally? Was he hurt?"

"Seriously. He was shot by the man. Though badly wounded, Lord Gance then attacked and overpowered him, stabbing him with a knife he'd been carrying."

"Were there any witnesses?"

"A servant, I believe. According to the report I was sent, the woman was too hysterical to question. Now, I'd like to ask again, do you have any thoughts on why two men, bookstore owners with no criminal records, would suddenly become thieves?"

Winnie shook her head. "The usual need for money, I suppose. But I can swear, sir, that I never saw James Sebescue before he broke into my house and attacked me. As for his father . . ." She hesitated long enough to get the inspector's undivided interest. "If he was truly infirm, his son's death might have unbalanced him. Robbing Lord Gance could have been a simple act of revenge on someone else who was a native of Exeter. Then again, robbing Lord Gance is somewhat akin to suicide, don't you think?"

"I really don't know. I suppose that it's possible." He seemed suddenly anxious to go. He stood and handed her a card. "If you can think of any other connection, please contact me."

"I'm sure more will come to me. Is Lord Gance staying in London? I'd like to send him a note. Perhaps if we confer on this, we can find a better connection."

"I believe he is."

"Then until we speak again . . ." She smiled sweetly, as if she'd just made him a promise, then led him to the door. "Good day," she said and closed it softly behind him.

After dinner that evening, Winnie told her husband everything that had happened to Mina. Like Jonathan, he believed Mina to be unbalanced. Unlike Jonathan, he had no valid reason for assuming otherwise.

"I am going to London tomorrow, Emory," she declared, the use of his Christian name making it clear that she was utterly serious. "I have to see Mina. It's the least I can do."

"After being attacked by a fanatic, and lying to police about his motives, I think you've done enough, Mrs. Beason." He waited for her scowl before adding, "But since you'll undoubtedly go whether I approve or not, I might as well give my blessing. You have a tremendous heart, dearest. It's your greatest virtue."

"Is it?" She walked to the other side of the table and lifted her skirts, straddling him on the dining chair. Before he could protest, she kissed him with so much enthusiasm that she nearly tipped over the chair, and the table as well.

"One of your greatest virtues?"

"Better." She kissed the bare spot on the top of his head.

"You're not going until morning, are you?"

"On the earliest train. I'll stay with Patty Walker."

"Be sure to take an extra five pounds," he said.

"Whatever for?"

"The fines, dearest. The last few times you stayed with Miss Pat, weren't you arrested for stoning members of Parliament?"

"We merely demonstrated for the vote," she said and gave him a good-natured jab in the ribs before leaving him just long enough to lock the doors and shut the drapes.

CHAPTER TWENTY-THREE

I

The day after he received it, Gance's wound threatened to become infected. The doctor treated it with alcohol and poultices, the patient's pain with morphine, until Gance was no longer certain that he would survive.

And in his delirium, his dreams grew terrible—of torture, of demons, of a hell he'd created for himself so many years before.

A less-determined man might have peacefully passed on; Gance fought death with every bit of effort he possessed. When Winnie Beason arrived, she found him sitting up in bed in a mauve silk dressing gown, devouring a huge plate of eggs and sausage and fried potatoes.

"You look remarkably well for a man grievously wounded just a few days ago," Winnie said.

"Willpower, Mrs. Beason. I hoard it for truly important matters."

She laughed. He started to, then winced and settled for a smile instead. "What brings you here?" he asked. "Certainly not concern for my health."

"I'm looking for Mina Harker."

"Here? Have you heard rumors I've somehow missed?"

"Mina said she was meeting you in London. If she is not here, I would think you'd know where I should look."

"For what reason? Do you have the rest of the translation?"

"The rest of what?"

"I went with her to find Anton Ujvari. He had burned the book, I assume just before he was attacked, since the cover must have been pulled from his fireplace. The man would not have burned it if he hadn't finished the work. According to a letter he never mailed, he had placed it in a safe place. I assume he meant that he'd sent it to his client, one Mrs. Beason of Exeter." Gance laughed. "You aren't Mina's only confidant, Winnie dear."

"I see that, but sadly Anton Ujvari took his secret to the grave. Now, where is Mina?"

"I don't know, though I have a good idea where to start looking for her. Now, if I am to crawl off what until yesterday was my deathbed to help you, I need some incentive. Winnie, don't scowl. Reach into the drawer in the night table and look at the sheets Mina gave me."

Winnie did as he asked and recognized them immediately. She sighed. "I'd give you the rest of the translation to read if I had it. I do not. Now, please, for Mina's sake, where is she?"

"You're certain that she's not at home?"

Winnie nodded.

"Then she has to be at Seward's," he said.

"Are you certain? If we go and aren't certain, Seward can lie."

"Seward will lie in any event. But, yes, she's there. My driver took her and Harker there. I would think that someone like Mina would be too precious for Seward to release, and he is persuasive enough to convince Jonathan that his wife's hysteria could be protected there." Gance's logic was impeccable, and his grin implied that he knew it. "The question is, now that we're certain, what shall we do?"

II

Each night the mists closed around the asylum at Purfleet. Each night Mina stared out at them then went to sleep on the bed she had pushed close to the window. With the breezes soft and damp against her skin, she dreamed of her last visit to this house. The Maudsley book implied that a recurring dream meant something more than its face value.

If so, Mina thought, hers meant freedom.

From convention. From conventional relationships. And, God knew, from Jack Seward.

She recalled how Lucy had described Seward's straightforward, rather nervous proposal. When Lucy turned him down, he'd asked if there was another suitor. He must have been pleased to hear that there was and that he had not been rejected for himself alone.

Mina wondered why he was not married, for truthfully any intelligent woman could control him easily. Perhaps they all saw through him, as she did. The more she infatuated him with her wit, her helpfulness, her glowing references to him in her journal, the more she understood the incredible ego of the man.

Yet he trusted her too, enough that she might have escaped that morning. They had been walking the grounds when a sudden emergency in the asylum called him back. She had asked to wait for him on the terrace, and he had agreed.

Had she been certain that this was not a test of her reliability, she might have gone. Instead, she was content to bide her time here with the staff and the lunatics, not certain to which group she belonged.

Today Mina had achieved a breakthrough with the blank-faced girl who'd cried when she heard Browning. She had taken the girl to her own room, helped her bathe and wash her hair. When she was clean, Mina gave her fresh clothes then combed out her hair in front of the mirror. The work took most of the afternoon, and when she was through, the girl smiled and shyly whispered her name, "Annie." She beamed when Mina said her own in return.

"Annie is reaching out to you," Seward said when she told him. "You're a woman. Perhaps she feels more comfortable being with you. You would be a great asset to this place."

"Is that an offer, Jack?"

"I hadn't meant it quite that way, but yes, I think it is. When you're well enough to decide what you want to do, consider it."

Night six, she thought, as she brushed out her hair and extinguished the light. A long howl coming from the lawn, like the cry of a wolf or a large dog, made her heart race with fear. She ran to the window and stared down at the grounds.

Near the wall, she saw a figure of a man dressed in a dark inverness, a large hound walking beside him.

As she watched through the bars of her window, a carriage rode slowly by on the road. In its light, she saw the man in the inverness more clearly, the whisps of white-blond hair falling over his forehead. At that distance, she could not have been certain that Gance had come for her, but the presence of the dog made it clear. This was a wolfhound the size of Byron. Gance had told her that there were few so large.

She hastily lit the lamp, held it up to the window and extinguished it again.

The carriage lamp dimmed then flared once more.

Signal received, she saw Gance open the carriage door. When dog and master were inside, the carriage moved slowly on in the direction of Carfax.

She heard the howling again after sunrise, ran to her window and saw the carriage in the light, dog and master once more walking on the edge of the road. She grabbed a white scarf from her dressing table and waved. Though Gance must have seen her waving, he wisely gave no indication.

Again the carriage moved on; this time she saw it turn into the old drive leading to Carfax. At the place where the wall between the estate and the asylum was highest, it disappeared from view. Though Mina watched for some time, it did not reappear farther down the drive.

Gance waited for her! She dressed quickly, then sat and wrote quickly in her journal.

I asked Jack yesterday if he would have some work for me, and he said he would when I was well. I asked him when that would be, and he said when Jonathan decides so. "After all," he noted in his logical way, "if you thought Jonathan delusional or despondent, would you want him to determine when his treatment would end?"

"Do you think I'm ill?" I asked him.

"Obsessed," he replied. "But so much better."

And it's true. I am better, and if Jonathan would only come, I would show him how much better. I find it terrible that he would leave me here so coldly after all we've been through.

I've made a decision. Jack, I know you will read this and I want to put your mind at ease. I am going back to Jonathan. I will face him and demand to be released from my marriage. He had grounds, and once it is done and I am free of him, I will come back and work with you if you will still have me.

Please do not be concerned. I have the means to travel. I will write as soon as I am home.

She returned the book to its drawer, then knocked on her door until one of the aids unlocked it. "I would like to have breakfast alone with Anne," she said. "Dr. Seward gave me permission to work with her."

"It will be ready in an hour, madam. You can dine in the room where you read to her."

They ate together. Mina talked a great deal. Annie, as always, said little, though Mina was certain the girl listened and understood. Seward joined them for tea, then agreed to Mina's request that the three of them take a walk on the grounds. "She looks so much better, doesn't she?" Mina asked him, knowing it was the clean clothes, the combed hair, the kindness that made it appear so.

"She does," he said. His arm was linked with Mina's while Annie moved ahead of them going in the direction Mina had pointed out to her, toward the corner of the grounds where the wall to Carfax and the main road met, moving faster than Mina walked, increasing the distance between herself and the couple.

When she was near the road, Annie turned to Mina and saw her nod. With a shriek, the girl bolted, jumping the low wall and disappearing into the stand of willows and brush on the opposite side of the road.

"Go after her, Jack. I'll get help."

Seward ran. He caught Annie easily and took her, squealing with happiness at how she'd duped him, back to the house. Only after he'd given her to the care of an aide did he realize that Mina had gone.

*   *   *

By then, Gance's hired carriage had pulled out of Carfax with Mina, Gance and Winnie hiding in the back. Though Mina was fairly certain that Seward would believe her letter to be true, they did not return to Gance's house. Instead, they traveled south through London, stopping only long enough to give the dog to the care of a servant before continuing on to Croydon. After they made arrangements for rooms, Gance suggested that they eat.

"Rest first," Mina said. "You're hurt. Your wound even opened on the ride." She spoke of it so naturally, as if his bleeding were common knowledge. He lifted the corner of his shirt and saw the tiny circle of red. Winnie gaped at her. Mina shrugged. "I just know," she said.

They compromised and dined in a private room, Gance stretched out on a bed, the women at the table beside the bed. Gance ate carefully, almost as daintily as the women, taking small bites and swallowing with some difficulty. His breathing was shallow, his expression somewhat strained, as if hiding his pain were becoming as great a trial as the pain itself.

"Now that you're a free woman, Mina dear, where do you want to go?" Winnie asked.

"I never thought of that. I only wanted to be free of Seward,"

Mina replied. "You've brought me this far, Gance. Where would you take me?"

"We can go to France. I have friends in Paris. Your husband won't be able to touch you there," Gance suggested.

Winnie shook her head. "Don't," she said.

"What should I do, then? Go back to Jonathan?"

"You have to face him."

"He will do what Millicent wants. He will do what convention demands. I'll face him, Winnie, but only when I have proof that what I feel is not some delusion that Seward or another like him can repair."

Winnie pointed to the translation. "Give him this. Tell him how you feel."

"It isn't enough. I need proof, not just for him but for me. I'll find it . . ." Her voice trailed off, the sudden thought of what she needed to face having unnerved her.

"At Dracula's castle," Gance finished for her. "I'll go with you."

"You're in no shape to travel," Winnie snapped.

"I will be soon enough. A day or two in Paris followed by a luxurious trip east in a private car will be easy enough on my recovery. By the time we reach Transylvania, I'll be ready for the overland ride. If I'm not, we can find Van Helsing. We ought to find him anyway, unless we want to end up permanent residents of that castle."

"You would do this for me?" Mina asked incredulously.

"No, Mrs. Harker. I do it for me. This is the sort of adventure Old Uncle Byron himself would have relished." He raised his mug of ale in a jaunty salute to the dead.

"Since it's settled then, Winnie and I will leave you for the night," Mina said, kissing him on the forehead.

As soon as the women were in their own room, Winnie took her friend's hand and said, "Mina dear, may I request a favor?"

"Of course, anything."

"I want to take the translation home. Then, in a week or two, I'll take it to your husband."

"I was going to ask you to do that. I also want you to give Jonathan this." She handed Winnie her little book.

"This is your journal!" Winnie exclaimed. She knew what was written there.

"There will be no more secrets between Jonathan and me, not even as to where I've gone." She waited to see that moment of understanding in Winnie's expression then went on. "Tell him that I'd like him to wait in Exeter until I write him. Tell him to please try and understand why I have to go back."

"What if Dracula is still alive?"

Mina smiled bitterly. "Then I'm still cursed, and I'll have to deal with that."

"How?"

"I don't know. Perhaps I'll ask Van Helsing to kill me. I'd trust him to do it well. Perhaps I'll weaken and choose that terrible life. If so, I will do my best to practice control and hope I'm not suffering from self-delusion. Whatever I choose, I promise that you'll get word of it. Don't look so sad, Winnie. Isn't knowledge better than ignorance?"

"Dearest Mina!" Winnie said, holding out her arms.

Winnie cried that night while Mina lay beside her, holding her, comforting her, feeling Winnie's broken breaths warm on her neck, Winnie's anguished pulse so strong against her cheek.

III

April 12, Lille, France. *Gance bought me this journal in Calais. The cover is gray leather, embossed with fleur-de-lis; the pages are parchment edged in gold. I have never written in so grand a book before. Its beauty seems fitting somehow, as if I, like the Countess Karina, am setting down the most important moments of my life. As I write, I feel that I have come full circle, with this journal recording the end, as my other did the beginning, of this adventure.*

Gance and I parted from Winnie at Croyden and went on to

Dover. Our midday Channel crossing was much calmer than my last. I even went on deck, something I had been too ill to do on our last crossing. The cold wind blew across my face. My cheeks stung from the salt spray, yet I gripped the rail, feeling the boat move beneath me, listening to the power of the waves pounding against the hull.

Gance joined me, though his face seemed even paler than usual and his lips were pressed together. He did not hide his pain well, perhaps because he'd never felt a need to do so before. A sudden lurch of the boat made him slip on the wet deck. He caught the rail to keep from falling and jarred his wound. He cried out, then cut off the sound.

I pulled up a deck chair for him and made him sit. "You should have stayed inside," I said.

"I never miss coming outside on a crossing," he replied, though he took the seat gratefully. I stood where I was, gripping the rail, looking down at the water so black and cold beneath us.

One of the crew noticed me and came down, intending no doubt to suggest I go inside. He noticed Gance sitting in the shadows behind me and went on with only a polite greeting.

How much easier life would be if I had been born a man. The world would be so much kinder to my excesses, my eccentricities. I would have no need of protection from Gance or Jonathan or anyone.

We spent the night at a tiny stone inn in Lille. Gance made no advances save that he kissed me before rolling over and going to sleep.

I lay awake thinking of Jonathan. By now he must know that I have left him. Has he gone to Seward? I alternate between fear for what I have done and incredible joy that I have at last freed myself from all the restraints, all the secrets that bound me.

April 17, Paris. We've stayed here five days in the beautiful stone house of a friend of Gance's, an aged artist whom I will not name or describe too closely for his sake. The crossing was hard on Gance, and he is taking something for the pain. Nonetheless, his constitution is so strong that healing continues quickly.

I have my own room. It has an iron balcony and stairs leading down to a magnificent courtyard. There, among the carefully tended flower beds, is an ornate stone-and-tile fountain and delicate iron chairs and tables for guests. I often drink coffee there in the morning with our host. He asked me to pose for him soon after we arrived. It passes the time, and he paints while I sit and read. He is a delightful conversationalist, well traveled and well versed in folk legends and beliefs.

Yesterday, as I sat sideways on the bench, posing as he requested with my hair falling over my shoulders, my chin resting on my hand, my legs slightly apart, with the fabric falling between them (a position Millicent would undoubtedly describe as "hoydenish"), he told me the most incredible story about a woman who turned into a werewolf while mesmerized. He said that this beautiful woman—titled, he added, as if this made her transformation even more bizarre— howled and bared her teeth, then returned to the present to describe quite vividly having devoured a lamb.

"Do you believe it?" I asked when he'd finished.

"I saw it," he replied.

"Isn't that enough?"

"I may have been mesmerized as well," he concluded with a dry laugh.

I wondered how much Gance had told him, or if the man had seen the mark still so dark on Gance's neck and guessed my obsession. There is no way to ask. Yet the man's point is a valid one.

I pray that when we finally reach the castle, we find no one there at all.

After my last sitting, he invited me to see the nearly finished portrait. I walked around to the easel and stared at a woman far too beautiful to be me, with her lips slightly parted as if ready to speak, someone with both trust and passion in her eyes.

"It is a fine likeness, don't you think?" my host asked.

"Is it?"

"Oh, yes. I painted your soul as well as your face." He raised my hand to his lips then looked directly into my eyes. "If you ever need a friend, or a place to stay for a while, come to me," he said.

"Thank you."

He must have sensed that I would not impose, for he quickly added, "I could think of a dozen portraits to do of you the way Dante did with his Lizzie. But unlike Rossetti, I'm far too old to demand anything but your undivided attention and some small bit of adoration for my genius."

"Not that old, I think," I replied, for though his face was lined, he was also terribly thin, which made him seem older.

"Then you are too young," he replied smoothly.

I laughed. Actually, sitting with him in the little enclosed garden with the sound of falling water, the sun on my face, the easel and scent of oils, I felt more at ease than I've been since this ordeal began.

April 19. *Last night Gance dressed and joined us for dinner. We dined in the courtyard and, after the meal, extinguished all the lights and sat beneath the stars drinking wine. It was another night of carefree conversation, all the wittier because of Gance's presence. And yet, perhaps because our host is so genuinely kind, I see the emptiness at Gance's core, and know his wit is nothing more than an intellectual exercise.*

Dracula, it is said, no longer has a soul. Gance, of course, does, but he hides it so well. It's no wonder that I was attracted to him. But later he did something so inexplicably at odds with his usual behavior that I cannot comprehend it.

We retired together. I thought he would say good night at my door as he has every night, but instead he followed me inside and kissed me with that intensity I have come to know so well. His hands moved as they always move, so skillfully over my body. As always, I wanted to give him the intensity of pleasure that he gives me. I reached for him and caressed him, but as soon as he began to stiffen under my touch, I heard him gasp in surprise. His hand covered mine and pulled it away. "Not yet," he whispered.

And though he kissed me and though his hands continued to pleasure me, he would not enter me or allow me to straddle him. Finally, unable to respond any further to his touch, I lay beside him. "Does your wound pain you so much?" I asked.

He did not answer, only moved away from me on the bed and said quietly, "I wish . . ."

I waited; he never finished. "You wish?" I asked.

"I wish I'd met you years ago." He brushed my cheek then added ruefully, "I suppose my near death just makes me sentimental. You could not have altered my life even then."

I put on my chemise and stole across the hall to my room. Before going to bed, I stood on the balcony for a few moments and noticed my host sitting in the dark courtyard, his white robe just visible in the dim starlight. I wondered if he had fallen asleep or if he sat alone with his thoughts. I wondered what he thought of Gance and me, if he had some guess as to where we were going and what we would face.

We decided at breakfast to leave tonight. There is a private car available, and Gance hopes that by beginning the journey with a night of sleep, he'll be even stronger in the morning.

He seems in a greater hurry than I am. Actually, since I made my decision to go, my nights have been restful and without dreams. Often I think it's because now that I am going to that castle, whatever wants me to return there grants me some peace.

April 20, early morning. *Our private car is at the end of the train. There are gilt moldings around the top and a pair of crystal chandeliers hanging from the ceiling. Though we did not hire any servants, we seem to have acquired one anyway, a tiny Indian man who politely let us know that he would do his best to meet our every demand. Gance whispered an order to him, and he returned some time later with champagne and a cold plate of pâté and cheeses. He bowed with exaggerated servility before leaving us.*

I told Gance of how wondrous it seemed to travel in such luxury. He responded by pouring me more champagne and saying with a wry smile that he was too used to it to see it as anything but common.

"Are you in pain?" I asked.

"A little. I'll check the wound in the morning."

I saw the need growing in the intensity with which his gray eyes

*focused on my face and my body. As quickly as desire rose, it vanished.
"I should sleep," he said.*

*I knew that raising his arm was still painful so I helped him un-
dress. Once he was in bed, I turned down the lights nearest him, said
good night and went back to my place at the front of the car. He did
not ask me to join him, and I didn't feel inclined to make the first
overture. Though Gance volunteered to come on this journey with me,
now that we are constantly together, there is little real intimacy between us. In the past, all our discourse began and ended with sex.*

*As I write this, I think of Jonathan—his vulnerability, his need
for comfort and how, in spite of his terror of that castle and the things
that lived there, he risked his life and his soul for me.*

*I am thankful that I left him behind. He has done enough. It is my
turn to be brave now. I pray my courage does not fail.*

*We have just pulled out of Strasbourg. When I wake tomorrow, we
will be somewhere in Germany. At least I will have little time to reflect on the danger I face.*

CHAPTER TWENTY-FOUR

After Mina had left, Winnie took over her fund-raising duties and cut back on her work in the hospital wards. The social calls, the witty conversation over tea, the constant presentations of hospital needs took Winnie's mind off Mina and the terrible journey she had undertaken.

One afternoon, when she had stopped at the hospital to catch up on some work, a volunteer nurse walked by the tiny office. "We didn't expect to see you today," she said. "Since you're here, you might want to look at the mail piling up in your box."

"Mail?" Winnie went to investigate and found a number of letters and flyers as well as some larger packages. She opened the packages, mostly donations of bandages and other supplies, and stuffed the envelopes in her handbag.

At home, she passed the time until dinner reading the letters. There were the usual notes of thanks, many from the children who had been treated at the hospital. Among them was a large envelope with no return address. By the time she pulled the sheets from it, she had guessed what it must be. With shaking hands, she looked down at manuscript pages, then read the unsigned note that accompanied them. It had been printed as if the sender wanted to hide even a small link to his identity.

Mrs. Beason. On his last day of life, Anton Ujvari left an envelope with me. He made me swear that, should something happen to him, I would send it to you. I confess that after he disappeared, I read its contents.

When I heard the details of how he died, I wavered. I very nearly gave these sheets to the police, but I know it is not what Mr. Ujvari wanted and, from how he spoke of you, that you would have had nothing to do with his terrible end.

If there had been a way to contact Mina, Winnie would have waited to read this account. Under the circumstances, however, she could hardly be blamed for reading it herself.

She sat in a rocking chair close to the little fire. As she began reading, she recalled the likeness of the countess that Mina had shown her—her delicate features, her golden curls, her tiny red lips in their tight, willful bow.

My desperate search for the man I had met was eventually found out, and I was confined to the house, and the gardens surrounding it, while my mother, deciding that I was having a liaison with some poor peasant lad, made plans to leave. I did not protest. Indeed, convinced that I was spurned here as I had been at court, my despondency made me unusually pliant.

Late one night, I woke and saw a woman standing by my bed. Though the room was sultry, her hands were cool and dry as she brushed back the locks of hair from my forehead. I knew the servants. She was not one of them. Besides, a servant would not have been allowed in my chamber without my request.

Nonetheless, I was not afraid. "What is your name?" I asked.

"Illona," she replied. Her eyes glowed in the light of the single candle burning beside my bed. Her hands were long and delicate like my mother's, her face smooth and pale, and her voice as she spoke her name had an incredible timbre that reminded me less of song than of dance. She resembled the aristocratic Hungarian women at court with their powdered faces and painted lips, but her hair was dark rather

than pale and fell like raven's feathers across her shoulders and the white cotton blouse she wore.

Her very beauty calmed me. I sat up in bed, tossing my hair over my back, trying to make myself look passable in her magnificent presence. "Why are you here?" I asked.

"To take you to him—to Dracula."

I frowned. I did not understand.

She smiled, a slash of red lips against the pale face, the white teeth. "So he was not foolish enough to call himself that," she whispered and laughed. "To your lover then. To Vlad? To Tepes?"

I recognized the last name. "He sent you? Yes, take me to him!" I exclaimed so loudly that Illona looked over her shoulder at the door.

Anyone who came would have died before they could make a sound. I know that now. Then, I only assumed she feared discovery, and I felt so foolish for speaking so thoughtlessly. I pulled on my clothes as quickly as I was able. With her moving before me through the darkness, one of her hands holding mine to lead the way, we stole silently through the dark house and into the night.

Clear, moonless. The stars shed some light, enough to show us the road as we ran to the edge of the estate. A horse was waiting beyond the wall, a coal-black stallion that answered to Illona's call yet shivered with fear as we mounted. She pressed her knees into its side, and with me sitting in front of her, we rode away.

I spoke to her, asking where we were going, how long it would take. She did not answer, but her hands dug into my wrists painfully. I cried out, I trembled. I heard her laughter again. This time it did not sound so beautiful.

The walls of this ancient castle were not so weathered when I first saw them. The upstairs halls were not so damp, and the furnishings were still rich and colorful. Illona lit a torch and showed me to an upper-floor chamber. There was wood for a fire, water to drink, even some bread and dried meat and wine.

"Where is he?" I asked as she showed me into the room. "Is he here?"

"He comes in his own good time. Sleep well," she said and pulled the door shut behind her. When I tried to open it, I found it locked.

Even if I had been able to explore, I was far too tired to do so. The bed was soft, the blankets warm. I slept until night, when Illona called my name.

She had brought another woman with her—a woman with hair even darker than hers and eyes that same shade of smoldering green as my lover's.

"This is Joanna," Illona said. "Dracula's sister."

"You resemble each other," I said, uneasily now, for though they had been polite, their presence in my room was too abrupt, had been too soundlessly accomplished. They seemed to be specters rather than women, their bodies long dead and buried in the caverns below us.

"Yes, we do resemble one another," Joanna said in that same strange accent as my lover had. Illona laughed, the brightness of it so at odds with Joanna's tone.

"We must prepare you," Illona declared and moved closer to me, her delicate fingers unhooking the front of my gown, her hands sliding it off my shoulders, my breasts, while Joanna was content to stand by the door and watch, an indecipherable upward turn to her lips that seemed less a smile than a sign of distaste.

The places where Tepes had drunk from me were scarred and bruised. Illona's fingertips brushed each one of them. My nipples hardened from the memory of what he had done. I am certain I blushed. A woman had never touched me there before.

"He fed on you often," Illona said.

Joanna laughed, too hard it seemed, though I understood her contempt easily enough later.

"Do you please him?" Illona asked, her dark dry eyes, so like his, fixed on mine.

To say yes would have made me feel too wanton, too full of conceit. To say no would have been a lie. I kept silent.

"Of course you do, and will continue to do, unless we turn you first." Her face moved close to mine. Her breath was cold and cloyingly sweet like a garden in midsummer. For the first time, I noticed that her teeth were long and sharp like his. I expected her to kiss me. Instead she rested one hand against the back of my neck and lowered her

head, pressing her parted lips against a wound he had made, biting down.

I wanted to scream, to beg the other woman for help, but for a moment I was unable to move. Then the spell broke, and my hands pushed against her, but I might have been a kitten or a little bird for all the effect my struggles had.

I don't know how long we stood there, me fighting impotently, her feasting on me, but she did not take much blood. Then she raised her head and released me so abruptly that I fell backward against the bed.

"Come, Joanna," Illona called sweetly and stretched out beside me. Her face was flushed from even that small amount of blood, her breath warm against my neck. "Come. Drink. When it is time, I will give you the privilege of her death."

I know I begged for my life then, but Illona did not notice me. Her attention was fixed on Joanna, her intensity drawing the smaller woman forward. As she moved toward the bed, Illona raised my hands above my head. Only when the second woman's teeth had opened a different wound did I hear Illona say, "A taste only, sister. It will be days before he returns." Whatever relief I might have taken from that last comment vanished as she added, "Then we will feast."

She smiled, her incisors long and white against the red of her lips. "Oh, yes. You welcomed his touch, did you not?" She ran her hands over my cheek, slapping me when I tried to look away. "Do you think we are so different from him?"

Of course they were! I stared at the creature, convinced that she was insane.

"Once we were male and female. Now we are only takers, and you only exist to give. We cannot love. We only devour."

I looked from Illona to Joanna, standing so silently beside her. "Is this really true?" I asked, begging her for the answer I wanted to hear. In our nights together, it had seemed that the creature they called Dracula, the man I called Tepes, had truly loved me.

Joanna did not answer, but when she looked at me, I thought I saw some softening in her expression, a look almost of sympathy in her eyes.

I will not speak of the nights that followed, only say that they were careful with me. Joanna especially saw to my comfort, making sure my room—my cell—was warm and my food adequate.

The fall from my window was long and steep. I had always feared heights. The door was barred. In time, I learned to live on their cycle, sleeping by day, wary at night. I learned too to accept their silent comings and goings, as they drifted in and out of my locked room on tendrils of fog and dust.

Some nights they came to me, their hands caressing me, their lips against the wounds, drinking until I nearly swooned, then forcing me to drink from them. In the beginning, I gagged. Later their blood tasted sweet, the nourishment it gave relished by my soul. On other nights, I stayed alone, pacing my chamber, inventing hopeless, useless plans for escape. Once, Joanna came and, after building up the fire, sat with me, taking my hand so timidly that I did not pull away. "Tell me about your world," she whispered, her voice trembling, her dark eyes glancing toward the door as if she were frightened that Illona would hear and come.

I did, in the same low tone. She asked about the clothing, more about the music, the books and plays. I did the best I could, telling her the stories I had read, singing the songs I knew. Though I did not dare say it, I knew the truth about her. She was a prisoner here. Now I understand why. Then, I only pitied her. It was preferable to pitying myself.

Dracula returned by night, sitting beside the gypsies on the cart. I recall that as they rode up to the walls, they were all singing. It seemed so strange to hear his voice mingling with theirs. I have never thought of the women as human, but I thought of him then (and still!) that way. It is his will, his human will. It is too strong to be overpowered, even in death. The gypsies unloaded the box of earth that made it possible for him to travel, and left. I have often wondered how he can be so trusting of those men or they so honorable when he is at his most helpless, yet the bond has existed for centuries. He gives them gold, that is true. But even if he did not, they would die for him.

As I leaned out the window, it never occurred to me to cry out for help. I don't understand my silence to this day. Perhaps I knew it was useless to place my hope in his servants; perhaps I already knew that the life I had lived before coming here had ended with his kiss.

The women entered my chamber as silently as always. I felt their presence behind me and turned from the window. Joanna, as ever, hung back in a subservient position. Illona moved closer. "Do I die now?" I asked.

"You do," Illona responded. I have never seen such an evil expression, such a sardonic smile. "Help me," Illona called to Joanna, as she began to remove my clothes.

Joanna hung back. "Let him have her," she said.

"Him!" Illona laughed derisively and went on, ripping the last of my clothes from me. When I was naked, she lifted a gown from the bed.

Once it must have been beautiful, for the lace was still delicate. But age had destroyed some of the most intricate designs. Once it must have been white, but now it was yellow and there were brown spots of mildew on the lining of the bodice. The laces in the back were rotted, so the top could only stay up if I stood very straight. When she'd finished Illona put the veil on me, more a web of dust and tiny seed pearls than the lace that it had once been.

"My wedding dress," she said. "Ideal, don't you think, for this profane marriage."

"Marriage?" I asked dully.

"To Joanna."

Joanna shook her head. I began to understand what made her so reluctant. She feared Illona, but she feared Dracula as well. Sometimes it seems that only fear gives her life.

"Then she is mine, as you were, Joanna, remember?"

With a cry that might have been despair, or rage, Joanna vanished from the room, though I sensed her presence, safely watching, unable to act.

Illona tore at her neck; she gripped my head; forcing me to drink as she had before. As I struggled, he came, his bellow of rage filling the room, the strength of his presence more potent than both of the women's

*had been. Illona gripped my hair and turned me toward the door, forc-
ing me to look at him.*

Her hand curved around my throat; her nails just touched my flesh.

"Let her go!" Dracula ordered.

"So you can take a bride after me? No, husband. Never."

*Later, he told me that his death in her arms was the most exquisite
act of ecstasy he had ever experienced, the little death, as the French
call it, extended into a momentary blackness of real death, then the
sudden wrenching instant of rebirth. I felt none of the glory, all of the
fear. Indeed, the last moments of my struggle raised so much dust from
the crumbling veil that my last human act was to sneeze.*

*Then her nails dug into my flesh, ripping at my throat like some
animal's claws, and the darkness fell over me, profound and silent as
a winter night.*

I dreamed of life as life left me.

*How I would sit and watch my hair glowing like gold threads in
the sun.*

*How I rode with my brothers through the hills, my stallion white
and powerful between my legs.*

*How I danced at court, laughing too frantically at the jests, crying
in my mother's arms at night because no one loved me.*

How I dreamed of another world, cities, countries, oceans.

*How I lay in Tepes's arms, my body trembling at his touch,
thrilling to the taste of his blood.*

*Illona denied it all to me. Her nature is utterly dark, with not a
ray of her past life able to pierce its blackness. How I loathe her. How
I envy her freedom.*

*And then there was nothing but darkness and, for a moment only,
the promise of life everlasting. I sensed it, desired it—peace, incredible
and eternal peace!*

*It abandoned me as it had the vampire women. I returned to life as
suddenly as I had died. My eyes opened. Though the room was undoubtedly dim, lit as it was by just a single candle, the brightness of it
hurt my eyes. I lay across the knees of a young man who was washing
the blood from my neck and chest. The warm water reeked of its scent*

as the room reeked of his fear. It reeked of his passion as well, for sometime during my death, the tattered gown had been removed and I lay naked before him.

Had he touched me while I was helpless? I was certain of it from the blush on his cheeks, the way he looked only at my face. I knew he could not help himself. I held up my hand and saw its incredible pallor: my legs felt thinner, longer, my hair when I touched it finer than before. In life, I had been beautiful. Death had made me exquisite.

I pushed away from him and stood, but there was no reflection in the mirror beside the bed. With a moan of anguish, I turned toward him and saw him looking from the mirror to me and back.

Though the others do not speak of it, I know there is a moment of choice for our kind, the moment when we decide how terrible a creature we have become. Do we kill? Do we use? Do we feast on ecstasy? I know this now, but Illona made certain I would be a killer like her.

If there had been no mirror, if the boy had not known what I was, if he had not shook with terror as he backed away from me, if he had not turned and bolted for the door, pounding when he discovered it locked, my pity might have conquered my hunger. I might have even loved him.

Instead, the need for blood hit, a terrible searing agony in the center of my body, and I moved toward him. Unable to stop myself, I gripped his hands, pressed his body close to mine, feeling his pitiful struggles to escape as I drank.

And drank. And felt him die.

Ah, the magnificence of that moment when you realize that you have consumed death! The potency of it! The fulfillment!

Afterward, mere tastes of blood are nothing, no more than kisses are after sex, no more than water is after fine red wine. Words fail me here.

Days passed. Weeks. Dracula did not come.

Sustained by the life I had taken, saddened by my lack of remorse, I fell into a sort of languor in which time had no meaning. Often, during my waking hours, I would think of the life I had left behind. Though I could not shed tears, I could cry—dry, terrible sobs. Joanna *would come and sit by me, stroking my hair, telling me to hush, that despair was as useless as hope in this place.*

I tried to leave, to go home and find the comfort of my family. But as each night drew to a close, I was forced back to the castle, until I understood that the legends were wrong. Your native earth is not the earth where you were born but the earth in which you died, and your master is always the one who killed you.

I have no will to fight her hold on me, but he does. When he returned, when he finally had the strength to face me, I stood separated forever from him by my death, and listened to his promise.

He will leave this place, he said. And when he has prepared a way for me, he will send for me and leave the others to the ruins and their own despair.

I trust him. I have no choice in that, either. And sometimes, the memory of his love returns to me and gives me comfort.

Perhaps someday Tepes and I will be free of this place, free to roam the world, to see its wonders, to live as best we can in this eternal life-in-death.

The gypsies come more often now, they and no one else. Illona dares not touch them. Yet we go on. We have no choice.

Today Illona returned from one of her hunts across the countryside. She brought with her another fair-haired girl like myself. She promised this one to me. I will have no choice but to obey and turn her.

What I have become cannot be altered by age or infirmity. I loathe myself, but I cannot control what I will do.

But if you live, and come here by day to read this account, take pity on me. Look below the room where you found it and where our servants rest in their own earth-lined coffins. Raise the lids of the boxes holding our mortal remains in their daytime sleep. Drive a wooden stake through the heart of the dark-haired woman with the ruby ring on her finger. Then, if you still have the courage, drive a stake through mine and through Joanna's.

Joanna and I agree on this. Death is change. We welcome it.

Dear Lord, Winnie thought, then read the translation again. There were answers in it, terrible answers to all the questions

Mina's strange actions had raised. Winnie sent a note to the Harker house asking Jonathan to visit her as soon as possible. A day passed and he did not respond.

Had it only been months since Mina and he had wed? Could this man have actually risked everything, even his soul, for her? And now, when there was just as strong a possibility that she could not help her compulsion, he turned his back on her!

The betrayal infuriated Winnie. The next morning she collected every bit of proof she had concerning Mina's actions and appeared at Harker's firm. The clerk told her that Harker had not come in that day. "Then I'm sure he would want me to leave him a message," she said and walked past the astonished young man and into Harker's office.

The desk was clean. The lights were cool. Jonathan Harker had not been there.

She walked to the Harker home. At the corner of his street, she flagged down one of the local bicycle messengers. "I'd like you to deliver a package to Mr. Jonathan Harker," she said.

"But his house is right there, ma'am. You could go yourself," the boy responded, pointing toward the bend in the street.

"I want you to deliver it directly into the hands of Mr. Harker. You are to say it is from his firm."

"Ma'am?"

"I'll wait outside. If you are able to deliver it, I'll know that he is home."

The boy opened his mouth, no doubt to protest again. Winnie pulled five pence from her purse and handed it to him. "Not a bad amount for five minutes' work, is it?"

She waited at the corner of the front yard, hidden by the old lilac bushes that separated the lot from the neighbor's. The front door opened, Millicent, sounding annoyed, asking what the messenger wanted.

"I'll give it to him," she said.

"I must deliver it myself, Ma'am. It's necessary."

She heard nothing else for a while, then the boy came past

her on his bicycle. "He took it as you asked," he said and went on his way.

Winnie waited a half hour then went and knocked on the Harkers' door. Millicent answered. "Oh, it's you," she said.

"I must speak to Mr. Harker."

"I heard you'd spoken enough," Millicent replied coldly and shut the door.

Winnie pounded on it, refusing to stop even when no one came. "Please," she shouted. "I must—"

The door swung open. Jonathan turned and walked back to his study. Winnie caught only a glimpse of his face but saw clearly that there had been tears in his eyes.

Millicent placed herself in front of the study door, her face red with anger. "How dare you come here," she said. "Can't you leave him in peace?"

"Aunt Millicent, please," Jonathan said wearily. "Mrs. Beason won't listen to reason, so you might as well let her in."

Winnie swept by the older woman. Millicent began to follow, but Winnie closed the door too quickly. To lock it would have been an insult. She decided that she could rely on the latch to keep the woman out.

She fixed her attention on Jonathan Harker. His prematurely gray hair had never made him seem old before, but now, with the grief and worry etched in deep lines across his eyes and forehead, he could have easily passed for fifty. "Did you read the note I sent with that package?" she asked.

"I did. And I also read the beginning of Mina's journal and I stopped reading exactly as she asked. Should I follow her instructions or yours?"

"She asked me to implore you to read it. She said there should be no secrets between you."

"Would that there were," he responded woodenly. "Mrs. Beason, do you believe my wife is sane?"

"I do." Winnie saw the grief grow in his expression and added, "But her problem is not a matter of sanity, at least not exactly."

She reached across his desk and picked up the translation. "Read this before any of the other things. Mina read this part." She handed him the first half of the translation, then the last pages. "These came after she had gone. When you finish, it will be time to talk."

Winnie moved from the desk chair to the little sofa in the opposite corner and occupied herself with the lastest copy of the *Strand* while Jonathan read. She did not look at him. To do so would have been an invasion of his privacy, and a distraction as well.

"Mrs. Beason," he called when he had finished, in a tone that, for the first time, expressed real concern. "What do you think this means?"

"That she has never been freed of the vampires' control—not just his, but the others' control as well. You can guess what they plan."

"I don't understand. The vampires were destroyed."

Winnie pointed to the little journal. "Mina told me that she wishes you to read this. When you're through with it, come and talk with me."

Winnie retrieved her coat from the chair where she had tossed it. When she opened the door and saw Millicent sitting on a chair outside the door, she turned toward Jonathan and added, "Mina is right. There have been too many secrets in this house, Jonathan Harker."

"I'll see you out," Millicent said coldly.

Winnie walked behind her to the door. Just before she left, Winnie turned to the older woman and squeezed her hand. "Be a comfort to your nephew," she said. "He is so in need of comfort now."

Millicent closed the door, then turned and leaned against it. She could think of nothing to say, nothing at all. It occurred to her that she had raised Jonathan to be so strong because she had never known how to deal with weakness.

"Aunt Millicent," Jonathan called. "Come in here please."

When she did, she saw that he had opened his wall safe and was pulling a stack of pages from it. As he held it out to her, it seemed that she had never seen her nephew's expression so determined.

* * *

MILLICENT carried the pages to her room and read the accounts of Jonathan, Mina, Van Helsing and the others for the better part of the day. When she had finished, she took the pages to Jonathan. She found him in his study with Winnie Beason, the both of them typing furiously. Jonathan paused when she entered the room, taking the pages from her, then holding both her hands as he told her why Mina had gone to London and what had happened afterward. "Now you know the story we did not want to share with you or with anyone."

"But it came out anyway, didn't it, Jonathan? Secrets always do." So much had been answered, but one question remained. "Why didn't Mina tell you of her doubts earlier?" Millicent asked.

"She didn't want to burden me with them. You can understand that, can't you?"

Millicent was a strong woman. She understood it all too well.

CHAPTER TWENTY-FIVE

I

April 26, Varna. *Gance and I are in the same hotel where I and the others waited months ago for the ship* Czarina Catherine. *It seems that we must wait here again, for Gance needs a day more to recover.*

I noticed his fever the night we pulled out of Lille. When I went to bed, his body seemed warmer. I thought it might be the closeness of the room or the champagne we had had at dinner, so I took a blanket and pillow and slept on the sofa.

In the morning, he lay uncovered, his nightshirt stuck to his skin. His face, usually so pale, was ruddy from heat. Alarmed, I called for the steward, who found a doctor to treat him. While I sat in the dining car, the doctor examined Gance, then opened the wound and cleaned it. After changing the dressing, he sent for me and suggested to both of us that we stop in Munich until Gance is better. "The wound may be abscessing. If the infection begins to spread into the lung when you are in some backward country . . . "

"We go on," Gance said.

"I'm leaving the train in Belgrade," the doctor explained. He looked at Gance, hoping to see some wavering in his resolve. There was none. "I'll look at you again tonight," he said wearily and left us.

"Gance, there's no rush," I said.

"If we stop and I become really ill, we could be trapped somewhere for weeks. Varna is a city. They have physicians there."

By evening, his fever was so high that I had to bathe him with cold water to keep it down. "We have to stop, Gance," I said. "Otherwise, you'll die before we reach Varna."

He only looked at me stubbornly. "Tell the steward to bring me some cold oranges," he said. "Winnie Beason told me that they feed them to the hospital's children to ward off infection."

"Gance!"

"We go on."

The night after the doctor left the train, I dared not go to sleep. Instead I sat beside Gance's bed with the pan of ice water, changing the compress on his forehead, holding his hand when he became restive. Finally, his own strong constitution came to his rescue. The fever broke and he slept peacefully. I have never seen his expression so innocent. He said in the morning that he'd had magnificent dreams.

He demanded to get dressed. When the steward came, Gance requested that the man change the linens on the bed and ordered me to sleep. We were an hour out of Varna when I woke.

Gance was sitting on the end of the divan, a map of the Carpathians spread beside him. "Mina, come and show me where we're going," he said when he saw me sitting up in bed.

"We're going to spend a few days in Varna," I replied. "I won't have your death on my conscience, Gance."

"I promise not to die."

"An easy promise to make. You won't even have to feel regret if you break it."

"Excellent!" he said, commenting on my wit. "But I'm sure to feel regret in the afterlife, particularly since it's common knowledge that I'm going to hell. Now come here, show me where we're going . . . eventually."

I did as he asked, exaggerating my confusion with the location, the steepness of the climbs, the chill in the air, the remoteness of the area.

My eloquence won. When we reached Varna, I recommended that

we come here to this hotel, and here we have stayed for the last three days. We keep to ourselves, Gance because he is recuperating, me because so many on the staff recall my visit here with my husband just months ago. Though Gance and I have separate rooms, they still look at me oddly, wondering, I suppose, where my husband has gone. I shouldn't care but I do. I feel as if some of the essence of our little band remains alive in these rooms. The feeling is impossible to shake, as is my belief that one day a ship or a train will bring Jonathan here looking for me.

Gance was much better this afternoon. A local physician (not at all the sort of quack the doctor on the train had said we would find!) examined Gance and told him that the infection had subsided. He gave Gance permission to bathe and instructed him to leave the wound uncovered afterward so the scar could dry.

"We ought to talk to someone who knows the area around the Borgo Pass," Gance said after the doctor had gone and we were together once more. "The physician had a suggestion on where to begin. Go and dress for dinner. We're dining out."

The hotel had the western flavor of all port establishments. But as we walked up the hill away from the harbor, it seemed that we had stepped into another land, one of many races. The women all seemed to share an affinity for white cotton skirts but covered them in wildly embroidered aprons tied in both front and back. These seemed to serve both as protection for the skirts and to give some warmth. Their chests were covered with woolen shawls, their heads with detached hoods that Gance told me were believed to date back to Roman times.

I had sufficient opportunity to observe a great deal because we walked very slowly and stopped often. Gance may be better, but his wound still pains him if he breathes too deeply. Once we were on level ground, however, we went on at a good pace. It is heartening to see him healing so quickly.

The instructions the doctor had written helped us find a small restaurant, no larger than a common English pub. A hostess wearing a magnificently embroidered velvet jacket that any London socialite might envy, showed us to a table covered with a blue crocheted cloth. The napkins were trimmed in similar blue lace. The hostess knew enough Hungarian to bring us the wine Gance wanted, but it took far longer for Gance to explain to her that we also needed to talk to someone who knew the area between Bukovina and Bacau.

She beamed with pleasure at finally understanding, nodded and said a word Gance told me meant "later."

In the meantime, we dined on the most magnificent goose, baked with apples and cinnamon, an odd pickled squash and a dessert of paper thin layers of dough that dripped honey down my fingers.

Each time the woman returned with bread, more coffee or dessert, Gance would ask about the guide. Each time she would repeat the same word.

When I thought the seam on my skirt would split from my gluttony, the man who had been tending bar in the front came and joined us.

There was danger in consulting a guide. We knew that, but we had no choice. Fortunately, the man was well versed in the roads around the Borgo Pass, but if the tales of the area meant anything to him, he gave no indication.

"Good land," he said of Bukovina, not once but often, then suggested we take the coach that traveled there every few days.

"Ask him if we can purchase horses at a coach stop," I suggested.

"If there are horses, I can purchase them," Gance replied in a quick whisper. He asked the man to come to the hotel in the morning, and paid the bill, including a handsome tip for the advice.

It was almost dark when we left the restaurant. As we stood on the hill overlooking the port, the entire ocean seemed to have turned to glass, reflecting the clouds and the many shades of the evening sky. The scene was so moving that I stopped and tried to etch it in my mind, as if its beauty could erase the horror of the past.

Someday when all of this is behind me, I hope that Jonathan will come here. I want him to look at this place with an artist's eyes and see its true beauty. And though I know that it is most likely impossible, I want to be here with him, to sit beside him as he draws.

I see this all in my mind so perfectly. Even as I stand here, my arm linked to another man's, I feel so close to Jonathan.

April 27. *Gance saw me to my room and followed me inside. Since he was so much better, I expected him to spend the night. When he turned to leave, I stopped him, kissing him with all the passion he had taught me to show.*

He shook his head slowly, sadly. "Gance, I'm sorry," I said. "I thought you would welcome it. I should have known that it's too soon."

His hand brushed the side of my face. He kissed my cheek sweetly, with all the affection of a brother to his sister.

"What's happened?" I asked. "What has changed?"

He seemed to be weighing an answer, or looking for something deeper than just a witty remark. "I care for you, enough that I never want you to feel any regret."

"Me, or yourself, Gance?"

"I'm not a coward, if that's what you mean."

"It takes great trust to love. You have to reveal so much of yourself." I touched his hair, soft and white like a small, fair child's. "You are no coward, Gance, but you are afraid of something. What is it?"

"I wasn't speaking of love. Everyone I ever loved has died, and none of them pleasantly." He sat on the edge of my bed. "I suppose I simply feel afraid for you, especially now."

"If the vampires are still alive, and I believe that some of them are, they won't kill me. Perhaps they want another prisoner to amuse them."

"Or your help in escaping those ancient walls."

I had never thought of that. Some of my shock must have shown in my expression, because he held out his arms, and when I sat next to him, he said, "Look at London, filled with thieves and murderers, men who would cut your throat for that brooch you are wearing. There would be no shortage of food for creatures such as them. Actually, London would be all the better for their presence."

"Dracula did not dine on thieves, Gance. He chose Lucy Westerna instead."

"Perhaps, in his own way, he loved her."

Why was I so shocked at his words when I already knew they were right? Why was I so saddened by them? I still do not know, but I cried, sobbing for her and for me and for the marriage that never had a chance to grow. Gance took my hands, and I looked up and saw that there were also tears in his eyes. Suddenly I understood why he backed away from me, for all the affection for him that I had held back surfaced, threatening my control the way the dreams had my sanity.

"How did those you cared for die?" I asked him.

He went to his room for a bottle of brandy. I had only meant to have a little, but as I listened to his sad tale of his mother's suicide and his father's slow degeneration into lust and insanity, we shared the bottle.

We drank a great deal and fell asleep, fully clothed, in one another's arms.

When I woke in the morning, Gance had gone.

I went back to sleep for another hour then went and knocked on his door. He didn't reply. Thinking him ill once more, I went in and found his bed still made up. Though there were clothes on the chair, the room seemed emptier. I went to the closet and found that his bag and heavier coat were missing.

The hotel staff sympathized with what they thought was my plight. The owner took special pains to assure me that the bill had been settled and an account left to see me through another dozen days or so. I could stay on or go as I wished.

He also gave me an envelope Gance had left for me.

I opened it in the privacy of my room. Inside was a draft for two hundred pounds and a note that simply said, Perhaps I do love you. Else why would I be foolish enough to go to his abode without your knowledge and protection. I took my own precautions, and now I am gone. A fitting adventure for one who shares Lord Byron's blood, don't you think?—Gance.

His own precautions? Something of last night came back to me, and my fingers brushed over a tender spot on my chest. I felt the cut. He had tasted my blood, and through it Dracula's, once more.

The fool! The terrible fool! I considered everything that had happened on my last journey here. An idea came to me, one I was amazed I had not thought of before. I changed into my simplest traveling clothes then went downstairs and asked the staff to give me directions to the nearest church.

"Catholic or Lutheran?"

"Neither." Dracula's religion, I thought. The one he had practiced all his life. The one he believed in. "Orthodox," I said.

II

Brother Michael Kozma, prior of St. Peter and Paul Monastery in Varna, seemed to be accustomed to the presence of unbelievers. He had a keen curiosity about the world, asking me many questions as he explained the history of the retreat. I was astonished at how well he spoke English and commented on it. He replied in German, then French, then, in English once more, he said I should be more amazed at his pride.

Astonishing. I came here looking for a holy man and found another Gance instead.

He told me that women were not allowed in many sections of the monastery, then took me into the church and showed me the sacred icons. After I had finished admiring them, he asked for a donation for their preservation.

This pragmatist was not the sort of holy man I had come to see. "When people come to discuss matters of the soul, do they also speak to you?" I asked.

"Me? No, madam. Those I hand over to the abbot, Brother Sandor, who has all the virtue that I do not possess."

"May I speak with him?"

"He does not give audiences to women."

I suppose I should have known. "May I ask for an exception?"

He looked surprised. Had no one ever asked this before? "For what reason?" he questioned, his voice now gentle, prodding a reply.

"One I prefer to discuss with him," I replied.

"Unless you speak Rumanian or Russian, you will be discussing it with me as well. And if you wish an audience with Brother Sandor, you need a reason and that must go through me." From anyone else, the words might have sounded harsh, but Brother Michael's candor made them seem no more than truth.

I considered how to begin, then said, "A year ago, my husband, a solicitor from London, came to this country at the request of one Count Dracula, whose castle is in the Borgo Pass. While he was there, he was attacked by strange creatures who live in that castle. It is of those creatures, called nosferatu in your language, that I wish to speak."

"Those creatures are legends. Whatever your husband saw was a dream."

"You asked me why I wished to speak to the abbot. I told you. Now, please, go and convey my reason to him."

"He will agree with me."

"Is he a holy man, a truly holy man?"

"Truly? That is between him and God, but I believe him to be holy."

"Would you tell him that I do not expect him to believe in the things I saw with my own eyes. I only wish him to hear my confession, and to bless me when I am through."

My sincerity must have been clear to Brother Michael. He excused himself, leaving me alone in the sun that bathed the front wall of the church.

He returned a short time later, carrying a brown hooded cloak much like the one he wore. "Put this on," he said. "Pull the hood over your hair and follow me."

Once the monastery had been a fortress, he told me. The original design was still evident as we walked through the center court, past the dining hall and the kitchen, past the rooms where the monks received guests, to the long, dim passage that led to the tiny quiet cells where they slept and meditated and prayed.

I had expected to see an office such as our ministers at home use. Instead, Brother Michael led me into a cramped room with only a pallet,

a table and chair and a single candle for light. The wax had not begun
to melt. It had just been lit for my sake.

"Brother Sandor?" I asked.

I could not see his face or his hands beneath the protective cowl and
shapeless sleeves, but I had a sense of age in the way he sat so stiffly on
his bed, the way his head was moved up and down in a slow assent.

"Will you hear my confession?"

Brother Michael translated. The monk on the bed replied in a
whisper. "He said he cannot give absolution," Michael told me.

"I do not believe in that sacrament, but there is a proverb in my
country. Confession itself heals the soul."

Another exchange. "He said to sit and speak."

Each time I told the tale, it became longer, more complex. This
telling took well over two hours. When I had finished, I began to ask
Brother Sandor detailed questions about his faith.

CHAPTER TWENTY-SIX

I

Gance had never lied so beautifully as he had in his final note to Mina. In the days they had been thrown together, he had given no indication of the reason for those lies or the quiet panic that had gradually taken hold of him.

Every physician who examined Gance's wound agreed that he had lost the use of one lung. Their advice was likewise similar— if he wished to live a normal life span, he would have to get adequate sleep, avoid nervous exhaustion and be careful not to exert himself physically or emotionally. They also added that sexual relations would be imprudent, and that if he must have them, he must practice great restraint.

The prudery of old men, Gance thought. He was young, vital, and he would not be condemned to a voyeur's existence. That night in Paris he felt well enough, and had gone to Mina as he had so many times before. She had learned so much in their times together—just how to touch him for the perfect arousal.

And then, in the midst of his growing excitement, he had felt his heart begin to race, found himself gasping for breath, smothered by his own excitement. He'd willed himself calm. It had taken far more effort than he ever cared to expend again.

He could easily picture himself in his mortal future. He would be seated at one of his many fetes, wearing black to make him look even weaker than he was. People would crowd around him to listen to him, admiring him for his perfect wit, his perfectly orchestrated socials, his cryptic remarks on the exploits of his past. The story of how he had defended a lover against a lunatic and paid with his health would be so perfectly romantic. He would have cherished an acquaintance such as he would become. And yet he knew he could never exist in his past. Better to die than go on for decades, trapped by caution and fear.

Mortality should be the concern of old men and the infirm, not someone as alive and vital as he. Gance considered this often as he traveled from Varna to Bukovina on the most desperate quest of his life—and quite likely his last.

The coach was nearly empty but reeked of sweat from previous passengers. A drunken old man rode on top with the driver, singing with keyless enthusiasm. The man beside Gance was a well-dressed Austrian taking the scenic route back to Vienna. Across from him, a little Romanian girl lay sideways on the seat, sleeping with her head on her mother's lap. The woman had a hood pulled down on her face. Often he saw her peering at him from beneath it with curiosity and fear.

Mina had warned Gance to expect this kind of scrutiny. Strangers were few in this land, and his coloring would remind them of the *nosferatu* who ravaged it.

Gance leaned against the window frame, letting the fresh breeze beat over his face, consulting his map frequently as landmarks came into view. "The Borgo?" he asked the woman and pointed to a break in the jagged peaks.

She nodded and made the sign of the cross on her sleeping child's forehead.

Yes, Gance thought. Dracula's country.

Bukovina would have been called a town only in an area of

the world such as this. In England, it would have been considered no more than a crossroad with its three small cottages with neatly thatched roofs and its stone-walled public inn and stables.

The owner of the inn was a Hungarian of an age Gance's father would have called somewhere between sixty and the grave. As Gance had assumed, the man had horses to sell. "Choose one," he said as Gance eyed the collection grazing in the corral behind the inn. One seemed too spirited for Gance to trust on the climb, and the second was lame, which left only a sturdy bay mare. "That one," Gance said and pointed to it.

"You will want it in the morning?"

Gance recalled what Mina had told him of the first journey. It would take a day at least to find the right road to the castle. "Yes," he replied. "I need to purchase tack and bedroll and some food as well. I intend to be in the pass for some days."

"Alone?" The man stared at Gance's face. He seemed to be seeking some clue to Gance's foolhardiness, or perhaps some proof of his nature.

Gance nodded, "Are they still there?" he asked, the question deliberately vague.

The man pretended not to hear.

Gance pulled a pair of bills from his wallet. One he gave for the horse. The other he held back and repeated the question. "You might as well tell me," he said. "If only to warn me."

The man looked curiously at him then took the second bill. "Who can know? Sometimes they sleep. It is said that they can sleep for months or even years then wake when someone of interest comes."

"Do you suppose I will interest them?"

"There are easier ways to die," the man replied.

Gance laughed then inquired about meals and a room.

The coach that had brought him here left after lunch, but later a second, more crowded one arrived from Galati. That night, the tavern was filled with music and life. Gance ate and drank more than usual, reminding himself that the innkeeper's meals could be his last.

As he sat listening to the conversations around him in languages he did not know, he considered how carefully he had ordered his life until Mina so radically altered it. Did he love her? More likely what he felt was nothing but self-delusion.

Yet he did care for her, enough that he did not want to see the look of regret on her face when she realized why he had been so eager to come here with her. Now he would stand in her place, and if luck was with him, he might win the greatest prize of all.

*   *   *

HE set out just after breakfast. By noon, the castle was in sight, but it took nearly all the remaining light to make the final climb to its walls. The mare had been an easy mount for most of the journey, but as the shadow of the castle fell over her, she shied and whinnied. Gance had never been troubled by heights before, but his wound made breathing difficult. His head pounded. When he dismounted, his legs gave way and he had to grab the saddle to keep from falling. A few shallow breaths steadied him, and he led the mare inside and tied her bridle to a post near the entrance.

The massive carved doors were still hanging open as they'd been when Mina left this place. In spite of the months that had passed since the fire, the smell of smoke was still strong inside. Dust and soot coated the stones of the floor. Dry leaves had blown into the corner by the stairs. The droppings of bats and birds left lines on the floor below the rafters where the creatures roosted.

Gance had come prepared to spend a few days here, but the lower hall would not have been hospitable if he'd been in perfect health. Hoping to find a room that had been more protected from the elements, he climbed the stairs and tried doors on the second floor until he found one that would open.

The room's tall, narrow window still had its shutters. The fireplace appeared usable. Gance lit a cigar, blowing smoke into the chimney to be certain of the draw. The straw mattress on the bed, along with an old wooden chair and table, could be used to heat the space. He returned to the courtyard and tended the mare. Concerned about the wolves, he led her into the lower hall, then closed and barricaded the doors as best he could.

Duty done, he returned to the room with the things he had purchased. His bedroll gave him a place to sit. His candles shed a dim light. In the darkness that grew more intense as night fell, he ate sparingly of the food he had brought with him, then built a fire and with all the surety that Mina had instilled in him, waited for the vampires to come.

II

Gance slept fitfully, dreaming of a great weight pressing against his chest. By the time he woke, the first of his candles had gone out, and the fire had died. He groped for his bag and lit a second candle, then sat in the little pool of light, slowly reciting the speech he had intended to make to the creatures that existed here.

"I am Winston Gordon, Lord Gance. I have wealth. I have houses in London, in Paris, in Bonn and in Budapest. I can give you shelter there. I can give you freedom from this place."

He thought he heard a woman's laughter, followed by another's and another's.

He stopped, his eyes straining to see in the darkness around him. The foolishness of what he did seemed terribly obvious. Oh, he had fallen in love—that much was certain—not with Mina but with her delusions. He had even been foolish enough to ignore his illness and come here. The irony of it made him laugh. He continued in a lighter mood, speaking to the air, he thought, seducing it as he might one of his shy conquests. "Press your lips to my skin, your bodies against my body," he whispered. "Use me. Make me one with you."

As he spoke, the wind rose outside, beating against the shutters of his window, howling through the cracks in the outer walls as if his words had summoned a hoard of demons from the craggy rocks beneath the castle. Downstairs, the horse whinnied with fear. The castle itself seemed to sigh, and though the door to his room was closed, a sudden draft of air blew out his candle.

He reached for it and groped for the matches he had dropped somewhere. Only the dim red glow of the coals broke the darkness pressing around him. In the silence, he heard his ragged breathing, his racing heart beating faster, ever faster, fueled by his fear.

"Use me," he repeated, less certain now that he meant the words. "Make me one of you."

The fire on the hearth flared of its own accord. The still-glowing wick of the candle ignited. Gance shut his eyes, and when he opened them again, the women hovered around him. The forms had all the substance of mist, the delicate hands solidifying as they reached toward him. Bodies followed, flesh growing as he watched. Their teeth were too white against the darkness of their lips; their eyes glowed red in the firelight. Diaphanous gowns floated around them in the stillness of the room. If Gance had not known what sort of creatures the women were, he might have thought them ghosts, or dreams, for this castle seemed ideal for dreaming.

The three were as Mina described—inhumanly alluring, impossibly beautiful—but their collective expression he knew well.

Lust. Greed. Hunger.

Yet he felt nothing for the women beyond an admiration for their beauty and a desire for the immortality they could give him. Like them, he was a hunter who preyed on the unsuspecting and corrupted the innocent. Like them, he could only devour.

There was one difference. He sensed it in how the fairest of the three looked so coyly at him, how she covered her mouth with her hand as she laughed and, above all, how she backed away as he reached for her.

He thought of how young she had been when she'd been taken, and how cruelly she must have died. Since then, she might have killed, but he was confident that she had never used her victims for sexual pleasure.

"Shall I be your first willing lover, Countess Karina?" he asked and held out his hand.

She took it, her own still a delicate child's hand, the nails sharp and translucent against the whiteness of her skin.

He moved his face close to her, whispering though he knew the others could hear. "Devour me slowly as he devoured you. Want me, as he wanted you, and I will give you all the pleasure I have learned to give. It is my gift. I know that compared to the one you can bestow on me, it is nothing, but I can offer you no other, Countess Karina."

Karina looked from him to the taller of the dark-haired women. She drew a breath into her lungs and asked in Hungarian, in a voice both eager and shy, "Is what he suggests possible, Illona?"

The woman nodded. "Use him as you wish, though I think you will be disappointed. Then let him live. Later, we will feast on him together."

Gance wanted to ask if they would share their eternal life with him, but Karina was already pressing close, her lips covering his. They were so cold against his that he shivered. Illona turned her dark eyes toward the flames. As they rose, she vanished into the glowing yellow pool of their light.

The third woman remained, standing motionless in the shadows. A strange, mad smile grew on her face as she watched Karina slip her gown off her shoulders, watched it fall and disappear before it touched the dusty stone floor. With a quicksilvery laugh, she vanished, leaving the pair alone.

Karina floated toward Gance as if her body had no weight at all. Her arms drew him close. Her hands that should have been so innocent moved knowingly up his body, finally brushing away the soft whisps of white hair that had fallen over his face. For the first time, he noted the color of her eyes: the brilliant blue of the daytime sky. He held her tighter, his desire real this time, and felt his arms close together, her presence leave him.

In the morning when he woke, her eyes were the last thing he could recall. There were no marks on him, no sense that he had done anything except sleep, and dream.

A piece of pale blue lace was caught in the splintered table leg. He reached for this joyfully, but as he fingered it, its ancient threads crumbled in his hand.

Perhaps the scrap had been a part of Karina's gown once, but no more. She had died. They had all died. I'm as insane as Mina, he thought, then laughed aloud. At least now he could fully appreciate her terrible delusions.

No, he would not tempt insanity any longer. He gathered his things, intending to leave.

At the top of the stairs, Gance saw the light from open outer doors, halted and whistled. There was no sound of hooves on the hall stones, no tinkle of bridle chains against one another, no snort or whinny. Not certain what he would find, he pulled his revolver from his pack. Gripping it, he started downstairs.

He'd descended only halfway before he saw the horse lying on its side—its belly ripped open, its entrails savaged.

But there was no blood on the stones, no marks on the animal's forelegs to show that she had fought. Gance would have walked toward the carcass, but a gray wolf padded between it and the stairs, eyeing him as if he were a rival moving in on the kill. As Gance stood motionless, the revolver cocked and ready, the wolf sat back on its haunches. Six others padded through the door behind it. Three were nearly as large as the animal who apparently guarded Gance; three were half-grown.

Gance might have stood against one or even two, but a pack was more than he cared to challenge. Still facing the beasts, he retreated backward up the steps and down the hall to his room.

He waited until he was certain the bones must have been stripped and then opened his door again. The wolf that had first faced him as he stood on the stairs now sat in the hall outside. It stared at him with almost human confidence, then bared its teeth in a soundless warning. Gance slammed the door then pried open one shutter. The rest of the pack lazed in the sun-drenched courtyard below.

Gance could shoot the wolf outside, he thought, then wait for the others and take them one by one.

If they came at the sound. Most likely they would not, and he would have to face them in the courtyard, or on his flight—on foot, he reminded himself—down the mountain.

Gance had no lack of courage, but he knew the limitations of his strength. He closed the shutter, built a little fire and ate a bit of bread and cheese. He chewed slowly, savoring every mouthful and stopping as soon as his hunger pangs subsided.

If the wolves were still outside in the morning, he was a prisoner here. If so, the food he'd brought could be the last he would ever eat.

When he'd finished his sparse meal, he lay down and closed his eyes. Tonight, when his beautiful jailors appeared—whether in flesh or in dream—he wanted to be alert and ready.

CHAPTER TWENTY-SEVEN

Sundown! Karina moved from sleep to waking with all the swiftness of her first rebirth. For an instant the closeness of the space, and the scent of the ancient earth beneath the silk and velvet of her coverlets, panicked her. When she had been alive, she had feared such places, and death had not vanquished that fear.

She willed her soul outside the box, and as she watched, fascinated even after centuries by her power, her body thinned to a mist that leaked from the lid of her marble coffin and swirled around her, slowly taking form.

"It is the soul that gives substance to the body," Illona had told her the first night of her second life. "To destroy us completely, someone must also destroy our soul."

"Can that be done?" Karina asked.

"With great difficulty. Perhaps someday you will learn how."

"I don't want to know," Karina said, for at the time even the strange half-life of her new existence seemed preferable to death.

"Time has a way of twisting perspective." Illona laughed, throwing back her head as she did. The sight of her teeth, so long and white, made Karina shake with the memory of her human fear.

Then time had done exactly what Illona had predicted. Karina, who had longed to be free of her estates and her duties, had been trapped in the castle for over a hundred years. Often, she willed herself to sleep through the nights as well as days until hunger made any rest impossible. But tonight she had risen eagerly, as she had last night. Someone was here, someone who gave more than blood and life.

A shard of hope.

So much that her human body had valued was lost to Karina now, yet surprisingly much still remained. Human comforts—the need for warmth and the pleasure of food and drink—meant nothing, but the trappings of human life took on a more profound meaning, as if by reclaiming them she could somehow reclaim a part of her lost humanity.

When had she last worn a new gown? Or listened to music? Or danced? Or laughed! Once the clothes had been possible. Now it had been months since the gypsies had camped near to the castle bringing with them bolts of cloth and beads and delicate lace. And when they had, they'd danced and sang in their encampments, never coming within the castle walls unless Dracula himself summoned them.

Now he was gone. They would never come again.

And so this Englishman's presence took on a deeper meaning for Karina.

Lord Gance could give her all she desired and more; he said as much. And he had known what she was and shown no fear when she kissed him. Strange, magnificently strange.

Though as cautious as all her kind, she went to him as soon as she woke, eager for his touch.

He slept. She moved through him, imagining herself mortal for a moment—warm, breathing softly. The heartbeat that was so imperceptible to the human senses seemed so clear to her in its soft and steady march towards death.

She pulled away and, hovering above him, drew her body over her soul like a cloak. Her fingers brushed Gance's lips; her hand moved under his loose shirt and up his bare chest. She called his name.

He opened his eyes and looked up at her, smiling when he recognized her, lifting his head so their lips could touch. "Last night?" he asked.

Breath was needed to speak. She paused, inhaled and said, "Last night was a test, a dream. Tonight will be real."

"Can I be certain?"

She smiled because she knew the sight of her teeth would please him, would convince him of her nature. "Certain? Is my power that great?"

"If you were the one who controlled last night's visions, it is."

Those had not been visions, and she hadn't been alone. She saw no reason to remind him of that. Instead she asked, "Will I be Lady Gance if I let you share my life?"

"Lady Gance should have a grander chamber for her wedding night," he replied.

"So should a lord. Come with me."

She took his hand, and he followed her on faith through the darkness of the outer hall and up a winding staircase in the tower. If he had not gripped her cold fingers so tightly, he would have believed himself alone, for only his footsteps sounded on the stairs, only his breathing hissed in the stillness of the dark.

He climbed past the pale shadows of open doors, past drafts from open windows. A bat skittered by his face, one leathery wing brushing his cheek before it swept on, following the cold draft toward the night sky.

At the next turn, she led him into a room. As they entered, the fire flared, revealing a space that still held all the beauty of its medieval past.

Candles were lit everywhere, illuminating the wealth contained here. Gold chains circled the velvet-draped bedposts. Tasseled pillows covered the velvet-draped bed. Fur rugs lay scattered on the slate floor, and a shield nearly the height of a man hung above the hearth. Beneath it, a thick sword that seemed even longer was mounted on pegs. Its polished brass hilt seemed to be waiting for someone to grasp it, though Gance wondered what man could wield so huge a weapon.

He heard her indrawn breath, listened as she said, "His sword. Even now, after so many centuries, I can smell the blood on it."

"Where is he?"

A pause, another indrawn breath. "Gone."

"Dead?"

Emotion flared, glowing red in the depths of her sapphire eyes, but he could not tell if it was anger or triumph. "Gone! Gone beyond the realm where he can touch any of us, but do not assume that a will such as his can be vanquished." She walked to the center of the room, threw up her hands and pirouetted to music vivid only in her memory.

And laughed, rippling waves of mirth that he could feel brushing his body. "Shall I be your partner at our dances? Shall I sing for our guests?"

"Sing for me."

Eyes closed, head bowed, she let the music grow in the silence of her memories, then lifted her chin and began.

He had expected something childish. Instead she picked an old Hungarian folk tune about a couple who had just met, pledging their love for a lifetime and beyond. The irony of her choice did not escape him, and her singing voice was not as he expected. It had a deep, trained richness that her speech lacked.

When she'd finished, he pulled a green silk scarf from his pocket and handed it to her. She unfolded it carefully and saw a gold ring in the middle, with an emerald of deep clarity, the fire in its center visible even in the dim light. "It is yours, Karina, a sample of all the gifts I will give if you let me share your life."

She cupped it in her hand, watching the emerald flicker in the firelight. "No one has given me a gift for so many years."

"Share your life," he repeated. "And I will take you from this place."

"It isn't so simple, my lord. If only it were."

"You know the way." He held her in a manner that no mortal who knew her nature had ever held her before, his face close to hers, ready for her kiss.

"And if I could bring only death to you, would you rescue me anyway?"

"Death is coming soon enough," he responded. Hints of anguish in his tone convinced her that he spoke the truth.

"Poor mortal," she whispered, and stroked his cheek.

The bed, as he had expected, was luxuriously soft. As they fell together onto it, she kissed him. He found himself astonished at the intensity of his response.

He had made love so many times before, but never to a woman as exotic as this. The countess Karina was soft, voluptuous in a youthful way he knew so well. Her scent was sweet—hyacinth and narcissus. Yet there was no heat to her body, no breath quickening at his touch. Her breasts were flawless, but if he rested his head on them, he would hear no heartbeat. She had died long ago, moving beyond any pleasure his touch could give. The thought would not leave him, and he fought down a sudden surge of revulsion, of fear.

"Do not tempt me," she whispered. "Fear brings death. Love me instead."

Her eyes were hungry for the life he offered her, as hungry he was for her eternal existence. "I will," he whispered and kissed her again.

She broke away, moved her lips to his neck. "So soon?" he asked.

"Your passion is my passion, my lord. I cannot respond, I can only echo."

Her teeth broke into his skin, sinking deeper. He felt the trickle of blood, the pressure of her lips as she drank. Her hands that had moved so languidly over his body became more insistent. Her legs brushed against the outside of his thighs, drawing him into her.

"Wait," he said. "Let me give you pleasure."

"Pleasure!" Her laughter rang clear and tremulous as crystal bells. "My lord, my only pleasure is that you love me."

With a growl of frustration, he did as she asked and found that he was indeed ready. As his body moved above hers, her lips pressed against the wound. She drank, trembling as he trembled, her cry just after his own.

When he lay beside her with his eyes closed, trying to force his useless lung to breathe, trying to still the frantic racing of his heart, he felt her hand move down his body once more. "You drank from Lady Mina, did you not?" she asked, her voice light.

The act could hardly have been of any consequence. "I did. I was already wounded. I hoped to tap the strength of her blood."

"Of his, you mean." She sounded weary, terribly sad. The weight beside him vanished. When he opened his eyes, she was gone.

"Karina, will you share?" he whispered to the emptiness around him.

He thought he heard laughter, but he could be sure of nothing, not even that the laughter was hers.

But there was a presence lingering here; he sensed it hovering in the darkness, watching him as the women had watched him before they chose to appear. "Karina?" he called softly. "Joanna?"

The door to his room swung slowly inward. From higher up in the tower, he heard a woman chanting, her lone voice rising and falling, repeating a string of words that included his name and another that he had come to know well.

"Dracula," she chanted.

Another test, he thought, this time one of courage.

With a candelabrum held high to light his way, he climbed the twisting stairs, listening to the chant grow louder. On the last turn, he saw light as well, and he continued more quickly to the open doors above him and into the room where torches shed a smoky light.

The narrow, vaulted room might have been a chapel once.

The stone slab at the far end might have been its altar. But whatever function the room had once possessed had been twisted like the castle itself from one of succor and protection to one of terror and death.

Symbols had been painted on the walls around him—horned men, owls, snakes, bats and the dragon's tooth herald he had seen on the shield in the room below. Interspersed with these were pictures of Mina's face drawn hastily in coal and lampblack. Many of these had been made on the stones themselves, others on scraps of paper and cloth. Discarded near the stone was a woman's cape, thick and fleece-trimmed. He could hardly know whose it was, yet he was somehow certain that it had belonged to Mina and that what was happening here was to blame for all her fears.

Illona sat on the stone, her back to him. Her hair fell in a dark cascade that covered her back and the stone itself. Her bare legs were crossed, her bare arms upraised. The chant did not waver, though Gance was certain that Illona had sensed his presence. This was her sacred space, her place of worship to the dark god that Mina said had given her the secret of immortal life.

He halted just inside the door and listened, hoping to make sense of her words, hearing only the constant repetition of Dracula's name and his own.

He took another step into the room, and the door slammed shut behind him. The smoke from the torches seemed to increase, filling the space until the pictures on the walls blurred and the walls themselves vanished. Only Illona was visible, in her place on the altar, her voice rising and falling, speaking his name.

Calling him.

The thickness of the air made him fight for breath. The candelabrum seemed suddenly so heavy. He set it down and walked toward her. As he did, she rose to her feet and turned to meet him with arms outstretched.

He saw that her body had been painted with bold strokes of red and black. The nipples of her breasts were circled with black, her pubic hair outlined in red. Red drops, undoubtedly meant to be blood, covered her breasts, red trickles marked her thighs. Her expression held a desire more intense than he had ever witnessed before. Her arms rose, and he saw that they were covered with the same symbols that adorned the walls. Multihued snakes circled her arms. Bats fluttered across the palms of her hands; owls sat solemnly on their backs, their brown feathers painted down the length of her tapering fingers.

Gance had always toyed with evil, but he had never seen real evil firsthand. He did now, and his first thought was to flee the room, the castle, the mountains, to put as much space between himself and this creature as he could. He had begun to turn when her voice, tender and serene, called his name. "Winston."

Flee, he thought, yet he paused to look at her.

And saw the wound she had made on her chest, real blood flowing this time, the offering to him.

As he paused, uncertain, she smiled. Her fangs had been painted as well, so that they seemed to curve inward, mimicking the dragon's teeth of her husband's shield.

"Did you think that she would be the one to turn you, Winston?" she asked. "She is a child, a charming child, so charming indeed that I have granted her wish. Come to me, Gance. Come. Drink."

"Drink?"

"My blood. Eternal blood. It flows in me through the power of the Lord of Darkness and Life. Come now. The invitation will not be given again."

Everything Gance wanted was waiting at that altar. All he needed to do was walk forward and take. He had come for this. He would not permit his courage to fail him now.

Yet as he moved toward her, his fear intensified and his heart began to pound. He felt faint, and the room seemed to grow suddenly smaller, with only swirling darkness for its walls. Her eyes glowed red, providing the only light he could focus on. He moved toward them, welcoming what she could give, fearing for the first time what he would become.

As he approached, she held out her hands. "Winston Gordon, Lord Gance, do you take freely the blood I offer you?" she chanted.

The instinct that had served him well through life was utterly overcome by the strongest fear of all—the fear of death. "I do," he responded. He took her hands and reverently pressed his lips to her chest, tasting her essence, her power.

Bittersweet. Cold. Lifeless.

Mina had told him that this was a passionate moment, one of release. Gance did not feel the ecstasy. Instead it seemed that death moved through him, slowly numbing his throat, his trunk, spiraling outward in his limbs. His legs gave way, but Illona supported him, holding him as a mother holds a child.

Still he drank until he was incapable of swallowing any longer. She let his head drop across her arms, then lifted his body and laid him on the stone slab. Unable to speak or to move, he heard the chant begin once more.

"Dracula . . . Gance . . . Dracula."

There was a presence in the room, one he had sensed earlier in the hall of the castle. It was not Joanna, not Karina, but something far more powerful.

"My lord," Illona chanted. "Take this vessel. Make it your own and return to me."

"No!" Karina's voice screamed for him, petulant like a denied child's. "You promised him to me. You promised!"

Gance wanted to say that it made no difference who turned him, so long as it happened. He wanted to tell her that he would indeed make a place for her in his world. But he could not speak. Could not even turn his head to look at her.

Then she was gone, her shriek of anguish hanging in the dense air. The chant continued. The presence grew stronger.

"Gance . . . Dracula . . . Gance . . ."

Something was moving in him, some ancient power filling him. His limbs grew heavy, the pressure in his chest increased. But as he looked up, past the whiteness of Illona's painted skin, and through the dark cloud of her hair, he saw Karina slowly taking form, and in her hand . . .

The huge blade fell, severing Illona's head from her body. A gush of blood covered Gance's face, blinding him. He heard it drip from the slab onto the floor, heard a steady pounding of metal on wood.

"Cold," he mouthed, without breath.

Karina wiped the blood from his face, blew breath into his body, trying to force him to live. "You fool!" she said. "What use did she have for Gance the man? Though she was far more powerful than he, she existed only for her husband. She needed a creature who had shared his blood to bring him back. Mina would have served, but a man would be so much better. She would have made you his vessel, your memories and your fortune his to use, nothing more. His will is stronger than mine. It may already be too late to save you."

She lifted the huge blade from the floor and made a deep cut on her wrist. The blood flowed down his throat once more, but it did not have the numbing cold of the other. "Drink!" she ordered. "Live long enough for me to turn you."

He managed to do as she asked. As his strength grew and he sucked hungrily at her wound, she pressed her lips to his neck and began the slow drain of life from his body.

A sound he had never consciously heard save in illness ended when his heart stopped beating. Still not certain who would wake in his shell, he died.

CHAPTER TWENTY-EIGHT

I

Soon after Gance abandoned Mina, Van Helsing received a wire from Jonathan informing him that Mina was returning to Castle Dracula. Jonathan also wrote he would post documents that would explain a great deal about her decision.

Van Helsing had no patience for the mails. He wired back, asking for details immediately.

The following day, a messenger from the telegraph office came to his door carrying a thick envelope. "I am to tell you that this is no message, but a damned epistle," the man told him. "And a strange one at that."

Van Helsing pulled out the pages. There, in its entirety, was the Countess Aliczni's story and a longer communication from Jonathan giving details of Mina's apparent breakdown, Ujvari's death and the Sebescues' attack.

Once, Van Helsing and Ion Sebescue had been allies in the struggle against the undead, and friends as well. Then Sebescue had lost his daughter and a good part of his sanity to the creatures in the Borgo. As soon as he had recovered from the shock of the girl's death, he had taken his son to England to start a fresh life. Had the memory of the creatures gnawed at Ion's reason even after so many years? Age could be to blame, for Sebescue's mind had been slipping when Van Helsing saw him a decade ago. As for the son, being raised with such bitterness could have accounted for his own obsession. After all, it was the poor child's sister that the vampires had consumed.

He raised his glass of slivovitz in a silent toast to the tragic family. As he reached for the bottle to pour another shot, he realized how much he had drunk.

"Fool!" he bellowed to himself. "Fool! You have sat here waiting for something to happen. It was exactly the laziness those monsters wanted." With a sweep of his arm, Van Helsing pushed the glass and bottle off the table. The contents of both dripped slowly across the already filthy floor, in a clear sweet puddle.

Van Helsing's clothes and books, and the journals he had kept of his work, had long since been crated for shipping back to Amsterdam. Yet he had remained here, doing none of the work he had come for, indeed doing nothing at all in the last month but drinking. At first, it had been in the company of others; lately, he drank alone, and the little house that was supposed to have been a refuge had slowly turned into a cell. There was nothing keeping him here, yet he could not leave.

As soon as he'd finished the reading, Van Helsing wired a message to the hotel in Varna asking Mina to come to him. Afterward, he went home and stared at his reflection in the little wall mirror he used for shaving. He looked younger than he felt, and the two-day stubble on his chin gave him an uncivilized air.

He shaved. He washed. He put on clean clothes. Mina was coming. He had to be ready. There was work to do.

Days passed, but his belief did not waver. Mina had a choice, even now. Though Jonathan hinted that her blood was still tainted by Dracula's, her will was strong. She would come.

And so he was neither disappointed nor surprised to see her standing at the end of his walk one evening, the brilliant setting sun painting golden highlights in her hair. He threw open the door and went outside, taking her hand, staring into her eyes.

"It isn't over," she said. "Do you feel it too?"

"I thought I was just an old man who had to have an enemy if he wished to survive," he said. "You were always the perceptive one. You saw the truth." He turned and went inside, noting carefully how she followed him without any need of invitation.

II

May 6, Bukovina. *When I saw the inside of Van Helsing's house, I had the urge to cry,* Mina wrote. *Van Helsing, who has always been scrupulously neat about himself and his work, now lives surrounded by filth. There were dust balls in the corners, dishes on the sideboard caked with moldy food. The few books he possessed were stacked on the single bookshelf, many with their spines turned inward. Saddest of all was the fact that, in spite of the mess, his bed was made and the table in the center of the room was clear and washed. He had known I was coming and prepared. What would the place have looked like if he'd had no warning of my visit?*

I sat at the table. He sat across from me. I was afraid that he would touch me. Aware of the dangers I would ask him to face, I felt terribly guilty and I took his hands. As I did, I looked at his face and saw, in his eyes, the same concern I had seen in Brother Sandor's as he had spoken to me.

"Whatever still lives at Castle Dracula will not rest until we go there," I told the professor. *"Jonathan feels it too. I know he does, but he has his work to keep his mind off the compulsion. I have nothing."*

Nothing but Gance, I thought, and he gave respite for only a little while. *"I am the life the creatures crave. I am the one who can appease their hunger, and I can never rest until I face them again."*

"If you knew all this, why didn't you write me? I would have come. I would have translated the journal, and tragedy would not have been necessary," he said.

"I held Lucy's death against you. I still do, but I understand that need to protect. I have done the same with Jonathan."

"You are a strong woman," Van Helsing said.

I heard the caution in his voice, as if even my admission of past anger frightened him. "And Lucy was not, is that what you are telling me?"

There were tears in his eyes as he began to answer. "Yes, Madam Mina, Lucy was not. I would not go with her to the Borgo Pass, not once but twice. I would not place my life in her hands as I do in yours. As for Lucy, I have prayed for her soul, and for mine for what I did to her. It is all I can do." He began to cry openly.

I kissed his hands, and then, because it seemed so right, I embraced him as a daughter would a father. We held on to one another until we were both in control once more.

"If we are to go tomorrow, I must prepare," he said. "There is a priest here in Varna who will bless hosts and water for me. It is best that this be done tonight."

Holy water! What good would water do in the face of a need for blood? "They are no use to us," I said. "Leave them."

"What will we use if not those?" he asked simply.

"Nothing," I said. "We will go armed with faith."

"Madam Mina! It is suicide."

I shook my head. "There are things you must know before we leave."

We talked the rest of the day. When I had finished, he asked simply, "You do not need me. Why did you come for me?"

I answered with the truth. "I was afraid to go alone . . . No, not that my resolve would falter but that someone would stop me before I reached the castle."

"Madam Mina," Van Helsing replied gravely. "I will take you there, and this time I will trust your judgment." There was nothing more to say. While Van Helsing made coffee, I read the final pages of the countess's translation, thinking of Gance and what he had done out of love for me.

My hope that Gance has somehow survived the meeting grows stronger. His wealth and the force of his personality would be a great temptation to the countess Karina. And if what I read is true, she and the others are still there waiting for me—my sister-kin.

I slept that night on a stack of cushions in the corner of his room. He was old, and from what I could see, far from well. I would not let him give up his bed for me.

In the morning, we spoke again and consulted Karina's translation. How odd it feels to write her name. It seems an act of intimacy, as if we are old friends. By noon we were ready to leave.

The journey has been so different from the last. We are on horseback rather than in a wagon. Though we brought heavy coats to keep out the nighttime chill, there is no need for furs or boots.

And the land is so green! Last winter when everything was dead and shrouded with snow, I would not have imagined such fantasy shades in needled and leafed trees, such beautiful little flowers in white and blue and bright russet covering the meadows around us.

Van Helsing says that the summer is so short that everything must bloom quickly. And die just as fast, I thought, while around us the mountains stand as a testament to time. I did not dare to tempt my resolve by thinking of parallels then. I see them only now as I sit in Bukovina, setting down this brief account while I eat my meal alone in the same inn where Gance stayed only days before.

Van Helsing, it seems, has friends here. I left him to his conversation because I do not speak the language and he was too polite to let me sit with him without translating. Before I went, I asked one question through Van Helsing.

Gance looked well, I was told.

May 7. We are in sight of the castle and have stopped for one final meal before going on. We are in no rush. The creatures we have come to face awaken at dusk, and we wish to be rested. The walls, outlined by the setting sun, are black and sharp, the rocky cliffs around them treeless, flowerless, forboding. Van Helsing says it was this way before. I cannot remember. Last time I came here, I was possessed by the vampire. Now, though I am called back, I feel freer, as if the burdens of my past have been lifted from me.

Do I have a choice? Dracula said I do, but it is here that I must make it.

I paused, to stare out at the land and to let the ink on this page dry for a moment, then I looked down at my writing, so stiff, as if forced from my hand. I promised Winnie that I would let her know the outcome of this struggle—this final struggle—and I will set every detail of it down. I have all the money that Gance left for me. If I die and wake in their life, I vow to see that this journal is sent to her. And, Winnie dear, if it comes to that, see that Jonathan reads it. Even after all that has happened, I love him too much to leave him forever wondering at my end.

These seem such terrible words, yet they are not. I feel no despair, only acceptance for whatever will come. In this state of calm, the meditative state that Brother Sandor had taught me was easy to achieve, I felt the grace of God move through me as potent as blood.

May 8. The struggle has passed. The beautiful night has come again.
I have never felt such peace.

We had just finished last evening's meal and were packing up our belongings when we saw the wolves moving silently up the winding road to the castle. They might have been coming to stop us, more likely to hurry us on. Nonetheless, Van Helsing helped me onto one of the horses. "Go up, Madam Mina," he cried. I rode furiously. At the next turn, I saw him following me, his pistol drawn. There were so many beasts chasing him that I knew he would die if he paused to make a stand.

As my horse thundered into the courtyard, I heard Van Helsing following behind. I dismounted then paused, unwilling to go into the castle without him. As I stood outside, uncertain of what to do, the gates of the outer walls, huge slabs of rusted metal, began to close. A second groaning merged with their sound. The castle doors were also swinging shut.

"No!" I screamed. I would not be stopped, not after coming so far. As Van Helsing thundered through the outer gates, I ran inside. The great doors slammed behind me. Van Helsing was a prisoner outside, for what reason I did not know, and I stood trapped in the castle alone.

The great hall was dark, reeking, silent. As I stood, not certain where to go or how to light my way, the torches of the room flared of their own accord. Rats that had been gnawing at the carcass of a dead horse looked up at me; then, as if sensing I was no threat to them, they returned to their feast.

I heard Van Helsing screaming my name. I went to the door and called to him, saying that I was all right. Though he pushed and I pulled, the doors would not move. I had not expected them to open. Whatever waited for me here wanted me alone.

I heard a steady, distant beating from some place far above me. "Gance?" I screamed. The pounding stopped. I called his name again and climbed the stairs to the second floor, following the noise to a winding tower staircase, a rising black tunnel with crumbling walls. My pace slowed as, with my skirts in one hand, my other hand pressed tightly against the wall, I began a slow climb. As I did, torches flared around me as they had in the hall below. I was meant to come this way, and quickly.

Faith, I reminded myself. Accept.

I went on, and with each step the rightness of what I did became more clear. Outside the barred door at the top of the tower, I called to Gance once more.

"Mina! Is it truly you or some other trick of these creatures?"

"I've come. One moment, Gance."

I paused, my mind moving inward, silencing the turmoil of my hopes, the distraction of my fear. I performed the simple exercise as Brother Sandor had taught me. With my mind fixed only on God, I said a simple prayer of rebirth and renewal, slid back the bar and opened the door.

A pair of candles on the table gave the only light to the room. I saw no sign of fire on the hearth, no food or drink. Gance seemed paler than I remembered him, and his eyes glowed red as he looked into the more brightly lit hall. I shuddered and reminded myself that his eyes had caught the light in this way the first night we met.

His expression was another matter. There was an intensity to it that I had never seen in Gance save in the midst of my first seduction or at the height of passion. Now, with his hand resting on the table for support, he seemed less ready for either than for collapse.

"Gance!" I cried and moved toward him.

For an instant, his expression changed to one trapped, desperate and a little mad—an expression I would have expected from him or any mortal under the circumstances. "You came," he said. "I knew you would."

His voice was his own yet not his own. The inflections were wrong. The way he looked at me seemed too full of need. I understood, even before he spoke, with such cold and terrible passion. "This body must kill if it is to serve me. Mina, dearest, come willingly to me."

"Dracula."

He nodded. "And Gance," he said. "His memories are my memories, his will mine to control. I need only you to make my possession of this body complete."

"Will I live or die?" I asked.

"That is your choice," he replied and held out his hand.

I went to him eagerly, kissing him, kissing Gance, accepting all the passion of my nature. His lips moved to the side of my face, brushing my cheek, my neck.

I held him close as he bit, marveled at how even now the act of giving myself to him could create such pleasure. For that moment, I did not care if I lived or died.

Then the arms holding me fell slack, the teeth withdrew from the wound, and a shriek, more desperate than any I had ever heard, came from deep within him. As he fell, a whirlwind seemed to fill the room, reminding me of the storm that came on so suddenly the evening our little band believed that Dracula had died.

"Mina." Gance's voice, so soft in the center of the storm.

I knelt beside him. "I'm sorry," I whispered.

"I saw eternity, Mina. Just for a moment, I saw it."

"I know, darling," I whispered. I said a prayer for his soul then held him close while he died. As he did, the whirlwind subsided from a storm, to a breeze, to the misty unformed presence I knew so well.

I stood. Dracula was all around me, impossible to see or to touch. "Tepes! Will you exist like this, an impotent ghost in a deserted castle?" I asked him. "You were the servant of God, the savior of your people. You are a saint to them, even now."

"Tepes! What is blood but life and water? This vessel is blessed by a holy man, a priest of the Orthodox faith. Your blood in me is blessed as you were once blessed before you rode into battle. Take my body. Use it to reclaim the heaven that even now you deserve."

The mist coalesced at my feet. It whirled around me, then vanished.

I felt him move through me, felt the drain of my life, an energy pull so much like the pull of blood I'd felt before. My body, blessed as it was, gave no welcome, but he remained, a warrior with no fear of pain or death, a warrior with the promise of heaven to keep his soul resolute.

"For all the years of loneliness, of damnation, accept the sacrament I offer you, the sacrament of my body. Take it, my lord, my lover. Accept the grace of this sacred vessel to redeem your soul. End the torment for both of us."

I expected another whirlwind, a painful good-bye. Instead he was present in me one moment, gone the next. I sat alone, beside Gance's body, crying for them both.

Karina formed in the air beside me. Though I was astonished at her beauty, I felt no enmity. We were sisters, she and I, bound by how we had been used. She looked at my tears as if she had never seen such a thing before. "You grieve for him? No, Mina, you must not. In time, Lord Gance would have had no choice but to be as I am. No will is stronger than our power and our need.

"Still, I tried to make him one of us," she said in her beautiful voice. Her accent was quite lovely, her English almost flawless. "Tepes and I learned the language together," she said, reading my thoughts as Dracula had done.

"What will you and Joanna do now?" I asked.

"Joanna." I sensed the feeling words could not convey. Joanna, always mad, had hidden herself in the caverns below the castle. On her own, she would never have the courage to leave this place. Instead she would remain, company to Illona's ghost forever. The walls would one day crumble around them, and they would haunt the land and the caves below.

Or perhaps she will eventually find the resolve to flee far enough that no one will recognize what she is. The world is full enough of half-mad creatures, feeding off the lives of others. I can picture her walking the nighttime streets of Paris or London, her dark eyes and red lips luring men to the shadows and to death.

"And you?" I repeated.

"I killed Illona, the one who made me. I am free to go wherever I wish."

I thought of the words she had written, the end she had asked for. "Shall I remain until dawn and give you death?"

"Death?" She shook her head. "If only I could live."

She did not look like the others. With her golden hair, her eyes such a brilliant blue that I could see their color even in the dim light of the torch mounted on the wall, her tiny hands and bow-shaped mouth, she could have been alive. Rouge would hide the whiteness of her face, gloves the pallor of her hands. She could live anywhere now. I wanted to ask her to return to London with me.

As what? A replacement for Lucy? A friend for Winnie and me? An exotic animal to keep in my cellar as the infamous poet Rossetti had the menagerie in his yard?

No! Not the last, though the others were true enough. I held out my hand to her. She clasped it and moved close to me. Softly, passionlessly, she kissed my lips, then tilted my head up and back as her maker had once done to her.

She must have known how Dracula had died in me. Nonetheless, I tried to warn her. "I am blessed. My blood will destroy you," I said.

She nodded, lowered her head to my neck and began to drink from the still-bleeding wound. She drank in death as she once had life, growing ever weaker in my arms, until I was the strong one, able to push her away.

I sat with her as the sun rose. It touched her flesh, and slowly she crumbled into dust as he had done, and blew away in the light dawn breeze. The presence left me. She was gone, soul as well as body, truly gone.

I buried my head in hands that until a moment ago had held her. I cried.

* * *

I had lost a great deal of blood, enough that I could never get down those stairs alone. I sat and waited. As I expected, the doors had opened at dawn. Van Helsing came to me.

"It's done," I said.

"I know. I felt him die."

I was as surprised by his look of triumph as Karina had been by my tears. Perhaps both our emotions were wrong. Perhaps this was something that needed to be done, nothing more.

He helped me down the stairs. We rested together in the courtyard until I was steady enough to ride. It was nearly nightfall by the time we traveled the few miles to the town from which we had set out the afternoon before. We took rooms at the inn. I needed sleep, but I could not find it.

Instead, I kept seeing Karina's face as it had looked in the last moments of her earthly existence—transformed from its vampiric magnificence to the charming childish beauty it had once possessed—and I knew that in the last moments of her life, she had found redemption.

After centuries of slavery, she had chosen peace over freedom. I sat at the table in my room and mourned her and our lover both.

And then, stilling my thoughts and emotions, I contemplated my life.

The passion Dracula awakened in me has not died. I am no different than the Mina Harker who came here with Gance days ago, and I must accept this fate if I wish to find happiness in this fleeting life.

And so I have written a letter to Jonathan, telling him all that has happened and how nothing has really changed. I told him that I loved him, then asked him to decide if he can love me with the passion I need. I enclosed the address of the artist in Paris and told him that I would wait there for him to decide.

If there is justice for both of us, I will meet him in that little garden. I will kiss him as I kissed my other lovers, and he will respond.

If he does not come, there will be life and happiness without him.